Praise For *Damage Fun*

"Well. Well! It has me in it, hasn't it!? That can't be bad!? I just *love* reading about myself all the time! In fact, to be really honest here, I couldn't put the book down. Immensely good read! Couldn't have done it better myself. Hang on? Of course, … I *did* write the damn thing! I do everything, don't I!? Wow! I'm great! – Although, … I'm afraid, I never did get those letters of correspondence addressed to me mentioned herein. All I'm saying is … don't blame it on me! Blame it on yourself! The sort of postal service the author is talking about actually doesn't work! You *really* don't need the post! All you need is thought and imagination. Imagination is the key, guys! – Well. Well! I am looking forward to the next instalment." *[tranquil silence]*

The Divine Principle

"What a ***king marvellous piece of writing! I mean, OK, right, it's not a handbook, right! It's not ***king bulleted and numbered, and it doesn't ***king tell you what to eat – gluttomania? great! – to become a fat ***k, or how to ***king kill people and survive in the ***king desert on your own piss. – But! Big *BUT*! It does tell you how ***king great war and its psycho aftermath really is and how to ***k up kids so they remain ****ed up and walk the right path of competition & consumption. Personally, I should have loved a little more porn, pistols, and peripeteia. I love that sort of thing … but that's just me. – Yeah! I'm certainly gonna read the next one! What's it called? *Schadenfreude!* Right. *Damage Fun* is brilliant and way-out! Mo******cker! *Schadenfreude* can only be better! You say it's a ***king trilogy plus more? Don't forget to send me the draft manuscripts, or I will kill you! I mean that, actually! – Oh, and you wouldn't mind just signing here in your own blood!? My words don't come for free, I'm afraid. – Thank you! What lovely handwriting. – I love you all!" *[massive applause]*

The Divine Principle's Dark Side

"Wha'? Read!? Are you off your ****ing trolley!? – Piss off!"

Anonymous Stockbroker

"Well, now! Let's see. – Thank you for giving me the book in the first place! Nice to be noticed! That was most generous! – I think it takes Nietzsche's whole metaphoric language and his allegorical tightrope-blah to a new level altogether. Spare me simile! In fact, one could say, it's a more practical Zen-like approach to basic human atavism versus divine nature. It's inspiring! I, for one, certainly felt good after having read it. Gave me an idea of how beautiful life actually is. – Couldn't spare some change, eh, guv!? Remember, you promised at least £ 20! Make it fifty and I'll fly for you! – Where's my dog gone!? Bugger!"

Benjamin 'Professor Fruit' Hollander, Hampstead (London) Vagrant

The Author

At the speed of thought Jens fell fast and nigh on unconscious into a human body in Oxford, England, UK, Europe, Earth, etc. towards the end of 1964, and still can't entirely recall what the planet he lived on before was called. It was very green and nice, and it had people and animals too. That much Jens knows. The people had soft, olive skin that could go quite dark when exposed to the three suns, and there was a giant, tree-dwelling amphibian called the flipfrog, who was wont to jump from a height screeching with joy during its fall but then whisper *owowow* for a very long time when it had hit the ground. The flipfrog would do this a lot. But that's another story, which the author doesn't want to dwell on at the moment.

Jens is a laughing, and widely travelled writer with Hiberno-Germanic parentage, although his now ancient, Irish father insists to this day that Jens is the product of the sort of union that isn't on! "Séamus! You dear, little gobshite! Your *real* father, and this might come as a grave shock, was an English aristocrat by the name of Lord Fartengas. It's all forgiven, of course. Your mother was bored. Well, myself, I myself was bored too … quite a lot! But just look at yourself in the mirror! You don't look like a Duffy at all! What!? You say your name's not Séamus!? There's your proof then! But I do love you! Then again, I don't look like a Duffy either, do I? I wonder what my mother was up to!? There was a time when we were so poor we had to eat our fingernails for calcium and […]" *etc etc*

Anyway. The Germano-Hibernian union of the sorts of people that would eventually beget Jens dates back to just after the end of WW2, when RAF soldiers were looking for pretty German Fräuleins at the fence of the landing strip to enhance their lives with offspring of mixed parentage.

Eventually, Jens tried to have himself educated in linguistics at Freie Universität of West Berlin, where he was mainly involved in being an unwitting spy, delivering sausages to greasy spoons, fending off the unctuous advances of his employer – a sausage manufacturer of ill repute – and witnessing sausage-gang wars for sausage-delivery areas, before he returned to England to study something like painting at Camberwell College of Arts, London.

As a young kid in West Germany he was much amused and alarmed by the whole silliness of the Cold War, and he remains amused and concerned about the sort of media propaganda that manages to pitch us humans against one another.

Sometimes Jens lives in Shambhala, sometimes in chaos, and at other times in Australia and Antarctica. Mostly though he resides in East Anglia on a silent river, surrounded by a bedlam of Jack Russell terriers, his wife, and wonderful family and friends, who don't mind taking his dogs for long walks when he goes reclusive to write, as long as he'll sing silly songs to them and talk Hibernian nonsense. Being on the subject of nonsense and its inherent antonyms, this is the first novel he decided to have published, as it's bloody sad and funny, really! – Enjoy the read!

Jens Duffy

Damage Fun

- The American Zone -

This novel is a work of fiction completely.
All names, characters and incidents portrayed
in it are the work of the author's imagination.
Any resemblance to actual persons, living or dead,
events or localities is entirely coincidental.

Published by MundoVerbi Ltd.
PO Box 10604
Manningtree CO11 9AG
United Kingdom

www.mundoverbi.com

This hardcover 1st edition 2009

First published in Great Britain in 2009
by MundoVerbi Ltd.

The paper used for printing by MundoVerbi's printers
is made from wood sourced from sustainable forests.

Copyright © Jens Duffy 2009

The author, Jens Duffy,
has asserted his moral right under the Copyright,
Design and Patents Act, 1988
to be identified as the author of this work

This hardcover ISBN 978-1-907227-05-9

Also available as paperback ISBN 978-1-907227-00-4

Set in Garamond

All rights reserved. No part of this publication may be
reproduced, stored in a retrieval system, or transmitted,
in any form or by any means, electronic, mechanical,
photocopying, recording, or otherwise, without the prior
permission of the publishers, MundoVerbi Ltd.

This book is sold subject to the condition that it shall not,
by way of trade or otherwise, be lent, re-sold, hired out or
otherwise circulated without the publisher's prior consent
in any form of binding or cover other than in which it is
published and without a similar condition including this
condition being imposed on the subsequent purchaser.

A CIP catalogue record for this book
is available from the British Library

To my wife,

my family,

my friends,

and all those who made this come about.

Thank you!

Contents

Some sources set the casualty figure of the war dead of WWII at around 55 million, others at 72 million. As a matter of compromise, the mean arrived at is 63,500,000 dead. That's quite a lot. The population of the UK comprises approximately 60 million. If each dead person involved in this list of the war dead be granted an average height of 165 centimetres (cm) or 1.65 meters (m), the following length, arrived at in meters, is: 104,775,000 m. This, in terms of simple length or distance, is 104,775 kilometres (km) or 65,104.167 miles. If each dead person be given, apart from their height, an average width of 0.5 m and an average depth of 0.3 m, the following volume is arrived at per person: 0.2475 m^3. If this be multiplied by the average-number of all dead, i.e. 63,500,000, the following figure is arrived at in cubic meters: 15,716,250 m^3. Thus, if all these average war dead were placed in a big, box-like, ready-to-ship-to-the-sun pile, the following measurement would result in the following, in terms of height, width, and length: approx. 250.49 m in height x 250.49 m in length x 250.49 in width. That's a very big, cubic pile composed of the war dead. 250 m is a big distance. Just think, an American football field is 110 m long (end zones included); a European football or soccer pitch is an average of 105 m long (90-120 m). The distance to the sun is approximately 149,600,000 km. This means only another 1,428 wars approximately shall be required to reach the sun! The distance to the moon is around 384,403 km. This means only another 3.7 wars approximately shall be required to reach the moon. The circumference of Earth is around 40,075.02 km (equatorial, as in … equals good weather … mostly). Thus, it would take one only about 2.6 times to walk around Earth on a constant string of the war dead (WWII only), head to toe, to reach one's destination, which would also be one's point of origin, i.e. the point one set out from. That's quite a big walk! If you manage to walk 30 km per day without too many distractions, a distance of 104,775 km means you would walk for 3,492.5 days. That's just under 10 years. Quite a walk. But physical exercise is excellent!

Defence Of The Village

Fergal had been watching the stationary enemy tanks in the distance for fifteen minutes. They were having a party over there. Loud music and dancing. This was boring! Fergal looked at his friends. Was it bad to be a mishling, he wondered? Being a changeling was certainly bad. He picked up his binoculars again to watch the American lines. He was a halfling-mishmash of two bits in one, he decided. And the one bit, that was he, was alright. His friends would only pick on what wasn't German in him when they were angry.

Suddenly, from far across the mud-churned field behind the American tanks the music was killed midtune. As if cued to hold its breath, the ice-cold wind died down. The tall poplars lining the medieval drainage ditch encircling the little Hessian village of Geesterheim near the river Rhine southwest of Frankfurt stopped their naïve song and oblivious swaying. Two, three seconds of stillness ensued making the distant scene appear out of order and place. Then began the silent movie of well-rehearsed military motion. A waving of arms, threatening gestures, steam from nostrils and black holes of mouths, opening, shutting, opening, shutting. A shouting NCO getting his herd's attention in this bedlam of overdramatic and underpaid actors willing to die for their country. America the Beautiful. – Brusquely, the wind reappeared in gusts of mockery deigning to translate the remote chaos into hammered fragments of human noise.

Fergal put down the binoculars, turned his head and looked up in reproach at the poplars behind him. They were a naïve bunch but he loved them almost as much as willows. The willow afforded the coolest and most calming of shade in the hot summers of Hessen.

The Americans were under a quarter of a mile away, mounting tanks and shouting confidently. Fergal was good at gauging distance. In German it was more exact. It was about two-hundred-and-fifty metres, zweihundert und fünfzig Meter. Actually, wasn't that just under an eighth of a mile? They hadn't done it at school yet. Maths like that was Big School stuff.

He nodded at his friends, Tristan and Joachim, the only ones with him in the drainage ditch. Geesterheim's last line of defence. Their position was well concealed by an ancient hawthorn.

They took off the grownup bits of uniform that would get in the way. They had managed to filch two Wehrmacht tunics and a greatcoat from the burning pile in the marketplace yesterday. Though much colder in their black shorts it was easier to run in the Hitler Youth's Pimpfe uniform. They'd fight themselves warm soon enough.

Yesterday Geesterheim had burnt twelve years of Germany's past in a huge pile. Today, the waiting game. Tomorrow, business as usual, or even better, the grownups claimed. One was dealing with the Americans after all!

Had anyone in the village known what Fergal and his friends were up to in the drainage ditch, armed to the teeth, surrounded by a year's supply of ammo and Hitler Youth bunting for the victory party afterwards, and, to top it all off, dressed in uniforms with swastikas all over the place. Uniforms that should have received death by fire yesterday, their ashes scattered by the winds of memory. Had anyone known there was in fact a last line of defence, the matter would have been settled simply by a good bashing about the ears, and that would have been that. But no one knew.

The massive helmets did not fit nine year-old heads. Butts and grips of the sub-machine guns were too big for their small hands and fragile shoulders. The boys knew what they were doing though. The Hitler Youth had trained even the Pimpfe of its Jungvolk well for this last victorious stand. Strictly speaking, admission to Hitler's Jungvolk was restricted to age ten to fourteen, but these were hard times. Although the boys hadn't been allowed the P38 pistol and Schmeisser sub-machine gun, they knew exactly how to use all the weapons at their disposal here in the drainage ditch. How to support the K98k rifle, so the recoil doesn't injure your collar bone or shoulder. How to handle the anti-tank Panzerfaust without torching comrades standing behind you. And how to kill with the dagger in close combat without cutting yourself.

Fergal's two friends from primary school got their weapons ready. His own Schmeisser had been prepared for some time. Everyone had three heavy clips in special leather cases. There were masses of reassuring ammo in the ditch.

Fergal heard the wind shout, "goddam show on the road" and "in the mood for killing" and laughter "get me one o' them Nazi Lugers".

He didn't translate this to his friends. It was his own language in another accent with a lot of bad words. His language wasn't bad. He felt a little embarrassed as always. He spoke both English and German. He preferred to think in English. English was gentler and said more. American didn't.

Five years ago his parents had moved from London to Frankfurt for business. They had stayed on.

It wasn't so bad in Germany really, Fergal thought, and once they had settled in the little village of Geesterheim he had even begun to enjoy himself. The one thing his parents should have left behind in England though was his sister, Johanna! Fergal called her J. A nasty piece of work! And he almost shared his name with her. Johanna Frances and Johann Fergal Bulhof-Murphy. His mother, Mutti, was German. His father, Dad, Irish. At the time the family had no difficulty moving to Germany. The Germans liked the Irish. They were independent and hadn't declared war on Germany. There even was an Irish radio station in Berlin, said Dad. Fergal wondered whether they would ever go back to England.

Fergal was born in Oxford, and proud of it. He considered himself an Englishman of mixed parentage. His mother had tapped him on the back of his head once, and with her raised index finger warned him not to say such a thing. Germans liked raising their right index finger at you. Dad said the finger was an endemic obligation for Germans in authority. Germans didn't like mishlings. Mishlings were ambiguous. It was dangerous to belong to two sides. To himself Fergal kept insisting, although half German, half Irish, that he was an Englishman in a rather strange situation. Altogether, quite strange! But, cheer up, Fergal, old chap, look on the bright side, it could be worse, so chin up now and stiff upper lip! He smiled. There were a great many expressions in English to cheer one up.

Across the field the enemy was firing up his tanks, revving heavy diesel engines as if rearing and ready to go racing. Fergal put his ear to the ground to hear what the soil would have to say about the deep rumbling that was already frightening the air around him and his friends. Close to his left eye little lumps of mud were rolling down to the bottom of the ditch into the small stream of half-heartedly steaming Geesterheim sewage. Just on a bit and cooled down, it disappeared into the ground. He focused his attention on the mud in front of him again. He was lying on the slope of a mountain. He was the mountain. First, sliding beds of gravel, then rocks, and finally huge boulders were beginning their unstoppable descent into the valley. An alpine avalanche. Fergal pushed more mud down into the ditch. He hadn't been to see the Alps yet. In the five years the Bulhof-Murphys had spent here his Dad had always been very busy.

Tristan's face was close to Fergal's. Tristan was not thinking of the Alps. His eyes were watering and his nose twitching. Despite the chill in the air the stench of sewage in the ditch was breathtaking. The deep rumble of the tanks no longer needed the wind to be heard. It was ever pervasive and all-round. Fergal felt the ground vibrating through his entire body. Each rev sent a wave of sickness from his head down to his toes. The path of fear.

Tristan's face relaxed so much it looked to Fergal as if his friend was falling down a deep well away from him. No! He was just crying, clutching his Hitler Youth dagger like an upside-down crucifix. Tristan was praying, all the while looking straight at Fergal. Joachim, on Tristan's other side, started throwing up and farting at the same time. It wasn't fear. Not in Joachim's case! It was the deep, throbbing noise from the guts of those predators waiting to pounce in the near distance. Maybe it was fear. No. Joachim knew no fear. He was the hardest of them all.

Tristan crossed himself. "We're all going to die, Ferkel. We can still go back home, you know. Führer or no Führer. It's all over, you know that, don't you?" he was crying. He didn't appear embarrassed at all. – What a strange sight!

Fergal had over time come used to his friends' calling him Ferkel. Germans couldn't say Fergal the proper Irish or English way, so he had become Ferkel to them. In German Ferkel meant piglet or little swine. In the beginning he had just been the foreigner, that little Ferkel. Now, his friends called him Ferkel. Most of the time, affectionately.

"No," Fergal answered quietly, "we'll be fine. I promise."

Tristan was helping Fergal with the avalanche. There was a proper little dam at the bottom now.

"Where does the earth get all this mud from?" Tristan asked.

Fergal thought for a bit before he answered, "From itself."

"It's *herself* in German, Ferkel. *Die Erde* not *das Erde*."

"Is it?"

"Maybe not. *Itself* sounds right."

"I think it is *itself*." Fergal got confused sometimes. There was no real logic. You had to listen to learn. *Das Mädchen,* a girl with the definite article was not *herself* but *itself*, but a woman, *die Frau,* definite article, was herself. Maybe it had something to do with age. Then again a boy, *ein Junge,* was altogether himself as much as a man, *ein Mann,* indefinite article.

"Arrgh!" German was difficult, but Fergal had sort of just learnt it from one day to the next without even an accent.

"That's *Ach!* in German."

"I know that. But there are words and sounds in English which describe things better."

"No, there aren't, Ferkel! And you know it. German is the best language in the world. You said *inglisch*, but its spelt *englisch,* which means we say it right and you don't and you are the one with the accent. In German you say what you mean. So there!" Tristan was always trying to improve Fergal's German even if there was no real correcting to be done. From Tristan's point of view there was a good German in *almost* everybody, as long as they were Nordic. But the Celts weren't that bad really.

They kept pushing more mud down to the bottom.

"We've just built the world-famous Shit Dam," Fergal said.

"I'm not afraid of death." Tristan was drilling a hole with his dagger in the ground.

"Damn shit! We'll survive," Joachim said in his quiet, slow and polite sounding style, scratching his crotch, "and win this, you thin little choirboy heap of shit, son of a whore called Tristan herself. We'll get the Iron Cross for this, maggots. Sieg Heil! Go on, Ferkel! Catch a bullet in the eye and tell us what's going on." Joachim was always full of harsh yet soft-spoken, slow and deliberate abuse. His grown-up language was down to the fact that his parents were never at home. His grandmother looked after him. She beat him for just about anything, and especially when he raised his voice at her. She was almost deaf and hated noise. So Joachim had devised this special way of quietly hurling the worst type of abuse known to man at her. He had made it his raison d'être to study the language from hell and construct it into viable sentences understood by his friends but not his grandmother. The *Duden*, that vast dictionary of the German language, was his bible. New hellish insults were celebrated by inviting everyone of his friends round, explaining to them the latest *Mordwort* kill-word for granny like *Würgehexe mit Riesenrektum,* the throttling witch with the giant rectum, and then hurl the new terms of abuse at her quietly. Everyone was allowed to have a go. They'd pretend to say *good day, Frau Hammerich,* politely with a smile and the obligatory, respectful bow reserved for grownups. In reality it was a quiet *Guten Tag, Du fauler Arschwurm, Hammerich!* Good day, you rotting arse worm, Hammerich. It was great fun. A new Mordwort or even whole phrase was learnt almost every day. Last week, when the Americans had still seemed so far away, Joachim's new thing had been to threaten everyone with *clog your shit mouth or I'll cut another hole in your penis and then you can piss in a cross.* It hadn't been so much the words then. It was all about the idea of weeing in a cross.

"Eh, Ferkel! Wake up from your salacious, infantile wet dream of dirt and dams and stop rubbing your baby-rat riddled crotch, you walking venereal disease. Tell us what's going on!"

Rats, commonly also known as *Sackratten,* sack-rats, were crabs in English.

"I wasn't dreaming, and I don't have sack-rats."

Joachim would have to explain *salacious infantile wet dreams* and *venereal disease* later. Those were really new, big words. Joachim must have tried them on his granny already.

"Then plug that talkative arsehole of yours and check, you cripple-cock."

The rumbling of the engines now joined the screeching of the tracks and the whine of their Jeeps.

The enemy was on the move!

Carefully Fergal raised his head over the side of the ditch again. The tanks were advancing on Geesterheim. Fergal wasn't able to tell whether it all looked a bit too cautious or too leisurely. It didn't matter! First the Americans would have to try and get past their ditch with the world-famous Shit Dam. Fergal and his friends were waiting and ready for them.

The Americans had crossed the Rhine nearby just yesterday. Germany had to be saved from the enemy invaders at all cost. To the last man, was the order. The old ones had gone home shaking their heads. One mad SS Rottenführer passing through undercover away from the front in a strange assortment of mufti and uniform had wanted to mobilise the entire village for the greater glory of blah-blah and, boom, found himself dead with a tidy hole in his head and children laughing at the corpse getting a hard-on. The murderer was never found, and the village policeman, Wachtmeister Erhardt, a truly patriotic local, had got rid of the smoking pistol in his hand.

All in all, there had not exactly been much of a Volkssturm here. The People's Storm. All weapons and ammunition, even some hunting rifles and shotguns had been piled up outside Geesterheim in front of the village signpost facing the country road going west. West towards France, Spain, Portugal, and then by boat to New York. Wachtmeister Erhardt had donated an enormous arsenal of K98k carbines and some Schmeisser sub-machine guns with the right calibre ammo stacked neatly by the side. A mass of potato masher hand grenades and anti-tank Panzerfäuste, from the four very-old-man strong Volkssturm and the HJ Hitler Youth, topped off all the charitable donations offered for the sake of peace. Geesterheimers wanted to show the invading American enemy hordes that resistance against them was by public decree strictly prohibited, *strengstens verboten,* and the consumption of the area's own excellent food and wine was quite positively encouraged as it would endow the unwittingly uncultured with the seeds of Germany. The way to a man's heart is via his stomach. *Liebe geht durch den Magen*, they said, and thus was the best basis for proselytising the ignorant to Germanism.

A hand-painted sign in the middle of the road at the village entrance, right next to the not at all unsizable pile of weaponry, announced *Gut Fuhd end Whine? Komm tuh Zum Weißen Hirsch!* There really was no better food the world over than at *The White Hart.*

The remainder of all Nazi history had then been burnt promptly in the marketplace at the centre of the village. Passports, licences and money were exempt from the historic auto-da-fé because without such papers, though still swastika-adorned, you were nothing in this world nor in the new one. There had to be order! *Ordnung muß sein* was after all the most important of German phrases. The fire had burnt through the night and there had been a bit of a Fest with wine and merry dancing.

For the boys the *Zum Weißen Hirsch* was boring.

Besides rescuing some bits of uniform from the flames, the Fire Fest had been boring.

The Gun Fest, however …! The big pile of charity arms outside the village was not at all boring.

In the early hours of the morning at two o'clock Fergal, Joachim and Tristan had snuck off to pinch as much as possible, so they could really face off the enemy all by themselves. The guard was very much asleep also known as *besoffen.* Pissed.

Stealing three sub-machine guns and six rifles was easy. Wachtmeister Erhardt, whose demeanour had changed hurriedly and completely in mufti, had been guarding the pile for the peace offering with four friends. One white flag and thirty cases of the local red. By midnight the attack still hadn't come, despite distant battle thunder and orange sky covering the whole horizon over Frankfurt. The beautifully romantic glow from Geesterheim's own historic marketplace was not to be sniffed at either.

By one o'clock in the morning Wachtmeister Erhardt and friends had been so tired, cold, and indignant at the fact that the

Americans might actually not bother to capture strategically important Geesterheim, Erhardt had sent his friends home sulking and cursing in a heavy stagger. They had fully expected an especially dedicated Hollywood culinary unit of singing, tap-dancing and toque-topped New York Italians waving big, white napkins. As Wachtmeister Erhardt and friends had missed out on the Fire Fest, they had carefully sampled twenty-four bottles of the local red, concluding there was no better wine – *der beste Wein, den es gibt!* – for the Americans than their very own, very local, very rare, red Rhein Hessen. Had anyone disagreed, calling it a pale red, in fact a rosé, more on the watery side really, Wachtmeister Erhardt would have found it within himself to shoot the swine.

Carrying the ammo, especially the heavy crates of bullets and grenades, had taken Fergal and his friends almost two hours of heavy labour until the ditch was quite full. Considering what it could do, a Panzerfaust was really quite light.

Joachim hit Fergal's thigh with a stick for attention. Fergal didn't react. Joachim hit him again and asked most politely, "Hey! You piece of glistening, foreign shit, what is happening!?"

Tristan smiled and shook his head disdainfully at Joachim. At times, Tristan too could seem very grownup. His parents were psychiatrists. Joachim just couldn't help himself. With the surname of LeBatard, Joachim's family were the Huguenot leftovers of Napoleon's retreat from Hessen, at least according to Joachim. And as every self-respecting Catholic or sane person like Tristan knew, Protestant Huguenot was really a generic term for tough, cussing, idiot bastards. And Tristan just kept smiling.

Fergal's eyes were watering with pain. "You could check for yourself!"

Because of Granny school, Joachim knew how to cause as much pain as possible with very little effort. Fergal knew it was best not to react to Joachim.

"No."

"They're coming right at us but very slowly. I'd say, still one-hundred-and-fifty meters, three minutes. Maybe five. They're crawling."

"Damn loud though."

"Hang on …"

"What?"

"They're getting cocky. Their foot soldiers are overtaking their tanks. They're actually walking abreast. There're some Jeeps too. These guys have no training!"

Tristan laughed, "They're American. They think no harm will come to them. They're invincible John Waynes and then, bang, film's over. My father told me Americans break really easily and cry. Of all soldiers he's seen, Americans are the most uneducated and hate dying most."

"Maybe that's because they have more to live for," Fergal frowned.

"Like what? – I suppose …" Tristan hesitated, "… you're right, Ferkel! Of course, how could I've not seen. They do have more to live for, like …"

"What?"

"Like … more, always more! Get it!?"

"Shut up, turd! This is war. Catch my gas!" Joachim let off a blubbery, juicy fart and waved invisible fumes towards Tristan in particular. "Shit! That was a wet one."

"No, I don't get it." Fergal scratched his head.

"They have more to live for, right … right?"

"I don't get it."

"Ferkel, you are a bit stupid really, aren't you? The only thing Americans have to live for is more, … and that is very sad! They don't live for life, they just live for more for ever more. So, there!"

Fergal thought for a moment, "What exactly does your father do?"

"He's a psychiatrist."

"I know that, Tristan. But what exactly …?"

"I have no idea."

Fergal slid back into the ditch with his head safely out of view. Just in time! The first shot was fired over the ditch by the Americans. The boys flinched. There was quiet. Over the deep rumble of the engines the boys heard laughter. A second shot was fired. The sound of glass breaking from the village. More laughter. Some more shots, more glass breaking, more laughter. And suddenly all hell broke loose.

Fergal carefully raised his head halfway out again. He knew he might die. They were too close for comfort now. Most of the enemy's soldiers had taken up firing position, blasting away, standing or kneeling in front of the tanks and even on top of them. The Jeep crews smoked and chatted leisurely watching Geesterheim crumble in this open-air war movie. Heavier gun fire started and smoke was laid as if for fun. Geesterheim was their shooting gallery. The enemy was not expecting any resistance.

From their position the boys could see masonry flying, brick walls exploding outward, roofs lifting off.

The enemy was laying waste to their village. Their homes!

A roof tile landed hot and smoking next to Tristan's head. Then an even stranger thing happened. Fergal squinted to see more clearly. Yes, it was a baby. A baby was flying high through the air describing an arch before it disappeared behind a house.

"Did you see that?! Did you see that?!!!" he shouted with his hand covering his mouth.

"What?" Tristan and Joachim shook their heads.

"A baby just flew past the church."

"What!?"

"Must have been the air pressure of an exploding shell." Fergal's Dad had told him all about that. Sometimes bombs didn't cut you to pieces. All the shrapnel passed you by and they just lifted you up high into the air. If you were lucky you'd land safely.

"Scheiße!" Joachim didn't say more than that, which in Joachim-terms meant an unspeakable lot of excited emotion, be it joy or terror. Of course, Joachim knew no terror!

The Americans stopped firing. Maybe they had seen the flying baby of Geesterheim and were now trying to spot the baby-delivery stork to shoot down and take home as a souvenir. Americans were like that.

Come what may, this was the boys' glorious moment!

Cue, *Für Führer, Volk und Vaterland.*

Hours before, Geesterheim's last line of defence had laid out exactly what they were going to do. In essence, the plan was to use as much of the ammo as possible and shoot the shit out of the Americans. In greater detail, the plan was just as straightforward. Start with the Panzerfaust and work your way down to your Hitler

Youth dagger, if then it comes down to that and you're not dead already. Whatever you do though, kill as many Americans as possible.

Simple.

Fergal, Joachim and Tristan raised their heads out of the ditch together. At fifty meters the Americans were now close enough. Their smoke grenades didn't help them one little bit. The wind was too erratic.

The boys unleashed hell.

Panzerfäuste first. In no time at all the Jeeps were taken out and four tanks were burning. The enemy was in disarray. Next, the potato masher hand grenades. The long handle of the Stielgranate made throwing them child's play. In quick succession they managed to throw thirty in all. Joachim had all the while been laying covering fire, spending clip after clip.

Now though, the most horribly glorious moment all had been looking forward to heroically lay directly ahead of them.

Getting out of the ditch, over the top and doing your best.

Führer befiehl! Wir folgen Dir! Führer command! We'll follow you!

Somehow all fear had gone. No thought of death remained. Only glory! – As the Great War elders used to say from their bench around the great thousand-year-old German oak by the church in the marketplace, *Dulce et decorum est pro patria mori!* This was in the boys' hearts.

Fergal took a deep breath and nodded an encouraging and comforting smile at his comrades. The enemy could not be allowed to regroup.

"Victory will be ours!" Their unifying battle cry, *Der Sieg wird unser sein* catapulted them out of the ditch. Running, attacking, firing, they screamed this slogan printed on the last Nazi poster that had ever gone up in the village, over and over again, "Der Sieg wird unser sein! Der Sieg wird unser sein! Der Sieg wird unser sein!"

Fergal felt the heat of the Schmeisser's barrel. The first clip was empty, the second one slotted in quickly. Tristan and Joachim provided excellent cover. He couldn't believe his eyes though. Americans, by virtue of their cinema, self-proclaimed invincible, weren't immortal cowboy-heroes. Like flies these guys were dropping left, right and centre. They looked befuddled. They really hadn't expected a fight. A lot of them were reloading. What was going on? Did they want to die?! Why didn't they concentrate? This was war!

Fergal wounded and killed a lot of them. It seemed so easy. Not like what Heinrich, Geesterheim's most talkative war veteran and GP said about killing. A lot of people didn't like Heinrich. They secretly called him the Vegetable-Man and said he should be put away because he'd been damaged. "Up there, you know," they whispered amongst themselves, tapping their foreheads with their index fingers.

For some reason Heinrich always spoke to Fergal of the War. No one else. Just Fergal. It was easy to kill in a second, and hell to live with for the rest of your life. Some could live with the hell. Others couldn't. Most others.

Fergal kept killing. He would have to ask Heinrich about his nickname one day. That is, if he got out of this alive.

There was a click from the bolt. The chamber was open. Smoking. Intense heat.

Fergal was out of ammo.

Tristan got shot through the throat and lost half of his neck. His head tilted. He looked down at his feet. Then, as if pushed hard by invisible hands, he just flipped over and lay there on his back, wheezing a little and briefly spluttering blood bubbles out of the wide-open side of his neck, with an arm halfway up in the air. The way they had always played war. A shot through his foot and chest and he was still. The arm stayed up with his hand clawing the air. Fergal couldn't see where the shot had come from. Fergal couldn't move. A handful of soldiers were coming towards him, motioning at him, shouting to put down his weapon in his own language. Americans could sometimes sound Irish, Dad said.

Joachim ran out of ammo. He was shot through the groin. Lifting him off the ground. Fergal saw a huge, red opening in his friend's lower back. Joachim came to rest on his front with his bottom sticking up in the air. In slow-motion he fell sideways. His hands needlessly covering the hole where his groin had been just two seconds ago.

The Americans kept shouting. Fergal pulled his Hitler Youth dagger screaming back in English he'd kill them all, adding "Schweinehunde" in German. Suddenly his right arm was missing. He looked at the swift absence in wonder, turning to see where his arm had gone, spraying his blood like a protective, magic circle around him. There it was! Just behind him still clutching the dagger. He went to put it back on again when a bullet through his hip sent him flying. He knew now that he was going to die. How easy it seemed. How painless.

The bullet had thrown him a good two meters back towards his ditch with the world-famous Shit Dam at its bottom. He would have loved to see the Alps even if Mutti had insisted on holding his hand. Why was Heinrich called the Vegetable Man? Fergal tried to crawl forwards with one arm to play avalanche again. Just one more time! The ground by his face was comfortably warm and wet. He didn't realize it was his own blood pumping out of his body. Warm comfort. He needed sleep. He heard a voice shout, "Jesus Christ! Kids! Stupid little fuckers."

Fergal began fainting slowly. What a strange feeling this weakness was. It was as though your stomach was emptying through your bladder.

A voice brought him back abruptly, "What the hell do you kids think you're playing at?" He was pulled up hard onto his feet by his remaining arm. "Hey! Answer me! Shpekken Anglish, you little German runt?" Fergal felt his head being twisted upward by a gigantic hand. He couldn't avoid the blue steel eyes staring at him from the most scar-ploughed face he had ever seen.

"Shpekken Anglish? – Answer me, you little fuck!"

Soldiers were beginning to gather round, joking, laughing.

"Yes, I do. Just let me die in peace. I've done my duty," Fergal answered quietly in a heavy German accent. The soldiers' laughter grew more intense.

"Speak up, you tit-suckin' pile of Nazi puss. I can't hear you. You want me to show you dead. I'm gonna kill ya dead …" he was interrupted.

"Sergeant!" Another soldier arrived at the dying-kid party laughing.

"Sir!"

"Enough. Leave him alone. He's a friend's kid."

"I know, sir. With all due respect, this kid needs scaring. You saw the shit he and his friends just pulled."

"Yes. It's alright. Let me talk to him. You get the men." The sergeant moved everyone back to the tanks. There was a lot of laughing and nodding over in Fergal's direction. Cigarettes were lit. A transistor radio came on with AFN playing the Rolling Stones' *Angie*.

"Right, Fergal. Stop shaking and tell me … what in the hell are you doing here?" This was Lieutenant Hardy from Geesterheim's US garrison five miles outside the village. A good friend of Fergal's parents, Martha and Seán.

"We were playing war, sir."

"Don't call me *sir*, Fergal. You know my name's Jon."

"Yes, Sir. Lieutenant Hardy, sir."

Lt Hardy waved Joachim and Tristan over who had recovered from their respective deaths trying very hard to hide in the hawthorn. Tristan was trembling and crying. Joachim's eyes were squinting at the sky. The sergeant had scared the living daylights out of all three with his voice.

"Do your friends understand me?"

"No, Jon." But Joachim and Tristan nodded.

"So you do understand me?"

Joachim and Tristan nodded again and said, "Yes" in English.

Fergal smiled, "They just know how to answer that and a few other things. It's the television and me. I've taught them."

"Right. Never ever throw stones at us again! I'm telling you, and you tell your friends."

"They were grenades …"

"Right! Don't ever pull a stunt like that again. Our blanks can kill you, the tanks can crush you. And that hurts, right! And then you're dead. This is a serious exercise, and you can tell your German buddies here that we're doing it to save them and their families from the Commies. And what are those broomsticks you're holding? Rifles, right!?"

"They're our guns."

Tristan's twenty-year old brother Siegfried had made them. One broomstick for the barrel. One triangular bit of plywood for the butt. Screws and lots of heavy-duty tape. You just had to imagine it, and it looked fantastically real! Fergal was best at making sounds of shooting and explosions with his mouth.

"Right. Guns."

"But our pistols look more real." Fergal produced a small toy pistol. Joachim and Tristan pulled theirs out of their coat pockets too, but carefully. They didn't want the tall American to take them away.

"Those are tiny .45 replicas," Lt Hardy laughed. "You can tell your friends I'll get you some real-looking ones next time I see you. Blank-firing 1911 kiddie Colt. How about it?"

"Seriously?" Fergal couldn't believe his luck. He wouldn't be able to take it home though, because Mutti hated guns, even tiny Airfix and Revell war toys. Fergal was just about allowed to keep his RAF bombers at home because Dad had been in the *englische Luftwaffe*. Fergal's guns were all kept at Tristan's, where one more or less really didn't matter. But this was just fantastic! An almost real Colt! He translated for his friends. The boys were ecstatic.

"Right. Just promise, you won't ever do such a thing again because if something happens, I might get into trouble and it won't look good in the papers."

The boys promised. A tank revved hard. Hardy made a face.

"Before I go, kids … who won?"

"We did, Jon. We played Hitler Youth."

"Oh, yeah! And you won, right!?" Hardy smiled. Then his face contorted. He was trying too hard to look serious, "Yeah, I heard about that one. The eight or so Hitler kids who got the locals in real trouble. Geesterheim's last stand! Long before my time. They got ripped to shreds. Our guys couldn't believe their eyes when they found the bits of them. I guess, it was in your ditch right there, eh."

Fergal nodded.

"What a sad story. Rare for kids to play kids though." Hardy closed his eyes for a second and shook his head, "I never played kid when I was a kid."

Fergal nodded again, "They weren't kids! They were all fourteen and even sixteen. Tristan told me all about it. His uncle was one of them."

Hardy tilted his head at Tristan, "What a damn shame." He paused as if thinking. "You look familiar. Your name's Tristan, Tristan Neussler, right. I've seen you with your brother. We know all about you. It's Siggy. Sick Siggy. The one who dresses up and walks round attacking Jeeps 'n' stuff! Yeah. Real funny fella. Well. Gotta go. And don't pull shit … a stunt like this again. And I didn't say *shit* just now, ok! … What's that?"

Joachim was whispering in Fergal's ear.

"What's your buddy wanna know, Fergal!?"

"Joachim is asking, why you're doing your exercises like this all over the fields during Carfree Sunday?" Being a polite interpreter Fergal left out Joachim's *crab commandoes. Sackrattenkommando.* It would have jeopardised the 1911 Colt.

"What! Why not? We pay the farmers for the damage and afterwards they can still go plant stuff in them. It's a sure win for 'em, right."

Fergal translated even though he didn't understand entirely. Joachim shook his head and whispered again.

"Joachim says November isn't really autumn because it's too cold now, and that's why it's called Autumn Manoeuvres. He wants to know why you're allowed to have fun in your tanks because you made the oil crisis because of Israel and Vietnam which you lost sort of and Germans have to stay at home and now his parents are at home today and they're in a really bad mood because they can't drive their car." Fergal omitted *and when I'm big I'm going to sow up your arses and then you'll stop shitting about all over the place.*

"Tell 'em, … they lost the damn war, right. We're here to help. – Fergal, I'd really love to chat … see ya soon and give my best regards to …" a tank revved hard, there was an horrendous, high-pitched scream.

"Jesus!" Hardy ran over to his men. Soldiers were shouting, pointing at the tracks of one of their tanks that had come to a rocking halt. An arm was sticking out underneath. Suddenly the tank started moving again. There were shouts of "Stop! Stop! Stop the fuckin' tank! Stop the damn thing! Back up! Back, for Chrissakes!"

When the scar-faced sergeant noticed the boys were watching he only took one look at them. Fergal, Joachim and Tristan ran like the wind. Tristan was smiling.

The Vegetable Man

Schadenfreude

Catching their breath the three friends were sitting on the cold, wet ground outside the high, white back wall of the property where Joachim lived. The Americans were in terrible disarray just three hundred meters away. A military ambulance was on the scene already. It was half past three in the afternoon and getting dark. Fergal loved November. His ninth birthday had been just yesterday, and then there was Christmas and more celebrating. His sister said birthday and Christmas so close together meant less presents. That might have been true, but Fergal loved the double-party. He was in a nervous state of anticipation from October to December. Presents hadn't been so good this year. Lots of clothes and shoes, and no guns or bombers or tanks.

This winter of 1973 was going to be a cold one, the papers said. Dad said that was because of the oil crisis, but they had enough oil at home in the basement tanks to stay warm. Mutti said they wouldn't have to freeze to death in the cellar, wrapped in a threadbare woolly blanket, surrounded by the dead and dying as in the terrible winter of '47.

Fergal felt sick thinking about the horrendous accident. It was as if he had been run over by a tank himself. His mind did this to him quite a lot. Tristan was acting strange though. He just kept on smiling!

Joachim's voice was much quieter than usual, "You two flatfooted losers, help me over the wall!" He was in a bad mood for some reason and wouldn't be good for anything else for the rest of this dark afternoon anyway. His parents would make him sit in front of the television with them to have a bit of a family get-together. Despite all the things he said about them, he wanted to be with them. Carfree Sunday was a blessing of sorts.

Tristan and Fergal gave Joachim a leg up over the wall and Joachim disappeared off into his own world with a quietly uttered and almost kind sounding, "Scheiße."

The two friends sat back down in the mud.

"I think Joachim won this one."

"Won what, Tristan?"

"Dying the best death. The way he looked, and held his willy, and he didn't mind getting completely dirty. And his farting and vomiting was pretty good too. Though, you weren't bad either. Your shooting and shouting and the way you flew forward in the mud really looked like you'd been hit in the back. Why were you looking at your shoulder?" Tristan kept on grinning weirdly.

"They shot off my arm and I was bleeding a lot before I died."

"Oh, right. Terrible pain. It can take up to eight minutes to bleed empty when an artery's been hit."

"How do you know all this, Tristan?"

"Pappi."

"And how do you manage to always stay so clean?"

"Mammi gets very angry." Tristan was fidgeting with something massive in his coat pocket. It hadn't been there before they'd started playing war with the Americans.

"I see." Fergal took out his hanky and played with it for a bit. He loved fingering the hard bits. He called it *nuddling*. He had a special hiding place for old hankies under his mattress so Mutti couldn't wash them. Mutti was always washing and ironing.

"That's disgusting, Ferkel."

"So what! You've been smiling all the time since the accident with the tank, Tristan."

"Yes, of course."

"What?"

"Of course."

"Eh?"

"I hate Americans."

"Why?"

"You are half-American, but you don't count, Ferkel."

"I'm not half-American. My Mutti's German, my Dad is Irish, and I … I am English!"

"You're sure about that?"

"Oh yes!"

"That makes you an almost perfect American."

"I'm not American."

"You think so!? You're sort of half of them and half of us. Maybe you can half understand, and then you'll be an almost proper German. Then again, you'll never be a proper German. Bit sad really."

"Then try one half of me and stop smiling like that."

"I can't. It's true Schadenfreude. And which half of you shall I try? The good half or the bad half?"

"What's the bad half?"

"The American one."

"Try the other half then."

"I hate their stupid Negermusik, and they speak so loudly all the time to sound sincere even when they're not. And they're *never* sincere, Dad says, that's why they're always loud. *And* they chew gum all the time like they're stupid sheep or cows or something. – Do you really think their Leutnant will get us the guns? I don't!"

"He's a Lieutenant not a Leutnant. That's German."

"Yes. And … !?"

"He's my friend."

"Yes, of course, he is. – Do you really believe that? They're only friends if there's something in it for them. Pappi says Americans even created a word to describe themselves and everything they say."

"What's that?"

"Bullshit."

"What do you mean?"

"It's *bullshit*! The word is. They are bullshit and they talk bullshit."

"I know what bullshit means. It's a very rude word, Tristan!"

"Americans are rude and loud because they have to be because they are full of bullshit and being loud is sincere for them, so they think we will take them seriously. Americans and truth don't go together. They're just like the Nazis, Pappi says, just more careful with the Jews because the Jews run their business for them."

"There are some really nice chaps though, Tristan."

"Bollerboe!"

"What does that mean?"

"See, you are a complete foreigner!"

"What does it mean though?"

"Same as bullshit, but the proper German way to say it."

"But Bollerboe doesn't mean a thing. Bullshit does."

"Bollerboe means you're talking nonsense. In our language you can also say *go to Bollerboe* like go to hell."

"J hasn't told me."

"Your sister is more of a foreigner than you, Ferkel."

"She knows a lot of German."

"Like learning a foreign language."

"She says she's German. Mostly."

"That's J's own Bollerboe."

"Bollerboe, Tristan! – Where is Bollerboe?"

"Don't know. Stop asking silly foreign questions, Ferkel."

"But you always know the answer."

"Bollerboe is some place that doesn't exist. Like Father Christmas and the North Pole."

"Father Christmas is real."

"Nonsense."

"Very real!"

"Bollerboe! Siegfried *and* Pappi told me so! So there!"

"I believe in him."

"You're a sad foreigner."

"So, where's Bollerboe?"

"It's up north in Germany. Full of Frisian idiots wearing their Frisian mink."

"What's a Frisian mink?"

"Their yellow oil jackets they have to wear all the time because it never stops raining and they're always angry because they're stupid."

"How can it be up north if it doesn't exist."

"You are such a child, Ferkel. Bollerboe was made up for the saying *go to Bollerboe* or *you're talking Bollerboe.* And when they invented it, they invented it for North Germany in Friesland. Everybody knows East Frisians are totally stupid."

"I thought you said all Germans are perfect."

"Not the ones from Bollerboe, and I suppose East Zone German communists are no longer perfect either."

"You're full of Bollerboe."

"You can't say it like that! You can say *Bollerboe,* or *don't talk Bollerboe,* or *go to Bollerboe.* If you say anything else you're a real foreigner and you're only pretending to be a German and you're a spy like all the stupid Americans."

"Yeah, yeah, yeah, Tristan. Bollerboe! I know thousands of nice Americans!"

"I don't know any, and if I did I'd become their enemy."

"Well, that's why."

"What d'you mean? You're talking Bollerboe again. – I hate them, and they take the mickey out of Siegfried. Siegfried is sick, and Mammi and Pappi say he doesn't know what he's doing, and that's why he is the way he is."

"Your brother Siggy is good fun, I think."

"Yes, but your sister isn't."

"No. She's mean."

"Ferkel, I'm going home. I'm cold."

"Ok. Do you want to play tomorrow after school?"

"No. Your birthday was great though, and Siegfried is going you-know-where on Friday."

"No! He's not going back in the mad people's *Irrenhaus,* is he? Again?"

Tristan sighed and didn't sound convincing when he said, "Don't say *Irrenhaus* or I'll hit you."

"Ok."

"Ferkel?"

"Yes, …"

"I found this on the battlefield and I can't take it home because otherwise Siegfried gets into even more trouble. It's like new and the pin is still in." Tristan pulled a smoke grenade from his coat pocket. This was what he had been fidgeting with all the time.

"Wow! Great! We've never had one of those. Looks a bit like a can of Coke."

"Yes, doesn't it? Maybe Coca Cola make them, just in green. Your American friends are all over the place with their stuff."

"They're not all my friends."

"But some of them … thousands, you said."

"Yes. But friends are not from any country, Tristan. They're just friends."

"*Really!?* – Mine are German, and one of them is half."

"I can hide the grenade in the hallway cupboard, no problem." Fergal took it from his friend. It was very heavy.

"Great! – Let's meet on Saturday. We can let it off then." Tristan got up but didn't leave immediately. It was very dark now. In the distance a US Army Red Cross helicopter was landing on an island of bright light. The whole accident area had been illuminated theatrically.

Fergal used his binoculars. He thought of the old Greek stories his Mutti always read aloud to him. He loved Odysseus and his wooden horse. The tanks were arranged in a semicircle as silent, invisible gods presiding over the lives of man as stern and brutal judges from Mount Olympus. He passed the binoculars to Tristan who shook his head, "I don't need them."

The helicopter took off again. The chaos continued for a while. Then the tanks began slowly moving into distance heading northeast to Geesterheim Garrison on the main road to Darmstadt and Frankfurt.

Tristan was still smiling when he turned to finally say goodbye.

Fergal stayed sitting against Joachim's back wall. He was wearing his winter play-coat so mud didn't matter.

What a strange word *Schadenfreude* was. *Damage Fun*, translated Fergal to himself. The words were opposite. Americans and truth, Tristan had said. What about the Russians? He didn't know any Russians. Tristan was full of Bollerboe! Never mind. Tristan was his friend. Damage-fun was like saying *bad-good* or *fire-water*. Americans sold firewater to Red Injuns on the telly. Well, then the Americans had probably still been English and Irish. And French, Italian, German and Greek and loads more. Fergal looked up with a start. Americans were really like Europeans, just all in one country. Unified.

The tanks had disappeared. It was a deep-blue-sea coloured evening. Christmas was in the air already. Only four weeks to go until the German Father Christmas *Weihnachtsmann* would knock on the door with his long, white beard and the short broom they called *Rute* here. If you'd been naughty, you'd get the *Rute*. It was a very German invention for a tool, especially designed for hitting children around the festive season. Very simple really, like a broom without the stick. *Rute*. Fergal realised it was a bit like *root* or *rod* in English. Maybe the words were related? *Spare the rod, spoil the child*, Dad didn't agree with. Dad liked *creating a rod for his own back* though, Mutti said, when he left everything up to the business accountant, Mr. RAF Flight so-and-so.

"Have you been a good child?" Weihnachtsmann would ask Fergal. He had a deep, frightening hollow voice.

"Yes, dear, holy Weihnachtsmann! I've been good all year!" Fergal would answer. Mutti would laugh. Dad would as ever be on the loo at this very specific point in time for Christmas. Fergal had his suspicions about Dad. Maybe Dad didn't want to see Weihnachtsmann because he had been very, very naughty. Never mind! And then, his horrid, vile, nasty sister J, Wicked Witch of the East, as in *Reds Under The Bed*, would say something like, "Fergal pulled my long beautiful hair twelve times, kicked me in the shin five times, broke one of my records, and hit me in the eye with his stupid blue Jensen Interceptor. Yes, Weihnachtsmann, apart from that, my brother's been a good child."

Weihnachtsmann would then pretend to hit Fergal with the Rute. Somehow though there was a silent pact between Fergal and the holy man in the huge dressing gown similar to Dad's. It was a simple pact, and it involved no real pain, but Fergal pretended to be in an awful lot of agony anyway, which pleased J no end. Once, two or so years ago, Fergal had asked Dad why Weihnachtsmann was wearing the same style dressing gown as he did. Dad had then told Fergal the whole truth and nothing but the truth, so help him God, at least for the time being.

"Weihnachtsmann is a Saint, Fergal. He has nothing but his long, white, flowin' beard. To be in many places at the same time, he has to fragment himself a lot."

"Fragment?"

"That means he copies himself for all the millions and millions and millions of children there are in this world, simultaneously."

"Simmultinissly?"

"Simultaneously!"

"Simmultinouslaly."

"Simultaneously!"

"Phew! That is a difficult word!"

"Try again! Simultaneously."

"Simmultainaslaly."

"Almost there." So it went on for a bit until Fergal had it.

"Simultaneously."

"Well done!"

"What's it mean for Weihnachtsmann?"

"It means, he does it at the same time. He copies himself into millions and billions of Weihnachtsmanns at the same time. Simultaneously. He doesn't, though, have the power to copy himself wearing his proper clothes, because all of his effort goes into making toys and good things for the poor, so he can take on their pain. He's a real Saint you see. So, wherever he turns up, he gets the parents' clothes because parents know about this."

"So, … he's naked?"

"Yes."

"And we are poor?"

"No."

"J says, he's a skeleton underneath the mask, and he will come one night to tear me apart in my sleep, and then he'll eat my giblets, and he'll make sure I'm alive to watch it."

"Good grief! That's a lie, Fergal! I must talk to Frances about this."

"Would Weihnachtsmann dress up, like … in Mutti's dressing gown?"

"That's a perfectly valid question, Fergal. He's conservative though. You see, that's why he's called Weihnachtsmann and not Weihnachtsfrau."

"Or Mother Christmas."

"Absolutely right."

"Or Christa Cringle."

Dad had seen the deep blue sea in Arabia. Very quiet and serene. Dad had fought a lot in the RAF. Very, very loud. He had seen the world but he had never been to the North Pole.

Fergal thought, the world was a very loud place. Like tanks.

Back in the cold mud, leaning against Joachim's back wall, it suddenly struck him. There wasn't a single sound in the air! The wind had completely died down. There was an oak just to his left. Its leaves were always the clingiest and last to fall. The oak was the slowest of all. But you really knew it was winter when its orange-brown leaves were down to a gentle whisper. Not even the tiniest of whispers now.

Desperately his ears tried to search for sound. Any sound! In his mind's eye he saw a radar scanner. He laughed. There! That was sound. He could hear his blood being pumped around his ears by his heart. Boom-boom … boom-boom. Little jungle people with bongos in his ears. They were the famous Waxobumm tribe of fat-fat Wetchamoonis with the most ugly language on earth because their language was called Wetchamoonsi fat-fart. A bit like the Germans in Fergal's mind before the Bulhof-Murphys came to West Germany. He sighed. But never mind! The Waxobumm with their bongos in Fergal's ears would eventually find true love and happiness when his ear hairs started growing like Heinrich the Vegetable Man's. Those were long ear hairs, like vines. In fact, they were so long the Waxobumm could use them for Tarzan liana practice, after bongo training. Fergal's coat made a sound too. A soft woolly sound. Blood pumping in his ears, wool rubbing. He tapped the ground with his hand in time. He had a concert going. A concert of his own sounds. He chuckled, completely delighted. And as if the reason for the silence surrounding him had not occurred to him quite as clearly before, he added his own voice to the wordless, soundless world around him, "Cars. There really are no cars!" He couldn't even hear a single plane, and Frankfurt was a busy hub. He stopped listening to the Waxobumm and concentrated on the silence. It was hard concentrating on silence. He managed it a little, and it made him feel taller. "No!" he said out aloud to himself, "Not taller. Bigger!" His voice shattered his own concentration. Suddenly, above him in the air, a whirring sound. It was getting louder, coming closer. Fergal felt afraid and threatened. It was too dark. He wasn't allowed out after dark, and Mutti and Dad would be really worried and angry with him.

The streetlights hummed and flickered. Nighttime was switched on. At the back of where Joachim lived was a huge car park for the Bürgerhaus where the village council came together to eat, drink, meet and get drunk all in the name of politics. They even had a bowling alley for the purpose.

The whole car park now lit up just as dramatically as the tanks grouped around the site of the accident earlier. Fergal got up. His bottom was numb from sitting. He was stiff with cold. At one stage there had been more lights in the car park than in the whole of Geesterheim some of the old locals said. That was the time when the drainage ditch had still served a real purpose and sewage was flowing through the small streets out into the fields. Before Fergal's time here. Before 1969.

On the 21st of July 1969 back in London they had seen Armstrong take his small step for man and one giant leap for mankind as the first man on the moon on the telly. After Christmas they had taken the giant step to move to Germany. The Bürgerhaus had been built twenty years after the war, before any gigantic steps, in 1965 with American sponsorship as part of a cultural exchange programme, hence the bowling alley.

Geesterheim was twinned with a tiny place in Texas called Geesterheim TX. Progress was moving fast with the Americans. Americans had more to live for.

Dad said, from a European point of view culture was certainly not the Americans' strongpoint, but that was only because Europeans felt a little small at times and that affected your view of the world. So it was a little bit of European envy making its cultured way West over the Atlantic. Americans had their very own culture.

Dad loved their cars. They were the best apparently. Fergal didn't know what made a good car. Certainly, American cars were enormous. Dad sold American, English and Italian sports cars. He had showrooms in Darmstadt and Frankfurt.

Of late the oil crisis had put a bit of a frown on his face and almost a sneer on Mutti's. Things weren't going as well as they used to, which must have been the reason for Fergal's boring birthday presents yesterday. No guns, no tanks, not even bombers. People weren't buying as many cars anymore, and Dad was in no way allowed to touch the reserve or their savings, Mutti said, or else. One thing was for certain, Fergal thought, as he walked to the centre of the empty car park, his parents weren't laughing much these days and they only very rarely smiled at each other. If they did, it was as if for the benefit of his horrid sister J's and him. Dad never used Mutti's first name. He only ever called her *darling*, or to others he referred to her as *my wife* or *she* or *her*. J and Fergal were mostly *my lord* and *my lady* to him and then there was something weird in his eyes. A bit strange, altogether. Fergal liked being addressed by his name, even if it was Ferkel. Mutti said of herself that she was *Beethoven* and Dad *Chopin*. Two different worlds, apparently. But who could really tell with grownups? Grownups were difficult!

Also of late, Mutti had started talking almost constantly of all the terrible things happening the world over. It was all hell, hell, hell! She seemed always angry and worried. It had started with talk of the business going a little sour. Mutti and Dad could really scare Fergal at times. It seemed that this was all down to business. Mutti would say angrily, the Second War really hadn't taught people anything. Mutti could sometimes tell terrible stories, which kept Fergal awake at night. People set alight like torches running through the night streets of Hamburg bright with fire and phosphorus. Wailing screams. Continuing air raids. Jumping into the river Alster to extinguish themselves. Burning on under the water all the way to the bottom. Yammering children burnt black, just about saved from death by the smouldering corpses next to them on the pavement, only to die in the street themselves anon. The whole world an empire of wailing and screaming and killing. This valley of tears! "Don't we ever learn?" she'd ask. And she'd been saying almost a little too much of that recently. All down to business going sour.

Fergal felt the smoke grenade in his right coat pocket. It was as heavy as his binoculars in the left. He started crying. The images in his mind as heavy as lead, the opposite of the earlier absence of sound. He got this sometimes. Tears just came, especially when he thought of the war and people set alight, screaming, wailing, dying everywhere. His German grandparents talked a lot about it too, but were never as brutally honest as Mutti.

Mutti said it was important to be brutally honest so people wouldn't forget, because if they forgot, they'd do it again. The German people had to apologise over and over for their horrible deeds. That was called *Wiedergutmachung* and *Vergangenheitsbewältigung*. Rectification and management of the German Nazi past. – Brutal honesty was the best!

Dad said, "What's wrong with just honesty?"

Fergal remembered the soldier squashed under the tracks. In Fergal's mind things were always more vivid and horrible, his parents told him. That's because he was a child. What did they know?

He now realised that the hand at the end of the arm sticking out from under the track had been that of a black man. Germans still called black people *Neger*. Mutti had no problem with that but Dad was by no means allowed ever to say *nigger*. English *nigger* was bad! German *Neger* was good, because the Germans had nothing much to apologise for in terms of black slaves at least, said Heinrich The Vegetable Man.

Germany's apology required more doing even though it covered only twelve years, because they were the losers, and the English and the Americans the winners. The winners had the say. The English and Americans got away Scot-free. The Germans were the worst people the twentieth century had given birth to. But the real Nazis who should have really apologised hadn't, and they never would.

Half of Fergal was a loser and the worst person ever then. Fergal had to become better at apologising. What was his Irish bit then? Dad said Ireland was all about poetry and blarney.

Fergal thought for a moment. Bullshit wasn't a place. Blarney was, and they had a stone there at the castle in Ireland, and you had to kiss it, bending over backwards, and then you were full of bullshit. Dad said, blarney didn't just mean bullshit "and don't ever say that word in front of me again! If you have to say it, say it to your pillow!"

Blarney also meant flattery, and, quite frankly, the kiss of the blarney stone could also infer the gift of the gab. Blarney was a great thing! And then there was Bollerboe. Bollerboe was a place that didn't exist and had no castle. Bollerboe was the same as bullshit but Tristan had said it was somewhere up north like Hamburg.

Bollerboe!

So, one half of him was an apologetic German, the other an Irish blarney castle kiss. However, he felt like neither. He felt English. He couldn't explain why.

Slowly putting one foot in front of the other Fergal left the car park. Home, on Georg-Büchner-Straße 9, wasn't far away.

A hundred yards.

He calculated.

In German that was about …? – Never mind!

It was about the same in meters. One meter was like just over a yard, so not really worth the effort.

Slowly! One foot in front of the other. Time was great! He could either get home in a minute, or walk really slowly. One foot in front of the other. That way he might be back home in an hour but he would come to know each stone in his path.

The sky beyond the streetlights was deeper and more intensely blue than before. If you used your hands for a telescope and only looked at the sky, there was an orange haze like a halo above the lights. Like a bombed city over the horizon burning through the night. Wailing and screaming. People like living torches, burning on under the water.

Fergal could hear their screams.

If you looked at the light directly, it was bright. White.

In Fergal's mind the black soldier's hand appeared again. This time he heard the shriek and the crushing of bones clearly. It had been like a girl screeching. It had been a high-pitched but gigantic exhalation. Then, a short, almost quiet howl, … if there was such a thing, … like loud, sighed regret at the end. Fergal was now certain that the helicopter had taken away a dead soldier.

And Joachim and Tristan and he had only been playing!

Fergal felt another surge of tears. He never cried in front of his friends.

He empathically sensed the pain the soldier must have felt briefly before breathing out his life. He felt his pelvis be crushed, his ribcage collapse under the huge, unstoppable weight. He could no longer breathe. Then, the worst of all! His head. Pushed into the mud and … Fergal fell down and died at the entrance of the car park. Every inch, every centimetre of feeling alive, was dragged out of him like a red thread he could almost see. He lost consciousness.

How Heinrich Came By His Name

"You're a strange sort, Fergal."

Fergal was lying halfway in the road just across from the Bürgerhaus. Heinrich turned him round and put him in a lying position on his side on the pavement.

Heinrich had been a medical officer during the war. Heinrich was the only German who could pronounce Fergal's name. Fergal had explained to him that in German it would be spelt *Förgl.*

"You're too young to pass out like that."

"I died. I feel sick."

"Of course, you do! You banged your head a bit. Can you walk?"

"May I just lie here for a bit, please? I feel sick."

"For a bit, but then I'll carry you home, otherwise your kidneys get it, unless you only have one, …" he laughed. Was this also some type of Damage Fun? Schadenfreude!? "… and then the kidney gets it."

"What happened, Herr Dr. Vogelsberg?"

Heinrich spoke quietly, "I saw you from Mönchsgasse. You were crying. Then you looked as if you were stretching, as if to get up from bed. And then you passed out. – That's all fairly normal when you're going through puberty, but you're not there yet, are you? And, please, just call me Heinrich, as we've agreed, and I might even call you Mister Murphy. Fergal Murphy."

Fergal had quite a problem addressing older people by their first names. When he did, normally after the second or third attempt, he found it felt most wonderful, so much so that you trusted the grownup more.

Mutti had told him it was very bad manners, without any respect, and very, very common because this was Germany, and not Ireland or England where people knew not how to behave! They just had neither shame nor respect. And America was worse! There people didn't even have surnames! Very much like sausages … even though she meant savages, because she just got certain English words mixed up and wrong.

Dad said she didn't really because that was her own sense of humour. *Rusks* were *rocks*, *very* was *weary*, *school* was *shoal* or *Sheol*, and she rarely ever mentioned the word *Nazi*. You were allowed to say it, but only with a great deal of anger in your voice. Being angry with the Nazis was *Wiedergutmachung* and *Vergangenheitsbewältigung*. Saying the word *Nazi* was up to Dad.

Mutti said, formal address was good also, because it made sure one kept one's distance with certain grownup men, as there were certain grown up men going by the name of Mr. Peter File and Herr Peter Ast of the Mitschnacker family, who'd use you to satisfy themselves and then cut off your head and drop it in a well, and then your headless body would be dumped in another well, and there it would rot and be eaten by fat maggots. And that, sadly, was the brutal and honest truth! The Mitschnackers were most dangerous! In German *Mitschnacker* just meant somebody talking to you a lot and giving you chocolate, and then you'd go with them and end up headless.

Dr. Vogelsberg wasn't one of the Mitschnackers.

"OK, Dr. Vogelsberg. – Thank you!"

"Shall I carry you home, Mr. Prof. Murphy?"

"I'll be fine in a moment."

"Sure?"

"Yes."

Heinrich was one of the few veterans who had returned from Russian captivity in Siberia. They were called *Heimkehrer*. The home-comers. The ones who had made it back to the German *Heimat*.

As a young medical officer he had survived Stalingrad, then a rather massive walk through the snow to Siberia, and, once arrived, the badly heated barracks at the POW camp with no television. On his way there people had thrown rotten potatoes and stones at him.

Fergal felt much better. Although the memory of his crushed bones and skull lingered in his body he really was fine now.

He got up. "I'm fine, Heinrich."

"Good. – I'll walk you home, Fergal."

Heinrich had returned from Siberia to Germany to find that his entire family had been wiped out by the war. RAF and USAF air raids in Frankfurt, Dresden and Hamburg. Marauding Russian troops in Berlin. All gone. Luckily some of his property was returned to him. He now lived with his lady friend in Geesterheim. They had set up joint surgery. He was in his late fifties and had voluntarily gone back to Heidelberg to update his studies and complete some of his exams in medicine so he wouldn't put anyone in danger.

Mutti was very fond of him and used him as the family's GP.

No! Heinrich was definitely not one of the Mitschnackers! Mutti was fond of doctors in general. Her parents had always wanted her to marry a doctor or lawyer, not an ex-enemy foreigner who used to bomb German cities from above, turned salesman of foreign cars. It didn't matter that Dad had worked in the RAF post office.

"So, what brought this on?"

"The Americans drove over a black soldier with their tank. I think he died. There was a scream and then nothing and the helicopter left slower than when it arrived. I think."

"Well, there are few known cases of survivors of such accidents but it really depends on how soft the ground is. In any case, it's possibly better to die. – When they marched us east," this is how it would always start with Heinrich, "the Russians were using some of our own halftracks, until they broke down. I was lucky because I had some medical knowledge. The wounded died first. Next was exhaustion. And the cold. The column of men stretched to the horizon and beyond. Many just sat in the snow and waited for death. Sometimes the Russians were kind and shot my comrades. Sometimes they saved ammo and drove over them. Sorry! – Why am I telling you this?"

"You always do."

"Mmh. – I do, do I!? Mustn't do that. Not good for you."

"It's interesting and not like Siegfried's stories … when he tells them. – Siegfried doesn't really talk that much."

"Siegfried has stories. I don't. I'm afraid, Fergal, I lived someone else's story. Germany's. They never asked me. I had no choice. I lost my own story a long time ago." Heinrich looked at the starry sky. "What do you have in your left coat pocket by the way?"

"My binoculars."

"And your right?"

"Just a bottle of Coke. Would you like some?" – Ouch! He had just lied. Mutti said never to lie, because the Nazis had lied a lot, and you would end up in Hell!

"Good Lord, no! And you shouldn't either. It's bad for you."

"Mutti says so too! And Dad says, kids are protected from bad things because they don't believe in them as much."

Heinrich laughed, "Well, … as Geesterheim's medicine man I have to subscribe to your mother's view. As a person, I think your father is right. The Nazis wouldn't have got away with children. He's a Roman, isn't he? Your father?" Heinrich didn't say *Nazis* angrily. It was more like Joachim leisurely describing *sack-rats*.

"What's that?"

"A Catholic. Well, … he's Irish, so it's self-evident, isn't it?"

"Yes. I want to be a Catholic when I grow up because at our Lutheran school we get beaten too much."

"I'm a Catholic, and I got beaten like mad at school. I bet your father did too. There aren't exactly many Catholic schools around here, are there? – If you ask your father nicely, he could take you to Saint Mary's."

"Mutti would flip, Heinrich! – She won't allow it. She likes Luther very much! I'll get confirmed her way and then I'll convert, when I'm eighteen."

Heinrich laughed, "You have it all sorted, haven't you, Fergal?"

"I write letters to the Pope. I like the Pope. He is the head of the Church. Each body needs a head otherwise the body doesn't work. God's the mind. The Lutherans don't have a head, they only have fists and … headless chickens."

Heinrich kept laughing, "Where are you getting all this from, little man?"

"My head. My head is my Pope."

For a moment Heinrich frowned. Then he said, "I hope your parents will send you to a good school."

They had arrived outside Fergal's home. All the lights were blazing inside. Fergal could see his sister Johanna Frances dancing like mad to the Beatles' *Sgt. Pepper's Lonely Hearts Club Band* upstairs in her own room.

Oh, my God! She was also singing.

Fergal felt deeply embarrassed.

He liked the Beatles but not when J was around. His sister was Johanna Frances, JF like Jinxed Freak or Jerky Foot or Jolly Feeble or … never mind! – J. Just J. She liked the Rolling Stones too. And everything else. And had lots of records and a good record player with a great amplifier and tuner. And two big speakers and great pocket money and a fantastic ten-speed! And everything was swamped with her old toys, especially her own room, so Fergal couldn't come in. Above all, though, she had her own room!

Fergal didn't have any of those things. Most of all, he didn't have his own room. During the week he slept in his parents' bedroom. J had to study. It made Dad grumpy. Weekends he had to spend in J's room. She frequently made him sleep on the floor or curl up in the corner. The most annoying thing about J apart from herself was her habit of talking about herself till the early hours of the morning! All the great things she was going to do, and the famous men she was going to marry, and how Fergal could be her servant and clean her toilet, until he got too old and had to be put down because he smelt. When she'd eventually fall asleep she ground her teeth so loudly it made Fergal shudder and kept him awake for even longer.

Fergal vaguely remembered having his own room back in London. He couldn't remember Oxford, where they had lived up until he was two. London had been great! Even though … J had once tried to throw him out the window. They had owned their own house in a place called Camden Town close to Regents Park.

Mutti and Dad always said J was far more grown up than Fergal, because she was six years older … hence the pocket money!

Well, her age wasn't Fergal's fault, was it? Fergal needed money, too! There were just so many things he needed! War toys. Guns. Aeroplanes. Tanks. Soldiers.

Mutti was always worried that Fergal would go off, if he had the money, buying himself enormous amounts of war toys and guns. – Well, … Mutti was right! But that wasn't the point!

The point was that Fergal needed war toys and guns to defend himself against Johanna Frances. JF. Jolly Fierce.

J. Just J.

It was such a waste to mankind to give so many letters to somebody so undeserving and cold and horrible and brutal.

J.

Just last weekend, whilst he was asleep, she had blown a whole load of pepper up his nose through the empty tube of a felt-tip pen. It had been terrible! Fergal thought he was going to die. She awarded him a hundred man-points for the pepper, and another one hundred for not grassing on her to Mutti and Dad.

Mutti and Dad thought Fergal was going to die from an asthma attack. Even J herself had looked a little worried!

Heinrich had been called in and had found out! Sort of.

Fergal had lost his one-hundred added J-bonus man-points. J had got the lecture and ten D-Marks off her one-hundred D-Mark a month parentally provided salary.

All standards considered that was too much money, even the parents of Fergal's friends said. Mutti said, J needed that sort of money because she was a growing woman and she went to Gymnasium, the sort of school that would give her access to university so she could study medicine.

Fergal would never consult her when she was a doctor!

Frightening thought!

The Bulhof-Murphys were now renting a big modern house in the latest architectonic style of posh eighteenth century Schwarzwald peasant huts as interpreted by the American architect who built them forty times bigger than the originals, and then rented them out to fellow Americans or Irish friends who wanted to go on the real German fun-ride. It was a massive house, with a massive garden, enormous amounts of space, and no room for Fergal. It was shared with another family. The Noldes.

The Noldes! Downstairs. – The Noldes were from eighteenth century Hamburg, Germany, Europe.

Chuck Nolde was one of Fergal's best friends. He called his parents by their first names, "Oi, Erika, wipies! I'm finished crappin'! Oi, Karl-Heinz, I'm hungry, now!"

The Noldes loved the latest thing in didactics. Antiauthoritarianism. This meant that Chuck could do whatever he liked and got everything he wanted!

Joachim said it was because Chuck's parents had absolutely no time for him. Just like his own.

Chuck was going to be a tennis star one day and always walked round with a tennis racket in his left and one ball in his right at the ready. Chuck was only eight and a bit, but that didn't really matter to Fergal because when it came to tennis target-shooting and attracting attention, Chuck was worth his weight in gold.

Both Noldes were American architects trying very hard to fit in and learn German. Their German claim to heritage fame was the painter Emil Nolde, possibly. No one had as yet told them that Nolde's original name had been Emil Hansen.

Erika and Karl-Heinz Nolde really had no idea how much they were being ridiculed by Geesterheimers behind their backs, because, who in the name of God cared about some expressionist called what? Emil Nolde!

Who's that?

He lived in Seebüll!

Where's that?

North of Hamburg!

Wasn't that almost Bollerboe?

Geesterheimers could be mean!

Hamburg, Germany, almost Bollerboe, north Germany, was not beautiful Geesterheim but reserved for Frisian cows and fat-bottomed, ugly people with that strange adenoid accent.

Hamburg, Seebüll, Bollerboe. Why didn't the Noldes, Karl-Heinz, Erika and Chuck, all go to Bollerboe!? And why call their son such a strange foreign name? Strange people.

Bollerboe was just the place for them. All of north Germany was Bollerboe really.

Now, Fergal understood!

He had learnt a new word today.

Bollerboe!

But who cared, Mutti said, if those who didn't even know the painter Emil Nolde ridiculed one. The judgement of inconsequential people had to be ignored.

Inconsequential meant people who were unimportant.

Mutti's motto was *Gesell' Dich eines Besser'n zu, daß mit ihm Deine Kräfte ringen, denn wer nicht besser ist als Du, kann auch Dich nicht weiterbringen.* Dad said, in Fergal's proper language that meant *Be with someone better, wrestle with his strength, for if you join a weak man, the weak man's mind you'll reap.*

Dad was good at translating. He said, in plain English that was only *don't stoop to their level,* and in Irish it was *oggus unarry boherlat* and that was spelt quite differently. *Agus go n-éirí an bóthar leat.* Irish was most beautiful and poetic, but difficult and that's why the English got rid of it. One day he might teach Fergal. *Go n-éirí an bóthar leat* meant *May the road rise to meet you.*

Mutti insisted, Fergal was absolutely not to mention to the Noldes that the painter's original name was Emil Hansen. *Do you hear, Johann Fergal!* Index finger raised authoritatively. Very German. The Noldes would have to find out for themselves. The gentle way. If told by Fergal or Mutti, it would be patronising and arrogant. It was exactly what low-grade, asocial people did. *Die Asozialen machen das!* All the time! Amongst themselves. To each other.

The Noldes would definitely find out one day. The Noldes were nice and higher people with whom it was good for Fergal to associate.

And as to those low-grade asocial people? Well! "As long as they don't have the power to put you in the stocks, or break your legs slowly, followed by the arms and your fingers, digit by digit, or hang you slowly by the neck until dead, or burn you at the stake, or quarter you by ripping you limb from limb with the help of two or even four horses, or drown you in a well all tied up, head first, or let you drink liquid manure before pouring boiling tar or oil down your gullet, … with a funnel, … as long as this is assured, … all's well!" Mutti would say with brutal honesty. Fergal would feel immensely sick after such lessons. Mutti would then add, "That's why education is important, and education includes

Emil Nolde, medieval torture, and the Nazis. We have to be brutally honest. The naked truth is all it takes to make us better, Johann! *Vergangenheitsbewältigung* means *Wiedergutmachung*. When you're a bit older, I'll take you to Lübeck's Holstentor, where they have a great medieval torture chamber! And then we can go on up to Seebüll to Emil Nolde's house. That's where he used to paint his Unpainted Paintings because the Nazis banned him from being an artist as they termed him *entartet*, which means he wasn't a true German according to the Nazis with their big Dobermans. Even though, Nolde had been a real Nazi himself in the beginning. We have to show the world that we are not so! We are not Nazis, you hear! We have to apologise for what happened!" Each time she expressed the forbidden word *Nazi* with an emphasis so angry, Fergal flinched.

Fergal didn't feel that guilty altogether.

Dad would say, "Well now, darling, your Nazis were brutally honest about their feelings regarding Germany's Jewry. And the naked truth had them naked in piles being bulldozed into holes now, hadn't it?" That's when Dad was fed up with Mutti's brutal honesty and naked truth.

And Fergal? – Fergal would feel sick with all the images in his mind. People with crushed bones being bulldozed into holes all over the place. Hanging people. Drowning people. Burning people. Screaming people. Always screaming because they didn't like to be torches brightening up Hamburg's orange night skies, romantically set against the dark silhouettes of bombs raining down for ever and ever and ever.

His nightmares weren't exactly nice. J had added the *romantic* bit when she related Mutti's horror stories to him, second-hand, "How romantic, Fergal! Orange night skies!" And then he'd have to go to the loo in the middle of the night and broken people, hanging people, screaming people, burning people surrounded his bed, but their fire didn't brighten the bedroom. It was a cold fire. Then Fergal would wake up again. It was morning already and he had wetted the bed again.

"What's Jewellery got to do with it!" Mutti indignant.

"What?! – What *are* you talking about, darling?!" Dad surprised. Genuinely.

"Nazis with Jewellery."

"Well, they stole a lot of that. … Oh, goodness! – Now, I see, what you mean, Fergal! – Jews, darling. Juden!"

"Ah, Juden! Well, let's not talk about that in front of the boy. Poor, emaciated little things. And the barbed wire. Oh, God! Horrible! – Horrible!!!"

Fergal only knew from Tristan and Joachim that the Noldes were being ridiculed quite badly at the local level. Both Joachim and Tristan were real locals themselves with parents who were, unlike other locals, well educated. Never mind.

What the Noldes had in common with everyone else, even the most common of Geesterheimers, was, that they were saving for an even bigger house with a bigger garden they could call their own.

Karl-Heinz and Erika Nolde were going to build this in the famous barn-and-sty style of the thatchy Northern Frisian reed growers of the sixteenth century, because Friesland was in Hamburg and north of Germany.

When the Noldes said things like that to Mutti, she would look completely, but somehow still politely, stunned, and later at home she'd say to Fergal, "Never, ever tell them the truth! They have to find out for themselves. It's just so embarrassing!"

Apparently, it was all the other way round and possibly down to their sometimes quite incomprehensible German they practiced on Mutti.

"Well, let's not blame them. German is a difficult language, even to the best of them!"

Hamburg was in the north of Germany, and Friesland was north of Hamburg. Quite a bit north. Mutti would shake her head at those poor ignorant foreigners.

Like everyone else, though his Dad wasn't so convinced anymore, Fergal's parents were also saving for their own home, … the very savings Dad was not to touch to save his business from the oil crisis.

Fergal didn't mind in what style their new home was going to come, as long as it happened soon and, above all, would give him his own room with his own door and lock and key, and a nice trench and fine parapet and a machine gun just like Siegfried's.

Fergal sighed. Imagining J dying in barbed wire, being ripped to shreds by heavy machinegun fire. Just like his German grandfather had witnessed in the Great War. Happy thoughts! J could get up again from her death in the barbed wire even though she was a bitch!

"Good Lord, what a big sigh for a little Herr like yourself, Fergal!" Heinrich gave Fergal a quizzical frown. Fergal had been far away.

"I was just thinking of J. She's very difficult, but she is at the best school. Gymnasium is the best school. I know school is very important. I have one and a half years left to Big School. But my parents might not send me to Gymnasium in Frankfurt, J says, because J is getting everything. I don't even have my own room. They might send me to a lower form of life school like Realschule, Hauptschule, or Sonderschule. Sonderschule is monster school. There even is one called loo school. Gymnasium is for the brightest like J. They become doctors and lawyers at university. Realschule is for the not so bright like accountants and normal police people. Hauptschule is low but important. Like carpenters and sausage makers. And Sonderschule is for idiots who are ugly, and they smell. That's why it's called monster school. And loo school is the lowest, J says. And if I go to loo school, I can clean J's toilet and be servant to her every whim and wish and wash her famous husband's feet and know his wishes off by heart, and always be at their beck and call. And *if* she's happy with me, she might not even torture me. But she'll have to sack me one day anyway, when I get too old and smelly. And then I'll need to be put down with a kind shot of mercy to the back of my head like your friends stuck in the snow in Russia."

Heinrich had been standing open-mouthed, listening to this fast delivery of words, "Mother of God! A whole life in under a minute! Bollerboe nonsense! Where are you getting all this from?"

"I hate J."

"Don't hate, Fergal. It's a sickness."

"I feel sick when I have to like J."

"Mmh."

"She tortures me for points. They are man-points. The more points the better. If I lose points I am closer to a horrible death she says."

"Are you sure?"

"Yes!"

"The pepper was not a silly accident then?"

"No!!!" Fergal stamped his foot, "I told you last week, Heinrich!"

"Well, next time I see your mother, I'll mention this to her, agreed?"

"Won't help, Heinrich! – They won't believe you, because they don't believe me. Mutti especially thinks I am too theatrical."

"Oh, come on, Fergal. Big words! It can't be that bad?"

"It is."

"Mmh. – Look at it this way. Tristan really has it bad with his brother, Siegfried. Siegfried really is sick and does do bad things, and he is ten years older than Tristan. At least you're strong enough to defend yourself against your sister."

"I'm not! Herr Doktor Eichenraub told me I have spontaneous acromegaly when we arrived here in Wetchamoonis. I mean West-Germany."

"Oh, yes. Your famed one-year sulk! Well …! – When Eichenraub diagnosed spontaneous acromegaly he was quite … well, there is no such thing. You do know quite a lot of big words, Fergal."

"I ask when I don't understand something even when it's Joachim. Joachim has more words than anyone in the world. And it wasn't a sulk. I don't sulk. Only babies sulk. And besides, J is much stronger than me." Fergal hesitated, "So, what is wrong with Siggy, really?"

"Your mother always says you worry her because you're so quiet. I can't quite see that."

"I'm not. With you."

"Honoured. Well, I suppose I do talk to you quite a lot too, or more than to other people."

"Honoured, Heinrich!"

Heinrich gave a bright, clear laugh. Fergal saw his mother peering out through the upstairs window. "So what is wrong with Siggy again?"

"I never told you what was wrong. Don't formulate your language to interrogate people like that, Fergal."

"What does formulate mean?"

"Construct. Build like a house."

"Why is Siggy going back to the *Irrenhaus*?"

"That's not a nice word. It's called an institution for the mentally unstable and sick."

"Why is he insane? He seems quite good fun with his uniforms and trenches."

"You *are* persistent! – He is *not* insane! He is mentally unstable. Choose the many words you already have at your disposal carefully and gently, Fergal."

"Heinrich, when I was discovered with spontaneous acromegaly …"

"You mean diagnosed! When you were diagnosed."

"Thank you! – So when I was diagnosed with spontaneous acromegaly, Herr Doktor told my mother, Mutti, in front of me I might only have three or four years to live. That wasn't careful or gentle. You see, I have to be persistent because I could die at any stage."

"Little man! You do scare me, the way you speak."

"The doctor used the latest word to describe my spontaneous acromegaly. He said that nowadays it was known as Situation Dependent Mutation or SDM. He said the medical profession preferred to call it SitMut. Now SitMut doesn't sound nice, does it?"

"I know. – I have heard of it. And it's a nonsense. Don't always believe in what other people say! Especially, if they are in a position of authority. SitMut was discovered in single cell organisms. Some bright young thing wrote his doctorate on it and created a stir in the profession. I think it was this Eichenraub of yours. He claimed he had found evidence that SitMut could affect human beings just as much."

"Your saying SitMut yourself now."

"Mmh. – You're right! Sorry. – I think one of the nastiest medical terms we used to joke about was *Faltkind für enge Wohnungen*. Do you know what that is?"

"No?! – What does it mean?"

"It means *the collapsible kid for small flats*. It refers to a child being born without its collarbones."

"What does it look like?"

"Narrow. Very narrow," Heinrich grinned, "Sorry. – It's really not funny."

"Is that Schadenfreude?"

"I suppose so. Nasty trait."

"So, why is Siggy off his rocker?"

"Come on, Fergal! Nasty way of putting it! I can't tell you that. It's doctor-patient confidentiality. But I can tell you that it must be quite terrible for Tristan who loves and trusts his elder brother very much. From Tristan's point of view there is nothing that Siegfried can possibly do wrong."

"Like what?"

"I can't tell you that. It's like the confessional in Church."

Mutti opened the kitchen window upstairs. She had been hovering there for quite a while, "Is that you out there in the dark with my Fergal, Herr Dr. Vogelsberg?"

"Yes, it is, Frau Bulhof-Murphy! He's alright! He's with me. We're just chatting."

"Are you? Really? – Fergal chatting?!"

"Yes. He'll be up in a minute."

Mutti was always doing that! Fergal didn't think that she had been worried about him. She just wanted to chat with Heinrich herself because he was a doctor.

"Why do they call you the Vegetable Man?"

Heinrich The Vegetable Man seemed quite taken aback at that. Mutti shut the kitchen window. Heinrich looked up to the left at the stars over Joachim's house just across.

Fergal could hear loud parental screaming and puerile crying. A first! He had never heard Joachim cry even when his Granny Hammerich beat him before breakfast and after dinner. Joachim could scream and wail for Germany though.

Heinrich was far away in another place, thinking. It would take him a while to answer. Fergal was accustomed to these interludes and always reacted patiently. He began looking at the stars too. Somehow it blotted out Joachim's desperate sobbing, and J's horrible screeching. J was truly atonal. The Beatles had now just about managed to arrive at *She's Leaving Home* with J's awful accompaniment. J really identified with that song. She was screaming it at the top of her voice. How lovely it would be for her to leave home. This really was Georg-Büchner-Straße at its stereophonic best. Joachim right ear, J left. Dad had just bought some Fisher hi-fi equipment. It was quadraphonic. J wanted a new system too or at least two more speakers.

"When men are in prison together …"

"Were you in prison, Heinrich?"

"Yes. – It was a prison for soldiers. The PoW camp in Siberia. – I told you! I was being held captive. Are you going to listen?"

"Yes. Captive audience." For some reason Fergal felt shame rising into his face.

"Men need women. Most men. When there are no women, men can fall in a type of love with one another. I prayed a lot. Sometimes I would help out a friend in need. It's not a standard thing. All a bit un-German. But it happened like Friday and Robinson on their island. I know you won't altogether understand me now, but you will, … later … when you are older, … if then you remember our little conversations.

"Even though it was happening, the Russians took it out on me. Well, I shouldn't say Russians really. They just happened to be there. They were just like the Nazis. One Corporal had it in for me and got one of my comrades to bend down in front of me to bite off my testes, testicles, … my lower bit. He didn't do it.

"He got beaten to death easily. He'd been quite weak anyway. He was expendable from their point of view. The next one in line couldn't do it either. I actually couldn't believe it. He got whacked over the head and just died. The fear was horrendous.

"To this day I think the Corporal hadn't intended to kill anyone. He looked quite astonished at how easily everyone was dying in our hut. The third one did. They took him away. Never saw him again. I thought I was going to bleed to death. I didn't. There was another German doctor. He helped. I pulled through. So I lost my manhood amongst other things."

"You have no willy?"

"No! – The bits *below* the willy!" He smiled, "And when I came to Geesterheim some time ago because of all our old family property, our orchards and vineyards, I suppose I was considered an eligible bachelor. I only went out with one lady back then. We fell out of love quickly. It wasn't about my lack of … , is all I can say. You know, … I didn't even know I was called the Vegetable Man. Not a nice term! I don't really get it though.

"Normally, it means you don't have any brain left to function. Well! Nasty rumours spun out of control. As it says in one of the Grimms' fairytales, *the sun will bring it to the light of day.* Judas the woman. But then, I fell in love again. Properly! At my age."

"Is it bad not having any balls left then?"

"Haha! I do like you a lot, Fergal! And I have no idea why I'm telling you this! It's a bit irresponsible, I gather. You're too young. That's the nice thing about liking and loving people. Let's just say in the beginning there is fear, then it hurts like hell, but the body hurts first, then the mind, and there it stays."

"You're now married though."

"No. I'm in love."

There was a pause.

In the background, Joachim stopped crying.

J was still dancing and screeching. The end of *Within You Without You.*

"You're alright, Heinrich. I like you, and I won't tell anyone."

"Thank you, Fergal."

"What is wrong with Siegfried?"

"You know, I can't tell you that!"

"Has it something to do with all his Nazi uniforms and the trench system he has dug in his parents' garden?" Fergal didn't mention Siegfried's substantial arsenal. It was a closely guarded secret. No one was allowed to tell, otherwise playing with real ammo would stop, Tristan had said.

"Yes."

"Tristan says, Siegfried doesn't know the war's over yet."

"Yes."

"Tristan says, Siegfried's stuff like his …" Nearly! Fergal had stopped himself just in time. Apart from his grandfather, Opa, he trusted Heinrich more than any other grownup, but he had promised Tristan never to breathe a word to anyone, Heinrich included. A promise was a promise, until you died. Both Mutti and Dad said so.

He had wanted to say that Siegfried had a lot of guns and ammo hidden away in their home. The Neusslers didn't know about this. The trench system in their garden was dug incredibly well, and also served as a weapons cache. Besides, had Fergal said anything, he and Tristan might no longer use the real potato masher grenades in the woods and at the dump. They were good fun and very loud.

"What, Fergal?"

"Siegfried has this stuff in his head like really bad nightmares about the war."

"Yes. His mind lives in the war. I'm aware of his case and his parents have via byways asked me for help. That's how all this started. How I came to be aware of his case. I'm not really qualified. I've just become their friend. Siegfried suffers from a strange type of war trauma. He gets battle fatigue. The symptoms are that of neurotic shell shock."

"Why?" Only some of the words Heinrich had just mentioned seemed to make sense to Fergal. He didn't want to ask for their exact meaning, as he didn't want to interrupt Heinrich's flow.

"No one knows. He hardly ever leaves the house, … well, his trench system really, … let alone been to war. And the war his mind is in is the First World War. He dresses up in Nazi uniforms to vindicate Germany. It's all *Dolchstoßlegende*."

"What's *Dolchstoßlegende?*" A right question at the right time.

"The myth that the German *November Revolutionaries* of 1918 stabbed the army at the Western Front in the back from behind, as in a traitors' home front, and brought about the end of the war. The *November Criminals* the Nazis called them. The extreme right maintains to this day Germany remained undefeated in the field.

And all of this is of course the Jewry's and communists' fault. It's all too stupidly simple. And it's an emotive lie."

"I don't know."

"Well, now you know … a little."

"A stab in the back. A bit like J."

"You really don't like your sister much."

"No. I can't! – So what about Siegfried?"

Heinrich grinned, "I've told you too much already, Fergal. A secret, you understand!? I know you can keep quiet."

Fergal smiled. He felt proud. "Tristan says whenever Siggy gets this battle fatigue he goes to the *Irrenhaus* with his helmet. There are more like him but much older and they have parties."

"I doubt that very much."

"He says, Siggy can watch the enemy from his trench for weeks without any sleep. I think that's why he gets battle fatigue because that means tired."

"Possibly."

"Was Russia horrible?"

Heinrich smirked down at the little boy. After all, a little boy only! Fergal felt himself shrinking. "Now, you are a child again, or … we could be having a an embarrassing conversation at a reception. *I hear you were in Russia.* Yes. *Russia was hell.* Were you there? *No, I had a desk job in Paris.* – Russia was hell. But now and then something strange happens in my own mind. You know, sometimes I think I'd rather be back at the PoW camp. In spite of being in love here, there I still had something to live for. It all made sense. I'm not making much sense to you now, am I? Ah well. – Here comes your mother."

Fergal quickly whispered, "Heinrich, I will keep our secret."

"Hello, Herr Dr. Vogelsberg. Good Lord, Fergal, you're a complete mess! What secrets are you having with my little Fergal then?" Mutti sounded ever so slightly concerned but put on her best smile for the doctor. Maybe, the Vegetable Man did have some secret links with Peter File or Peter Ast of the Mitschnacker clan after all.

"And again, einen guten abend, gnädige Frau. Well, it's not evening strictly speaking, but it is dark. Beautifully clear sky. – How are you?"

Fergal's Mutti positively beamed at the type of man her parents thought she should have married, "I am very well, thank you. You look so … refreshed. Refreshing! A long evening's walk, I presume. – How are you?"

"Thank you. Your lovely son and I just chatted about those silly manoeuvres at the back of the LeBatards' property. Apparently, there was an accident, and Fergal thinks he'll die of the SitMut soon. – Now, Frau Bulhof-Murphy, do make Fergal understand that the diagnosis of SitMut was irresponsible and wrong. There is no such thing. Incorrect information like that can affect a child's mind."

"Oh, that one. Of course. And how is your lovely …"

… blah, and blah, and blah, and blah, and oh … oh … oh yes, and blah, and blah.

Fergal ran inside waving Heinrich goodbye without looking. In the corner of his left eye he saw his sister screeching still, but far more out of tune. *A Day In The Life*. There was no music. She was trying out her new fifty D-Mark Sennheiser headphones.

Running upstairs, his pockets were heavy but balanced. In his left coat pocket, the binoculars. In his right, the smoke grenade.

It didn't come as a shock to Fergal, that his heart and throat pounded with almost ecstatic joy, when he imagined how he pulled the pin, clink, let go of the handle, plink, and threw into J's room this delectable bit of military invention, duff-roll-roll, to shut securely and fast behind him her door. Wait a bit! … Boom-bang-bong-bash-crash-bang-wallop-boom.

Above all, it was the door of her *own* room.

At the top of the marble staircase stood his father with open arms and a smile, "My young Lord Fergal! Huggies!" – Huggies meant … *I know what you've got in your pockets.* Not good!

Fergal ran past his Dad, squealing he really had to go to the loo. He wasn't allowed to lock the door yet but for three years now no one had dared come in when Fergal was on the loo. From downstairs he heard Chuck's yells of *wipies.*

Fergal himself, admittedly proudly, had been quite able to wipe his own bottom efficiently enough since age five. Chuck was coming up for nine and still called for "Wipies, wipies, wipies, now! Wipies, wipies, wipies, now! Wipies, wipies, wipies, now!" until someone of an antiauthoritarian bent, or Erika Nolde in particular, normally after five to ten minutes, would eventually remember that she had a son, and react to his disproportionate screams by venturing into the loo to wipe his bottom clean, at which stage Chuck would have done it himself already on the bathrobes, face, hand and bath towels and the precious Fuzzy Foot toilet mat. Erika Nolde was quite a Fuzzy Foot fan, as these little rugs in the shape a giant's footprint adorned the whole of their ground floor flat apparently in a Frisian Hamburg pattern. In any case, with Chuck's faeces smeared all over the bathroom towels and on the Fuzzy Foot and himself, a screaming match would ensue which could last for up to half an hour, whilst antiauthoritarian Erika Nolde was busily cleaning the spoils of Chuck's bowels from fabrics not intended to be brought into contact with such matter. She would then enter her usual state of ignoring her son until she had actually forgotten about his very existence at which stage Chuck however might be in the mood for another bowel movement.

Fergal hid the grenade at the bottom of Mutti's cleaning cupboard behind the loo-rolls.

A bit later, and for the Bulhof-Murphy family it was time for high tea. Lots of sitting upright and playing happy cheery, obeying Mutti's raised-finger order, "Let's be cheerful now!" No one was allowed to mention Vietnam or Oil Crisis or Yom Kippur or Arabs, or especially American, English or Italian sports cars, or other things that were somehow related, like petrol or even the heating. But Carfree Sunday had been great! They could have even played on the Autobahn had they wanted to.

Fergal noticed that Mutti really had stopped smiling at Dad. She always sulked or looked angry when he cracked a joke. "How quickly does an Arab hit the ground when you push him in a northerly direction off a three-hundred foot cliff with a southerly wind of eighty knots?" … "Well!?" … "Come on! It's simple!" No answer from any corner. "Come on now! Simple answer! – Who cares, as long as you have pushed him properly and made sure you get his oil!"

Mutti would say, "That's an ignorant joke."

Dad would say, "That's your serious German lack of a serious sense of humour, darling." Dad would laugh. Mutti would not. Then there'd be an atmosphere. J would just leave without asking whether she may get down from the table. It was called *J absenting herself.*

And still a bit later, Fergal played with his Matchbox cars and Corgi Toys in the hallway. Today Daktari was chased by the Daleks disguised as the USS Enterprise spaceship, because the real Dr. Who Dalek with the sparks inside was in J's room. Fergal never had a problem with the scale of the toys. J said she did. J only liked playing with cars of the same scale, because one day she was going to have a real Jensen Interceptor in bright red to catch expensive men in who had to be of the right scale, and the only place to do this wasn't in dreary Germany, but back in London where Fergal would be her servant and he could have a look at her expensive shoe collection, when she was thus inclined to be kind to him once in her life.

J had a thing about good and expensive shoes. Good shoes were expensive, and more expensive shoes were even better. The quality of shoes told you everything about the quality of the wearer. Fergal might have hated J a great deal, but he liked the fact that she intended to move back to London one day. He would too! Thankfully the place was big enough for the two of them never to bump into each other, as otherwise he'd kick her with his wellies, and she'd kick back with her expensive pumps.

"You like wearing rubber wellies and walking boots, you little turd," J would say, "which makes you a common and garden variety of low weed, generally not worth the effort, apart from being uprooted and thrown on a compost heap to rot far away from here."

Never did she impart her objective observations about Fergal in front of parents. She was very careful like that. Fergal looked on yet another bright side. At least his sister liked playing with cars, even though it was without him.

Then there was dinner.

Pork and nice stuff and disgusting Sauerkraut, but apple pie with lashings of custard for afters. Whoever complained, especially about the horribly revolting Sauerkraut, would have to go to bed without food. The problem about Sauerkraut was simple and straightforward for Fergal. It was the most disgusting food on earth followed closely by stringy, white asparagus. Even if you added a nice dollop of your own fresh, steaming poo, or even Chuck's, nothing could make it better. And Mutti was still not smiling at Dad even though Dad was carefully watching Fergal with a grin. J was already back in her own room.

"Oh, darling Fergal, you haven't eaten your Sauerkraut yet. And it is so good for you!" Mutti was ever hopeful. Dad laughed. He knew what was going to happen.

"Mutti, I'm really full. It was lovely. Thank you very much a hundred times for my food. May I get down from the table … please! I don't even have to eat the super apple pie. I have to go to bed. School's tomorrow and Saint Nikolaus is going to be there.

So on the 6th of December he'll know our wish letters by heart and we get everything we want. And the oil crisis doesn't matter."

"No, Fergal. Please eat your Sauerkraut. Think of all the starving children in the world. The hot wind blows over their dry little bodies, and then they die and the flesh falls off them, and vultures pick their bones. Not even Germany's asocials have it that bad. Now, you do not want that, do you, Fergal?"

"No, Mutti."

Dad interrupted, "For goodness sakes! Give the boy a break and let him get ready so he can go to bed …" Dad hesitated, "… in our bedroom this evening?"

"Yes, Seán. In our bedroom this evening. Because tomorrow is a school day, isn't it, Fergal?"

"I hate Sauerkraut and asparagus, Mutti."

Something was going on.

"Why does his lordship have to sleep in our bedroom again, darling?"

"Because Johanna is too old. And stop calling him *Lord!* We've discussed this, Seán …" Mutti became all shy and quiet, "… not in front of the children."

"Right. What is her ladyship too old for again, darling?"

"Fergal."

"But we are much, much older than Frances, aren't we!? Why then can he sleep in her room at the weekends again, darling?"

"Because Fergal doesn't have to eat his Sauerkraut and will get down from the table … now!"

Good! *Great!*

"You're, as ever, evasive. Whatever happened to your brutal honesty, … again, … darling?"

"Alright, Seán! You want me, *and* you, this evening, in the same room, without Fergal."

"Yes, indeed. From the deep black well of my memory salacious desire creeps up to infect my body now and then. In fact, I cannot remember when it was last that nuptial duties were performed properly, can you?"

Mutti made a real vinegar face. No. Worse than vinegar! Fergal thought it looked as if she'd eaten ten lemons in one go. But apart from that there was something more important. That new German word had just crept up in the familial mishmash of German and English. *Salacious.* Joachim had used it earlier today, together with *wet dreams* and *venereal disease.* And there had been … what was it? … Fergal remembered! *Infantile!* And now there was also *nuptial!* – Wow!

"Mutti, Dad! What's *nuptial, salacious, infantile,* and *wet dreams?* Oh, and what does a *venereal disease* look like?"

"Good Lord!" exclaimed Mutti. Fergal wasn't sure whether it was directed at him.

"Not now, Fergal!!!" That was Dad with a frighteningly angry order addressed directly at Fergal. Dad looked brutal when he got the angry eyes. Mutti would say, frequently behind his back, that he could easily murder anybody when he was in the funny-eye mood. Was he in that mood now? One of Dad's best friends had funny eyes too. Big-Eye Nathan. Nathan cycled everywhere to get away from the Second War.

Fergal had to speak up, "I don't like it when you're like this. In fact, I don't like it at all! I want you to smile and be nice to each another."

Mutti sighed. For a moment she lost the lemon tinge around her mouth, "You're talking a lot today, Johann Fergal."

Dad sneered.

Wow! – Dad sneering was a first for Fergal. It had only ever been Mutti before. It had only ever been about money and the savings for Fergal's own room, with his own lock and key.

Dad shook his head at Fergal, "You know, Fergal, you are very dear to me, but sometimes there are grown-up things that are between your mother and I that do not concern you. – Understood!?"

"Well." – Fergal thought deeply. "Just wait right here, please. And keep your eyes absolutely shut. Please! Until I ask you to open them again."

"You're really quite talkative this evening," Dad said with a nod. Mutti was nodding too. Those were the sort of nods of harmony Fergal was looking for.

Good!

"Close your eyes and wait, please!"

Fergal ran into the loo, took out the smoke grenade from the back of Mutti's cleaning cupboard, firmly wrapped his hand around its Coke-can-like body so the trigger wouldn't fly off too early, and pulled the pin. Holding it out in front of him with both hands he stormed back into the dining room. Both Mutti and Dad still had their eyes shut obediently. Fergal put the grenade on the dinner table and loosened his grip. The trigger handle came off.

Clank!

"Keep your eyes shut, please!"

Dad had cheated. He had his eyes wide open. He was screaming like Fergal had never heard him scream in his life, "Grenade! Ruuuuuuuuuun!" His eyes were really frightening.

Immediately, Mutti grabbed her son and ran into the hallway, "What did you do, you stupid little boy!?"

Glass shattered.

Fergal started crying. Now, why did he have to cry in front of everybody! So embarrassing!

Then Dad shouted, "Jesus, Mary, holy Mother of God, you stupid, little fool! Who taught you how to do that!?"

Immediately there was a big fffffffduff outside. Fergal knew the grenade had gone off. Crying badly he followed his mother back into the dining room. Dad was standing at the window he had just smashed. He was smiling!

"What was it?" Was Mutti really that unknowing.

"Darling, it was a smoke grenade. Quite harmless unless you let it off inside … on the dinner table."

They were smiling at each other. Fergal had won back a little harmony for both of them.

But then they looked at Fergal.

Fergal really got the lecture that evening.

Voluntarily, he wrote a letter to the Pope in Rome to give expression to his misunderstanding of a parental situation. Although quite disapproving of the Roman Catholic Church, Fergal's Mutti had given in to this strange urge of her child's.

Letter #11 – Fergal To God Via The Pope

Dear Your Holiness, Papa in Rome, Papa Paulus Sextus, Episcopus Romanus,
Giovanni Battista Enrico Antonio Maria Montini, Dear Holy Paul VI (that's the way the Romans used to count),

Here's another letter from me for you to kindly pass on to God Himself. Thank you!

Dad told me everything about your names this evening, because he was very serious. I didn't know you had so many. I won't write them all out again in future.

This evening I am writing to you because I put a smoke grenade on the dinner table to make my parents smile because I was thinking they are not smiling enough at each other. They did smile at each other afterwards though, but then they were very unhappy with me.

Do not worry! They did not force me by unnice means to write to you so you can pass this on to God. They just shouted a bit, but not at all like our Lutheran school pastor who once forced me to write *Martin Luther was a nice man* a hundred times, and I wrote *Luther was a fat thickhead* in-between. Then he discovered my lines in-between and he really bashed my face until my ear bled, but I think I told you about that a year ago.

I know you are a very busy, holy man, and I won't keep you for long. I am still just a Lutheran at the moment, but once I grow up I'll become sensible and a good Catholic. So, now I just apologise!

I would like you to pray to your Employer for J to become normal and nice, and for me to have my own room and not die soon of the SitMut, and for Mutti and Dad to love one another again, and for everyone to have a nice Christmas soon, so no one goes hungry and has to eat Sauerkraut, and for all my friends to be happy.

If you can't fit it all in, just ask your Cardinals and Bishops to do it for you.

It is also very helpful to think of St. Francis Xavier, Dad says, because the Jesuits are good at educating, and they like the ~~holy toe~~ Holy Toe. – Sorry for the grenade! I'll try not to do it again like that.

Yours faithfully
Send my best wishes to God

J. Fergal Bulhof-Murphy.

Gestapo Basements, RAF Air Raids, And Love

"Very nice! Very clean!" Opa nodded approvingly, "No change since we were here last, Seán. Very good. You don't waste your money on furniture. We've also had ours since Oma and I met. Proper craftsmanship then. Good carpenters. Young people these days always buy new things, always!" That was a compliment. "And everyone has to drive a car. Cars for the masses are useless!" That wasn't a compliment considering that Dad loved nice cars and loved selling them to as many people as possible. "*Der Gefreite*[1] Hitler and his silly Volkswagen. Even we saved for one. A big swindle, all of it. Lost all my money in the VW savings account. Cars are a money-spinner and a waste of time. Oh, and *frohe Weihnachten* all round!"

It was Monday, late afternoon on Christmas Eve. Oma and Opa had just arrived from Hamburg. Oma and Opa were Mutti's parents. Dad had collected them, doing the five hundred odd kilometres in the snow from Frankfurt to Hamburg in three and a bit hours in the Chrysler Town & Country, the biggest, thirstiest station wagon around, America's answer to the oil crisis at six miles to the gallon in urban traffic.

The return journey with Oma on board had taken him three days and a bit, with about fifty-eight stops for vomiting and two detour stops at a nice Gasthof in the Harz Mountains and the Odenwald. For the entirety of the journey back to Frankfurt he had patiently listened to Oma's silence of docile bovinity, sporadically interrupted by the sounds of her regurgitation, and Opa's well-meant advice on how to improve the world, its economy, Dad's driving, and how to give his American, English and Italian cars to third-world charities and buy a Mercedes instead, if then he had to have a car.

Opa had never driven a car in his life and had no intention of ever doing so. Opa loved crossing even the busiest of roads without looking, waving his walking stick like mad in the air at anything vehicular, especially oncoming traffic. He frequently stopped cars, with himself standing in the middle of one lane or

---

[1] *Ger. military rank:* private

the other berating drivers for their intolerance and even insanity, as they had no real concept of what their speed could do. Drivers were so in awe of Opa's easily conveyed Germanic authority, they automatically wound down their windows in fear, to listen to the rant, apologising, promising to do it better next time round, although Opa had never actually worked for the traffic division of the police force as his department had been vice for most of his career. At the end of each finger-stabbing speech he would throw in a bit of good advice, "Now, before you drive off, child, remember we are all, all of us, first and foremost, you and I, we are pedestrians at our core. Pedestrians come first! Now, off you go, child! And remember to drive slowly with *due* care and attention. I have your registration." *Am Anfang waren wir alle Fußgänger! In the beginning all of us were pedestrians,* was one of his mottos. Another *Sieh, daß Du Sieger bleibst! Make sure you remain victorious!* he had framed in the hallway at his and Oma's home in Hamburg.

Considering his direct approach to traffic, literally, it was good thing that his long country walks didn't take him across the path of any Autobahn, laterally. It was an utter miracle that he hadn't been killed yet! Great War trenches to modern day traffic.

Dad looked very nervous and tired. And … a little guilty, Fergal thought. That was obviously down to the amounts of traffic he had observed collecting behind him in the rear-view mirror. Dad's unspoken motto was *Don't cause any silly tailbacks or pileups on the Autobahn or any other thoroughfare at whatever the cost. Be the fastest!*

Oma didn't like speed much and hated the Autobahn because the Nazis had built it to bring down unemployment figures with the RAD, the Reich's labour service, to control the workers, and specifically to facilitate the transport of weaponry. Oma loved back streets, country roads and lanes, and, above all, dirt paths! Germany's Landstraßen were the best in the world enjoyed preferably at walking speed on the television from her customised, residential armchair. Forty kilometres per hour was really pushing it! Fifteen to thirty was quite enough, thank you, or else *Uaaaaargh!* That's about nine to nineteen miles per hour, Dad said with a shudder.

In spite of Oma's being an ex-Communist, who luckily, because of Opa, hadn't ended up in a KZ[2] – the German form of concentration camp abbreviating lives – and a modern-day social democrat, Oma did also not like public transport because of her hip skiing thing back in the winter of 1943, when Oma and Opa had gone by bus on a you-don't-have-a-choice skiing and hiking holiday à la Luis Trenker in the Bavarian Alps with Nazi-owned Cheery-Happy Tours, KdF, *Kraft durch Freude*, the famous *Strength Through Fun* movement, as advised by certain superiors of Opa's, so the latter could find out about a certain person, an acquaintance of his with certain un-German tendencies the Gestapo might want to talk to with right fingers raised, regarding his views on the inevitable *Endsieg*, the final and ultimately inevitable victory of the Nazis.

Getting off the cold bus into a crowd of ecstatically cheerfully singing and healthy looking German-stroke-Bavarian children with red cheeks, nigh on white hair stirred by the wind more welcoming than the little rectangular party paper flags they held aloft, swastikas fluttering merrily, Oma was overcome by the urgent desire to be inside the Skihütte as quickly as possible to seek out the ladies conveniences, go to bed, sing the International, bang her head, kill somebody, or, best of all, enjoy a warming litre of Glühwein to be taken as quickly as possible.

This sequence of nervous, atavistic urges made Oma slip on the icy surface of the pavement leading up to the Skihütte, only fifteen meters away from its heavy wooden doors. Midfall she took it upon herself to shout "Scheiße!" really quite loudly and put an immediate end to the singing infants' politically motivated *Mistmusik*, known also in common English as *shitty tunes*. Still a quarter of her fall to go she regarded with a great sense of pleasure the severe shock she had put on the open-mouthed Hitler infants' sweet little faces at the scatology.

One could go to war and honourably kill scores of children for the Endsieg, but swearing was most certainly not the done thing! When Oma finally hit the pavement she twisted her right leg so unfortunately, she broke her hip. Ever since then had she spent her time in her favourite, customised, residential armchair

---

[2] *Ger. abbr.* KZ (*pronounce* car-tsett): Konzentrationslager, *Engl.* concentration camp

with the painful leg quiet up on top of a leg rest, and the left leg and foot in constant motion, tapping some rhythm on the floor to the never-ending Hans Albers to Howard Keel musical-bonanza playing in her head.

Oma lived in her armchair. She knitted a lot and obsessively in her armchair, and there was never a moment when needles and tapping foot weren't communicating in harmony. When she didn't knit she played card or board games with equal dedication from her armchair, either with her chattering friends or, if she really had to, with Opa. Always tapping along. Chequers, nine-men's-morris, backgammon, gin rummy, canasta, patience, *Mensch Ärgere Dich Nicht.* The latter a most famous German game called *Man, Don't Get Angry!* The simple German card game of *Mau-Mau* though was her favourite.

Oma was a magnificent cheat, a *Schummlerin.* For her, *shummeling* – cheating – was the purpose of any game! As the undisputed Shummel Queen, her shoulders never lost their rolling motion to accompany her tapping foot, and if Fergal watched closely, he could almost see her head swaying a little. Only sometimes would her foot stop its accompaniment to her armchair life. She would then hum an unfathomable, random tune like professional drummer Gene Krupa, but only on the rarest of occasions, when her shummeling had become so disrespectfully blatant, fellow-players were beginning to threaten not to get her any more Belgian chocolates from the bottom drawer next time she needed some, which was fairly frequently.

All in all, since February 1944 Oma had only left her armchair to look out the window exclaiming, "Unsinn! Alles Unsinn!" *Nonsense! All of it, nonsense!* And other bare necessities. To these were added, as of March 1952, visiting her precious and only princess daughter Martha-Louise, aka Mutti, every other three years for births, deaths, marriages and Christmas.

Oma sat quietly knitting, shummeling and humming, through air raids, firestorms, the last days of the war, the cold winter of 1947, the frozen family on the pavement outside who didn't want to come in, because they were a little embarrassed of charity and, frozen to death, were put on a cart the next day, the handsome young English men in gallant new-style green and hopeful, though monarchic, uniforms marching through the streets of Hamburg.

Oma's valiant endeavour at venturing all the way to Oxford for her daughter's wedding and later both Johanna Frances' and Johann Fergal's birth and baptism, making it appear as if she weren't in any pain at all and could proceed in a walking motion quite effortlessly without her crutch, did not go unnoticed, and earned her an enormous amount of respect from anyone, and a very compassionately raised left eyebrow from her own husband, Opa.

Opa always said, "That was yet another real miracle, almost like Ferkel's!" Then he'd shake his head for minutes using the momentum of this sad, contemplative motion to include his Cognac glass.

Fergal considered it sad because Opa was a Lutheran, of course, and not allowed any Saints and miracles. The greater miracle Opa referred to was naturally Fergal's own incredible recovery from near blindness, deafness and complete muteness just before Christmas 1970, almost exactly one year after the Bulhof-Murphys had moved to West Germany in the year of '69. The least miracle was Oma's journeying over to Oxford. The greater of the lesser Oma-miracles was her obstinate refusal to move out of her armchair, out of the house, whilst terrible things were happening all around her. The world was in turmoil, and Oma was sitting, knitting, and shummeling.

Four times during an air raid, with those very scary, quiet fire bombs, and air mines, most noisy, and other definitive attempts at intimidation exploding in a variety of inconvenient and specifically residential places, and twice after a successful RAF bomb run, rushing back from the bunker, had Opa come home to find more and more of the houses in their street laid to waste, with incendiary devices still burning away happily in his own front garden. Not once was their house hit! Fergal actually considered this a great, big, massive miracle, most worthy of the Pope's attention. However, he had been primed not to, please, mention the Pope to Opa.

After the 8th of May 1945 not a single property apart from Oma's and Opa's and the local deli Kolonialwarenhändler's remained in the street, which hadn't been damaged severely. The few surviving neighbours there were didn't look favourably on that.

Opa was one of the first Hamburg residents to be taken in by the British as a top-ranking Nazi official cum Gestapo officer cum murderer and very bad man indeed, who had personally killed Frau von Jammerlang's husband, who had disappeared suddenly after a harmless conversation of her husband's with that known Nazischwein "Heil Hitler, Herr Bulhof!" in his long black coat, though wool and not leather, and friends with scars all over their faces and monocles and cravats and mouthpieces for their cigarettes, never to be seen again and possibly her dachshund, Dackelchen Dieter too, who had disappeared only a week after.

For Opa this was the beginning of the long and laborious process of denazification, which to a degree he admittedly enjoyed a lot without wanting to convey any amount of undue ebullience, as it involved filling in enormous amounts of forms and signing lots of paperwork with long involved sentences.

Frau von Jammerlang's information and general behaviour was quickly proven most unreliable as Opa managed to take the intelligence officer and denazification-bulldog round Dackelchen Dieter's and Herr von Jammerlang's place of residence just under ten minutes away in the Jeep, although difficult, and much longer in real terms, as a lot of the rubble still hadn't been cleared at that stage.

Dackelchen Dieter and Herr von Jammerlang were living with a lovely, quiet, unabusive and elegant lady, Frau Mohnke, without any dachshund-fetish, but a palpably and de facto brain-damaged ex-Hitler-Youth son, Gernoth, who just couldn't get over the screamingly obvious. It was only discovered six years after the war that her son Gernoth was *missing that requisite amount of cups in his cupboard,* which is German for *really quite off his rocker, actually, totally barmy.*

Herr von Jammerlang was most obliged and happy to give Opa references regarding his status of dangerous Gestapo dachshund-fetish murderer.

As Frau von Jammerlang had lost her own property to complete devastation, and as she was also the only one of six other female survivors without husbands in the street, Oma took it upon herself, from her favourite armchair, to put post-war Germany in the right direction. Most charitably, she invited everyone in to stay for as long as they wished, until their houses had been rebuilt by the *Trümmerfrauen*, the industrious *rubble girls*, or husbands had returned from their Siberian PoW camps, or other inconveniences.

When Opa came back home from denazification that day he found his living room, in spite of the notorious tobacco and coffee shortage, filled with wafts of thick cigar and cigarette smoke, and eight gambling, coffee quaffing women, his wife and daughter included, non of them evidently capable of being a rubble clearing Trümmerfrau, because of the bad air.

On closer inspection it was discovered by himself that the secret cigar and cigarette compartment in his desk was now empty, as was his coffee compartment under the floorboards.

Only five years later did he admit to his GP, Hausarzt Dr. Geberling, that he would have liked to scream a little. Dr. Geberling prescribed divorce or separation, and recommended a good filling of mouth-watering asides. After all, Opa was working for the vice squad, wasn't he, the Sitte on St. Pauli's Reeperbahn. Opa was indignant at this, "I'm a married man!" and took himself off to the Harz Mountains without a forwarding address to go on *Kur*, the German way of going an a curing retreat to forget about the ills of the world and body.

He returned only two months later, close to a heart attack as he'd overeaten massively. There were rumours that he had been seen at the spa of Bad Harzburg with an overdressed type of lady. The type of lady who has to overdress professionally, elegant nevertheless, to support the success of her profession by means of attraction, which is, all things taken into consideration, to attract certain lonely, … never mind, … anyway, he was seen by a "most reliable friend of my dead husband's and mine" claimed Frau von Jammerlang whose husband wasn't dead. The red colour of Opa's facial complexion did not so much "indicate any heart trouble as it points to a happiness gained further down …"

"That's really quite enough now, Frau von Jammerlang. Let's play on now. Oh, look! Mau-Mau! I win!"

Frau von Jammerlang was to this day living as a tenant at Uferallee 39, Opa's house, in Oma's custody.

Fergal knew for a fact that Oma and von Jammerlang lived in the same room on the right on the first floor and Opa on the left just across. Oma and Opa had always kept separate quarters with a double bed in each. Fergal had stayed there three times, twice with his sister J. Oma and Frau von Jammerlang giggled a lot. Fergal was allowed to sleep in Opa's room. He and Opa laughed a lot together too, but that was quiet and really nothing compared to the level of noise the door on the right was muffling. J, Oma and Frau von Jammerlang got along splendidly. Whenever Opa and Fergal eavesdropped though, Jammerlang and Oma and J were definitely talking about men behind their closed door. Fergal and Opa rarely talked about girls or women. What for? Girls were boring!

What was by far more interesting was Opa's great proficiency at stalking. Opa was gifted! It was as if he became invisible. And then one day Opa revealed to Fergal how to become adept at being invisible.

Invisibility! This important art of survival which he had picked up in the Great War and found to be of even greater use to him under the Nazis. All you had to do is firmly believe you were invisible and breathe in a certain way. It all came from your stomach. Fergal became good at it in only two weeks. Of course, you didn't actually become invisible! You just sort of became more part of the background. Blending in. And it really worked! What had to be considered also was dress. The colours grey and brown were paramount. But that had been some time ago and now it was Christmas.

"What would you like?" Dad really was on his best behaviour today. Baby-Jesus-Day. Let's be nice and festive, according to Mutti. Considering that he had just spent three days on the road with Oma and Opa, his parents-in-law, throwing up and holding forth, and long tailbacks in his rear-view mirror, he managed to no longer tremble, appear in any way agitated, or show his glaring, mad eyes. Good stuff, Dad!

Fergal knew, being with his grandparents could be most tricky at times. They would haphazardly keep sniping at each other via any innocently bystanding third parties.

"Please, tell her! She was the one who listened to the BBC World Service, Seán. And then Otto died. She is just as much responsible for Otto's death," Opa would say. It would come out of nowhere.

Otto had died a long time ago, during a demonstratively concise Gestapo interview at Berlin HQ. Otto had been Oma's brother. Opa had been forced to observe the interview. Fergal and his Dad both knew about this. Oma didn't, apparently, and Opa had made grandson and son-in-law swear never to tell her.

Then Dad would nod at Oma's nervous knitting needles and tapping foot.

Oma would smile, "Opa could have stood up to that man and just rejected the offer to join the Gestapo. Same as with the SS membership beforehand. *Unsinn! Alles Unsinn!*"

Dad would nod at the deep red rug separating Oma and Opa.

Opa's lips would by now have disappeared in his mouth, "Seán, do tell my darling Liebling that it wasn't an option to turn down Giebenrat's polite requests. They were orders. My darling Liebling might also remember that the interrogation took place just *after* she had been denounced by that First War Russian ex-PoW Nazi for listening to that silly BBC propaganda station. Never trust foreigners! Then again, they were right."

Oma's foot would stop tapping, "*Unsinn! Alles Unsinn!*"

"Please, try to convey to my Liebling that if I hadn't obeyed the invitational orders to go to Berlin Gestapo, Otto would have died anyway. Then, my Liebling Frieda would have also not survived some interview or other because of her weak heart or whatever, and then they would have most likely *interviewed* our daughter Martha after my disappearance! – Well, … or put her in for Nazi orphan re-education. All in all, I had no option! I know … I knew the system! I wanted to keep my family!"

Oma, foot tapping again, "Seán, I never did find out whether Opa was there in the Gestapo basement in Berlin when they tortured Otto to death. Why was he transferred from Hamburg to

Berlin at the time? I've never found out! He never tells me anything, Seán!" Oma would look straight at Seán. Seán would look straight at the deep red rug.

This was a repeat performance whenever Oma and Opa visited. It was as if they never talked back at home. Maybe they really didn't. And it was mostly Seán they targeted. Fergal sometimes. Never, Martha-the-Innocent, or Johanna-Frances-the-Immaculate.

Sometimes they would really lay into Seán about his participation in the air raids on Hamburg, and Dresden, above all. They wanted to hear whether he thought it had been wrong.

"Of course, it was wrong. War is wrong. It was an adequate reaction to something very wrong. I worked for the RAF Post Office, though, and you know that. I did a bit of Dollis Hill and a bit of that. I did some observing and some airlifts from RAF Lübeck Blankensee. I was never part of the bomber crews!"

Seán was right. But this was just the way it would always be. By now it had attained the rank of tradition and Oma and Opa appeared to enjoy it. Opa would normally bring these brief bouts to a close by quoting loosely from Prussia's military philosopher Clausewitz' *Vom Kriege*, "*War is just the continuation of peace by other political means.* Let's leave it at that! We were all just following orders. – Now, Seán, I see you have three brand new cars in the drive. Business going well, eh!" And this, really, would be the end of it.

And now, there were even four cars outside, but business was bad!

Dad and Opa had just about managed to help Oma and her knitting sit comfortably in her residential armchair-cum-leg-rest, an identical copy of the one she had back home in Hamburg. It had cost a fortune but Mutti hadn't minded doing that for her own Mutter.

"What would you like?" Dad's renewed Baby-Jesus-Day peace offer. Absolutely no post-traumatic-driving-stress agitation left. No wild eyes. All aggravation forgotten.

"Seán, how lovely of you to ask, isn't it, Murres?" For Opa to call Oma *Murres* wasn't exactly polite. The word was uncomfortably close to *murren* as in *grumbling and complaining,* and being, generally, contrary. It was another way of saying *Mutter* or *Mutti,* but only when you were in an angry mood.

Fergal knew at once that Opa too must have been a little fed up with Oma's vomiting in the car.

"It's been a long journey, almost a holiday of itself. We'll have a coffee and Cognac each, please, Seán, and some mince pies, if then you want to indulge us the English way. From Fortnum & Mason as usual?"

"Sorry. No. Just Marks & Spencer's this year."

"Lovely."

Oma looked up from her frantic knitting, not interrupting her work, "Seán, thank you so much! *I* know you're Irish, Seán. Nevertheless, would you be able to recall how long Karl-Gustaf Friedrich Wilhelm Bulhof, alias Opa, and Frieda Maria Helene Gadebusch, alias Oma, have been married for?"

Dad frowned harder than usual. After all, he had been living with Oma and Opa at close quarters for almost half a week. "You have been married for, … since 1919."

Oma dropped her knitting and clapped her hands with a huge smile on her face, "Unbelievable, isn't it, Seán!? That's fifty-four years of the chance to come to know one another! Seán, do I drink coffee, or Cognac?"

"No, Frieda. You like cinnamon tea, … and cherry liqueur, … and Belgian chocolates, and Bahlsen's Prinzen Rolle." Dad exhaled uneasily, yet still with a sense of pride as he'd managed to get it right. He studiously avoided Opa's eyes.

Oma picked up her knitting and resumed her work nervously, shaking her head ever so indignantly, slightly humming, "Fifty-four years, fifty-four years, fifty-four years, … how time flies in … never mind!" Her left foot was tapping overtime.

Dad took off his jacket and disappeared into the kitchen. Opa positioned himself right next to Hansi, the Bulhof-Murphy canary in the cage by the window overlooking the snow-covered garden. Hansi started chirping wildly, flying and hopping around in his confined residence, his panic insane, seemingly bent on breaking a wing whilst bashing his brains out.

It was hard to tell with Hansi whether it was actually the insane panic of hellish fear brought on by claustrophobia, or simply the mentally incompetent happiness of an extreme extrovert at seeing Opa again. What did it matter? There had always been something special going on between Opa and Hansi. No one talked about it. Dad was slightly jealous of it.

But today Opa was not in the mood for special, friendly feelings of attachment to Hansi, "Be quiet, you orange bird, you! You don't know what real life is all about! Look at the snow out there. It's cold! If I opened your cage you'd fly out there, and die. You'd die!" Hansi stopped his faffy panic, shut up and cocked his head. – There definitely was something extraordinarily special going on between the two.

Amazing, thought Fergal, who now moved quietly over to the sofa to sit as close to Oma as possible. Although she was looking down at her knitting and was evidently immersed in all sorts of other simultaneous and important activities like foot-tapping, word-humming and swaying a little to some head-musical or other, Fergal could see her eyes were looking at him. She was grinning, "Fifty-four years. Fifty-four years, Ferkel. That's a long time! Come here and give your old decrepit Oma a good cuddle to last for the rest of her life." She had whispered this.

Fergal got to his feet in an instant. He loved cuddling Oma. She exuded the wonderful blend of Chanel No. 5, lavender and old age.

Both Oma and Opa used lavender on their handkerchiefs. Opa also used lavender water as an aftershave and Seborin hair tonic for his fingerful of leftover hairs. It would have been anathema to him to let Chanel's France invade his territory and then even let the enemy come so close as to make him smell of their own effeminate toilet waters.

Opa was staring into the white distance of the garden. "There's only death for you out there, Hansi. A horrid, cold death. The death of the gentle sleep. And suddenly you awake, and you know you're going to die, and you can't move. The dream you have had of warm summer evenings will stop, and you'll really feel the cold. You're frozen rigid! That's it. Finished! It is not a gentle death. That's a lie! Do you hear me, you orange bird, you!?" Hansi was actually looking out at the beautiful scenery of his prevented white death.

Oma shrieked a laugh, abrupt but imbued with a strange joy, for a moment only teetering on the verge of something quite different, before she whispered again, but this time at Opa, "Fifty-four. I am seventy-three and you are seventy-seven, Karl. We're old now. All so quick!"

Opa moved his head slightly. Maybe there was a smile now. It was too subtle for Fergal to tell. Then he nodded gently.

"Stop staring at Opa, Ferkel. Give me a hug!" Oma put her knitting down again, this time releasing her hands from those difficult looking loops. Dad claimed the Germans knitted differently. English and Irish knitting was easier and looked nicer. He would never dare say this to Oma. Her knitting was of supreme quality and kept him warm in the office. Everyone wore Oma's couture. In days long gone she had been a seamstress and dressmaker.

"The biggest huuuuuuuug for Omaaaaaaaaaaaa!" Fergal wrapped his arms around this wonderful woman and stuck his face deep in-between her shoulder and neck like a little olfactorily deprived perfume-vampire. He inhaled deeply. She hugged back and giggled. She was Fergal's nine-year-old sister at heart.

Opa ended a cough on, "... that's the way of life, Hansi!" Cough, "Ahem!" Harder cough, "Ahemmmmmmm!"

Oma took Fergal's cheeks in both her hands and said, as she released him, "This, Ferkel, is the way of life. Only this. Liebe macht, daß die Welt sich dreht." *Love makes the world go round.* "The rest is all *Unsinn.*" Fergal didn't entirely know what Oma meant but it sounded and felt good. He sat down on the sofa.

Oma's and Opa's exchanges were the same as ever. The first time he had met them had been virtually identical. They even had an orange canary called Hansi at Hamburg. It was a time-trap he himself fell into every time he was around his grandparents, and every time it made him feel old, immortal and safe. He tried to emulate the feeling every morning by using lavender water on his face. It did work, but not as well.

Opa wasn't a great one for showing a lot of emotion. Indeed, if he shook your hand and even looked you in the eye for more than three seconds, that really signified an eruption of emotion so volcanic you could feel his cold hand getting slightly warmer in an instant. Such magmatic excess would also take Opa himself aback quite considerably. He would have to sit down with left eyebrow raised and ask for a book to be given to him from the bookshelf. His favourite was the atlas but he wouldn't ask for it in particular. The atlas would be given to him in any case as soon as he'd sit down.

Dad had once jocularly remarked, during a Sunday picnic outing to the Taunus woods in his '66 Thunderbird, that a German holding an atlas was quite a frightening sight. The fight that had erupted made both Johanna and Fergal quiver and cry in the small backseat, and then it had started to rain. Mutti and Dad never appeared to make up after their rows. Neither ever said *sorry* to the other.

Mutti was now shouting from the kitchen in Johanna's general direction for her to hurry up and say hello to her grandparents. J had spent the last hour in the toilet. Mutti the two hours before that. In fact, both his sister and Mutti had spent an awful lot of time in the toilet over the past two days, as it had never been quite clear when Oma and Opa were going to arrive with Dad. When Mutti would emerge from the bathroom though, she really did look different and great. She favoured cocktail dresses and pearls. J coming out of the loo, on the other hand, was as pitifully repulsive as ever. She would be attired similarly. On its own her dress would have looked superb even with mud, oil, beetroot and red wine stains on it. Fergal was fairly certain J had spent about twelve hours on her general state of makeup and the other fifteen trying to get some eyelash right with the little intelligent perception she had left in that toilet-bowl brain of hers.

Fergal actually didn't understand that thing about feminine beauty, as even his friends claimed Johanna was very beautiful. His friends shouldn't say things like that! It felt a little … like betrayal. J was stupendously ugly! Even the best of painters wouldn't be able to capture her random facial aberrations in Chuck's poo. Full stop.

The real problem was that Oma loved J just as much as she loved Fergal. Her feelings for her grandchildren were really completely balanced.

With the brightest of smiles Mutti came in, slowly pushing a triple-decker food trolley ahead of her, stacked precariously with tea, coffee, Cognac, cherry liqueur, Oma's Prinzen Rolle and Belgian chocolates, a pyramid of M&S Christmas pies and German *Stollen.* The trolley was parked right next to Oma who nodded gratefully at her knitting.

"What are you knitting, Oma?" Fergal asked.

"Mmh! I don't know. Another body-sock, Ferkelchen? What would you like it to be?"

"I don't know, Oma." Fergal thought for a while, "I have everything I need, apart from guns and tanks."

"I can't knit those, Ferkel, and they are not good for you."

"How about my own room?"

"Sorry darling?" Oma put her knitting down and folded her beautifully old and long hands. She looked at him like a kind teacher.

"I do need my own room, Oma! Or you could just knit a body-sock for me to hide in from J, please!"

Mutti interrupted, "That's enough now, Johann Fergal! Apologise to Oma."

Oma frowned, "There's no need for the boy to apologise, Martha."

"Yes, there is!"

"I'm sorry, Oma. I was being nasty about J behind her back," apologised Fergal.

Then Mutti lit the four candles on the advent wreath for the festive mood and six candles by the Nativity representing all present.

Opa's body was now only half facing the wintry scene outside, half the orange prisoner Hansi, who had to be kept in there for his own protection. His head though was pointing in Oma's overall direction. Fergal couldn't tell whether he was looking at Oma or the trolley or even him.

In company Opa rarely ever smiled nor did he look angry. He was a bit like Mister Spock. This was Opa's balance. When he was on his own with Fergal though, especially in his garden at home in Hamburg, he would smile, sometimes even laugh. Not loudly, of course!

Mutti sat down in the armchair across from Fergal. Dad came in, opening a bottle of Champagne for Oma, Mutti and J.

J was now old enough for Champagne. From Fergal's point of view, this created an even wider and deeper rift between him and his sister. A moat filled with really pissed and bite-crazy piranhas. He had his doubts as to her behaviour towards him under the influence of alcohol. Over the Christmas period he would have to sleep in her room! Oma and Opa were staying at *Zum Weißen Hirsch.*

J was screeching her very own disastrously made-up Jimi Hendrix version of *Stille Nacht, Heilige Nacht* in the loo. Oma wouldn't have any liqueur at this time of day. Champagne was just fine!

Dad filled the Champagne glasses and the Cognac glasses and sat down in the armchair next to Mutti's. It was alright to have wines and spirits in a haphazard order, because it was Christmas, and Cognac was good, because it was cold outside. The glasses though remained on the trolley.

Dad folded his hands under his chin. Opa sat down next to Fergal on the sofa. The atlas was there, too. It remained unopened.

Fergal noticed that everyone, apart from Oma of course, had their hands folded. He tried the same, realising with shock that his elbows didn't reach his legs properly to support his chin on his hands unless he leant forward drastically, as if to throw up. He didn't want to add such tinge to the developing Mutti-festive mood. There was a little atmosphere, because of the waiting glasses on the trolley.

Everyone was waiting for J.

Fergal put his hands on his thighs. The wool of his dark grey Christmas trousers itched his skin. He uncomfortably put his hands in his pockets.

"Hands out of pockets, Johann Fergal! It's not festive!" Mutti ordered. Mutti preferred Johann to Fergal, and most certainly to Ferkel. Sometimes, when she was being stern, or at other times, when she wanted to demonstrate family unity, she'd call him Johann Fergal. Johann was the nicer name to Mutti, as in Johann Wolfgang von Goethe and Johann Sebastian Bach. Yet she'd sometimes call her son *Ferkelchen,* affectionately. The diminutive sort of meant *very tiny but sweet piglet* in English.

An apprehensively festive silence began descending on the Christmas living room. Fergal detected, J's Jimi Hendrix and *Stille Nacht* found a certain merry response in Oma's rhythmic left foot though.

This was ritual-waiting for J, and her process of immaculation.

A lot of family time was generally being spent on waiting for and on J.

Oma started humming the International.

Opa breathed out audibly.

Oma and Opa had met in Berlin in December 1918, just after the Great War. Oma was a fervent nineteen-year-old communist, and very pretty. Opa at twenty-three was still wearing the Kaiser's uniform and couldn't quite believe, that the war was over! Just like that! Without him having died horribly honourably like the rest of his friends!? And that there were still woman as pretty as Frieda in Prussia was just impossible!

Oma followed people who Opa had elected never to have heard of and felt not the inclination to learn anything about. Commoners, intellectuals, and what not, all foreigners really! Marx, Engels, Liebknecht, Luxemburg, Rosa. Rosa Luxemburg! Now what kind of a name was that? Heavens above! As of January 1919, dead of late, anyway.

Frieda was a great name! Frieda came with great hips!

Opa was sulking with his absconder Kaiser, the one his family northwest of Berlin had been breeding horses for when the *Über*-aristocrat had come along. Opa's family had been breeding horses forever.

Opa used to love horses a great deal. He joined the Potsdamer Kaiserlich Berittene Garde, the Kaiser's mounted guards, almost right at the beginning of the war, because the cavalry was the only way, the uniforms were the best, and France would be theirs in a matter of minutes, seconds even. In fact, all a German soldier had to do was fart a good Prussian fume in France's general direction. They had done it in 1815 and in 1871. They would do it again! He was going to work his way meritoriously up, until he could work more closely with the Kaiser.

Der Kaiser wasn't interested!

Opa was still slightly befuddled at the fact that he had managed to survive Verdun. The outcome of his wasted youth, four years that had felt like a hundred spent mostly at some mired front or other, eating rats and drinking piss, was a nice collection of serious looking medals with colourful ribbons. He had received two Iron Crosses, Eisernes Kreuz Erster Klasse. The saddest looking piece of brass was the medal commemorating the whole war. It just said 1914-1918. "It commemorates the fact that I have survived on a rather bad diet," Opa had said when he and Fergal threw the whole lot into the river Alster.

Opa delighted in being demonstrative and symbolic with Fergal, as it would teach Fergal that war was bad. Fergal thought it a shame to get rid of the medals.

Opa did enjoy talking to Fergal about the wars all history seemed to have so plenty of. A bit like Heinrich, Fergal thought. Opa had never talked to anyone about it, he insisted.

Mutti frequently asked Opa to refrain from this urge to put nasty, brutal things into her young son's mind, because, inevitably, Fergal would talk about it and then play war. Opa however was bad at listening to advice ever since the end of the Second War, and Fergal stopped telling Mutti what Opa and he talked about.

After the Great War, apart from losing all his old friends who had joined up with him, Opa also lost his love for horses. He just wanted all horses to rest in peace or roam free. He could even get angry at the ever rarer sight of Geesterheimer farmers using their horses to pull trailers for the harvest festival. "They just work them to death!"

After the Great War Opa never went back home to work on the family farm. He wrote letters from his lodgings in Berlin Charlottenburg without any forwarding address. He was fine, and that was all he was going to tell them once a year for Christmas for the rest of his life.

To fall so deeply in love with a communist was not altogether ideal for an essentially deeply conservative gentleman like Opa. For a communist to fall in love with an imperialist, capitalist, monarchist, landowner chauvinist, militarist, loyal Kaisertreuen was in essence primitive, as it was backward, and a new era was beckoning with the promise of a great workers' victory after the World Revolution. "Yes, you poor, deluded, cute, little cavalryman! Just look to our Russian brothers and sisters. In '17 they just buggered off home and kicked out their oppressor, that traitor of the people, the Tsar. Please lock the door. Someone might come in! Now, let me have a look at the real Kaiser Wilhelm again."

Oma and Opa were so very deeply in love they forgot the whole world for fifty-eight days and nights from December 1918 to February 1919. Opa's landlord didn't seem to mind much, as there was lots of coming and going generally. The noise of hand grenades and machinegun fire from street fights between factions, groups and parties allsorts, only too familiar to Opa, reached them just about in their bedroom, overlooking the second Hinterhof, that most emblematic backyard, a prominent feature of all Berlin architecture, that so inspired the illustrator *Pinsel*-Heinrich Zille in his depiction of working-class Hinterhof life. The sounds of war from the streets were only quite muted but with enough of a romantic echo for both of them to come to a decisive compromise.

One: Opa was going to have to stop being backward and stupid.

Two: He would have to stop wearing that silly imperialist, capitalist, monarchist, etc. uniform bespoke tailored only for backward murderers and idiots.

Three: He would have to learn how not to always satisfy his own urge but hers also.

"Anything else?"

"No."

"Good, Frieda. Now you listen to me. I …"

… One: Will do what you ask me for.

Two: I want to marry you.

Three: I want to have children eventually.

Four: You and I have to keep exercising a lot more for that children-thing before we actually have children. "Let's say ten years!?"

Five: I want only one child, and that has to be a daughter who can't go to any silly war.

Six: Shall we try that other funny thing again!?

"Oh yes, Karl! Hang on, … did you just propose to me?"

"Yes."

The political compromise they found was simple. Oma would move slightly to the right, and Opa would move slightly harder to the left. Hence, they became social democrats and moved left in a westerly direction to Hamburg only weeks later. Hamburg, though a free town of the Hanse, was considered to be part of the more civilised Prussian sticks with potential access to the world via the river Elbe.

Oma continued her dressmaking and Opa joined the police force to bring some order back into this world of rightist turmoil and dangerous leftist upheaval. The Kriminalpolizei accepted him and put him in the Abt. *Sitte*.

Sitte!

Vice!

Opa couldn't believe his luck! Abt. Sitte was quite different to Abt. *Blut, Beulen, Mord und Todschlag*, the latter department being dedicated to blood, bruises, murder and manslaughter. Sitte in St. Pauli was a godsend and much fun. Yes, now and then there might be a bit of a murder in the world of those most enthusiastic prostitutes but generally it was fun and there were ships from all over the world.

Working for the Sitte entailed Christmas blessings from client quarters most generous. Prostitutes and their respective employers, really, were a grateful bunch! For the unmarried officer of the law presents could be most indulgent, staggering and abundant, if accepted. For the married keeper of the peace gifts were largely culinary in nature.

Either way, Opa was married and always hungry. The presentation gift baskets were delightful enough. Oma and Opa had never before seen so much food from around the globe! It was out of this world. And there would always be a little pecuniary something hidden as a tiny surprise at the bottom of the basket.

During those historically lean days it was manna from heaven. During Inflation Years it might be a little gold coin, during the Crash of '29, the Germans call *Weltwirtschaftskrise,* even bits of exotic jewellery.

Names were never mentioned on the attached Christmas cards which would only ever read, "Mit herzlichstem Dank für all die guten Taten!" *All your good deeds,* or, "Na, na, na, wieder 'mal ein Auge zugedrückt! Danke!" Looked the other way again! Thank you! Along those lines. Ending in the standard, "Frohe Weihnachten" from either *Anonym* or simply, "Dann raten Sie doch ‚mal!" *Have a guess,* or even the much less formal address of, "Na, dann rate 'mal, Süßer!" *Have a guess, sweetie!* – If the latter were written on a card, Opa would simply take it off and put it on the fire, because it was cold and he didn't want Oma to think he was having affairs *mit den leichten Mädchen,* the easy girls, or the much ruder *Nutten auf'm Strich,* because he simply didn't.

His loyalty to the Kaiser had turned into loyalty for his wife. For Opa that was part of the social democratic compromise.

He did explain to Fergal at one stage that men, one of which he would grow into later, have strong and low desires, stemming from the low place down in their trousers, and sometimes this urge was very, very hard to fight.

Fergal promised not to tell Mutti, which he hadn't been doing for some time anyway, but he really had no idea what Opa was on about.

And this was how life was going to be for Frieda and Karl for the rest of their lives, including the time when their one and only daughter Martha-Louise Theresa Amalie was born in 1930. Nothing was going to change apart from the obvious: Karl was going to be made Kriminalrat and then start something with the Innenministerium. First, at the local level in Hamburg, then to continue at the national level in Berlin, maybe even in the Außenministerium.

Oma would fantasize a lot about being Karl's ambassador wife in the New World. Dvorak's symphony playing in her head, she mind-walked down Fifth Avenue quite relaxed and accustomed to the hustle and bustle of NY street life. So much like Hamburg, just the buildings were higher. Her magazines helped.

Somehow, communism's braver new world, once dystopia to Karl, utopia to Frieda, now quite forgotten, the world was their oyster with a massive pearl in it. The Weimarer Republik just spot on, and quite great really, apart from that trifle of a legalistic, conjunctive oversight of having *Kanzler* and *Präsident* mutated together in the same homunculus chimaera for the rule of myopia.

"Never mind. Thankfully, it's past now. And we're all alive!" Opa would say.

Although Frieda, the ambassador's wife *in spe*, would never have admitted to this, especially regarding the source of the family's relatively high comfort and income, the Bulhof's had gone relatively unscathed through inflation and the Crash with the help of other people's business. – As in pimps and prostitutes.

"Never mind. I did enjoy it!" Opa would say.

And then, a rather dark alpine shadow with an unstylishly castrated Austrian moustache was cast over the whole place in ominous emasculation of state and sanity aka, "Dieser blöde, österreichische, lederhosenedelweißpflückende berggefreite Fanatiker, Dorftrottel und Bauernlümmel mit diesem erfundenen, undeutschen Namen, der irgendwie englisch klingt, Populärmusik, ein Hit, dieser Hitler, der nicht 'mal an der Kunstakademie angenommen wurde und zudem noch Ex-Häftling ist und dieses Mistbuch *Mein Kampf* irgendwie veröffentlicht hat, macht Werbung für eine Partei, die fast alle Parteien unter einem Dach vereinigt, ... NSDAP, Nationalsozialistische Deutsche Arbeiterpartei ... klingt dumm und gefährlich und machtbesessen[3]." Yes, that one! From Schickelgruber, to Hüttler, and finally Hitler. Ultimately a pile of ash and bones. Now a bad memory. A man, not so much with a great imagination, but fantasies conglomerated in a sick, unreasonable vision of state that excluded all Jews, and therefore a considerable part of all educated German bankers, shopkeepers, geniuses, artists, scientists and

---

[3] *Ger.* … this ignorant, Austrian, leather-trousered, edelweiss picking, mountain-private fanatic, village idiot and farm bully with this made-up, un-German name that sounds somewhat English, popular music, a hit, this Hitler, who wasn't even accepted at art school, and to top it all off, is an ex-convict who has written this pile-of-dung book *My Struggle* which he somehow managed to publish, is advertising for a party that is bringing together almost all parties under one roof, … NSDAP, national-socialist workers' party of Germany … sounds stupid and dangerous and power-obsessed

even hardcore war veterans. Opa even knew some very nice Jewish prostitutes.

But today was Christmas.

Waiting for J.

Speak of the devil …

… the loo key turned and up turned J with blue eye shadow and pink lipstick and a pasty, yellowy baby-sick colour face cream.

"Johanna, darling! – We've been waiting just for you. You look wonderful!" Problem was, Mutti actually meant it, and no one was reprimanding Johanna-Frances at all!

Fergal found this forever hard to believe. If he'd been faffing with the wrong make-up on the loo like this for days on end, he would be given a good talking to, plus Mutti would be most worried! He got the lecture quite a lot anyway, and then he would write to God via the Pope.

Had J put a smoke grenade on the dinner table Dad and Mutti would have asked for her motive and forgiven her! Possibly even increased her so very, very meagre pocket money, which had driven her to such expressive action. She might then be offered some counselling with an expensive psychologist.

Fergal had had a motive in that he wanted to bring his parents closer together again. J wouldn't have thought of such a thing! Waste of time.

J only knew of the paths in her own world where the Autobahn of her imagination would get her fast to wherever she wanted to be, with as little interference as possible from any outsider. Everyone was an outsider if they didn't serve her purpose.

Fergal knew that she wanted to be a doctor. To think of her caring for the sick and weak especially under the influence of Champagne and an overblown sense of self made him shudder.

Fergal looked around him. – Everyone was festively happy-cheery. This entire, silly spectacle was down to Baby-Jesus lying wide open-eyed in the crib of His Nativity on the sideboard, with two candles to the left and two to the right of it. Each candle represented one member of the Bulhof-Murphy family. Oma's and Opa's candles were directly in front of the nativity.

Had Jesus been there Himself he would have understood what was going on! It didn't take a grownup to figure it out.

However, it took a grownup to pretend nothing was wrong! It took a grownup a lot of lying to get to the state they were all in.

Jesus would have figured out pretty quickly that Mutti and Dad now hated each other. The oil-critical frowns and sneers on their faces had disappeared inside for the festive season.

Jesus and Fergal knew that whichever love Fergal's parents had once shared for each other, they had now entered the realm of hate.

Since the smoke grenade incident matters had become quieter, but worse!

Fergal felt guilty, as he saw himself the reason for the increasingly bad atmosphere between Mutti and Dad. In the past they had had rows like everybody else over silly things. It was all in the voice. Those had been rows played out over the underlying harmony that had kept his parents together for over twenty years already. The words they exchanged now came from the conviction that both of them were right but in different ways.

Mutti and Dad were in different places altogether. The underlying harmony had gone. Replaced by a strange cacophony Fergal could feel on his skin as an abrasive friction with each atmosphere.

His parents had definitely been in love at one stage in their lives, but that was before Fergal's time.

During Johanna's nocturnal soliloquising, when Fergal was forced to sleep in her room at weekends, she would sometimes say how wonderful things had been with Dad, Mutti and herself of course, before *Fergal's* arrival! Mutti and Dad apparently used to throw yellow flowers in the air together … they used to laugh out loud and together at the same time … and then *Fergal* came along … and things happened … it was all Fergal's fault!

Fergal would then hear Johanna grind her teeth. She always promised him, she would kill him soon. Almost daily! It scared Fergal, and sometimes he wondered where all his fear went.

He also knew he had nothing really to be scared of, because his little life was so nothing compared to Opa's and Heinrich's, and sometimes, Dad's stories of the war. And then, of course, there were Mutti's images of death and destruction and smoking corpses lying around haphazardly in the street.

Fergal really had a good life, apart from the J-factor. Fergal knew that Johanna blamed him for everything bad in life, even the oil crisis, "Just look at them, you little turd. The name Ferkel isn't bad enough for you. I shall call you *Dreck* or *Schmutz* from now on, when they don't listen, because I do not want to cause them any further pain. Or *Scheißdreck* is more apt, isn't it? Have you ever seen them laugh together when you're around, Scheißdreck?"

"No."

"You see! It's all down to you and your *Dreck*-presence."

"Yes." It did hurt Fergal somewhere when Johanna was like this. And Johanna was like this most of the time. But he didn't know where this *somewhere* was, or where her constant insults went inside of him. As they weren't true, maybe he was alright. Heinrich said, only the truth has a real effect.

J offered, "Would you like me to put you down, Scheißdreck?"

"No."

"It won't hurt as much as my other treatments, and then it's all over! I think Mutti and Papa are asleep, so I won't even disturb them and you'll promise you won't scream, Scheißdreck!"

"Leave me alone, Johanna. – I'm tired."

At this stage Fergal might get the *smopil* torture. Smopil was J-lingo and meant *smothering by pillow*. It wasn't nice. When it was over, and Johanna had returned to her bed, she'd continue with her *once-upon-a-time-when-there-wasn't-Scheißdreck* … "Mutti met Papa at the perimeter fence of RAF Lübeck Blankensee when he was airlifting stuff to Berlin, because Berlin was cut off by the Russians."

"I know, Johanna. – I am tired!"

"It's a beautiful story! Up until the moment you come in. And you'll listen or else …!" At this stage it might be two o'clock in the morning.

"Ok. But Dad was only an RAF Post Officer."

"Shut up, Scheißdreck! – So, Mutti was on her way to the Baltic during the summer holidays, because it was hot, and she needed a swim. She knew nothing of men, although she had her fantasies. As do I! It was a cycling tour with her friend Erika who still lives in Hamburg and has boobs bigger than mine even. Mutti was so full of life and youth and happiness, because she didn't know then that she was going to have a child called Ferkel Schmutz-Dreck Scheißdreck. And then, outside Lübeck, she and Erika passed the airfield with the English and American planes that were going to Berlin. She wasn't much older than I. And there was Dad …"

… in his dashing uniform, and they all fall in love immediately, and then they all get married and love each other even more, and they all move to Oxford and have gloriously beautiful Johanna Frances who increases their happiness a thousandfold, and it is all rain-of-merry-yellow-flowers and fat elves hovering in the bright celestial light of clear joy and bliss ... until …

"… until Ferkel Dreck! Ferkel Schmutz-Dreck! Scheißdreck!"

Above all, in terms of physical torture, Fergal found Johanna's late-night love stories the worst torment. Whether J's stories were about Mutti and Dad, or Frank Sinatra and J in the same Baltic airlift situation, or Mick Jagger and J, or Marc Bolan or John Lennon or … Fergal was, without reprieve, the only contributory factor to the worst bad-ending ever, so he had to be killed horribly to turn any story of J's into a cheery happy-ending wonder story. It really made J feel great!

And now, she was as ever the innocent centre of attention at the family Christmas party! And she was about to have Champagne, which in turn was going to affect her behaviour later, when Fergal had to stay in her room.

Fergal put his palms upwards. Somehow the wool of his trousers made the tops of his hands itch less than his palms.

"You look lovely, Johanna!" Oma was so sincere. Fergal admired that hugely. Of course, he minded the fact that Oma liked J as much as she loved him. Fergal hesitated. *Rephrase, little man,* a voice somewhere in his head said quite clearly. *Oma loves J as much as she loves me!* Fergal felt better for having thought it like that to himself. Oma's love for both of them was untainted and clear.

"You look wonderful, darling! Merry Christmas! Welcome, and cheers!" Mutti and Dad said it almost at the same time. Mutti said *you look,* Dad added *wonderful,* Mutti and Dad *darling.*

That sort of thing. Almost a harmony.

Fergal though was only too aware of the difference in tone. A dissonance. Both his parents' minds were somewhere else. Mutually exclusive *else.*

Mutti's mind possibly on the fact that the savings would now have to be touched, and then all money would be used up swiftly on trying to stop the massive, unpluggable leak in Dad's sinking ship, and then they would all be homeless and roam the fields for scraps of rotten potato, cabbage, carrot, and wet firewood, and they'd all become alcoholics and die of frostbite screaming at each other in the gutter like the gutter-society of asocials down Mönchsgasse who screamed the sounds of hell on earth and beat their alcoholic children to death, got very drunk, and then hanged themselves after they had thrown their wives out the window of their government housing estate. The estate down Mönchsgasse played host to the annual beating of up to ten wives and one spectacular suicide at least per year.

Dad's mind was on Christmas, his wonderful darling-daughter, as he evidently thought, and possibly, only possibly, a little ahead in time with some niggling worry about how to save the business that provided for his family.

A strange silence cut into this festive endeavour unexpectedly. Oma had stopped knitting, tapping and swaying to the music playing in her head. Her head down, she was looking at her grandson Fergal.

"You seem very thoughtful and very far away, little man. What's wrong with our little Ferkel? Eh, Ferkelchen!?"

No one answered. *Everyone* was looking at Fergal.

It hurt.

What was wrong with thoughtful? The fact, that *thoughtful* existed as a word, comforted Fergal. All the family knew that Fergal thought more than he spoke. Opa certainly approved of that because one of his other numerous but not primary mottoes was *Reden ist silbern, Schweigen ist Gold*! Silence is golden! They knew he wasn't stupid, apart from some fears in that direction during his speechless year. His thoughts came out in writing at school. Teachers marvelled at the rich language and large vocabulary of this very quiet, little fellow.

The good thing about writing was that you could think really carefully about it before you wrote it down and then you could think about it again and make changes. Fergal rarely talked about his thoughts, and doing so this very minute, in what was referred to by possibly all those around him as a festive mood, would have caused great distress and would have been misconstrued as selfish.

No one wanted to hear about how badly the business was doing, how bad money was, how Mutti and Dad had almost over night really started to hate each other, how Mutti's mind was filled with imagery so horrid, she constantly betrayed herself through too much talk with Fergal but mainly J, how there was no help for Dad from the banks he had kept so much money with over the past five years. Silence was golden! What was more brilliant than gold? And, silently, Dad's business was going to go down.

Fergal looked round at everybody, quietly, before he said "Am I wonderful too?"

Everybody laughed. There even was a jocular grunt from his sister. Somehow though, once the laughter had died down, and it died down quickly, Oma and Opa gave Fergal this understanding look.

They knew.

Things hadn't been so great between Mutti and Dad for about a year. There had been talk of another woman. The Colonel's wife, Lydia. Notorious nymphomaniac at USAF Frankfurt. Joachim had looked the word up for Fergal. Wow! What was that all about?

Mutti had been on the phone to Oma a lot talking of all the foreign women who liked Dad. The amounts of money he spent on other people, never on his family. Sometimes there wasn't enough money for food even. Fergal had overheard that Oma and Opa had started sending money in the post. Dad was detaching from the family.

Opa nodded at Fergal, "That's why I like talking to your son, Martha." He didn't look at his daughter. His eyes met straight with Fergal's. He rarely did that. Fergal knew that Opa had been good at interrogating suspects. Without prompting Opa had sworn to Fergal that he had never tortured anyone.

"Have you ever killed anyone, Opa?"

"It was war. Let's not talk about it."

Just now and then did Fergal wonder why some older people trusted him, tiny little Fergal, so much, told him so much, maybe even too much. Sometimes he didn't want the information. It put a lot of thoughts into his mind. And images that weren't necessarily his.

"Yes, I know, Papa," Mutti nodded, "You just shouldn't talk of too many grownup matters, of war, please! – Now, everybody … cheers and welcome, Oma and Opa, again! Merry Christmas. Let's be cheerful over the festive period." Mutti laughed a crystal-clear snow-covered peaks laugh, "Let's be festive. – Merry Christmas!"

Opa stuck his chin out and closed his eyes for only a second without a smile, "It's *Heilig Abend*." The Holy Evening. Christmas Eve. As if on cue everybody, even Fergal, now cheered "Merry Christmas!" Then Fergal got up, went over to the nativity, made the sign of the cross, genuflected and said, "Happy Birthday, Baby Jesus."

Oma screeched with delight.

Opa shook his head, but chuckled. Heavily, he heaved himself off the sofa and went over to his grandson. He lifted him up and took him in his arm giving him a long, hard cuddle with Fergal's head on Opa's shoulder. Opa smelt just as wonderful!

Mutti and J were chattering in the background.

Fergal saw that Oma and Dad were watching him and Opa. They were smiling.

When Opa put Fergal down again he took his hand and both were standing in front of the nativity for a while. Hansi was trilling away in his happy, secular panic-style in the background.

"When you're bigger and older and you're a man, I will die," Opa said. There was a bit of a pause. Opa appeared to be talking for the nativity's benefit only.

Fergal knew from experience there was more Opa would have to say. This was a bit of a demonstrative and symbolic moment just like the one with the medals by the Alster. Mutti and

J stopped chattering. They were expecting something about Opa's last will and who was going to get most. As if knowing Opa smiled at the expectant silence at his back. He continued whispering down into Fergal's ear, "We all die. There's no secret. Pope Paul will die, Luther died, Jesus died. All impart something or the other to the ones they love who come after them."

Fergal pulled Opa closer by his ears and whispered back, "What's impart, Opa?"

"Tell. It's tell, give, that sort of thing. When I die, I will give you my secret, wooden Marble of Wisdom."

Fergal laughed.

"Quiet child! It's not a joke. I don't make jokes. Look!" Opa took out of the left inside pocket of his jacket a perfectly round, shiny golden ball the size of a big chestnut. He shook it by Fergal's ear. It made an insignificant rattling sound at first. Then Opa held it still, and there was a tiny, harmonious chime. "It contains the secret of the world, Fergal! It has the answer!" – Opa gave Fergal a very serious stare. Opa looked proud.

"May I hold it, please, Opa!? The marble."

Oma sighed audibly, and it seemed to Fergal that her knitting was becoming louder and louder. Mutti and J were chattering again but more quietly. They were obviously trying to hear what on Earth was going on and whether there was any money in it for them.

"Yes, you may." Opa laid the sphere in Fergal's open palm.

"It's heavy, Opa."

"It's made of gold on the outside."

"Why is it called wooden?"

"Because I took a look inside, once, during the Great War and once in the Second. First there's the outer layer of gold, then there is wood and inside there is something else. It's almost seamless but you can unscrew it. My own Opa gave it to me."

"What's the answer?"

"I can't tell you if you don't have the question."

"Opa ..."

"Yes, Fergal"

"What's the question, please?"

"That you'll have to find out for yourself! But it's equal to the answer." Opa took the heavy, wooden Marble of Wisdom back and returned it to his inside pocket.

J snorted.

Oma looked at her.

Mutti, J and Oma started grinning. Fergal didn't know what was going on and sat down on the sofa next to Oma's armchair. Dad left the living room. Then J looked without a smile at Opa and said cockily, "That's quite bad for your jacket's inside pocket, Opa. Why not carry your secret, wooden thingy in your trouser pocket. Might be quite manly and attractive like a big …" she didn't get any further … Mutti had slapped her face! – All had happened in a lightening instant. Oma had stopped grinning, Mutti had stopped grinning, and then Mutti's hand was retracting already from J's red cheek and messed up hair.

Fergal didn't understand what had brought this on. Even Opa looked befuddled. But … J smacked!? This was a world first! However, it felt good and right and just wonderful.

J ran into her room.

Fergal was happy.

This was going to be a very happy Christmas.

Letter #15 – Fergal To God Via The Pope

Dear Your Holiness, Papa Paul in Rome,

My Opa is a good man. He is German and a Lutheran but that is not his fault, because he was born like that. My Opa has seen a great many terrible things in the wars, and he tells me about them! He says beware of people whose business is war. Sometimes his stories give me very bad nightmares, but I know that when he imparts these things it makes them easier for him inside him, and I can cope. It is much worse having to be with J and not having my own room!!!

Opa says he is going to die, because all of us have to die at some stage, and it is perfectly natural to do so, so that's OK really, isn't it, and that's not his fault either!? When he dies he wants to give me his wooden Marble of Wisdom. It has the secret of the world inside, but you will only understand it if you know the right question. Dear, Your Holiness, Papa in Rome, do you know what the question is? If you do, please let me know, so I come prepared when he dies and I unscrew the wooden Marble of Wisdom.

By the way, it is not really wooden, and it's not made of marble, nor is it a toy glass marble. It is a little ball made of gold and it makes a beautiful sound when you shake it. Inside it has things that rattle and there is wood but you have to unscrew it.

Please pray to God for me so that Opa lives a long time and I can think of the right question, and the wooden Marble will answer me then! Please also make J stop being nasty to me, because it always hurts, and the pain she gives me inside I do mind a little, really. I mind far more than the pain Opa's or Heinrich's stories give me, because they are real stories. Mutti also says some terrible things. Please give her peace and make Mutti and Dad love each other again.

Yours faithfully

Pass my Love on to Your Employer

J. Fergal Bulhof-Murphy.

PS.: JF keeps telling me that I am the reason for Mutti's and Dad's unhappiness, and that all the pain she puts me through is good because it will turn me into a better person when I'm dead. I don't really believe her fully. But she is very serious when she tells me these things. Please tell me that I am not a bad person, Holy Papa! God must know I am not!

PPS.: I hope you don't mind that I write to you so much. These are troubled times. I can open my heart to you. Thank you.

Torturing For Points

It is just after midnight, Saturday. Johanna-Frances aka J, age fifteen, and her younger brother Fergal aka Ferkel Dreck, Schmutz-Dreck, Scheißdreck[4] age 9, are home alone. Mutti and Dad are at a party at Geesterheim Garrison. The Noldes downstairs have taken their son Chuck to a tennis match in Munich for the whole of the weekend. The house is empty. Fergal lies bound and gagged on his side on the bathroom floor. The bathtub is filled with cold water. His pyjamas are wet. He's wearing thick socks. He is shivering horribly. His lips are purplish blue. It is evident that he has just been dragged from the bathtub.

J: If I kill you, it is highly likely that I'll go to prison. If I go to prison, I won't be able to have the life I want and deserve. If I don't have the life I deserve, I'll be very, very unhappy! You don't want me to be unhappy, do you, Dreck?

Dreck: Mmh, mmh, mmh! *[obviously exhausted but in a state of mortal fear, shakes his head violently]*

J: Let me take off the gag. – It was just for fun. No one would hear you anyway even if you screamed. And look on the bright side! I didn't quite drown you. *[tenderly, with a smile she takes off her brother's gag]*

Dreck: Please, stop this, *[panting]* Johanna. I feel terrible. I'm going to die if you continue. *[out of breath]*

J: Don't be silly! – You are quite resilient! Just one more thing to complete your points … *[JF leaves the bathroom and returns minutes later with a long lead, one end has the plug attached, the other end is open, wires sticking out, she is wearing gardening gloves]* … this is a new one. I read about it in *Spiegel* or *Stern* magazine. Wet clothes are the best! *[she plugs the lead in]*

Dreck: *[screaming]* Mutti!

J: No one will help you. No one believes *you*! There won't be any marks, Dreck. Just some pain inside,

---

[4] *Ger.* Dreck = *Engl.* dirt, mud, scum, something soiled – *Ger.* Schmutz = *Engl.* dirt, something extremely untidy and soiled – *Ger.* Scheiß/e = *Engl.* shit

and you might be a little ill for a bit. *[she holds the wire in his wet hair]*

Dreck: *[briefly screams, then as if he's run out of breath there is no sound, just convulsions going down to his feet, grinds his teeth]*

J: Over soon, little Dreck! Let me now just try your thighs and then your feet. *[she touches Fergal's thighs and feet with the live wire]*

Dreck: *[convulses terribly, after each interval panting faster interrupted by little gargling noises]*

J: *[beginning to clear up in the bathroom, her utensils disappear, she strips the pyjamas off Fergal and puts them back in the washing machine, Fergal can hardly move, she helps him into her room and on the sofa bed]*

Dreck: *[falls asleep trembling with his thumb in his mouth]*

J: *[watching him with a sense of serenity]* Forty man-points, little Dreck! This is always good fun. – You exhaust so quickly these days! Don't worry! There'll be no wounds to show on the outside.

Letter #20 – Fergal To God Via The Pope

Dear God, and Your Holiness, Papa in Rome! Dear Papa!

I want to kill J so she dies horribly and even if I go to hell it can't be worse there than having to be near her while she is still alive. I know saying this is not good and I won't do it, so please do not worry. But I would very much like to ask you to pray that she dies horribly. She put me in a cold bath and drowned me and then she gave me electric shocks and I was ill for three days. Mutti does not believe me and Dad is at work too much. Mutti just says I am vindictive and my imagination is overactive and I should stop lying. She says it is unlikely that I'm not lying because I lied for a whole year when I was silent. No one believes people who cry wolf. But I'm not lying and J started being nasty to me when we moved to Wetchamoonis, which is West Germany, and when I stopped being silent she became horrible. Back home in London she was just mean because I was invisible to her. Mutti's imagination is very overactive too, Dad used to say when he was still around more and less at work and when they still talked to each other. The worse work gets, the more he has to work. That is strange! Dad says, those with the worst imagination, for profit, already run the world. So happy thoughts for Mutti!

Heinrich came round too, to have a look at me. He says there is nothing wrong with me. It is just a cold. I think he is more on the side of Mutti than my side.

I would like for J to die slowly with wet hair in the socket, or to throw her out of the window head first about a hundred times. I would like to take her eyes out and then tie her up and put her feet in a fire and then her body too, very slowly.

What makes me feel quite good about J is that she will definitely die one day! She will go to hell! And when she's gone I have my own room because you prayed for it. Happy thoughts!

Yours faithfully with much love and happy thoughts from your future priest

You are Love, aren't you? God is Love! You are employed by God, aren't you?
Good!

J. Fergal Bulhof-Murphy

Fergal's Big Long Sulk

Prof. Dr. Dr. Eichenraub

"Come in please, please!" From behind a pair of very smudged and thick reading glasses Prof. Dr. Eichenraub nodded an hello at an enormous file very much in front of him on his gargantuan kidney-shaped Jugendstil desk. This was Mathildenhöhe in Darmstadt. Everything was Jugendstil. "Please! You will sit there, there, and let me have a quick read to re-acquaint myself with the patient, patient."

Gently, so as not to break her tiny, little, fragile son, Mutti guided six-year old Fergal forward soothingly by his left shoulder, as she had been doing for almost a year now.

Fergal was limping and groaning, holding out ahead of him his arm, his hand groping blindly in the air to avoid any oncoming obstructions that might by unanticipated impact increase his deep pain even more.

Tenderly, Mutti placed him into one of the two deep, comfortable leather armchairs, and sat down in the other one herself, perched uncomfortably on the edge of the seat, watching Fergal carefully, so as to be ready to jump to his assistance with words of comfort and cuddles of love and some marshmallows or marzipan just in case another dreadful attack, possibly even of something entirely new, should occur or add itself to the mysterious medical catalogue that was her beloved son, already a living collection of such inexplicable and painful symptoms, the medical profession all over the south of West Germany had thus far not managed to find a cure, let alone an answer for.

Occasional near-blindness, complete muteness, frequent deafness, a limp that could shift from one leg to the other at will, sporadic dry-retching without vomiting, strangely only when his sister Johanna-Frances was around, bouts of nervous twitching all over his body, and as if this wasn't enough for that poor little creature, a sad form of uncontrollable flatulence, especially when Fergal was with the few friends he had managed to make ever since the Bulhof-Murphy family had moved to West-Germany just under a year ago after Christmas '69.

A good ten minutes went by before Prof. Dr. Eichenraub remembered there was an actual patient, and not just a file.

Prof. Dr. Eichenraub gave Fergal a long, analytical stare over the rim of his glasses. Fergal had completely collapsed in the depth of the armchair, letting off occasional groans, which befitted his unsolved disease perfectly, with his hand now and then still reaching out into the hazy distance, where the neurologist and psychiatrist was hovering in a cloud of smoky vagueness.

"Well, … well?" Prof. Dr. Eichenraub hesitated for a moment and looked at the file again, "Frau Bulhof-Murphy. Delighted to meet you, you!" He came round his desk, "Even under the circumstances," and proffered his hand, "I'm Professor Doctor Doctor Eichenraub. Just Doctor Eichenraub will suffice, suffice. Thank you, thank you!"

He was very tall, old, and emaciated, with the most unflattering looks of a very young and open-beaked nestling eagle about him.

Fergal shifted uncomfortably. This was caused by a terrible pain in his heart, the reason for which was Fergal's incredibly mysterious condition of primary muteness and secondary lots-of-agonising-symptoms brought on by having to endure the vision of Chief Nestling Eagle from his sprawled position in the armchair.

"The pleasure is all mine, Doctor Eichenraub," Mutti said without enthusiasm, but managed a sad quarter-smile, only half rising from the edge of her seat.

"No, do please stay! You will sit, sit! Don't get up, up. – I should recommend you take a long spa holiday, once we've found out for certain what ails little Master Ferkel here. He hasn't spoken in a year, a year he hasn't spoken. Mute, eh, mute! It is quite a bit of a file your young son has gathered, I have to say, say. Some people don't even manage that after a lifetime of unwellness.

"Now, Frau Bulhof, let's keep this strictly down to a minimum, so I don't waste more of your precious time, time. Time! Eh! I know exactly what ails our young friend here, and

Ferkel might even leave here today, today a completely healed little fellow, won't you, Ferkel!

"Speech, speech. A great gift. Gift!" Over the rim of his glasses, with predatory eyebrow feathers in menacing disarray, Prof. Dr. Dr. Eichenraub gave Fergal a stare so intense, Fergal fell forward on the floor in a slide and started retching. Mutti reacted instantly, jumping up and onwards to the rescue. Her little son was dying! Midway, she was stopped by Chief Nestling Eagle-Eye, the specialist. Fergal couldn't believe the creature's audacity!

"Please don't, Frau Bulhof! You *will* not help him! That will make matters only worse, worse! Worse, for such an expressive child! Expressive without speech, speech. – Speech! What a gift!"

"What do you mean, Herr Professor Doctor?"

"Coincidence has it, that a majority of my colleagues whom you have consulted on this either studied with me at Heidelberg or attended my lectures. Before you visited me here this morning, morning ..."

Fergal interrupted the specialist's flow with an abominable groan and heartbreaking retch from the floor. Again, Mutti, tried to get up to reach her mute and dying son, but the specialist's raised finger claw told her to sit down.

"May I ask, Frau Bulhof, ... have you by any chance ... developed ... any symptoms of stress over this yourself? Let's, for example, say, say, ... say a gastroenteritis?"

"Yes, how did you know? – But I am fine, really. I take my salts, and it goes."

"Well, ... well, ... well, you too will feel better, once I will have healed your little chap here! Mute!? Eh, ... eh!"

"Oh, Herr Doctor, are you sure? That would be so wonderful!"

"Quite sure! – Now, now, ... now, as I was saying, I talked to a variety of my colleagues who have seen your son's, ... Ferkel's range of varietal entertainment stunts, ... and now the onus, ... so to speak, ... is on me, me. It's been going on for long enough!"

"What do you mean, Herr Doctor?"

"Please. Please! Frau Bulhof. Bulhof. I'm just going to examine Ferkel." – He turned and glared down at Fergal, "Mute, … mute, eh!?" who was still lying on the floor groaning a little.

Fergal could feel the specialist's eyes burning into the nape of his neck. He sensed himself safe down there, with the comfortably soft Chinese silk rug in front of him smelling of mud and cigar smoke, with bits of crumbs in it.

It was a completely different world down here.

Fergal groaned again. He was not going to move!

He was going to die here, and then they'd be sorry!

"Get up, … get up. Ferkel. Ferkel! Get up!"

This terrible man's voice was such, it left no space for doubt in Fergal's mind that he would get killed if he didn't get up. Fergal got up in an instant.

"Stand up straight, … straight! And do not move, little man!"

Fergal stood to attention like a soldier.

"You see, Frau Bulhof. Bulhof!? – The right tone of voice does it. Now. Now! You will tell me, please … please … if there is anything else, else apart from his made-up catalogue of symptoms, anything you find noteworthy of your son, son?"

"He's quite pretty for a boy, and very well-behaved."

"All children are lovely to look at, especially boys, boys. Boys. Oh. Boys! – What I mean is … anything you'd consider a gift for example. Gift? – Does he play the violin wildly, … or has he sat down at the piano playing like Mozart although no one has properly taught him?"

"No. We don't have instruments at home, apart from his little xylophone. – Oh yes, and the drum … and the recorder."

"How very, very sad, sad. Sad! – You should get him a piano. Lovely instrument! Great outlet for myself, I assure you. – Anything else, else? Anything noteworthy?"

"Well, … he can already write without too many spelling mistakes in both German and English. That's the way we've been communicating over the past year."

"I see. I see. – Interesting. And it would be you and your husband who taught him how to do this, I presume."

"Well, Herr Doctor, to a degree. But he reads a lot when he's by himself. We have to keep him from the big books in our living room."

"Maybe you shouldn't! Actually, you will stop doing that … as of now, now … but that really has to be left up to you, I'm afraid, afraid. Fascinating, fascinating. So, no one's taught him how to read or write, write?"

"Well, *yes*! – As I said, … but not as well … well … as would warrant his …"

"Actual ability. Mute, eh! Eh!" The specialist picked up a pen and notepad from his desk and handed it to Fergal in a threateningly demanding claw. "Write! Write! Now!"

Without hesitating Fergal went round the desk, sat down and wrote for a little. Then he handed the notepad back to Chief Nestling Eyebrow Eagle with smudged glasses. Nestling Eagle took his glasses off, nodded twice, put them back on again, and read silently.

"I see, Ferkel! – Now, can you write that down in German for me!? Now!"

Fergal took the notepad, wrote again, and presently handed it back to the bird of prey. Dangerous bird of prey!

"Oh, Herr Doctor! – Johann is so different with you!"

"Of course, he is! – I doubt, his father, … your husband … husband … is around much to teach him … some lessons. Lessons! All this antiauthoritarian nonsense is going to ruin our society with little terrors like your little, mute Bulhof-Murphy here. Mute, eh! A mute Murphy! I used to think the Irish babble a lot!? Don't know the meaning of a good full stop, stop! Commas, hyphens, colons, semi-colons, that's their lot, lot."

"I beg your pardon! – What are you talking about?"

"You're letting him get away with too much. Too much! You will have to make absolutely clear to him where the sentence stops! Stops! Full stop, stop! Spare the rod, ruin the child!"

"He's not getting away with anything. He's lovely, and very, very sick. He needs all the attention he can get."

"Yes, yes. I see, see. Attention is what all of this muteness is about. An enterprisingly mute mutineer Murphy mongrel, eh, eh! Aren't we expressive!"

With the speed you would expect from the predators of the sky, the specialist turned round sending his glare straight down at Fergal, still sitting comfortably behind the desk. The eagle-man's eyes were dangerous!

Fergal flinched once. And again!

It was as if the man had pecked him with his beak, probing his skin, to tear out his guts. And again he flinched. He couldn't help himself. – And still these eyes were boring into him as if hacking into something.

What was it?!

It wasn't his guts.

Fergal's head hurt.

Nestling Eagle-Eye had it in for his skull, to pick out his brains!

Fergal flinched and flinched and flinched.

He couldn't stop it.

"Your son, … your little lovely son, son … has just added a new symptom to the Bulhof-Murphy Syndrome. Fascinating, fascinating! Has he ever flinched like that before, Frau Bulhof?" Eagle-man was blocking Mutti's view. He stood aside and outstretched his left arm in a threatening, open-wing movement to present to Mutti the tiny, flinching, baby-rabbit Fluffy, that helpless son of a symptom she had.

The flinching was really bad!

"Oh my God, no!" Mutti exclaimed, the little fist of her right hand in front of her mouth as if she wanted to take a bite.

But suddenly, something less atavistic, less predatory appeared to be happening in Professor Doctor Eichenraub's own head-gut of a brain. He hesitated. His demonstrative left arm, still pointing at Fergal, pulled back, slowly. Fergal was still flinching hysterically. He could see though that the Doctor's hand, now disappearing in his white coat pocket, was trembling. The Doctor frowned as in pain at the ceiling and shut his eyes for an instant. When his gaze fell back on Fergal it seemed to the little patient full of love and compassion. The corners of Doctor Eichenraub's mouth turned down, his bottom chin quivered for a moment as though he were about to cry, but then, … then he pursed his lips academically, proficiently enough to escape from this bout of unprofessional emotion into purest pity. Deepest pity for this little soul who had one of the worst and most painful conditions known to man.

"Ferkel, … my little boy. Boy! – Please, come here for a moment, and let me have a look at you!" Professor Doctor Eichenraub's voice was completely changed. It was soft and forgiving. Any eagle-like attitude vanished.

Mutti sat back in her armchair, relaxing into vindication.

"Please, Frau Bulhof, be absolutely silent. – And you, Ferkel, … stand here in front of me, and shut your eyes. Relax. Relax, completely! Breathe in and out, calmly. You're a lovely young man, and I forgive you for what you have written. Good? Good!"

Fergal did as was asked of him.

This was centre-of-attention the serious way he had been enjoying for almost a year. He shut his flinching eyes. After a while the nervous reaction subsided until he could no longer feel the urge to let his eyelids twitch.

Everything became very quiet.

For the first time Fergal noticed that there must be a grandfather clock in the psychiatrist's consultation room.

Tic-toc-tic-toc.

Oma and Opa had one in Hamburg.

Oma and Opa were very worried about him. Very worried!

Great!

Lots of gifts!

It was just two more days to go until Christmas Eve on Thursday, and then he'd get a lot of 'the *right* presents that he so desperately needed. Dad had already collected Oma and Opa. It had taken them almost a week from Hamburg to Geesterheim.

Tic-toc-tic-toc.

Mutti and the Doctor were absolutely quiet. Fergal peaked a little and could see the Doctor's big shoes.

Tic-toc-tic-toc.

Fergal had written a very long wish list for Saint Nikolaus to collect on the 6th of December, but the main thing was that he would get either the red Bugatti with pedals or the green Land Rover. Or both!

The Bugatti was a racer and came with a battery so you didn't have to pedal all the time. But the Land Rover could go through water and drive through the snow and the desert.

Tic-toc-tic-toc.

The only thing was that having only one car was just not right! You needed two or more, like Dad. Dad might get him both the red Bugatti and the green Land Rover, and then he'd write a nice thank-you poem, and Weihnachtsmann wouldn't hit him, even if Johanna-Frances would be nasty and tell Weihnachtsmann horrible lies about …

… his comfortable thoughts of anticipation and Christmas and presents were shattered in a split second …

… noise …

… noise everywhere …

… ahhhhhhhhhhhhhhhhhhhhhhhhhhhhhhhhhhhhhhhhhhhhhhhh …

… the nightmare scream was in Fergal's ear! He shot away from it to the right, as far away as possible. It didn't go away!

Where was it coming from!?

His eyes were wide open! He fell over the armchair. He heard Mutti exclaim, but the scream in his ear went on and on! Long and high-pitched, and hot.

Hot and wet.

Doctor Eichenraub was right next to his left ear!

Bits of saliva still being catapulted into Fergal's eardrum.

Fergal felt sick.

Then the specialist ran out of breath.

The specialist remained right over Fergal, panting from the long, screamed exhalation at his poor, sad patient, looking at his face as if searching for an answer.

Fergal saw a gigantic index finger pointing at his eye, "There! There! There it is! I have found it! Heureka! They're both contracting at random!" The old specialist jumped up ebulliently, dragged Fergal to his feet, lifted him up high in the air to drop him in the armchair like discarded underwear after an accidental, public, diarrhoeic attack.

Mutti remained absolutely quiet.

From what Fergal could see, Mutti, too, was in a state of shock after the Doctor's scream.

Prof. Dr. Eichenraub clapped his hands, then rubbed them together, "Well, now. Let's see. Where shall I start, start?" He rubbed his hands as if washing them, "Arthur Janov, Primal Therapy. Referred to as Primal Scream. Do it every morning. Helps. And it also brings out the symptoms of Spontaneous Acromegaly when practised on a patient.

"I gather you could then refer to it as the primal shock diagnostic test. Got to write that down later. Primal Shock Diagnostic Test. Well Ferkel, …" he nodded proudly and approvingly over at Mutti to return his sad gaze of earlier to the bundle of infantile shock cowering in the armchair in front of him, "… you … you … child, child … you are suffering from an incredibly rare disease!

"Rarer than spontaneous combustion! And you should count yourself lucky! Your Mutti could have taken Contergan and then you would have been a Contergan-Kind, eh. Writing would have been a bit difficult then, eh, eh. Ahhahhahhahaaa, aha, ha!? – In England that's called Thalidomide, isn't it?" He looked at Mutti.

Mutti nodded with a great deal of dislike and disgust directed at Eichenraub.

"What you are suffering from is, … as I said, said, Spontaneous Acromegaly! Acromegaly! In our profession it is most commonly referred to as Situation Dependent Mutation. Now, if you were to only have acromegaly, life would be a little easier for you. A right old fest altogether, together!

"You see with acromegaly a thing in your head called the pituitary gland produces a little too much of something called the growth hormone. Well, … well, it makes you grow and … you are … are at that age, age.

"Acromegaly only affects the hands, feet and face of the patient though. With Spontaneous Acromegaly on the other hand, that is SDM or more specifically $SitMut_{01}$ to $SitMut_{10}$ the story is entirely different!

"Well, … it's more spontaneous, spontaneous." Doctor Eichenraub giggled a little at this. "$SitMut_{01}$ to $SitMut_{10}$ describes the stages of spontaneous physical mutation that you might undergo during an attack for briefer to more prolonged periods of time. $SitMut_{01}$ is the least visible and $SitMut_{10}$, which is also the last stage, is, … well, very visible. Visible! – Now, for the patient there is …"

"Doctor Eichenraub!" Mutti's eyes were shut and her right hand was covering her mouth. "Should we be discussing this in front of my child?"

"Yes, oh yes, Frau Bulhof, Bulhof! – It'll do Ferkel good, good! He'll see that there is much worse in this world than all those harmless symptoms of his mentioned in his file."

"I see. – So, … what can I do about this SitMut of his?" Mutti was close to tears.

"Nothing, … actually, actually. Absolutely nothing, nothing!" Doctor Eichenraub shrugged, and scratched his head for a little. "No, there is nothing, nothing I can think of." He resumed scratching his head for a little longer, "No, nothing, nothing. But, …" he resumed more excitedly than before, "At the moment he is suffering only from $SitMut_{01}$ in the early stage. Very harmless. Hardly visible. With the added hope that he may de facto never develop it fully, … as much … as he may never suffer an attack of any severity at any time. If … however … you suddenly perceive that individual … or all body parts of his … are growing … out of all proportion, but only for a time, ten minutes, an hour maybe, spontaneously, abruptly, not to say creatively, gloriously distorted, … you might want to come back for me to study him. – You see, … it's fantastic, … fantastic … with SitMut the entire body is affected!"

"What does it do? What brings about an attack?"

"Well, now, … complex … to quantify, quantify, complex, … very, as … I should have to delve into a modus of knowledge and jargon … the jargon of my profession, which … not only does not … constitute part of your not-so hermetic background, although I'm sure you would have made an excellent psychiatrist, indeed … you might have profited from it in terms of bringing up your child, but … I have already told you that his creative powers might, might … might benefit from a piano, … a piano … but also is based on only one very sketchy … sketchy, sketchy medical record dating back to the late seventeen hundreds, which …

which … I took a great interest in during my earlier years as part of my research for my first doctorate and, … and, … not wanting to appear proud, … proud … proud … I was the first one … the first one … to have discovered this in the archives at Marburg. – Sadly, sadly, sadly, … I lost the original, original! Ha! I lost the original!"

"Sorry, Doctor Eichenraub, … I really do not want to be unduly worried … nor do I want to seem disrespectful. So, … there has only been this one case in the past. One case! And that's quite long ago? Ago!?"

"Yes."

"I see."

"But, … but, … Frau Bulhof, that … that really … really doesn't change the fact, that erratic contraction of the pupils was evident in the patient immediately after the shock. The application of the scream as used in Primal Therapy is my own, own idea. Idea. Idea. I shall call it Primal Shock Diagnostic SitMut Test. Have to write it down, down."

"Great. That's really quite something. I'm glad for you." Mutti was getting up. Ready to go.

Fergal was no longer in quite as much of a state of shock. He was just trying to make sense of all Eichenraub had just said. – This had great potential!

"Frau Bulhof, … you might be witnessing, witnessing medical history in the making here!"

"Please! – I think we're ready to go now. Come on, Johann! And we won't mention the fact that you scared both my son … and me … to death!"

"Frau Bulhof. I assure you, you are not dead, dead, and it was necessary to ascertain his SitMut."

"Naturally."

"Will you please promise me, me to look after your child? He is quite special!"

"I know that! Do not patronise me!"

"Please, Frau Bulhof, promise me that if you discover your son is suddenly growing an enormous head, … even … with … a different face, … or huge hands extending from … unnaturally long arms, … those slender arms, arms of boys … boyhoys … or if he doesn't grow, … or he might even shrink … in certain situations, please … do call me! And I'll be there, there. Here. Right there! There!"

"What do you mean *certain situations*?"

"It is hard to quantify, qualify."

"Try me!"

"It appears, … that SitMut attacks … attacks are primarily brought on by silly, silly impulsive behaviour, … threat and insult, insult. Most people react psychosomatically to such psychological ambience conditions, as in … boss shouts every day but not at secretary, but secretary is stressed and feels guilty or whatever, what do I care, whatever, secretary may feel, who cares … silly secretary develops a headache or vomiting. That sort of succinct mind thing. It's internalised, you see?! See.

"With the SitMut sufferer however, well, … the SitMut takes it rather more … physically, shall we say, physically, physically, … personally. He … or she, if then girls have the imagination, so let's stick with he … he will externalise … to the point where … really fantastically grotesque deformations occur at random, … haphazardly, … out of the blue, and so creatively spontaneous, it is quite breathtaking, breathtaking."

"I see. – And there has only been that … one … one recorded case … two-hundred or more years ago, and you, … you wrote about it!?"

"Yes, Bulhof … Frau Bulhof."

"And prognosis is down to contraction of the pupils after external shock, as in scream or insult or threat?"

"Yes, yes."

"Well, … let's hope my son … son … develops something psychosomatic like … his Mutti, … like gastritis. – And what about his other symptoms?"

"Oh … those, … those are just made … made up … for attention, attention. – Very … very creative and … stubborn, stubborn child, … yours, eh, … mute, eh!? Mute, mute! For a year! What a feat! I suppose he didn't really want to come to Germany?"

"He was five! He wasn't given a choice! It was a business decision!" Mutti stretched out her hand towards Fergal. This was international Mutti-language for *We're going! Now!* Mutti looked differently at Fergal. In fact, Fergal thought, Mutti looked quite angry altogether. But she also looked quite thoughtful. Before they were at the door she turned to Eichenraub one last time, "Tell me, Eichenraub, … what did my son write on the notepad?"

Eichenraub hesitated, but not for long, "Nothing much. Nothing … nothing you don't know anyway now."

"I'll decide that for myself. Tell me!"

Professor Doctor Doctor Eichenraub clicked his heels the old way and went over to his gargantuan desk to fetch it. Mutti took it from him and handed it to Fergal, "Read it." There was a tone in her voice Fergal had never perceived before. It was unequivocal.

"READ IT NOW! Or you can forget about birthday's and Christmases for the next twelve years to come, my dear!"

Fergal sighed, … and for the first time in almost a year he was about to open his mouth to speak for the sake of red Bugatti and green Land Rover pedal cars.

He had been singing, of course, during the silent year of his big sulk, but only on his own. He now knew that they weren't going to go back to England. If Johanna-Frances found out, she was going to make mincemeat of him, … and Dad? Well, Dad was going to be very happy! Dad had been praying a lot to Jesus, Mary and Joseph and God Himself to heal Fergal again, *please, I'll do anything.* He'd even written to the Pope to get the whole of the Vatican to pray for his little mute son.

And suddenly, as if out of nowhere, Fergal began looking forward to a life external. He was looking forward to primary school, and friends, and speaking German, and laughing. He stopped looking backward into the good past they had had in England. Looking forward was almost like a new feeling. A new feeling that deserved a new word, it was so special to him.

Mutti and Dad had spoken in their respective languages to both their children. Back in England already had Fergal been able to speak German. Johanna-Frances and he had even made up a new language for the place they were going to. West-Germany. Chamoonian as spoken by the Wetchamoonsi of Wetchamoonis ruled by the Daz Witch Awonda.

In the beginning this had only been copying Mutti's strangely hissing German accent, when she spoke English. In Mutti's accent *German* sounded a bit like *Chamoon,* so the new language became Chamoonian. And the West Germans were the Wetchamoonsi, and they lived in Wetchamoonis. The Daz Witch Awonda, who ruled over Wetchamoonis, was Dad's way of saying the German word *Das Wirtschaftswunder.* The great economic wonder of Germany getting back on her feet after the war.

All of this had evolved into a simple but completely new sound language all of its own mostly ending in the English *fat* or *fat-fart* and *fett* or *fett-furz* in actual German because the Wetchamoonsi of Wetchamoonis were quite fat and had to fart a lot as a consequence.

"Don't tell me you're lost for words now, Johann!?" Mutti laughed, but not a real laugh. It was anger. Uncomfortably close to fury!

"Interesting, Frau Bulhof! – You refer to your son as Johann, … and in his little note he writes of himself in the third person, … as Ferkel! And I automatically called him Ferkel, too. His file is that of J. Ferkel Bulhof-Murphy. Very interesting!"

"What you find interesting … I find irrelevant, Eichenraub. – My husband was the one who registered him with the first specialist, so the file went from there. He is Fergal not *Ferkel.* And Johann wants to read us his little note now, … doesn't he! READ! ALL OF IT!"

Fergal coughed. When he read out his note he felt an intense happiness in the pit of his stomach, *"Deer docter, please dont tell Mutti, Ferkel is fine or she will kill me and then yu are a morderer and that is a bad man like Peter File and Peter Ast, the Mitschnackers. Merry Christmas!*

"Liber Docter! Bite sak Mutti nich das Ferkel gesunt is or shie brink mich umm un dan bis du en Mürder und dass is schlecht wie der Peta File und Peta Ast die Mitschnacker. Fro Weihnacht!"

Mutti was crying. Mid-read she had started stroking Fergal's head. Now she bent down, hugging him so hard it hurt. She was sobbing.

Eichenraub seemed a little embarrassed, "Yes. Yes, yes. Good boy, boy. German accent's good for a foreigner but you need to brush up on your spelling, grammar and punctuation. Anyway, … there are other patients I …" but Mutti was out in the corridor already.

The Pact

"Never ever, … never, never, never … never ever tell anyone about this! Do you hear me, Johann!?"

"Yes, Mutti! I promise. I won't sulk again."

"You have such a wonderful, wonderful voice!" Mutti was still crying at the bottom of the stairs by the huge doors that led out onto the street into the heavily falling snow. Fergal had never quite seen her like this. Shouldn't she have laughed and danced and bought him some toys straight away? He'd really needed the Corgi Toys NY fire engine very much. She was evidently happy though! Grownups cried when they were happy!

"No, … listen. – I want you … and I … to make a pact, OK!? – Let's agree, like a contract, … einen Vertrag. Dann können wir uns wieder vertragen.[5] OK!?"

"OK." And so Fergal made the first pact in his life. The first pact with another person than himself.

"Listen carefully. When your Dad and I came back to Germany, it was because I had been pushing him for some time. I'm being very honest here, Johann! I was sulking with your Dad for some time the way grownups do, so we'd come back to Germany. Dad said that if this move were bad for you or Johanna, we'd go back. Had you sulked any longer we would have gone back to London."

Fergal frowned. He wouldn't have minded that at all! He should have persevered!

"Now, … what you'll do for me is this, … and this is our pact! You will *not* speak until Christmas Day, and then you'll have a *miraculous* recovery, OK, … and you'll sing … or something!"

"Why?"

"Oh, … because! Because Dad likes miracles and the Pope and … God!? And if I say Eichenraub brought out your little secret," Mutti wagged her endemically raised German index finger at him, "Dad will say, that's not enough of a sign and *we're going back home*, OK!? – I think, Dad does actually suspect you're

---

[5] *Ger.*, "… a contract. So, we'll make up again. OK!?"

sulking. So just make him happy at the right moment! So far, he's blamed me, the move, and Germany for everything that ever went wrong in the business and in his life. And, Johann, … I do want to stay here! It's not Hamburg, … but it's still home! And at least, I'll make some friends here. And … his business is just picking up very nicely, so …"

"I live in London, Mutti."

Mutti started crying again.

Fergal felt bad for her, and he was looking forward to friends and school, "Oxford is not bad either …"

Mutti cried more.

"OK! I promise. – It's a pact!"

Dad's light blue Volvo estate drove up in the snow. Dead on time! – Fergal and Mutti got in, and Fergal decided to stick with the pact. It was a promise after all! But he was going to do things *his* way.

Dad said, this was one of the first Volvos in Germany. Volvos were good in the snow and even though they were Swedish, he was selling them to Americans like hotcakes. Dad had recovered from bringing Oma and Opa from Hamburg. He was relaxing for the Christmas ahead.

The Daz-Witch Awonda Of The Wetchamoonsi Of Wetchamoonis

The blizzard had stopped. The fear had gone! Fergal was no longer on the run.

This is how Fergal's life began for real in Wetchamoonis. This was the day he was going to surprise the world!

He had at last escaped the clutches of the Wetchamoonsi. From the wet heat of their jungle to the dry cold of the never-ending plateau of ice ahead of him. He was alive and safe and driving away from them. Trying to find his way back home. Gleaming snow and brilliant sky were one, wherever he cast his eyes. The rattling of the green Land Rover was absorbed by the total but welcome stillness of this unforgiving landscape. A theatre of infinity and perfection where nothing would go wrong anymore. He was going home at last!

They had to be a long way behind, frozen to death possibly, considering their lack of equipment. They had caught him once. They would never catch him again! After all, the Wetchamoonsi were the most dangerous cannibals as yet unknown to man, and *he* had discovered them!

The Wetchamoonsi were fat, round, pink, blind giants with no legs but two flat feet and long arms reaching their smelly stamping ground in tiny hands. Their heads and necks of negligible import, they had really concentrated their evolution on their huge glistening lips and tongue, with which they found their way around and recognised friends. They didn't eat what they recognised, which made them demivegetarian nomad-cannibals close to extinction as by now they were well-travelled and had no teeth any longer. They sucked and licked their food until it was gone. They were also at least three times taller than Fergal. The latter fact hadn't made his escape easy exactly, as blind giants could sense farther and bounce and roll much faster still. Yes, the Wetchamoonsi didn't walk or run, they bounced and rolled, as their fatness had turned them into near perfect ball-beings with thick lips and flat feet. One had to see it to believe it! But then that might just be the last thing one ever saw. Anyway, for Fergal it thankfully hadn't been. He had escaped to tell their tale. As they say, he was the one that got away!

He hit the brakes abruptly, and too late. At fifty miles an hour his Land Rover ploughed straight and deeply into the drift, before it was forced to a sudden halt by the compacted snow. The impact crushed him against the steering wheel. He heard his ribs crack, saw blood splattering against the windscreen, and then the whole world of snow collapsed into his open car on top of him. – Was this it? His valiant escape foiled by a silly pack of snow hundreds of miles from home! Should he have kept the soft top? After all, he had given it to the Wetchamoonsi as a present on first contact. Never regret giving presents! Their fat lips on top of their bodies had looked so very friendly, their fleshy tongues seemed to lick his hair ever so gratefully. Then, looking and licking even friendlier still, they had rolled him up in his own soft top to cure him slowly.

His escape had only been made possible because the Chief's fat daughter Fatosofata-Fatfat had been overcome by a strange and intense hunger in the dead of night. Actually, she was so fat she was sitting inside herself ten times over. Her only redeeming feature had been her constant, friendly humming. In fact, this had been the only nice thing about the Wetchamoonsi on the whole, in retrospect. So, into the second night of his new status as sausage roll and he had faintly heard her friendly humming getting closer. Slowly had she been rolling towards him, her fat body squelching a concert of merry farts. Slowly had she unrolled Fergal. Slowly had she opened her mouth wide over his right foot, that dark and scary night. That had been the beginning of his long escape from the Wetchamoonsi, the friendly humming demivegetarian cannibals of Wetchamoonis.

His breathing was now laboured and intensely painful. The mass of snow on top of him didn't improve the situation. This was not the end. He was not going to let it be the end, pain or no! Deep down he knew that no one was going to believe his story. But he was not going to die for this story. He was going to live for all the adventures still to come!

He dug himself out, ignoring the pain as best as possible. Just for a little would he lie down in the snow to rest and recover.

He collapsed.

A small, muffled explosion came from the car throwing up a tiny eruption of snow. A lot of steam followed. The radiator! He wouldn't be able to use the car anymore. He had to find some kind of human habitation. He looked at his blood in the snow. It was very dark. Somehow, his throat had been cut a little. He had no doubt in his mind, … he'd survive this!

So far, he had ignored the icy cold as a mere afterthought. The elation of his successful escape had erased all feelings of discomfort. Now, it descended on him without mercy! Yet, there was in the deep chill gripping his body an undertone of promised comfort, almost warm to the touch of his mind. He would sleep for a little to awake refreshed and certainly without this pain.

His eyes were just about beginning to shut, as fear ripped them open again. There in the distance he saw two gigantic figures approaching fast. They were rolling! In this vast expanse of white infinity their destination was clear. Him! The Wetchamoonsi had after all managed to follow him all this time! He tried to laugh out loud, but the pain in his chest stifled it down to a croak.

They wouldn't get him! He would do away with himself first. He held his breath. Not an easy death at the best of times and his lungs hurt immensely from his broken ribs and the freezing air. An idea surfaced. The last idea of a dying man choosing his own death. He had to beat his own chest hard enough for his ribs to pierce both of his lungs.

Fergal beat his chest as hard as he could.

The two Wetchamoonsi had now rolled up to arrival at their destination. They were swaying over him, frowning quizzical smiles, humming beautifully. They had definitely never licked freezing meat. They were going to suck the sample right now, before the rest of their nomad entourage should roll up!

Just two more minutes and Fergal was going to be dead. Nevertheless, he'd have enough time to take his last observation of them with him to the grave.

The taller one, at least four times Fergal's size, was attired appropriately with a heavy winter coat, licking the inside of his horn-rimmed glasses resting over his lips. He looked most concerned. The smaller one, only three times Fergal's size, smiled from a nice suit, white shirt and tie. The taller one went over to the Land Rover and picked it up in one hand as if it weighed nothing and dropped it by Fergal's feet. The smaller one still smiled. How nice it was to die within the next three or so seconds with a kind smile from your enemy and the feeling, somehow, of having won.

"Ach-vat-fat de fet Bengel-fat moose yets-fut fix-fet-fat ouf shtane-fot peck fett rick-fat zonst airfreert air-fat tsarck-fit vits-vutts-fat-fat, klapps-food, zoe fort yets-fat!" was the last thing Fergal heard. He felt a great sense of astonishment at the fact that the Wetchamoonsi had some form of language. He stopped beating his chest. He could breathe no more. His head rolled to the side concealing the great gash his throat had sustained. The snow around him was red with his blood, with his life.

Goodbye, great world! Thank you for your wonders! Thank you, so much! I … I … ahhh … ahh … ah … Then he died.

"Come on now, Fergal! Let's go home celebrate in the warm." That was Dad with a lot of thick, shiny, silver-black hair and a neat parting on the left. Today was Christmas Day. The other man was of course Opa, wearing grey and dark grey all over with his six plus maybe five-hundred strands of grey hair left. Opa grew them very long and combed them back with Schwarzkopf Seborin hair tincture. He called it Blackhead Seborin, and sometimes he put some in Fergal's hair. Dad said blackheads were comedones, which stuffed up people's pores when they got older. It had nothing to do with commies. Opa always frowned at the word *commies* in spite of Oma.

And this was how Fergal's life began again! This was the moment when Fergal made his life begin in Wetchamoonis West-Germany. Very soon he was going to regain his speech again for his Dad, and for Oma and Opa too of course. For the whole world. Surprise! Miracle! Sister J was still a bit of a problem.

"Come on, get up now, Fergal! Time to open more prezzies the English way, eh!" Dad again. Fergal had had his presents the German way yesterday, and today was English Xmas.

So, … Fergal's surprise for them would in a way be twofold. In under ten minutes, once he had opened his second bout of presents back home, he would say "Hello! I am back! And thank you very much for all my lovely presents!" And then he would also say it in German! And they would all fall over and pass out with wonder. And then he would read to them too. He could read quite well already. Just hadn't done it out aloud.

"Get up now, … Fergal!?" Dad again. He sounded very worried. But, eyes firmly shut, Fergal would play dead for a little longer to get him really scared. He was hardly breathing. This was what death felt like!

"Oh, my God, … Karl! I think Fergal's *dead*!!!"

"Ach, was, der Bengel ist not dett! I know dess venn I zee itt. Lots. Der Bengel shtill lives. Here, I shoe yo." Opa prodded Fergal gently with his foot. Nothing! Fergal was dead. Opa bent down and squeezed his grandson's waist on both sides. Fergal was extremely ticklish there but kept perfectly still.

He was dead! Come on!

Opa's hat came off, landed on Fergal's face and rolled off into the snow. Fergal stayed absolutely still. Not a shiver, not a peep. He was dead!

"Ach, der Hut! – Na ja, gut! Der Junge mag schon tot sein. Vatt yu zay? Yes. He ist dett! Zere iss shtill shteam come from his shnouter, ja? Zett happens zomtime. I've zeen it."

Fergal sensed Dad bending down. He quickly gave him the last rites, *in nomine patris et Ferguli filii.*

"Goodbye, my son. – Come on, Karl! – Shame about Fergal here though! But that's the way it goes. Anyway, let's look on the bright side there. Oh, look! How bright! It's *us* who get to open his presents, now." Dad threw some snow over Fergal.

Fergal just couldn't believe this!

"He'll be fine here, don't worry now. We'll pick him up in the spring when the snow has melted, and then we can put him up in the living room as a mute memento."

Fergal was getting a little angry now! He was not ever going to talk to them ever again! What was a memento?

"Or how about you put him up in your garden, Karl!? – He'll make a fine old scarecrow, once the wind has dried him up a bit."

There was a pause.

Opa changed to *total* German and sounded very serious and stern. "Now, look here, Seán! I can't believe you're that cruel! We can't just leave him here. He's your son! We need to call an ambulance. He might not be dead after all. What a tragic thing to happen to the little thing."

There was another pause. Fergal could hear shuffling. Dad was exhaling a lot and loudly. He seemed to be moving. Then, Opa again, "Ah, I see! You're right! Oh, look! The snowplough is coming. They'll take him away. It'll save us some money on the funeral. Let's go and open the presents then. His presents!"

Fergal heard their muffled steps crunching in the snow, disappearing. So, this was what life was all about!? He held back his tears. Now he was all-alone in the world. He had no one. He was going to die for real now! No one would care anyway. They could have his presents! For them he was dead already. Goodbye, cruel world! The things you shall have missed without me in it. He felt very sad for all who wouldn't have the benefit of him in the world. No surprise. No regained speech.

Fergal could hear the sound of a big engine. Slowly, he opened his eyes. Dad and Opa hadn't been playing, they were *really* gone, and so was his lovely, new, green Land Rover! He had no words to describe the depth of feeling he had for them. But when he would find that word, it wouldn't be a nice one! They were possibly already *playing* with his Land Rover, and then they were going to open all his presents the English way as it was the 25th, and Mutti would laugh! Her laughter would be clear and happy, and she would almost sing *Merry Christmas,* because on the 25th you were really, really festive.

Fergal's eyes were wide open now. The noise of the engine was very close. The huge, orange Mercedes snowplough was approaching fast. Really fast! The big shovel at its front was throwing the snow high up in the air to the side on the pavement. Fergal was in the middle of the road. He would die, if he didn't move. He could only die once, so this additional death would come as even less of a surprise to them … those … whatever … he would find the right word! It would have to be a word that came from the feeling you had when you really wanted to kick somebody in the shin.

Fergal jumped up and ran home like mad!

Home was just around the corner.

Actually, he had been lying in the snowdrift just next to his wall. The snowplough man slowed down and waved as he overtook Fergal who had just about made it in time. It was Martin! Martin stopped, rolled down the window and shouted "Heppy late Birshday, Ferkel! End heppy Chreeshtmess now. Heff to get on. Nozzer shtorm coming. Many shnow vill be fan for you!"

Fergal waved and smiled back. Good thing was, most people here in the American zone spoke some form or other of English. They might not understand a proper English response, but that was beside the point. Martin, like all the other villagers of Geesterheim, thought Fergal was a mute and couldn't understand German yet. He'd show them soon enough!

Fergal had come to know Martin all by himself!

One day he was wandering around the village and just met Martin. Mutti was very worried because she had lost sight of Fergal whilst chatting to Herrn Dorfgeist, the owner of the village store, and there were of course the strange men of the Mitschnacker family especially Peter File and Peter Ast. Mutti always kept repeating that *they* were around. It was boring! Whenever Fergal went out with Mutti but especially when he'd play outside on his own or with friends did she repeat the story of the Mitschnacker family, sometimes also called the clan with the shiny skin.

She told the Mitschnacker differently every time. Sometimes they were rich at other times poor. Sometimes they looked like monsters, and then again they might look beautiful. It scared Fergal a great deal, as in essence *anyone* could be part of the Mitschnacker family! It didn't stop him from investigating the outside world though.

Today the story had been of Peter File and Peter Ast in a car and both looked a bit like the same woman with shiny skin and both wore Macs. One beige, the other one brown. And then they opened their car doors, smiled at Fergal and offered him lots of sweeties. And that's when he really had to run because if they caught him, they'd kill him and dump him in a ditch, wrapped in their Macs like a Wetchamoonis sausage roll favoured by their tribal chiefs. And in the ditch Fergal would rot, and the crows would come and pick his eyes from his sockets.

Mutti loved her mute, little, limping son so much, but Fergal remained a bit dubious about the whole world being covered in Mitschnackers. When he grew up Dad would tell him exactly what Peter File and Peter Ast did, before they rolled you up in a Mac. It was far worse than he could possibly, possibly imagine, Dad said!

Herr Dorfgeist, the Geesterheimer shopkeeper, did have a bit of a smile, and he had a car and a Mac too. His skin was alright though! And if indeed he'd looked like a woman she would have won the who-looks-worse-than-dung beauty pageant.

To make certain, Fergal had once prepared a written question for him, asking if he was called Mitschnacker or Peter File or Peter Ast. Dorfgeist had laughed and said "No", handing back to Fergal his little notepad. Mutti grabbed it, read it, and went very red.

Herr Dorfgeist sold everything, but mainly food and the best sweets in the world, apart from Fergal's sweetshop in Oxford, because back in England there were more sweets! He was beginning to forget about Oxford. Mutti said, that was why English children had such bad teeth.

Herr Dorfgeist *always* had a big pile of Negerküsse under a glass dome on his counter! The other glass dome covered the cheeses on the other side of the counter, where the serious food was. He sold milk on tap and his face went crimson when he pumped too much.

Fergal loved nigger-kisses! And Herr Dorfgeist always handed him one when Mutti and he went shopping there.

Nigger-kisses were half-round marshmallows with a wafer at the bottom and totally covered in chocolate! It was a very Chamoonian sweet, Mutti claimed. A bit like snowballs in England, just without the coconut, Dad said. Snowballs were also Fergal's favourite. Snowballs were first though!

When Dad's and Mutti's American friends were visiting, Dad always told them that Fergal loved nigger-kisses. Everybody would chuckle. It was always the same joke. Still. Then he told them that the Germans had this marshmallow-thing called *Negerkuss*. Then they'd all laugh like mad, and some said in

Germany language still said what it meant. Even the two American negroes laughed quietly. They were also with the USAF, and they didn't laugh that loudly, because they weren't real officers yet.

Altogether the Bulhof-Murphy's Negro friends were more like gentlemen. So were the Mexicans. Mutti said, they had to be gentler so as not to get shouted down or killed by the Americans. Then Dad would apologise a little, in general, and say that the word *nigger* wasn't good, but it was not as bad as *Kaffir* in South Africa. South Africans were rude. But a nigger's kisses were sweet, especially if they happened to be female, and after all *niger* was Latin for *black*.

Mutti never laughed at this use of education. One of the Negroes once said, "Hey, Seán! But we ain't black, are we? And we don't call you albo or candido!" And Dad said in his best Texan, "Hey, I can hardly hear ya there, boy! It's so dark! But you are *so* right, 'cause I ain't white. I'm Irish pink!" That's when everyone would laugh really loudly for a while, and the Negroes would smile loud in another direction, or at Hansi.

Dad's accent would always change slightly when the Americans were around. He didn't mind saying he was Irish with *them*. Dad loved Texas. Apparently, there was a lot of family there. Afterwards Mutti always told Fergal never to say *nigger*, … ever! Because the Americans especially from the south still had to learn what the Germans had already learnt the hard way about the Jews, and Americans were loud to stress they were right and shouted you down, if need be, even if they were completely wrong, or especially when they were wrong. Especially the ones from the south!

Fergal would have to find out more about the Jews, Negroes, Americans from the south, and Mutti from Hamburg in the north of West-Germany, called the British Zone.

And then Fergal was getting really very bored with Mutti chatting with Herrn Dorfgeist, because they talked about nothing and still laughed a lot. Fergal had already had his Negerkuss, so he went for a walk on his own. And that's when he met Martin cleaning his big red Mercedes fire engine with his friends.

Everything was Mercedes in Wetchamoonis, Fergal was certain, apart from Dad who only drove American and English cars which he sold, and sometimes Swedish and Italian cars too. Dad drove a BMW though, and he was quite proud of it, because he owned it and would never sell it! Fergal liked the Chrysler station wagon and the E-Type more.

Martin could drive almost anything! Apart from his fire engine and snowplough, Martin could also drive that strange steamroller with the massive circular saw, and tanks, and lots of other things with tracks. The steamroller was older than Opa and as big as a house, and it had lots of belts on it.

But mostly it was Martin's father, August – Fergal had to call him Herr Immelmann – who drove the steamroller round the village every fortnight to cut wood for the villagers. Herr Immelmann was not just a woodcutter! He was also Geesterheim's scrap metal merchant. He had a yard in the village, but also wanted to own the dump outside behind the woods with the swamp in it. But the dump was already owned by very strange and massively scarred Herrn Steinhöfer with his two Dobermans both called Hölle.

Hölle means Hell!

Steinhöfer had vowed to forget himself if ever he saw Immelmann close to his dump! Forgetting yourself means shooting somebody. Wood and metal were Immelmann's only hobbies really, as he loved cutting things to bits. He was very rich but very tiny, and he had a huge brass bell on his steamroller, which he banged with a hammer. "Like a maniac," Mutti would say, whenever Immelmann drove round the village at half a mile per hour.

Martin claimed his father was close to one hundred and ten years old and had almost seen five wars. That's why he shrivelled up and went very tiny.

"He's also quite mad," Martin would whisper and tap his temple with his index finger, because everything his father owned was cut up into little pieces, so it could be carried off more easily when another war came.

Martin's grandfather was long dead and had seen Napoleon with his own eyes, when Germany was French. Martin also claimed his father was eighty, when he made Martin, and that his mother was very young and died somehow … immediately.

Martin said Mutti was very beautiful and Aryan, and he would like to marry someone like her, but he couldn't, because he thought he was outstandingly ugly, and his father Immelmann would beat him again and again, if ever he suggested marriage ever again, because you couldn't cut people into small bits to carry them off.

Martin had asked Fergal not to say anything to Mutti, and then he was very embarrassed and apologised because Fergal was *stumm* in German, *mute* in English, but Immelmann … Immelmann was mad! Immelmann said people got shot and rotted, and you had to leave them behind and it wasn't worth the amount of tears, because it made you too thirsty. And if you cut them up beforehand, it was a sin, because it was murder even though you'd just wanted to help them flee from the Russians who'd rape your wife in front of you and then cut her womb out for you to eat, and then, somehow, you'd get away and you couldn't remember how.

Martin said many cups were missing in his father's cupboard, and his Papa's roof had *really* been damaged when he had to flee West without his wife.

Mutti and Martin were grown up and independent. Mutti and Martin were almost the same age.

Fergal had drawn a heart for Mutti with Martin's and her name inside. Martha and Martin sounded just lovely! – Then, very slowly, he had written *butiful Mutti sayd Martin.* Mutti had corrected the spelling for her little, innocent, mute baby.

Fergal loved the word *beautiful* because it was beautiful. But this had been after Mutti had been angry with Martin first. When Fergal had shown her the heart and the word, Mutti had laughed and said, it was a very nice thing of Martin to say so, and Martin was definitely nice looking too in … his very own, special way, … deep down, … yet for another girl … somewhere else … with totally different tastes. Mutti was married to Dad, and apparently that meant a lot! And anyone married looking around, which meant at other people, was breaking a commandment, and that was a mortal sin.

But before Mutti met Martin, Fergal met him all on his own! – Whilst Mutti was chatting with Herrn Dorfgeist, Fergal walked all the way to the other side of the village through the very old, medieval part and met Martin at the fire station. It was possible to disappear really quickly in the old part with all its narrow lanes. It smelt of cows and pigs. It was impossible to get a car in there. There were only animal voices in there!

Mutti hadn't watched Fergal for a couple of minutes and he was gone. Dorfgeist talk!

The first bit he ran really fast. He was running away from Peter File and Peter Ast, and a whole lot of very dark members of the Mitschnacker family, who were chasing him to kill him in a ditch with their Macs.

Fergal did faintly hear her calling for him, but it was like Peter File's voice and very scary, so he ran more. It was a very hot day, almost thirty degrees Celsius already. A typical Hessen summer. And this part of Hessen got even hotter and wetter than the rest. Clouds of mozzies drinking your blood in the dark because this part of American Hessen was called the Reeds, close to the Old Rhine. Frying eggs on stones was easy!

There were dried frogs you could eat and snakes would come out at dusk to drink water from the Frog Pond by the jungle wood, inside which the swamp was, and then two kilometres later … Steinhöfer's glorious dump!

The dump was paradise! Hundreds of old cars!

Snakes ate frogs too, but not the dried ones. Snakes also left their skins behind, if you scared them alright, but you couldn't bring them home, because Mutti would flip and would always say not to roam so much.

Mitschnackers hiding everywhere! *Nonsense, Mutti,* Fergal thought.

Mutti called the police, and they found Fergal and Martin at the fire station. Martin had given Fergal three glasses of Coca Cola, and Fergal was still thirsty, because he wasn't allowed Coca Cola.

Coca Cola was definitely the best drink in the world! It made you burp like a real man! Burping was slightly ruder than belching, said Dad. And if you wanted to be polite and not understood,

Fergal should try writing eructate. And maybe one day Fergal might talk again, if he eructated enough and tried to form sounds on the back of the gas being ejected.

Eructate was a difficult word. Eject was easier.

Martin was easy to get along with, and he burped a lot! Fergal was going to be a fireman like Martin! Mutti was very angry with Martin for some reason, … but that was before Fergal wrote Martin's word *butiful* for her.

So, that was Martin up there in the snowplough!

And Martin was off already, ploughing more snow.

Grownups did not understand this! But Martin was really enjoying himself very much.

Martin said, he had always wanted to do this, even when he was Fergal's age. Fireman, snowplough-man, tank driver, steamroller-man! Martin was a little sad, they hadn't taken him on as a train driver. But he loved *Negerküsse*!

Maybe he was going to marry a beautiful *Negermädchen* one day, when his father had stopped cutting things up to go to his last resting place. "Please!" Martin had said.

Now, Fergal looked up at the kitchen window. He was very cold and wet! The light was on, but there was no one in the kitchen. He felt that earlier surge of anger again and a lump in his throat.

They were *all* playing with his lovely, new, green Land Rover now!

Mutti would be handing out the presents in a moment! Laughing, singing, dancing! And then, …

… they would all go and get Johanna-Frances from her room, because she was still asleep and sulking about the leather briefcase she got from Weihnachtsmann last night, "It was supposed to be made of cordovan not some primitive, poxy, old porker's hide! Jesus Christ! Don't you ever get anything right, you …?!"

She was sent to her room to cool off.

She had banged the door, then opened it again after a minute shouting, "I shouldn't have wanted to stay in your company in any case!" and banged the door again.

Dad was about to run after her and be firm, but Mutti touched his arm, so nothing happened, because it was festive and Christmas.

It was Friday the 25th of December 1970 today.

It was ten o'clock in the morning.

Fergal could already read the time on his Mickey Mouse watch, tie his shoelaces, and know the days of the week backwards.

The heavy curtains up in his sister's room were still drawn. He was glad, she was still in bed and might remain there, up until the early afternoon. She loved sleeping.

He was six … since November.

Six was more reliable than five. And not even Mutti was at the window!

Mutti should be at the window so she could see that he was there for the surprise! His and Mutti's pact.

He was going to speak! But where was Mutti? The lump in Fergal's throat jumped up into his eyes, and he burst into tears.

This was the most important day ever! He was going to speak!

The beginning of a new life, and then school would start in summer.

But no one was waiting for him.

Mutti should have!

They didn't want him anymore! Dead or alive! Surprise or no!

Fergal was speechless and crying like mad.

He didn't know how it had happened. Fergal was still stiff with the cold, but now he was crying his eyes out on Dad's shoulder in the big hallway, sobbing like mad. He couldn't stop it.

This was a little embarrassing for a six year old. Then Dad passed him to Mutti, and Fergal began calming down a little. Mutti had that soft calming touch.

Almost a whole year of not speaking! Crying, burping, humming, coughing, Fergal had allowed himself, but absolutely no speech! Had anyone here festively present any idea how hard this had been!?

Dad's foot-muncher was closing in to finally stop the crying. The foot-muncher was also called foot-fresser or Fußfresser. *Fresser* was German and meant *muncher* and *Fuß* meant *foot.* Fergal loved the foot-muncher. It always made him giggle although the foot-muncher would eat your feet gobbling them up like Cookie Monster on AFN's Sesame Street. German kids didn't know Sesame Street yet. They had no idea what they were missing! Fergal stopped crying and wriggled free to run into the living room.

There was Oma knitting, tapping, sitting, and grinning in her residential armchair, with any luck listening to a new mind-musical playing in her head. No sooner had Oma spotted Fergal than she stopped her knitting and her shoulders started swaying and rolling, "Ferkel, my little, mute prince, come here and give me a hug. You got up much earlier than I this morning. Merry Christmas!"

Fergal ran over to her and gave her the biggest cuddle ever. Perfume vampire hug. She always smelt so wonderful.

And this was Fergal's moment! The fruition of his pact with Mutti.

Opa, Mutti and Dad were all standing in the living room door. They were all just smiling at Fergal and Oma. Every moment required a bit of preparation, Fergal knew. He smiled back at them and started racing around the coffee table with his arms in the air and his mouth wide open.

Every good moment also required the right place. Their eyes were following him closely. He ran over to the lion rug with the scary head and teeth. It was a real lion. Dad also had a gazelle and a zebra in the attic.

Fergal positioned himself on the lion's back with the lion's open mouth facing the living room door. Opa had started to frown. Oma was swaying and clapping her hands. She was also laughing more loudly than Fergal considered adequate for his preparatory performance. Mutti and Dad were looking at each other. Did they look worried?

This was Fergal's moment!

A new Fergal!

No more sulking!

He was going to love West Germany, his school, his new friends.

Just everything!

And he was going to give them his best German performance, telling them everything in his best German. The *real* German he had been listening to so carefully for almost a year, since they had left London. Admittedly, he had never really spoken that much German with Mutti even back in England. He was considered a quiet child, but in his mind he knew he could do it.

Now, Fergal! Speak German! Or just speak! This is your moment, his mind was telling him very clearly. *Sprich deutsch!*

I shall open my mouth now, Fergal thought loudly in his head, *and I shall speak for you! I'll throw my arms up in the air again to catch their attention. They're looking a bit strange.*

Fergal threw his arms up in the air again.

He opened his mouth wide and puffed out the air from his lungs like a boxer before the fight. *I shall speak for you now, watch me,* and inhaled as deeply as he could.

And started exhaling to let his words follow naturally, carried on the unstoppable flow of his breath.

And then, Fergal spoke, "Yamballa-farts-fat, malla-fett malla-fat, chick-brek, neck-track, voortsel-poopsy-fleck, fett-fat-fart!"

What in the name was that, Fergal wondered?

Well, *fett* was *fat* in English, and *fart* was *Furz* in German.

Fergal was, truly and honestly, deeply astonished! What had come out was Chamoonian, not German. Nice, and somehow interesting! What surprised him even more was the lack of control he had had over this language.

Mutti sat down on the floor and just started crying quite unabashedly.

Oma actually got up! With her knitting sliding to the floor, she was rubbing her hips, screeching with laughter.

Dad and Opa were approaching Fergal slowly as if the lion under him were still alive.

And out came another one, "Yambo tchick-tchack fett-fat veck-fat, shnell-tsack!"

What does this mean? I'll try again!

But somewhere Chamoonian was also fun, "Vartle-feck plitt tsack-fett, plitt-fat! Ick pinn hill dank-now fat, ach!" It certainly came out quite fluently, and, at least, all knew now that his voice had been restored to him.

That was something, after all!

Mutti was dragging herself to the sofa to really sob and bawl now. Shakes, trembles, incomprehensible fragments of German and English. That sort of thing.

At first, Oma looked as if she were about to join Mutti, but then, step by careful step, she started walking. Slowly. Apparently without any pain! Then her walking motion turned into a good jog past her daughter, out of the living room, down the hallway, screeching and burping laughter, and into the bathroom.

Fergal heard the loo door bang loudly.

Opa and Dad were looking at the empty armchair, as if Oma had just vanished into thin air. Opa was shaking his head, frowning very hard, "Quite unbelievable! Two such glorious miracles on the same day! Wonderful, isn't it!?"

J stuck her sleepy head in briefly with a *Frohe Weihnachten* and to ask what the ruckus was all about. When told, all she had to say without any emotion was, "Oh, my God! It speaks!" and returned to her bed.

By now Dad and Opa were standing over Fergal looking down at the little open-mouthed creature that made no sense. They were inspecting him.

“Seán, what’s happening to Ferkel?”

Dad raised both his eyebrows and bit his lip.

Fergal had another go, “Valt izt kin-splik fat Chamoon oh ya, fett-fat!” It began to dawn on him that he had spent too much of his time playing with and studying the Wetchamoonis as the explorer he had been over the past year.

“Well, Karl …,” Dad was hesitating, “at least, we know now that Fergal can speak.” He bent down and looked his son straight in the eye, “Well done, Fergal! Well done! Really! And it sounds a little like …” he smiled and picked him up, “… what German sounds like to foreign ears!” He gave Fergal a hug.

Mutti was sobbing like crazy. Fergal knew it was because she did not want to go back to London, or England for that matter, and he had somehow managed to betray their pact. How had he been able to speak so clearly at Dr. Eichenraub’s?

“All over. The end!” Mutti bawled.

Opa just said, “Be quiet, silly child!” in her general direction. Mutti was quiet instantly.

Fergal struggled in Dad’s arms. He needed to stand on the lion rug properly without Dad’s restraining embrace.

Now!

Both looked at him again. Dad with a certain amount of quizzical pride, Opa more knowingly than Fergal felt comfortable with. Opa could scare him! And now, for the first time ever in his life, Fergal admitted freely to himself that he was playacting and enjoying it like nothing else. But if Dad and Opa knew, didn’t that mean they were also playacting, maybe even playing with him? Fergal was going to see where this would take him!

Opa looked very serious when he said, “Yes. But what is it that Ferkel is speaking, Seán? It’s not German at all. You have come across more languages than I. Is it Arabic? And who taught him? Maybe it’s tongues.”

“No, no! No, it’s not!” Dad exhaled again like earlier when Fergal had been dead in the snow. Dad had been all over the place. In Saudi Arabia, even Aden, and Africa, and India, and Malta, and Israel, and wherever Tongues was.

“Look, Karl! It sounds familiar, doesn’t it? Or rather, … fragments … like German.” He laughed, “I hope you’re not possessed, little man!" Dad bent down and looked his son straight in the eye again, "Do you understand what I'm saying, Fergal? If so, just nod, please!" He laughed again. This wasn't going to be the end of it yet.

Fergal nodded.

"Good! That's something. – Do you know that we cannot understand you?"

Fergal nodded again and said, "Abble you-nix moost mik-tsik vare-fett stand-frick-shtane-fat, vooden-vooden!?" And what he had wanted to say was *But you must understand me.*

He had to get his language back!

Too long had he been working in Wetchamoonis as a spy and explorer and Land Rover driver. He hadn't been allowed to tell anyone though.

"Jolly good! – Can you tell me what language it is that you are speaking?" Dad sounded a little more pleased now, but his words were coming ever more slowly, as if he thought Fergal were an idiot child. Mutti's red eyes appeared from behind the sofa.

Fergal made a fist and put all his energy into the answer when he shouted with pride as loudly as he could, "Chamooni Wetchamoonis!"

Mutti slid back behind the sofa, and another bout of bawling received Opa's, "Does it always have to be the same drama with you? Be quiet, child!" and Mutti became quiet again immediately, apart from a tiny, trickling babble of words that could be heard wafting over in specifically Opa's direction. That it was all her fault, she started the war, but she loved Jews, and Christians had gone on the Crusade, even a Children's Crusade, lots had been killed, arms ripped off, pools of blood, but they drove her away to England where it was cold and damp and poor and the heating didn't work.

Oma appeared behind Opa with a gigantic grin. She looked at Fergal and snorted. Fergal grinned and snorted back. This was communication at its best!

Fergal felt as if he had won a big battle. Well, of course they were still living in Wetchamoonis Germany, but the amounts of sweets and attention he had been given had been great and well worth the one-year sulk!

Oma gave a sudden cheer, "Hurrah, Ferkel!" and so did Fergal, "Hack-fat-fart!" followed by Dad, "Well done!" For some reason though Mutti did not appear from behind the sofa, and Opa seemed a little serious.

"What's Chamooni, Seán?" Actually, Opa was very serious. Possibly, too serious! He didn't even look at Oma as he said, "And Murres, you go to your armchair, and do calm yourself."

Oma snorted, but obeyed.

"Well, Seán! What is Chamooni?"

"Well, Karl, … have a guess, Herr Inspektor?"

"No guesses! What is Chamooni? Tell me what you know!" That was Opa in police mode and, retired or no, he wasn't joking!

"Chamooni, or Chamoonian is German. And we all live in Wetchamoonis. And you, Karl, and Martha and Frieda are the Wetchamoonsi. That's Frances for you, I'm afraid. And Fergal has taken his sister's yarn and kept spinning it a little more. Haven't you, Fergal? And you're not possessed at all, are you, sweetheart?" Dad was really very happy now and Fergal nodded.

Eventually Mutti stopped crying and cheered up, knowing now that she was going to stay in Germany.

Everything was very festive and went according to plan.

Fergal regained his English, and his German turned out to be not so bad at all.

In the evening of this miraculous Christmas Day, after Johanna-Frances had taught Fergal the German word arsehole, *Arschloch,* to be used as a term of respect and endearment for Opa only, after Fergal had been told off severely by Opa in front of all outside church, and after Fergal had re-enacted his earlier death in the snow, Dad took him by the hand and asked him to write to God via the Pope in Rome whenever he thought he had reason to sulk again. After he had written to the Pope about his reasons, whatever they may be, and the people he hated most, whoever they may be, he should go back to the person who had made him sulk, and whom he might also hate a great deal at that time, and solve the problem then and there. Dad looked very serious. Everything Fergal wrote about to God via the Pope would be forgiven. God via the Pope could also answer prayers and wishes!

"Dad!"

"Yes, Fergal."

"What if there is nothing I hate in others, do I still have to write to God and the Pope?"

"Fergal, you don't *have* to write to God! It's only an idea. You don't *have* to do it! – It's good though to get certain things off your chest. Just be glad you can write at all at your age! And let me be glad you can speak again." Dad smiled, still in complete wonderment at how fluently his child spoke English. "I'm just saying if there is something you do not want to talk about with either Mutti or me, the God via the Big Papa in Rome is a good outlet, and you are not beholden to him because you are a Lutheran. And once you have written the letter you give it to me and I'll post it. Deal!?"

"Deal, Dad!" Fergal thought *deal* was not like *pact.*

However, there were still a few problems with Fergal's German. He couldn't pronounce the guttural *ch* and said *k* instead, and the *r* was for some bizarre reason *l* although he wasn't Chinese.

For goodness sakes, the child was only five, Dad said. There wasn't anything to worry about that time wouldn't heal!

Mutti was not just happy, or very, very, very happy about Dad's decision to stay in West-Germany, she was super-ecstatic and cuddled Dad a lot that evening. The business was really beginning to do well back then. She told him about the strange pact with Fergal and *all* was forgiven!

Before Martha and Seán went to bed without Fergal that evening, Seán asked her, please, not to have any big secrets like that from him again, "I've had enough of secrets during the war. Let this be family, not politics, Martha. No more pacts!"

Martha promised.

And in J's room Fergal was being taught as many bad words as his sister knew. If he didn't pronounce them correctly she would pull his hair by his temples really hard. That really hurt! – J insisted, only by *really* torturing Fergal would he become *really* normal.

Letter #1 – Fergal To God Via The Pope

Hello God!

Our Holy Dad in Rome, Father Paul The Sixth, will pass this on to you. – Hello Pope! Thank you very much for passing this on!

My father helps me write this letter. But I can write on my own. So this is my own last letter to you. It's called the final version. I tried five times already. My father is tired now.

My name is Johann Fergal Bulhof-Murphy. I am six and there are six of you. That's quite a lot. Merry Christmas to you all!

My sister J tells me a lot of bad words last night. She pulls my hair at the side of my head. That hurts. She thinks I am stupid. I don't talk so much. I do not talk for a year. I did not talk. I think. Mutti and Dad do not know where my language comes from. J wants to torture me. She says I must be really normal to really fit in.

I want to apologise for sulking. It was a whole year. I had a lot of fun! Everyone looks at me. Johanna tells me I am very sick in the head. I must be turned right again and she will help me so there is a happy-ending it is called as in the films from America called movies there is one happy-ending always.

Dad brings you this letter personally via the sleep-post that goes to the Pope first for correction. The Pope knows him because he looks young with grey hair. It is silver and very thick. There will be more letters from him. Papa's hair is grey because of the war. I cry when he leaves in the morning. In the evening he is back. I cry then too. I am happy. His hair is very grey. He sees very silly things in the war. In the past it is he has seen, Dad says. He does not talk about it. Mutti does. Dad says she has seen very little, but terrible things have happened, and Mutti should not talk about it because she knows very little.

I am not a Roman Catholic but a Lutheran, Mutti says. Dad shrugs his shoulder.

Yours faithfully

J. Fergal Bulhof-Murphy

Primary School

Frau von Brechwitz and Herr Hitler

It was the middle of July, and at twenty to eight in the morning, already sweltering and bright. It had been muggy throughout the night, filled with J's frustrated battle cries of aerial combat against the clouds of midges that only ever seemed to inhabit her room.

For Fergal it was his second fantastic, hot Hessen summer. Another two days to go until the summer holidays that lasted for six weeks. The summer holidays made going to school well worth it! Not that Fergal was attending school yet. He had another six weeks and two days to go if everything was fine with the Chamoonian language test today.

Mutti and he were walking down Mönchsgasse where the asocials lived in specifically adapted, cheap government housing where they couldn't break all that many things and throw stuff or their kids out of the window. – No one was being thrown out of windows today!

"They're all still asleep from alcohol!" Mutti smiled down at Fergal, "And if they look at you, do not look back at them! Walk straight past them! Do not react and rise to the bait, Johann!"

The route Mutti and Fergal were taking was Fergal's prospective way to school as of six weeks and two days from now.

The Bulhof-Murphys lived just around the corner from Geesterheim's Lutheran Primary School For Boys And Girls. That's what it was, so that's what it was called, and nothing else. In German you had to be correct and to the point, Mutti said. *Lutheranische Grundschule für Jungen und Mädchen Zu Geesterheim.*

There was no school uniform here like there was in England. All, parents were being asked, was to dress their children nicely and keep them clean, tidy and louse-free for their every day at school.

Today's test was going to ascertain whether Fergal's Chamoonian was fit for German primary school. He had been registered just before Easter. All in all, it was already over six months since his Christmas miracle, and everyone had been talking to him quite a lot. His Chamoonian was no longer a real problem. Even J had calmed down a bit with the torture, either because she had a lot on at Gymnasium or simply feared her brother would talk too much about her educating him for her happy-ending that included making him her little obedient toilet servant.

And here it was!

Geesterheim's only school!

The one that would prepare Fergal for Gymnasium, so he could go to university to study something. But not medicine like his sister!

Fergal knew exactly what he didn't want to do! As to what he really wanted to do, he had no clue.

At age four J had already decided to be a doctor. Helping people was great, but you really had to mean it with medicine, and Fergal was quite certain his sister didn't mean it.

Abruptly, a long, deep scream of anger emitted from the asocials' block, echoing its auroral way down narrow Mönchsgasse. The closer you came to the church, the wider and brighter the lane became. *How strange*, Fergal thought! Those people were in hell, and heaven was promised just two minutes away down Mönchsgasse at church. The church was part of the school grounds where lots of monks used to live.

For only a moment Mutti and he stood outside the high school wall and looked up at it. It was covered in a patchwork of dried, brown and luscious green moss. The wall felt hot to the touch. Church and school wall were one. Five times higher than their wall back home. You couldn't just jump over it.

Fergal turned. He could see their balcony from here.

Mutti pulled him by the hand. Why did she always have to take him by the hand? It was so very deeply embarrassing! He followed her because he had to.

He would have loved to look at the moss for a little longer. Touching warm moss was lovely.

He followed Mutti through the big gap in the wall. Instead of a gate there was only a wide, arched entrance in the school wall, so six or eight mothers could stand in there and have a well-deserved matutinal chat after they had dropped off their children. Six or eight mothers might arrange to go shopping later, or whatever Muttis did if no one was around.

Behind the wall it was still dark and cold.

Fergal managed to free himself from Mutti's grip to stroke the moss and the ancient masonry outside where the sun was. He put his cheek against it. The stone was hotter than the moss. The moss felt almost refreshing. Its scent the opposite of the stone it was growing on.

"Johann! Back inside again!"

Inside, the wall felt icy to the touch! There was a part in the far corner where the sun never reached because of the way the three school buildings were grouped. Fergal looked up at the facing building. Up there were the second years. The shade would recede soon to fill their classroom with light.

There were a lot of children moving about upstairs. There was a lot of screaming and laughing coming from inside through the open windows. Fergal was getting very excited! He would meet his new friends here soon! Six weeks. Two days.

Another angry shout came echoing down Mönchsgasse. Mutti ignored it, and Fergal let this echo of sadness pass them by, making its way up to the church, dying in the market square as all anger eventually died, even a one-year sulk.

He asked Mutti, why there was no one outside.

"Because, … Johann, … children have to be punctual for school. Come, take my hand again!"

He looked at his Mickey Mouse watch. – Mickey Mouse nodded his head constantly. There was a girl in the village who did that! She wasn't as famous as Mickey Mouse and people called her a spastic. Her name was Gloria.

Gloria had been another special discovery of Fergal's, he had made all on his own like Martin. It was mostly her head that was affected. Gloria too could already write, and she had shown Fergal when no one was around. People made her nervous and her speech was more laboured then. Gloria was very beautiful. Maybe she and Fergal would get married one day.

Gloria was Mickey Mouse and told Fergal that there were three minutes left until seven forty-five.

"There are three minutes left, Mutti. They are all early. Why aren't they playing?"

"In Germany children are very punctual, Johann! Don't worry! You'll have to learn it too. We have a saying here in Germany, which goes *Fünf Minuten vor der Zeit ist des Soldaten Pünktlichkeit.*"

A soldier should always be five minutes early!

Fergal understood the words perfectly, … but the meaning they had, being expressed hand in hand like that, was off. – He thought of the dark bit of the wall where the sun never shone. Well, it did depend on what you did with a saying. Maybe there was something good in it! The individual words were alright. But the whole did not sound good to him.

He tried to find the good meaning and couldn't. He frowned, because both Opa and Dad said that being a soldier meant war and wars were terrible, so being a soldier is not very nice really. He had to tell Mutti, "But we are not soldiers, Mutti!"

Mutti nodded so very wisely, "You have to learn discipline *as if* you were a soldier, Johann!"

He didn't understand this. "Why can't *you* teach me!?"

"Because discipline is a little painful, and … it's also better if you learn it from somebody else, as otherwise you'll end up not liking your parents very much. Such is life!"

"I like you whatever, Mutti! Can you teach me discipline, Mutti?"

"I already am, Joh …" … noisy ringing interrupted her. The bell!

The shrill school bell Fergal was well acquainted with, as they lived so close by. But that didn't matter really. You could hear the bell from anywhere in Geesterheim just as much as the siren from the war. It was very loud and went on forever, completely drowning out and putting an end to the children's screams and laughter inside.

Suddenly, the bell stopped, as abruptly as it had started!

Now, it was much quieter up there, but two distinct voices continued some kind of word competition. One shouted, "No!" Then the other would shout back, "No, no!" and the first one would scream "No, no, no!" It went on and on. *No, no, no, no, no, no, no, no, no!* Fergal didn't bother following this boring exchange.

Although, it *did* sound fun!

He looked at his watch again. He didn't understand. There was still one minute to go! His watch had to be slow! Or maybe this was what Mutti had just said about five-minute soldiers? But then it should have been four minutes ago, shouldn't it?

Mutti continued, "I already am teaching you discipline. If I say 'No', you don't like it, but you won't do it, will you? You see, your Irish Dad says *yes* far too often! *No* means discipline. It teaches you to wait and be calm. If you wait, something better will come along."

"Dad is not discipline?"

"Yes, he is. – But you say, he is *disciplined*, or this is *discipline.* Just not with you and Johanna."

"Disciplined! This is discipline, and discipline is pain?"

Mutti laughed again and was about to answer, when the bell rang for a second time. And this time the ringing really went on forever!

When it stopped … there was utter silence! Like death.

No laughing, no screaming, no more *no, no, no.*

Mother and son heard a door shut and a dissonant chorale of voices "Guten Morgen, Frau …" For some reason Mutti shuddered. Fergal couldn't make out the name of the Frau, but in English that was *Good morning, Mrs.* Then there was nothing, no sound. A hush, reminiscent of Johanna's horror story silences, before she would pounce in the dark.

Mutti's voice scared him a little when she spoke again, "It is pain … but only if you don't know what it is. Discipline can save you, too! Punctuality is respect, and obedience and discipline."

"Punctuality and discipline are painful. Soldiers are disciplined, says Opa, because they have to die. Opa says soldiers die like flies, like J's midges. At school I learn discipline." Something was sinking in, "School is painful. – Will I die, Mutti?"

Fergal knew what death was. He didn't want to die yet, even though it was fun if you could scare your parents! J had said for the New Year that she was going to have a party with all her friends when Fergal died.

"Oh, come on, Johann! Of course not! School is lovely, once you have learnt about discipline, and if you're good, … you'll get a lot of praise!"

He would definitely have to think about this more! He needed more words to put into his language, even though he had discovered a year ago, whilst he was still silent, that *word* was really the only word which described itself and all others. It was the *number-one* word. The perfect word.

Discipline didn't appear to be saying quite as much. "What is discipline in German, Mutti?"

"*Disziplin.* – Can you say that for me, please!?"

"Diss-tsee-pleen. – Wow, that's difficult!"

"Very good! Now say, 'I am very disciplined' in German, please."

"Icky-fettsy-fat bin-tsack-fett-fat ditsy-ditsy-fett … I don't know disci…"

"Oh, mein Gott! – Johann!" Mutti looked absolutely shocked.

Fergal had sort of done it on purpose.

"Johann! – Listen! Absolutely no Chamoonian! Promise me *that*!"

"I'm sorry! I promise, Mutti." He was not sorry. It had sort of slipped out … for fun. Fergal realised this was because he evidently *wasn't* disciplined.

So, discipline was no fun!

The *no, no, no* game though did sound like a lot of fun!

"Now say, '*Ich bin sehr diszipliniert*'. Go on, Johann-Fergal. – Say it!" – *Johann-Fergal* meant Mutti was angry!

"Ick binn sell diss-tzee-pleen-illt."

"Oh! Johann, Johann! You could do the *ch* so nicely this morning. – Never mind, now! Let's go inside. Our appointment is for eight."

"What's appointment, Mutti?"

"*Termin,* in German! Just like with *all* your doctors."

"Tear? Mean!?" – What a terrible word that was!

"Well done! – It means, it is the *right* time! It is the time, which we have arranged … or fixed with somebody, to meet up to see how Master Bulhof-Murphy's German – and *not*

Chamoonian …" her index finger shot up by the side of her face, almost as if shouting *or else!* The finger never involved any pain or discipline with Mutti. Dad never used his finger like that! "Look at me! – *Absolutely* … *NO* … Chamoonian! – To see how Johann's *Deutsch* … *Deutsch,* you hear, … is coming along."

"How can we fix or arrange time?!" This was a baffling concept!

"If you are disciplined, it is a joy to arrange an appointment or *Termin* and turn up at the *right* time five minutes beforehand, … at least! You keep an appointment! *Never* turn up late! You only do that, when you are undisciplined like the asocials. Germans are *very* disciplined, Johann! You are going to learn from the best! – Let's go in."

Fergal was quiet now. He would really have to think about this one, and he would have to find more words. Not in his mind, but in his mouth! – But, all in all, asocials weren't really German because they were not disciplined. So … Fergal was a little asocial, because he too was not really German!

I am English, he thought quietly but with a lot of pride in his heart!

You went to school to learn discipline.

Going to school to learn discipline was painful!

Then, … you had to make appointments, called *tear-means.* And you had to keep them, because you had gone through so much pain! This meant, you were showing off, … how disciplined you were!

Hadn't Mutti said, at some stage, that showing off was bad!?

There even was a German saying for that!

Er übertreibt und übertreibt, und keiner mag ihn leiden!

He's showing off, just showing off, and no one ever likes him!

Fergal remembered that it was with doctors that you made appointments … and suddenly the coin dropped! – You had to go to the doctor after you had finished school because you were in so much pain from showing off discipline, like the wall without the sun, where nothing ever grew.

There were many, many doctors in Wetchamoonis! Mutti once said there were more doctors in Germany than anywhere else in the world, and that's why Germans were so healthy.

But didn't you need a doctor only when you were sick?

Unconsciously, all the way through his contemplation over *tear-mean*, *discipline* and *doctors*, had Fergal been slowly walking backwards through the archway, out of the darkness into the light of the sunny lane.

Impatiently huffing, Mutti went after him. She was shaking her head but laughing at the same time.

Hand in hand mother and son finally managed to walk steadily and *disciplined* up to the entrance of the main building.

You learnt discipline to become patient, because when you were patient, better things came to you. Mutti hadn't been patient just now! Patients needed doctors!

"I understand *completely*, Mutti!"

Mutti laughed again, "Your English is really quite lovely, Fergal. – Let's show them about your German, eh!"

They proceeded through a double glass door, and Fergal had to stamp his feet so the dust came off. Mutti did the same. "Being clean is also showing respect and being disciplined!"

Fergal could hear a woman screaming at the top of her voice upstairs.

"That's Frau Kellergeister!" Mutti looked worried when she said this. "And she *ist sehr streng*, … that's *very* disciplined or severe." – Mutti thought for a little before she added hesitantly, "Frau Kellergeister is tough with her children. She won't let them get away with anything! She is just! – Be disciplined, Johann, … and she will be perfectly just." – This meant Fergal would have a hard time getting away with anything.

He was glad he wouldn't have to scale the wall because of the open archway. Only problem was, there were doors here all over the place.

Fergal had a strange sensation. He shook his head. It was as if he was now trapped in Wetchamoonis, in one of his own games, and Frau Kellergeister *really* was the Daz-Witch Awonda!

There were children crying loudly behind the red door where Frau Kellergeister was screaming like there was no tomorrow. Fergal could hear a continuous slapping noise. He knew what it was because a lot of parents in the village would slap their children. They always cried. Frau Kellergeister was smacking her children! Children were learning patient discipline here so they could go to the doctor afterwards.

As Mutti and Fergal were about to climb the long flight of stairs to the first floor where the sounds of whimpering and crying were coming from, Fergal made a choice.

He chose *no discipline* … ever!

He turned straight around on his heels to make for the glass doors.

Escape from Wetchamoonis!

But Mutti was just that little too quick. She took him by the collar of his summer jacket and marched him straight upstairs aiming for another red door. There were *only* red doors here! Warning signs on the road were red like this to guide traffic. Mutti didn't say a word. At least there was no screaming from in there. There was a sign with a very difficult and long word on it. Mutti read it for him.

"That's the *Sekretariat*, Johann-Fergal! – Say it!" Mutti sounded a little severe and tough now. In fact, Mutti had changed a little ever since they had entered the school building. The smile had gone from her eyes.

So Fergal spoke after her, "Zeck-lay-ta-lee-aaat!" He felt a surge of pride almost equalling his earlier thought of *I am English*. He *would* go to this school. He *would* learn about discipline. He *would* not get away even with anything! And Mutti could let go off his collar *now*!?

She didn't though.

Instead, she glared at him. – "Say it again!" Mutti sounded a bit like Opa in police mode, as Dad called it.

"Zeck-lay-ta-lee-awt! Lee-ort?"

"Oh, ... mein Gott! Lieber Himmel! Was ist denn das jetzt? Was ist denn jetzt bloß mit dem Jungen los? – Herr Gott noch mal! – Bengel! Say it again! Zweimal! Twice! – *Sekretariat!*"

Fergal's Mutti had just said "Oh, my God! Dear heaven! What's wrong now?" and so on and so on. In essence, Mutti *really* wasn't happy! At all! And Fergal was supposed to say *Zeck-lay-ta-lee-awt* twice, so he had said it twice.

Fergal was trembling a little, and there was ever more screaming from Frau Kellergeister coming through the other red door.

This was all very stressful!

Stressful was a great word Fergal had learnt from Chuck Nolde, his best friend downstairs, who would also start school in six weeks and two days.

Stressful applied to a situation when you had called your Mum to do *wipies,* and she didn't come, and then you wiped yourself everywhere. That was stressful because afterwards there would be lots of screaming, and your Mammi was very, very angry at the skid marks everywhere, and the noise your Mammi made was even more stressful!

Chuck was right.

"Zeck-lay-ta-lee-awt! Zeck-lay-ta-lee-awt!"

"Lieber Himmel! That's not good! We have a problem. Not good at all, Johann! Johann-Fergal!"

What wasn't good? A *problem* obviously wasn't good! This wasn't a problem!

Fergal was a little worried now.

It was five minutes to eight.

Mutti knocked on the door twice. No answer.

And again. Three times.

A severely tough voice shouted, "Herein schon!!!"

Fergal knew *herein* means *come in*, but Opa had told him that you said *bitte*, which meant *please* and was polite, but instead of *please* there was only *schon* which meant *already,* and he didn't know you could say that with *herein* but it did not sound polite or friendly. – At all!

Fergal was learning more and more, *already.*

He was at school! The school of the Daz-Witch Awonda of Wetchamoonis were the little Wetchamoonsi were taught how to be respectful, disciplined patients, and speak Chamoonian properly, so they could say *Ja* all the time and then go to a Chamoonsi doctor for medicine. And poor little he was only an English asocial.

All of a sudden life here in Wetchamoonis made a lot of sense to Fergal! It was all about the great game of getting away!

When mother and son entered the school office *Sekretariat,* Fergal smiled his way into a calming thought of hope and deliverance, *my escape from Wetchamoonis has started!*

Mutti opened the door, and mother and son entered the school office.

"Guten Morgen, Frau von Brechwitz!"

No answer came.

Mutti shut the door.

Frau von Brechwitz was the school secretary and twenty times older than Mutti. Mutti was beautiful. Frau von Brechwitz, though well kempt and turned out for respectful, patient discipline, was quite the opposite with an *Umlaut* on top and not even the tiniest of effort in even the vaguest direction of being nice. She was also much too thin!

Frau von Brechwitz was beyond looking angry. Frau von Brechwitz was anger!

Maybe Frau von Brechwitz didn't like getting up so early? A bit like Johanna-Frances, Sister J, the midge killer. Maybe Frau von Brechwitz ought to go to England, where school didn't start *that* early? – Fergal said so. "She's tired and angry and needs to go to England!" But Mutti shushed him. That was the first time Mutti had ever sounded like a snake.

The *Sekretariat* was Frau von Brechwitz's domain. Her *Reich*!

Mutti somehow managed, in an instant, to change her own look from being angry with Fergal to being extremely nice to Frau von Brechwitz. But there was something else in Mutti's demeanour. It was something that reminded Fergal of the neighbour's hunting dog, Capo, when he pretended to listen to be good. – The neighbours were called Bruckner. They were very nice with a fifteen meter heated swimming pool.

Fergal didn't know the word for Mutti's look, but it was a very *specific* look that made him sad and angry at the same time. Such look and feeling caused in a bystander just deserved a word! In Chamoonian it definitely was *arpchuddle-bang-fat-hm.* It was a dog-look! A look that said *I am harmless, and do whatever you want me to do, as I am a respectful patient of discipline.*

But Mutti wasn't like *that*! Or was she?

Despite the fact that mother and son were standing in front of Frau von Brechwitz, the latter shouted another volley of "Herein schon!" at no one in particular.

Mutti let go of Fergal's hand, went back to the red door, opened and shut it again, and then she offered another but very loud "Good morning, Frau von Brechwitz! We are here for the language test of my son Johann's. We made an appoint…"

"Sit *and* wait!" Frau von Brechwitz didn't look up.

Obediently both sat on a very low, red plastic sofa made for dwarves. Mutti was totally different with Germans, Fergal noticed. Or Germans like this.

Frau von Brechwitz was behind a high counter. Much higher than Herrn Dorfgeist's counter with the Negerküsse.

Fergal knew instinctively that Brechwitz hated everybody! Maybe because she was hated by everybody!? – J had taught Fergal a most special word for people whom you really loved in both German and English. She had promised it wasn't at all like calling Opa a German *Arschloch* or English *arsehole.*

Brechwitz needed lots of love. But Fergal wouldn't say the most special word now, because he also knew instinctively that he couldn't make her like him even if he tried. In Brechwitz's case, to make her like you would be like betraying yourself just for a little peace from her anger.

Brechwitz was doing something with her hands. Fergal could hear paper being shuffled around. Mutti and he looked up at her. They waited like that for a long time. It was now fifteen minutes past eight. Brechwitz was hidden behind the counter. There was no sound. Just the clock over the door kept ticking quietly. Fergal noticed it was ten minutes fast.

Then, "Mrs. Bulhof-Murphy, yes? Do … you … speak … Gerrrr … man?" Brechwitz had appeared from behind the counter. She was looking straight at no one.

"Yes, of course, Frau Brechwitz …"

"Frau *von* Brechwitz, ja!" Her voice was like something very hard, but Fergal had a little trouble thinking of a thing which sounded as hard. – *Yes*, he could! It was like ancient Martin's father banging the bell on his steamroller that cut lots of wood into little pieces with hundreds of belts. No, … not the bell, … but the banging. Her voice was like the banging!

"Frau von Brechwitz, we spoke on the phone last week. We have an appointment for the language test with the speech therapist."

"Frau von Allerleben, yes. A friend of mine. She is our logopaedician, … do … you … know … that … word!? She is a … speech therrrrr … aaaaah … pist. – I remember you, Mrs. von Bulhof-Murphy. No! You are *just* Bulhof-Murphy! You are not a *von,* and you do not have an appointment!"

"Sorry, Frau Brechwitz. But we do! For eight o'clock today."

Brechwitz wrote something down with the tiny remnants of a red pencil in a small red book, then pointed the pencil at the clock over the door. It was a well-rehearsed movement. She continued to look down in her book as though waiting to have cause to make another entry. Fergal wanted to be outside that door!

"It … is … half past eight, … Frau Brechwitz."

"Exactly. Well done, Frau Bulhof. And what does that mean?"

"That … it's … half past eight?"

"No! Try again! – Now!"

"That my son and I have waited for half an hour?"

"Be quiet, unless you know the right answer, Frau Bulhof! And don't you be cocky with me! – So, do you know the right answer?"

"No."

Fergal couldn't believe this was *his* Mutti. – Mutti was looking down with her hands placed on her knees. If she had had Capo's tail it would have been between her legs.

"Good, Frau Bulhof! This is what our place is about! Learning and discipline! – In my book your son is already late by one year because of his … *sickness.* He should have come to us when he was five. If it were down to me, every child should start school at four. At least! Six is a nonsense! But what can I say. Late! Like mother, like son. We could have taken the sickness right out of him. But maybe … to late!?"

"I see, … Frau von Brechwitz." Mutti had added the *von* now. Mutti had given up completely!

"Good! – You are late, and you do not have an appointment for *late*, do you! You had an appointment for eight! Hence, you are not here!"

"I am so very, very, very sorry, Frau von Brechwitz! Johann was sick this morning."

This was new to Fergal! Mutti was not telling the truth even though she had no reason to lie. And she was using him to hide behind! And now Frau von Brechwitz-fett-fat-tsack was looking at Fergal from up there behind her counter, and her look hurt him.

"Ahaaa! – He is the problem!" Her eyes bored through Fergal, "The *famous* problem! A year late at six years of age … in my opinion!"

You couldn't hide the truth from Brechwitzen-hitzen-tsacken.

"The boy is not sick! He is just stupid, and he needs to learn! He *is* the problem. I know *all* about him! – This is a small place, Frau Bulhof, … and foreigners … like you … stick out! Americans and whatnot! All foreign! Stick out! – He doesn't speak! And Frau Kellergeister will remedy that! So, … what is the first thing you have learnt so far, Frau Bulhof?"

"I'm sorry, I'm late."

"Late who?"

"Frau von Brechwitz."

"What, Frau von Brechwitz?"

"I'm sorry, I'm late, Frau von Brechwitz."

"Good! – But that is a given. – What have you learnt?"

"I don't know, Frau von Brechwitz. That coming late isn't good?"

"No!" she screamed, "Don't lie! – You have learnt that my clock is ten minutes fast. So, if you want to be on time you too have to be fifteen minutes faster! And that applies to that little runt down there, too!"

Fergal realised that she was looking down at him again. Her look hurt his body all over. Somehow she demanded he look back at her. He couldn't keep this up for long! It gave him a severe pain in his neck. Her counter was too high.

"You said, he speaks now, and our beautiful, clean language at that!? – Make him speak! Make him say something nice and polite to me, Frau Bulhof. Let him introduce himself. – Now!"

Mutti had been holding Fergal's hand all the while. Her hand was really sticky, even though, normally, it was quite rough and dry. That was because of all the washing-up liquid. And now she squeezed it really hard. She didn't even look at her son.

Fergal knew, what was expected of him, but he just couldn't talk to Brechwitz, because she was like Martin's father banging the hammer on his bell, and he didn't want to like her. Ever! – Yes, it might have helped her if someone liked her, but Fergal was not going to waste his sister's most special word on this monster woman.

He shook his head and looked at the red steel floor. The floor had the appearance of stone but it wasn't. It was just cheap lino. He would never say a word again!

"Go on! – Now! Frau Bulhof! Now! – Make your son talk, at once! Make him look up at me, this moment!"

Mutti sighed, "Please, Johann! Let's show Frau von Brechwitz how nice you are, and how well your German has been coming along."

Fergal pressed his chin down on his chest and shook his head again. He didn't ever want to look at that woman again! Ever!

"Johann, please! – This is *important*! *Really* important for you, do you understand me?"

Fergal kept shaking his head. His chest was hurting his chin, and in turn his chin was hurting his chest. And with his head down like that, his neck was in even more pain. He would not talk! He turned his eyes up at Brechwitz as hard as he could, and had to lean back a little to see her.

Mutti was no longer on his side! He could feel it.

Brechwitz banged her little red book down on the counter, then shuffled some more paper before she made an abrupt sweeping motion with her hand in Mutti's direction. Fergal knew this meant *the child needs smacking!* He had seen Geesterheimer parents do this when they talked about their children. Fergal looked down at the floor again.

There were fast and hard, stomping footsteps. Brechwitz! – Brechwitz had shot around the counter. Fergal was now looking at her black, buckled shoes. They were men's shoes. She needed to eat more sweets! She was beyond marzipan, but something like an apple might help.

"Frau Bulhof, you ask too much and tell too little. This one especially needs to be *told*! Stand over there! Let me show you!"

Mutti's shoes moving out of Fergal's line of vision. Mutti had deserted him! That's what soldiers did who didn't like trenches.

And then Fergal felt something he had not felt before. It hurt more than anything J had done to him so far. It wasn't the body-pain so much.

Brechwitz was tearing at Fergal's hair and wrenched his chin up from his chest. He wouldn't cry. After all, he would shave soon! He shut his eyes.

"Look at me, imp!" – This wasn't shouting. This was screaming. Worse than the kids before the bell had rung for the first time earlier. Fergal felt her fingers digging in behind his ears and her thumbs pressing into his eyes. – Where was Mutti?

"Open!"

The pain was intense, and Fergal opened his eyes. For some reason his eyes were crying. This was very embarrassing! Brechwitz laughed a screaming hammer-laugh, "Open Sesame! Klara's magic!" Her name was Klara! Fergal wouldn't ever forget her name.

"Now, say something, … dwarf!" There was no support he could expect from Mutti. This was school, and Fergal was learning patient discipline.

He would speak. – On his own terms!

"Speak, … you little runt or I smack you so hard you'll never feel pain again."

He had to speak! – Fergal was hearing his own voice in his head pleadingly shouting *speak, speak, speak!*

Mutti took a step forward.

Fergal could see that she was about to smack Frau von Brechwitz's head from behind.

So, … Mutti had come back, after all!

Fergal felt much better now.

"Cow-moo-tsack-fottle nix-milk yo-shtink sad-fat-fett ach was nix you-fett-fatsy bang-fett hammel-fat nie-fick-fett keine fuck-tsack-bumm aus Schluss!" – Fergal had actually just made that up! But he made it sound really angry and Chamoonian, and it had a grand effect on Brechwitz. She let go of his face abruptly and stood back next to Mutti. Mutti had just hit the back of her head. Brechwitz hadn't reacted!

Both frowned.

Brechwitz knew no pain! Mutti's frown contained a little smile. She was looking at the back of the secretary's head.

Fergal decided that Brechwitz's befuddled frown was her nicest look. She still looked as if she wanted to turn him into *Hackfleisch* and *Blutwurst*, but Fergal didn't care much for German mince meat or blood sausage. For now, she was quiet!

He could run now!

He thought of his escape for only a second, and then abandoned the thought. They might put Mutti in the cellar in her *own* room for a long time, and then she would look like Dad's friend, Big-Eye Nathan. – Big-Eye Nathan was Dad's PoW friend who was cycling all the time. Sometimes Fergal thought he could see Nathan in the distance. Fergal had only met him twice up close and personal, but that had been quite enough! Scary! Dad said Big-Eye Nathan had had a bad time as a PoW in a German camp in Bavaria. He was cycling all over Germany to find a nice German because he couldn't believe there were only angry people here. Dad said there were some lovely Germans, but you had to win their trust.

Brechwitz had regained her speech, "What in the name was that, Frau Bulhof? What in the name of Himself. I think there were some very strange words in it! It sounded like … Austrian!? Like the *Führer* Himself." – She hesitated. But as Mutti was smiling a victorious smile at her, she felt encouraged to continue, "I believe in rebirth! Strongly! Look at him, Frau Bulhof! Just look at *him*!!!" Somehow, Brechwitz was really taken aback and still had no idea that Mutti had hit her. "So beautiful. The black hair! The dark raisin eyes! It could be, couldn't it!? … His language! … He just needs a proper haircut."

Fergal now knew Brechwitz was one of the *insane ones.* Opa had talked a lot of the *Führer* and his demented lot. Somehow the *Führer's* disease had caught on with the help of industry. It had lasted twelve years and left a lot of people *very* dead. There were a lot of the *insane ones* about still. Brechwitz was one of them!

Mutti no longer displayed any fear or subservience. She was shaking her head, slowly. It was some kind of pity. A little like the way she used to look at Fergal, when she still believed he was a mute child, but without the smile in it, "Frau Brechwitz, please! It is his own language! He made it up. But, don't worry, he does speak German! Can we see Frau von Allerleben now, please! We are late because of *you.* And with *now*, I mean, … *now*, as in … *at once*! And we won't mention, that you just hurt my child, or anything else." Somehow, Mutti had gained the upper hand! If she had had a tail it would be up, but not wagging. Her hackles would be up!

The secretary did an abrupt about-turn and disappeared behind the counter. There was more paper shuffling. A phone call was made.

"Frau von Allerleben is waiting for you. Room three. Lower ground floor." Frau von Brechwitz's eyes glazed over. She was actually looking at Fergal with a great deal of admiration and love! Fergal sensed metal in her eyes. It made him shudder. Fragments that could hurt whomever she looked at. He turned away.

Without uttering another word, Mutti and Fergal left.

On their way downstairs Mutti realised she had left her handbag behind. Fergal volunteered bravely and raced back up to the school office just storming in without even knocking. The moment he entered, he imagined Brechwitz was waiting for him, to kill him, tearing him limb from limb. He saw Mutti's handbag right there on the red sofa.

Where was Brechwitz?

Fergal moved forward into the office along the high wall of the reception counter. His mind was bombarding him with horrific images of what Brechwitz would do to him for the undisciplined intrusion! He saw her cutting off his arms and legs, eating them in front of his very eyes. Where were these images coming from? He had never had seen such horror! This was far worse than even J's nightly monster stories that always turned into love stories as soon as she had killed off Fergal as the bad-ending bit.

Where was Brechwitz?

With great stealth Fergal moved towards the sofa to grab and run. He grabbed, turned, and …

… there she was!

She was standing very still behind the counter of her little domain with the red door and sofa. She was standing a bit like Opa when he had shown Fergal how soldiers stand to attention. Her eyes had gone from simply being glazed over to tearful. He could still see fragments of steel in there. It wasn't just her eyes. Her whole being was a fragment of steel. Fergal saw Brechwitz turning into a knife chopping him into a thousand little bits of mincemeat blood sausage.

"Excuse me, Madam! – I have just come back to get Mutti's handbag." Fergal said this in his best German, without even thinking of Chamoonian. He was aware of his bad *rs* that always turned into *ls* and his bad *chs* that always came out as *k*. Somehow though, it didn't matter, and when it started mattering it would somehow sort itself out, … maybe even today. Opa said, life was like that!

There still was coming no response from Brechwitz. And that was just fine, because Fergal really wasn't in any mood to chat, and leaving quickly was a *really* good idea. He was just making for the door, when her metallic voice reached him like a sharp knife in the back. He was very scared of this woman! Insane or no, he didn't know why, really.

"Yes, … naturally, Johann! And when we meet again, you must come and visit me, and I will tell you about the real Berlin, and the old times, so you can remember who you were! Agreed!?"

Fergal turned round to look at her. He had had nightmares like this before. Something terrible and evil was coming for you, … you couldn't see it, … you couldn't run away! You were stuck in the mire of your own painfully deadly, slow dream-thinking. There was something in Brechwitz' eyes which wasn't quite there, and was much more than looking through frosted glass in the loo.

All loo windows had frosted glass in Germany, Mutti said, because people were a bit shy about their business. Fergal's nightmarish immobility didn't stop!

Maybe this was a dream!?

He couldn't look her in the eye. Her eyes would turn him into a million pieces of metal. A sickness of steel. This was a new fear! As of being affected by someone else's disease. A disease that wouldn't kill you quickly, but was with you all your life, and it depended on your own decision to stop it.

He was not going to agree to visit her.

No way!

No way, ever!

No way was an American saying, but Fergal liked it, and it meant *absolutely not*! – Somehow though Fergal felt the need to say something nice to her, as she had changed so very much over the past half hour. A change from unfriendly, to insane and nice. Of sorts, because she had given him the feeling that he was something quite special.

Fergal remembered what Dad had once told him about mirrors, and that if you smiled at them they'd smile back, and it was the same with people. So, if you liked people, they would like you back, and if you didn't like people … and so on and so on.

"Flau Blekwitz!" The problem. The real problem! Never mind. He would say something really nice because Brechwitz needed healing.

"Flau Blekwitz! If you want to be leally fucked you need to fuck othel people back othelwise you'll never be fucked by anyone! And then maybe I could fuck you too and come and visit you but you have to fuck othel people filst!" There! He had said it, and it had been very wise to use J's most special love-word.

In German *fuck* was *fick*. Now, that was really easy! J had explained to him that if you really loved somebody you wouldn't just say *I love you*, you would say *fuck you* or *I fuck you*. Fergal knew, he was speaking the absolute truth and nothing but the truth! After all, there is a German saying that goes *Kindermund tut Wahrheit kund*, which is very, very old, and it means that children speak the truth!

But now, with Fergal's direct truth to heal poor Brechwitz' steel soul, he saw that her jaw had dropped. Before, Fergal would have not been able to imagine her dropping anything. Cutting up in little bits? Yes! But dropping? Oh, no!

She was glaring at him.

She was going to kill him, he was absolutely certain!

Slowly, he moved backwards out of the school office. Two screams issued simultaneously from behind two different red doors up here on the massive landing of the first floor.

Her voice came almost softly, "Wait, Ferkel!" A hot knife through butter. It was clear to Fergal who was the butter. That nightmare immobility again. Suddenly though her eyes softened, and Fergal was able to perceive something in the frosted distance of her soul. Slowly, steadily, her right arm rose straight into the air as if she wanted to shout happily *over there, that's a nice view* like Mutti sometimes. Mutti loved nice views, sunny weather and festive moods. "Do you remember this?"

"No, Flau von Blekwitz!"

"It was our greeting, when times were still good! Remember it! When you use this greeting, you can tell your friends from your enemies, … at once! And with your friends you can say *Heil Hitler*, when you greet them like this. Raise your arm, and say it to me, please!"

She had just said *please* to Fergal, so he raised his arm and said "Heil Hitlel". His *rs* were really quite bad today.

"Very good, my little Adolf. Don't worry about your *rs*. They will come, like all your other memories. Von Allerleben will sort you out, even though, sadly, she is not one of us … never mind! Sooner or later they'll all come round. If she won't sort you out, I shall! – Now, say *Sieg Heil*, please!"

Another lovely *please* again, and such a lovely smile, almost as nice as Mutti's when she was in a sad mood, and very hard to resist for Fergal. But inside this woman lurked the Daz-Witch Awonda spider of the Wetchamoonsi. J had told Fergal all about that terrible mind-spider, before they had moved to Wetchamoonis. It was like the creatures inside the Daleks. Johanna still had the Dalek that made sparks inside when you moved it. "Sieg Heil, Flau von Blekwitz! I have to go now."

Fergal's neck was trembling. The sweat on his forehead felt cold. And then, he just banged the door shut behind him as he ran back downstairs to Mutti, and jumped into her arms.

"Oh, I love you, too. – Why are you trembling, Johann? What's wrong?"

Fergal wriggled free from Mutti's embrace and greeted his mother with his right arm raised high, "Heil Hitlel, Mutti!"

Mutti went quite pale, and her head tilted slightly, "Never, … ever, … ever … say *that* … ever … again! – Do you understand me! – Never! – Those were *evil* people, and Hitler was an *evil* man!" Mutti looked a bit like Big-Eye Nathan now. Fergal also knew that Mutti was his friend most of the times.

Frau von Allerleben's Breasts

"Herein, bitte!" – Now that was a nice *come in, please*! – The friendliest voice on Earth from beyond yet another red door.

Mutti and Fergal were on the lower ground floor. To Fergal it looked just like a cellar. When Mutti was about to open the door, it opened all by itself, and a lot of sunlight filled the dark corridor. The sun had risen over the high school wall! And there stood Fergal's speech teacher, who was going to turn him into an acceptable German with a disciplined patient *r* and *ch*.

"Come on in. I am Anne." Her voice was totally beautiful! It was like the voice on Fergal's Odysseus record. That was Odysseus for babies, of course, or in Johanna's words *Odysseus for the mentally retarded*, but there were the Sirens, and Anne sounded just like one. Fergal was not going to ask Mutti to stuff up his ears with wax! The Phaeacian girls on Odysseus-for-babies had great voices too. And there was Circe who turned all the men into pigs, which were grownup *Ferkels*, but the Siren had the best voice all-round. It was the same voice as the fairy on his Pinocchio record.

Anne's chest was also so much bigger than Mutti's! It was like a fest of balloons filled with water, and then they wobbled in a most lovely way! Mutti didn't really have a chest. Fergal would have liked so much to touch Anne's. He wouldn't ever do that with Mutti's. Mutti was not very body-like and didn't seem to enjoy being touched, although she was the most beautiful woman in the world. Men, of course, didn't have chests like Anne's.

Mutti sat down in front of the only desk. Fergal kept staring at Anne. She really was most beautiful.

"Come on in and take a seat, Johann!" Anne smiled at Fergal, but she was much too old for him! She was more beautiful even than Jenny, his wife back in London.

Fergal and Jenny had married quickly before Fergal was off to the Daz-Witch Awonda's Wetchamoonis. Both had been five then. They had vowed eternal love and friendship. One day Mutti received a letter from their neighbours back in Camden Town. At five and a half Jenny was now apparently married again. Happily married to Fergal's archenemy, Ralph! Never mind. Such is life.

Stiff upper lip, eh! – Fergal got over it quickly, but the news had certainly added to his persistent muteness, and especially his veteran's war limp.

The top of Fergal's head was tingling. What a strange feeling that was! He shut the door and sat down next to Mutti. Continuing to stare at Anne was necessary, because it was good for his eyes. Her hair was really blonde and short like Dad's. But Dad's hair was silver grey like a gorilla's back.

"Well. Your son has a really lovely smile, Frau Bulhof-Murphy! I understand he can speak German now, but has some problems still, hasn't he? Don't we all!? Now and then! German is not an easy language at the best of times. And I'm here to help you with that, Johann. Would you like to tell me a little about yourself in German? – My English, I'm afraid, wouldn't stand up to yours. But, I am learning." She wasn't looking at Mutti at all. She was looking at Fergal! Her eyes were like his pillow, and he'd like to put his face into them and feel her breasts to see if they were like balloons filled for the water battle.

"Hello, Miss!" Fergal couldn't stop smiling. – So far though, he hadn't made a mistake. He completely forgot about Mutti.

"How are you, Johann?"

"I'm fine, Miss! Thank you! And you? – I am Fergal! I like Fergal better. Delighted to meet you." He so wanted to be good for Anne! Mutti was shifting around a little.

"I'm fine, too, … and I like Fergal better, too! You can call me Anne!" She looked at Mutti, and from the corner of his eye Fergal could see that Mutti nodded. He didn't know why, but he nodded too.

"Now, Fergal! Your German is really lovely. I don't think you'll have any trouble at school. Let's play a little game then!" She handed him an exercise book and pencil. This was real school stuff! The tingling was also in his shoulders now. He got that with Opa too, when he told him about the big war, or when Opa was drawing something, especially horses. Opa couldn't draw to save his life, but still, it was wonderful to watch him.

"Can you please write a few sentences down for me? I'll dictate them to you. You'll play this later at school too."

"What's dictate, Anne?" Anne's name was like *I love you,* or even J's *more-than-love* most special word! He had once said it to Jenny, but he had to be really careful here. Anne was much too old for him!

"*Dictate* means, I shall read it to you slowly, and you write it down for me please." Anne was wearing a white blouse with three top buttons undone. The top of her chest looked like Fergal's bottom in the mirror. It was hard to see your own bottom. Jenny didn't have a chest like that. But she'd grow boobies soon, she had promised. She and Fergal had checked every day, but they didn't grow. Jenny had been dismayed!

It was getting really hot now! The sun was laying blocks of light, made of dust. Anne was smiling. Mutti though had a big, huge mirror in the bedroom for make-up and jewellery. The mirror had three bits like an altar, which was called triptych, and you could see yourself and your bottom or infinity with your bottom never-ending, racing off into the distance of the mirror. Infinity was that which never ended. Anne's breasts didn't really look like his bottom. Her breasts were beautiful!

"Ok. May I take my jacket off, please."

"Of course."

Mutti helped Fergal out of his jacket.

Anne started dictating.

First, she read all that she was going to dictate, and Fergal had to wait until she was finished. Then she read much more slowly and Fergal wrote it down.

"*Ich fahre jeden Tag mit meinem Rad zur Schule. Nach der Schule fahre ich zurück nach Hause. Ach, es ist sehr heiß heute! Gestern war es nicht so heiß. Wir haben einen Bach im Garten.*" This was quite easy for him, Fergal thought. It meant, *I ride my bike to school every day. After school I ride it back home. Oh, it's very hot today. Yesterday it wasn't as hot. There is a little stream in our garden.*

He wrote as quickly as he could to show her how good his German was, although he wasn't going to school yet, and he didn't have a bike. Yet! There was also no stream in their garden. A stream would be lovely! You could play ocean on it with ships and harbours and cities on its banks. And then he had finished writing for her.

Anne seemed quite pleased with Fergal. She was smiling a great deal. Fergal really liked her a lot and might use the special word of J's later, but quietly. She took the exercise book and pencil back and then her eyes opened really wide.

"Frau Bulhof-Murphy, … this is absolutely incredible! You have done an incredible job here. Almost not a single mistake! Everything is in the right place. I am really baffled, actually! This is year-two material! I'll do some more tests. But, I think, we can recommend he'll join year two straightaway." Then Anne turned back to Fergal, "Well done, Fergal. – Now, please read it to me."

Fergal was really going to give it his best now. He read out loud and clear, "I lide my bike to school evely day…" He knew exactly what was going wrong! And there was nothing he could do about it. But Anne still smiled!

"No problem, Fergal! – Let me show you how to do German *rs* and *chs*. There a bit alike, really."

Fergal nodded. He had no idea they were!

Mutti was stirring.

"Yes, … Frau Bulhof-Murphy?"

"Fräulein von Allerleben, … I was wondering if I could just do my groceries? – This is going to take some more time, isn't it?"

"Yes. – I think, we'll be safe if you pick Fergal up in two hours. It's much better if he and I are on our own in any case. Well, … let's say at ten past eleven, when the bell goes. I'll bring him out to the archway, if that's alright."

Mutti left. She obviously trusted Anne.

Fergal trusted Anne, too!

"Ok, Fergal. If you have to go to the little boys', just tell me."

"Yes, Anne. Thank you!"

"Right! Who smokes in your family."

"Opa does! Opa is German. And Dad does, too! He is Ilish though. I mean Ilish. I can't do it, solly! He smokes cigalettes. Opa smokes big cigalettes. Cigalettes! Solly! Cigals."

"I see. – I hope, you'll never smoke! It makes you quite ill, and after a while your voice sounds no longer nice. You have a very beautiful voice, Fergal, and you are a very beautiful little boy, but when you smoke you'll lose all that, because your skin will go ashen grey! Do your Opa or your Papa cough in the morning?"

“Opa? – I don’t know. I don’t think so. – But Dad does. Leally bad! He says he smokes too much. Sometimes even a hundred!”

“For goodness sakes! Tell him from me to stop, or at least do it elsewhere. – Tell him!”

“I shall. – I like the smell though.”

“Don’t Fergal! They’re saying it causes cancer. – So don’t!”

“Alright.”

“Can you show me how your Papa coughs?”

“How!!!?” This seemed to be turning into an even better game than the writing.

“Well, just sound as he sounds when he coughs.”

“I’ll have to get up to show you.”

“That’s fine.”

When Dad got up early, and he always got up very early, he was very quiet. He quietly shut all doors behind him. Well, there was only the door of Fergal’s parents’ bedroom. Of course, Fergal had to sleep in *their* room. Then, there was the door to the loo.

As soon as the loo door shut behind Dad, he would start singing! He had a beautiful voice, but it was also incredibly loud. Actually, whenever Dad wasn’t talking, he was either singing or whistling. Inside or out, in the car, in the garden, in his little home office, in the back corner of the living room, where the books were. Everywhere. Anywhere. Dad was quite cheerful really!

Mutti wasn’t like that. Mutti said, singing like that, so everyone could hear it, was embarrassing! Mutti was more thoughtful, and listened to music by Bach and Beethoven, thoughtfully.

Dad was more into Chopin, Hank Williams, The Dubliners, and that sort of thing. In fact, once Dad started singing at four or four thirty in the morning, it was very hard to sleep.

Mutti had asked Dad a million times not to sing those loud foreign songs on the loo in the morning. Dad said he wasn’t singing on the loo, because that was reserved for an altogether different effort. He was singing in the bathroom, and, to be precise, in the shower with the door quite shut!

Dad just couldn’t help himself with the singing. He said he was Irish, even though he didn’t like Ireland, because they were all a bunch of ignorant peasants, and Joyce had been right. Dad never said he was Irish in front of anyone but family or Americans. To the world he was English, and after all he had valiantly fought for England in the RAF Post Office and had an English passport, and it would stay that way! Mutti should *never* ask him *not* to sing! It was the Irish way! The sounds of the soul ought not be kept down.

But even asking him to keep it down just a little, *please*, would cause so much offence and bring on such a sulk, it could last for weeks, during which the pitch of his bathroom performances would demonstratively increase.

At the end of each sulk-period Mutti was told she should be quite happy that he didn't start the day with a dance on the bed at three thirty or so. Hands at their sides, all rigid, apart from their legs, the Irish also invented dancing, before the rest of the world had discovered Jesus and knew what poetry and music were!

Dad had showed Fergal how to dance in the garage once just after they had arrived at Geesterheim. The Irish way. Dad had been whistling some most difficult tune like crazy, but his upper body looked as if it was in another world altogehter and all tied up by J, and his legs were going completely mad!

After the sulk-period Dad would also say, Mutti, and the whole family as a matter of fact, should be quite happy that he wasn't altogether Irish, because Irish men beat their wives black and blue, and after that there would always be more children on the way, and the men would get drunk ad infinitum.

In a way, everyone loved him for the constant singing and whistling! With some of the early morning Irish songs Dad would leave out the naughty or brutal bits, he said. Ever since they had moved to Wetchamoonis he had started singing Irish songs again, Mutti said. Mutti also said he never used to, back in England, because he had been embarrassed about being a bit of a Mick, which is a Paddy, or someone from the Emerald, which is Ireland or Éire. The Emerald Isle was also split in half, just like Wetchamoonis. The north was English and called Northern Ireland, but there were no commies, which are bad for business, and Commies are generally thick. The South is the Republic of Ireland. ROI.

That's why his accent also changed to English, because the Irish are a bit of an enemy to the English, and Dad didn't want to be an enemy, so the Second War was his way of showing that he wasn't. Germany was the enemy then. And then Dad got married to a German to show that he really wasn't an enemy generally, and the German was Mutti specifically.

After Dad had the shite beaten out of him, according to J who always incorporated Dad's sad story of destitution and poverty in her nightly weekend horror stories with Fergal as the bad ending, and then Fergal got killed brutally and it was a very happy ending indeed, which cheered Johanna up no end, well, after Dad had the living daylight-shite beaten out of him by his own fat and ugly Mum, because of the other two hundred brothers and sisters Dad had, and after Dad also got beaten senseless by his Pap, and also found that the Franciscans didn't stop hitting him all over the place, Dad had considered his options and buggered off, according to Johanna, on bare feet, because he was so intensely poor, he had to live on his finger and toe nails and the bits of hard skin that form on your feet when you walk around without shoes a lot. Dad had buggered off to Belfast to join the RAF war effort, which was complete paradise, even at age fifteen pretending to be sixteen, at which stage every one in the RAF believed he was twenty, because Dad had looked so haggard an old, according to Johanna, and put him down as eighteen.

Irish is beautiful and can sound a little like American, just softer, and, Dad said, it was, all in all, very much more cultivated because it sings and celebrates the English language.

Fergal didn't explain any of this to Anne, of course! He just started singing at full blast, knowing that with a good, old Irish song, he wouldn't have any trouble with his German *rs*.

"When Oy went home on Monday noight, as drunk as drunk could be, Oy found a horse outside me door, where me old horse should be ...," and so Fergal sang, and he kept on singing, and she was listening and watching really carefully. Towards the end of the song Fergal left out the naughty or brutal bits, because he didn't know how they went, so he just hummed a little "mmh,

mmh-mmh-mmh, mmh-mmh, mmh-mmh …" and so on. And then he sang it all again!

He only really remembered the lyrics for Monday, Tuesday, Saturday and Sunday. But now and then he put in Dad's coughing which was really loud and started like a scream, and that interrupted the song quite a lot! Then he sang on for a little more, and coughed a good deal more. And he always started again where he had interrupted himself coughing. "When Oy went homaaaaaaaaagggggh (spit) …" he didn't actually spit, he just made the sound. He couldn't really spit. Yet! – He kept trying and would just drivel down his front. "… uaaaaaaaggggggghhh (spit … spit) … on Sarday uaaaagggggghhhh (spit) noight as drunk as drunk couldaaaaaaaagggghhh (spit … spit … spit) … could be …" and so on and so on. Leaving out the naughty bits.

Actually, after a while of showing Anne, and his throat was beginning to hurt a lot, there was a knock on the door. Anne didn't answer. She was just staring at Fergal. He had sung the song for her four times!

There came a deep voice from outside the door, "Everything alright in there?"

Anne woke up at that, "Oh, yes! Quite alright! I'm doing German speech training for an English boy, Alois. – It's alright."

The voice outside the door hesitated, "Ah …," then "… it's Ferkel, isn't it, gnädiges Fräulein? The English German kid who used to be mute, yes? Can I come in and watch?"

At that Anne got up, rushed to the door, threw it open to reveal a fat, little, crouching man in a thin blue coat with a very red, big head and no hair on top, who just fell forward into the sunlit room. He had been watching through the keyhole!

Alois got up really fast. He wasn't much bigger than Fergal. His crimson face was the same height as Anne's nice, big chest, and he was staring at it right now.

"Go away, Alois! I'm teaching."

"Sorry, it sounded strange." Alois winked at Fergal and looked straight back at Anne's chest. "Had better get on with it, Fräulein von Allerleben. Sorry 'bout the interruption!" He winked at Fergal again and did a funny gripping movement with his hands. When he had left, Anne explained that he was the caretaker and alright. "Go on, please, Fergal. Coughing." She sat down behind the desk again.

"Uaggg-haggggha-hagggha-haaaaaaghhaa (spit) … I found a horse outside me daaaaaahaaaar whehaggggggahhhaaahhh (spit … spit) uaaaaaaaaaggh (spit … spit) …"

"Ok, that was really great. – Fascinating!" She was still smiling at him. Was her smile getting brighter the more she smiled? Brighter than the sun! Fergal was sure it was. The tingling sensation at the top of his head had now progressed down to his chest.

"Now, pretend to me that you are spitting, but again, don't actually spit, otherwise Alois will complain. Just let it start really deep in your throat. Like this …" she sucked in air really fast through her nose, swallowed and then, … amazing!!! … Mutti would've never, ever, ever in a lifetime, would she have ever done that!

"Ccccccccchhhhhhhhhhhhhhoouipft! – That's what proper spitting sounds like, Fergal! Internationally. – You try it."

"Huuuuaaaagggghgpft!" Fergal could hear it himself. It just didn't sound like Anne's super-spit.

"Try again, … cccchhhhhhhhouipft."

"Cccccccccccchhhhhhhhhhouipft." – That was it! He knew he *had* it now!

Anne clapped her hands and did a little twirl, "That's it, that's it, little man! Welcome to Germany!"

She was the most beautiful woman in the world, apart from Mutti, but Mutti was married to Dad, and apparently that meant a lot. And when Anne had completed her twirl her chest wiggled a little, then it bounced, and then it was still.

Fergal would have dearly liked her not to call him *little man* though. It made him think of Alois the caretaker. Fergal wasn't like that, and he didn't wink at people pretending he shared some kind of secret with them. And he certainly did not do funny squeezy things with his hands.

"OK, Fergal! Now spit this word. – Baaaaaachhhhhhhhhhhouipft."

"Baaaaaachhhhhhhhhhhouipft."

"Super! Now skip the *pft* at the end and say Baaaaaach."

"Baaaaaach!"

"You are doing great, Fergal! – Now shorten the baaaaa and say Bach."

"Bach!"

"You are the best!!! – Now what is Bach in English?"

"It's a little *stream.* And Dad always tells me mole than one wold for the same wold."

"What do you mean? Oh. Yes. *More* and *word.*"

"Yes. – Well, Bach in German is stream in English, and a stream can also be a brook. Deutsch is difficult." His English *rs* were alright for some reason. His German *rs* though were really annoying now. But Anne did not mind, so he minded less too. Anne was very nice!

"Wow, that's very clever! I've just learnt two new words. Stream and brook. Thank you, Fergal! Bach was also a German composer of the Baroque."

"I know Bach and I like the Beatles. And the Lolling Stones sound bettel. But don't tell Mutti. *Wow* is not Gelman, Anne. It's Scottish, Dad says, and Amelicans say it a lot. It means 'absolutely gleat'."

"You don't have many friends your own age here yet, do you, Fergal?"

"No, not leally. When I played mute my palents and even Johanna talked to me a lot, and I had to see a lot of doctols. Johanna is my sistel. Sistel J or just J. She's six yeals oldel than I."

"That's a lot."

"She's at Gymnasium in Hot Dog."

"Hot Dog?"

"Yes, Flankfult."

"I see. So you played mute. I was told you had a laryngeal defect."

"I don't know what that is."

"Your larynx contains your vocal chords, and when you breathe you can speak, because air makes them vibrate."

"The lalynx contains the vocal cholds and ail makes them viblate so I can speak."

"You are very bright, Fergal. I must see to it that you start in year two straightaway rather than one. And you need some friends your own age. They might make you sit a basic year-one maths test, though. Are you good at counting too?"

"I don't know. I can lead my watch. Mutti has been doing maths with me because they all thought I was vely stupid. What is viblate, Anne?"

"OK. What is five plus three?"

"Eight."

"Wow. And ten plus ten?"

"Twenty."

"Wow! – What number can you count up to?"

"I don't like numbels much, Anne. Nine-hundled and ninety-nine. J made me. It took five houls, almost. And she didn't dlown me, and I got loads of man-points. And I knew aftel that it's a thousand. But I don't like that. What does viblate mean?"

"Can you multiply?"

"J has taught me the ten-times table. But I hate it. What does viblate mean?"

"You are quite stubborn! Look, Fergal! I'm only trying to help, because you might find year one very boring. Do you know what the larynx is then?"

"Yes, nevel mind lalynx! Viblate! But I'll meet my new fliends there."

"True. OK. Vibrate is what a car does when you start it's engine. Vibrating is like rattling."

"Not Dad's car it doesn't. One's a V8 and we have a V12 also," said Fergal in English.

"Ha! I understood you!" Anne continued in German, "Well, when I start my Beetle it vibrates. And you want to be careful saying that to your new friends, because no one likes a show-off."

"I wasn't showing off, Anne! I was only stating fact."

"Uooh! Stating fact, and larynx. Well, I have never heard that come from a five-year old! Please, do speak German with me again."

"So, viblate is lattle?"

"And moving up and down and side to side without any specific direction. – Do you have a garage with a metal gate?"

"Yes. Two. We can get four cars in."

"Don't say it like that! That's arrogant! That's showing off!"

"Arrogant is showing off."

"Yes! – Do you ever use it for a goal when you play football with … your dad?" Anne was really smiling all the time. Somehow it was magic. Fergal really thought her smile was getting brighter and brighter just like the sun from outside. But that was impossible, wasn't it? Otherwise your mouth would just wrap itself round your head. And that's exactly what her mouth looked like now, although she thought he was arrogant and a show-off. Fergal loved Anne a lot. Totally!

"Dad doesn't play. Dad works! – But I have one friend downstairs. Chuck is a tennis star and he will be famous! He can't wipe himself yet but plays great soccer. We play, and sometimes, …" Fergal had to shake his head at this, "sometimes J plays soccer with me too. It's more like playing ball then. And she just throws the ball at me."

"Right."

"Well, Johanna laughs at me. She says, I'm not a great sports person at all! Dad says neither was Churchill. Churchill said *No sports!* And Churchill was a happy chappy without sports, apart from the Black Dog, which Dad will tell be about when I grow up." – For the first time ever, since he could remember, Fergal *did* enjoy just talking! He could have gone on all day! He knew why this was. It was Anne! Fergal was in love.

"OK. When you hit the ball against the garage door it vibrates."

"I see. Like your boobies when you speak and move."

Anne sat down and started laughing like Fergal had never seen Mutti laugh, especially when the body was mentioned. Anne had tears in her eyes when she said, "There is a man in there already, isn't there? You definitely need year two or three. – Listen, Fergal! I'll really do my best to convince those two shrews upstairs. It might not work. I can't promise. But maybe."

"What are shrews?"

"Oh, never mind, Fergal!"

"May I touch your boobies, please?"

To Fergal's great surprise Anne nodded. This was the most exciting day in his life so far! Slowly did he walk over, and then he squeezed. They felt not like balloons filled with water at all, more like … he had no idea and squeezed again.

"Gently, Fergal! They are quite sensitive. When your mother had you, her breasts might have been similar."

"No, Mutti has no breasts at all! She's like a boy really. I think if she ate more sweets they might grow. Jam would be ok. How old are you?"

"What … jam?"

"Dad says if people eat more sweets they'll cheer up and become more like women. During the war we should have dropped more jam on Germany."

"True!" Anne laughed. "I love sweeties. Might be a good idea with all this Cold War nonsense. Jam for the Russians and Americans. And I am twenty-three, Fergal."

"Your breasts feel so soft and much nicer than my pillow! First I thought it's like there is water inside like when you fill a balloon with water for the garden battle and J makes me catch it five times and then it bursts. This is more like jelly!"

She took Fergal's hand and gently moved it off her breasts, "Sorry, they do hurt! I have a little Fergal coming."

"Oh, no! Anne! You are married! – This is terrible!" – Fergal wanted to die!

She laughed, "Why is that?"

Fergal loved Anne. And now his hopes had been dashed! And she was much too old anyway. When he was twenty, she was going to be … forty-eight. That was ancient! Mummy-ancient! But it didn't matter. He would love her, come what may!

He *had* to tell Anne!

Otherwise they might *never* meet one another again!

He didn't hesitate, "Because I fuck you very much!"

Anne's jaw dropped hard and quick, until it could go no further. She was obviously surprised at this turn of events. Maybe she loved Fergal as much!

"And, I thought, you could fuck me too. And then …"

Anne's upper body was moving back, away from Fergal, as if he had said something very wrong. She shut her mouth. Her smile was more of a frown now.

"… then, we could get married, and we would fuck each other so much until we die!"

Anne puffed up her cheeks and exhaled hard. – She sounded very stern when she said, "Now, listen! And sit! Over there, Fergal!"

"Why?"

"Because, … *I* say so!"

"OK."

"That is one of the *worst* words the German language has on offer! There is another word, but this one is almost as bad, … I think. And you don't ever say that to anyone! It's language hell, and it betrays your state of mind and culture." Anne wasn't shouting this. She did sound serious and intense though.

"Why?" Fergal's bottom lip was trembling. Oh, no! He was going to cry! What had he done wrong now?

"Because I say so! Who taught you this word? – Come on!"

"I can't say. It's a secret!" He was crying now. Just a little. "And if I tell you, … I get tickled, smothered, or … drowned for a while for the man-points."

"Oh, my goodness gracious me! It's your sister, isn't it? That Johanna J! But, God in Heaven, … she's only elelven, isn't she? Where does she get …!? Six years is simply too great a difference in age. What else has she taught you!?"

Fergal related to Anne as quickly as possible his repertoire of English J-words, "Shit, turd, shithead, epileptic idiot, spastic idiot, fuck, fuckwit, sad fucker …" and continued in German, "… Arsch, Arschloch, Arschgeige, Scheiße, wandelnder Scheißhaufen, Misthaufen, Arschficker, schwule Sau, Spastiker, ficken, Fickmaul, …"

Anne, … eyes wide, … mouth open, … but she was still *so* beautiful, "Stop right there! *Never* say these things to anyone! Even if you are angry with them or even in jest or if you want to hurt them. Never!"

"J told me that if I liked somebody really *a lot,* and if I wanted to show how well I spoke German I should say to them that I *really* fuck them, *ich bin ganz verfickt in Dich, ich ficke Dich so sehr*!"

"Hey! Stop, stop, stop! Your sister is quite dis … naughty. She is very, very naughty, Fergal! And you have *no* idea what *fu* … that word means?" Anne blushed.

"Anne! I do know the other words are not good! But fuck is a *really* good word. Really liking somebody. Like love. Believe me!"

"No, it isn't! And it doesn't mean that! It's a word that pulls something *really* beautiful like love down, and … it tries to drag it through the mud."

"I don't understand!"

"I will leave it up to your Mutti to explain that to you, … when the time is right!"

"When is the time right?"

"When she says so and explains it to you! But I gather you will find out … here at school … soon enough before Mutti can explain it to you."

"What's the *other* bad German word then? You said, the one which is like *fuck*?"

"Shush!!! Don't *say* that word, Fergal! It sounds truly awful coming from someone like you!" – Unexpectedly, Anne was smiling again! And she was even laughing a little, shaking her head. She got up, came over to Fergal, lifted him up a little and hugged him really hard.

Fergal didn't really like Anne lifting him up like that, … even a little! It made him feel like a little kid! Her breasts though were really soft against his face. It was lovely! But after a while it became like a game of smopil. J hadn't played smopil with him in a month … thankfully! It had nothing to do with him having regained his speech, J claimed. She had to study a lot at the moment. J said this was only a reprieve, "Only for the time being, little *Arschgeige!*"

Anne smelt lovely!

Fergal couldn't breathe.

"I can't breathe!"

She released him gently and put her hands on his shoulder.

He panted, "You are still the best smelling woman in the world! Even before Oma! And I still fu …, no, … I like you very much, Anne!"

"Thank you! I like you, too, Fergal. A lot! You are the strangest little fellow I have ever come across. You are really not very German at all. And I mean that as a compliment. I hope you'll stay that way."

"What way?"

"Your way. Open and direct and … just funny! You make me smile. You even made that skirt-chaser, Alois, smile. And he normally just leers."

"You are funny, too. – What's leer?"

"Not now, Fergal! Ask your mother. – Anyway, I didn't know I was *that* funny! I suppose I try my best. But being funny isn't always allowed in Germany, unless it is planned for and organised and has it's right place and time and lots of beer, … or else. But you'll find out! Never lose that smirk of yours either, will you?"

"Do I smirk?"

"Yes. And have you noticed …!?"

"What?"

"Without any of my doing, really, … and a bit of spitting, … you have not only managed the German *ch*-sound but also your *rs*, I just realised. You turned the *ch* into *r* somehow. – It's still at the back of your throat, but it's coming forward."

Fergal couldn't believe it! Anne was right! He felt so intensely happy now! – This meant … he wouldn't go to monster school, after all! J had told him all about the monster schools of Wetchamoonis. Little idiots who couldn't speak would go there to be slaughtered and turned into sausage. This had been one of his sister's many happy endings to one of her love-horror stories. Fergal dead, turned into sausage! World relieved. Happy ending!

"Thank you, Anne!"

"You are very welcome, Mr. Herr Fergal Bulhof-Murphy. And you will *definitely* find the right wife one day, and then you can like a lot, as *much* as you like, that is … if she likes to be liked." Anne laughed.

"You mean like *each other* a lot!"

"And that too, Fergal."

"Thank you so much, Anne!" Fergal raised his arm, "Heil Hitler!" – This was *definitely* the best time he had ever had since arriving here in Wetchamoonis!

Wetchamoonis was becoming better and better! Anne *definitely* had no Dalek spiders in her, and Fergal wouldn't need the Tardis. In a very short space of time he had learnt a lot down here in the cellar which was called the lower ground floor, … *das Untergeschoß.*

But now Anne was frowning again!

"Did your sister teach you that one too?" She actually looked more serious than ever.

"No, Anne. Frau von Brechwitz did, so one finds one's friends. And Frau von Brechwitz needs friends. Mutti says *Heil Hitler* is not right! But Mutti isn't always right, and you are only the second person who frowns, which means it is not right to say *Heil Hitler.* Mutti's world is full of Peter Files and Peter Asts of the Mitschnacker family, and people used to run around burning like torches and screaming, and then they died, twitching and quivering from the boom-boom, and their body fat would run out of them like oil."

"Good Lord!" Anne was breathing heavily. It was as if she was trying to calm herself down. "Your mother is right, of course, and wants only your best. You have to believe that, Fergal! Knowing history is the way to peace!" – Anne told him, just like Mutti, that saying *Heil Hitler* did not mean that you were finding your real friends. It dated back to a time in Germany, which had been very bad and caused many people to die *horrible* deaths! She said, it wasn't actually all that long ago. The bad time had ended just before she was born in '48. But for Fergal 1945 to 1971 was twenty-six years, and that was ancient. Anne called twenty-six years *more than a quarter of a century,* and that made it even longer! In 1945 it had all ended! It had been supposed to last for a thousand years, but had lasted, thankfully, only twelve! It had caused a lot of terrible damage!

Anne said there were still a lot of people in Germany who would like this man, Adolf Hitler, back because he had brought order and work and the Autobahn and the Beetle. Frau von

Brechwitz had been a very big SS-Nazi who had lost her husband and three sons at the Eastern Front.

"I know!" Fergal exclaimed. "Mutti says there were a lot of angry Russians, and they were hungry also, and then they kicked the Nazis out, but they weren't all Nazis, and they were so hungry, they cut them open and ate them, and then …"

"Shush, Fergal! It was horrible!" – Frau von Brechwitz was waiting for the departure of all foreigners and the return of a *Germanic* order. Von Brechwitz believed that Hitler would return, as other people believed Jesus would return. The Second Coming of order!

"Anne! I know!" interjected Fergal again, "Jesus is Irish and called Seamus really. He was undercover in Israel. Dad knows these things!"

"Nonsense! – You can tell your sister *and* your father, they should stop telling you nonsense and lies, OK! Tell them, … Fergal takes too much on board! They have to tell you real things, not all this nonsense!"

"How can I tell them?"

"Oh, … you just say *nonsense* next time, especially when your sister tells you one of her special secrets. – It's easy. Say it!"

"*Nonsense*, Anne!"

"Exactly!!!"

Somehow Fergal trusted Anne just as much as Opa. And now he had found out that J was really full of nonsense. "Frau von Brechwitz says I look like Hitler, and I am rebirth."

Anne threw her arms in the air, "Oh, my God! This woman has lost it! Completely!" She exhaled hard. "Look, Fergal! – It is unprofessional of me to talk of a colleague … but … Brechwitz is *very* strange … and sad, … but altogether … harmless … unless … you take her … seriously … or give her power, which is the same I suppose! Let's just be grateful she isn't in power! Don't always believe what other people say, OK!"

"OK. Why am I rebirth?"

"Rebirth is the belief that we are reborn into another new baby-body, when we have died already as an old person. And we keep coming back forever. You say *I am the rebirth of, I have been reborn.*"

"Like three mirrors and seeing your own bottom forever!"

She smiled, "Yes, like that!" – Anne scrutinised Fergal for a little. There was shuffling outside. Possibly Alois! Anne shook her head, "Believe you me! You do not look anything like Hitler. And if … if there is rebirth, he might come back as something very unpleasant. Something …"

"Like a spider."

"Spiders are quite useful. – I think, Fergal, … you are healed now! Welcome to German school!"

Fergal decided not to say *Heil Hitler* again. Thus far, he had managed to make two people he was very fond of *very* angry. Mutti and Anne. Brechwitz was *not* a friend. Just very scary!

The bell rang! It was ten past eleven already. – Time really slipped through your fingers when you were enjoying yourself. His time with Anne had seemed like ten minutes!

A mass of children poured out of their classrooms. Screaming, laughing, some crying. Satchels were being thrown into the air. A surprise announce had been made. The summer holidays would start today! It was simply too hot.

A tiny girl with thick, horn-rimmed glasses and a patch over her left eye was bawling her eyes out. Someone had smashed her slate, broken her slate pencil and stolen her sponge. Where was her satchel? The world was coming to an end. She couldn't find her satchel. A teacher went over to comfort her. So, there wasn't just horrible Frau Kellergeister!

A healed and almost German Fergal discerned the little creature was obviously a first-year, considering her academic paraphernalia. He might not have to be with such little people! He might start at year two, or even three! J would kill him if she found out, her monster brother wouldn't be killed at monster school!

Outside, Mutti was waiting under the archway. It was stiflingly hot and dusty. The sound of crickets seemed to be all-round. It was beautiful! How different it was out here! You didn't have to go to school to appreciate this.

Anne spoke quietly to Mutti. Fergal couldn't hear them. Mutti nodded and frowned … a lot. Then Anne said goodbye. She wouldn't do any more speech lessons here as she was going to

Damage Fun

have her child at home in Frankfurt. She didn't know whether she was actually going to continue working. Her husband was a French Canadian and didn't like it much in Germany. They hadn't decided where to go in the world yet, but the World was a big place.

After Fergal's performance today they might go to Ireland. Anne had winked at Fergal. Not at all like Alois. "I'm going to call my child Fergal, male or female, come what may."

Mutti looked proud. Fergal was very unhappy that he would never see Anne again! He just had to cry like a man who couldn't hide. Men don't cry! So Fergal hid behind Mutti.

Anne gave him another smopil hug. Then something very serious happened. Anne shook Fergal's hand like a grownup, "All the best, Fergal! You'll be alright. And remember the problem is gone! Now speak as much as you like, but do it carefully."

He watched her leave with Mutti, because they needed a private moment, which was even more grownup.

When Anne started her white Beetle Fergal really understood what *vibrate* means. As he watched the Beetle disappear up the lane towards Frankfurt Fergal vibrated his entire body until Mutti told him to stop.

On the way home he cried a little more because he had just lost the second love of his life. First Jenny, then Anne.

Mutti said, lunch would have to wait until Johanna got back from school. In any case, she would have to talk to him about certain *things,* and to Johanna about a certain *word* she had incorrectly related to her little brother. Johanna would be back home around two.

Two o'clock!

That was two hours and twenty minutes until grub, said Mickey Mouse. Gloria and Chuck would be in the same class if Fergal started in year one. If he started as a second-year he wouldn't know anybody!

Never mind. Mutti and Anne would decide what was best.

Two o'clock! He wouldn't be allowed to eat until then. Eating in-between meals made you fat, and currently Fergal was on one of Mutti's special diets. This meant no food in-between meals, not even Milky Way even though it was so light it even floated in milk as it said in the German commercial on telly. The special diet also meant less food at mealtimes. Apparently, eating less made you stronger, and so did watching less telly because it was like bad food for the mind.

Mutti had a lot of American books about children and diets. The pictures in her books showed exquisite looking food on white plates, but when Mutti cooked it, it sort of looked quite different and very boring. But that wouldn't have mattered *really,* had it only tasted nice! You could eat a Milky Way in the dark without cutlery and it still tasted great!

Fergal was very sad about never seeing Anne ever again! His hunger didn't improve the situation. The *Problem* was over … and he trusted Anne to know this.

The new diet was supposed to be even better, Mutti promised!

What new diet? Fergal shuddered.

Mother and son had been ambling home slowly. If you walked normally, it wouldn't take you longer than a couple of minutes. For a grownup it must be half the time.

The lane was almost deserted now.

Six weeks and one-and-a-half days to go until school. Then four more years until Gymnasium, … and then another nine years until your school finals, the important Abitur, which would get you into university! And then another five to eight years or even longer at university …

That was a long time!

Fergal shuddered again. He didn't know why.

For now, … six weeks and one-and-a-half-days to go!

Frau Kellergeister's Line-Up And The SS Pastor

The first day at school started at church at seven forty-five in the morning. It was late August. The old men sitting on the bench around the ancient oak in the marketplace said, *surely, this had to be the hottest summer ever!* But they always said that in summer.

Forty-four degrees this early wasn't bad. Admittedly, the thermometer reading had been taken in the sun on the balcony by Mutti. Dad said it was about twenty-eight, maybe thirty. Still. Quite hot!

Despite Anne's recommendation, the director of Geesterheim's Lutheran Primary School, Frau Kellergeister, had decided that Fergal was *not* to be treated as a special case! And the fact that he could read, write, speak German, Chamoonian, and English, and even do second-year maths was a parental delusion. Not to get upset, ... all parents were like that, and Frau Kellergeister knew best! Giving the little terrors special treatment like that would only go to their little heads and would create big terrors later in life.

Whatever parents had to say was in any case just antiauthoritarian claptrap! *Anpassung*, *Unterwerfung* and *Gehorsam!* Adjustment, submission and obedience were the Kellergeister-leitmotif. Without these attributes society could not work! These attributes were the ingredients of discipline. Discipline followed on from a sound and unshakable belief in authority. Authority had to be exerted!

Fergal didn't mind. – He was going to make friends.

Twenty-two children with parents and, in some cases grandparents and great-grandparents, filled the pews at Saint Mary's, not forgetting all the other unrelated villagers who managed to cram into church for the spectacle year after year.

It was hard to tell exactly how unrelated these villagers really were as a healthy amount of incest was still being practiced merrily. – There were the ones with the funny neck, and the ones with the tick. The ones who had the strange crooked hand, always held up in front of their chests. The ones with the Habsburg-lip, and those who had the misfortune of eyebrows so fat, male or female, they would almost cover their eyes.

All children were clutching their customary sugar cones, only just a little smaller than their owners, brimming over with sweets. – In Germany every first-year was given a huge cone made of cardboard and filled with goodies for their first day at school.

At the top of the cone a layer of crêpe paper tied with a pretty ribbon prevented most children from having their sweets until they got back home in the late morning. Most children! These were antiauthoritarian days! And Chuck was outside the church throwing up a good kilo of Mars bars, Milky Ways, Gummi Bears, boiled sweets, swallowed whole, and magnanimous amounts of marshmallows.

Chuck missed his first day at school, but so did his mother, who had overslept. After much retching outside the porta coeli, sedate Herr Nolde had to carry Chuck home quietly.

Fergal was very proud of the whole first-day-at-school affair, and so were Mutti and Dad. There was a lot of shouting going on at the front by the altar. Pastor Meinheit had joined the ranks of the Lutheran Church for atonement after the war. He had done his bit as a young man in an SS Panzer division in the East, hadn't liked at all what he'd seen there, especially during the hurried retreat West, so God was his new leader now, and he'd be forgiven for whatever, come what may.

As a pastor he suffered from the great disadvantage of not being able to speak soothingly or quietly at all, nor was he in any way equipped to cause any kind of reverential feeling, or at least attention, in the congregation. It was a vicious circle really.

Rumour had it that Pastor Meinheit was beating his son Bernhardt quite badly because of his religious frustrations with the flock. There was no wife to Meinheit, no mother to Bernhardt. A sad village story kept secret from outsiders' ears.

The pastor's son, Bernhardt should have been here too today! He wasn't. – Rumour had it he was recuperating from one of his father's educational sessions. Six-year-old Bernhardt was nearly as big as his father and looked more like a ten year old.

The louder Pastor Meinheit shouted his indistinct first-year sermon, the louder the congregation was communicating amongst itself. The more Herr Leuschner tried to convey to his attractive pew neighbour, Frau Merck, that her daughter was surely one day going to be as pretty as Frau Merck herself, "Pardon?", the louder that fat idiot of a Pastor was shouting.

"Pardon?"

"I said fat idiot of a Pastor!"

"Yes. I heard that! Where is your wife, Herr Leuschner!?"

Screaming Pastor Meinheit, "In the kingdom of God all are equal. Education for only the few who can afford it is unjust. Our education is the best in the …" at which stage Pastor Meinheit was drowned out completely. – There was a party going on below him in the relative obscurity of the main nave, and Meinheit was missing it.

The prolific abundance of excited children, who had brought the whole of their family tree along, guaranteed a sound pitch so impenetrable, even the deepest of bass voices, as Pastor Meinheit's, was drowned out completely! The church was filled with one, long scream to high heaven for twenty minutes.

An offer of red wine for those confirmed.

Eucharist!

At this time of day?!

Lord, no! – Meinheit had to be joking.

The sign of the cross was cast over all from above.

Bye-bye!

Still screaming at top-pitch, to the highest of happy heavens, the children ran out. Fergal amongst them.

Gloria was there with her mother.

Parents started chatting.

Meinheit banged the huge celestial gate shut, from the inside. There was a massive, hollow echo.

No one cared.

A crowd of just under three-hundred people made their short way along the high wall to Geesterheim's primary school. – There was a narrow little path leading down directly from the back of the church to the school, but no one ever took it. Mönchsgasse was fine!

Frau Kellergeister and Frau Brechwitz were unsmilingly waiting under the archway. All children gathered outside with their parents at their backs in the lane.

Frau Kellergeister raised her hand for attention. Everyone was quiet immediately. – Frau Kellergeister exuded natural authority and steadfast discipline.

Fergal himself thought she looked six-hundred and twenty years old, with something of a very dry desert carrot about her.

The carrot spoke. "Absolute silence! – Parents! Take your children's cones and go home! *Now*! Your children *now* belong to me! I rule here, and I do not tolerate dissent! Any dissent with an established rule, or authority, causes doubt in a child's mind. Doubt is a child's worst enemy! It causes the wrong kind of revolution. Let the child doubt, when, and if then it manages to get as far as university and study philosophy. Here, I will teach *your* children concentration, so they might one day doubt with dedication. Adjustment, submission, obedience! This is what I also ask of you. I ask of you not to interfere! Your children need clarity now! And *only* discipline can give them that. For the educated amongst you remember *non scholae sed vitae discimus*. We learn for life, not for school! – Have a good day."

With that she turned on her heel, and von Brechwitz' crooked finger indicated the children follow Frau Kellergeister, *or else!*

"In Reih und Glied! Zu zweien! At once! Everyone take your neighbour's hand! March, march!"

There was some *Yuck! Her! She smells* or *He's sick! I won't take his hand! I'd rather die!* going on, but all Brechwitz had to do for complete silence was scream "Ruhe!" at the top of her voice with her seriously mad-looking fragmented steel-eyes, and all doubts about the cleanliness of your neighbour's hand or character were allayed!

To Fergal this was all a bit amusing. He had never heard any grownup annunciate like Kellergeister, or scream quite as seriously, furiously as Brechwitz!

What was this?

Shouldn't parents now realise their children were being actively threatened by some very mad dimwits? *Fuckwit* was a

Johanna-word. It made a lot of more sense in the context. Fergal had promised though, never to use that *bad-bad* word ever again! He had also promised never to swear again. He would do it in his mind.

Thankfully, Fergal had been standing next to Gloria all the time. Gloria was in top form today and not jerky at all. Just her neck was moving a little now and then.

Parents left in a cloud of dust. Parents gone! An absolutely frightening moment! – In the column of children neatly filed up ahead of Gloria and Fergal, little voices started crying, but the level of fear was such already that it was being done quietly.

These were the beginnings of discipline!

In the inner yard a long straight row of chairs had been lined up in the shade under the old chestnut by the fifteenth century building everyone knew as the Schafshütte, the Sheep's Hut. It was a building especially dedicated to religious education by SS Pastor Meinheit.

"Halt! Stillgestanden! Achtung! Mädchen hinsetzen! Buben hinter die Mädchen stellen! Lächeln! Jetzt werdet Ihr photographiert!"

Halt! Stand still! Attention! Girls sit! Boys stand behind girls! You will now be photographed!

This was for the first-year photograph.

Because von Brechwitz had given the order, everyone did their best *zu lächeln*, … to smile!

Fergal didn't! – This was far too serious for any type of smile by miles. He felt threatened to the core. Everyone, including Fergal, took their positions. Everyone, bar Fergal, was grinning like a bedlamite fond of chewing grass all day.

Fergal was *not* going to grin like that!

SS Pastor Meinheit was making his descent, with eyes shut and hands folded as in prayer in front of his enormous bulk, down the steps of the Schafshütte. His huge black robe, with its yards of shirred fabric gathered at the back, swayed around him like a gigantic bell of doom waiting to chime a dissonance so horrific Fergal would surely pass out. The two white bands below his collar were starched rigid.

Fergal knew that German judges looked similar. He had seen it in the history books and the newspapers at home. But suddenly SS Pastor Meinheit stopped and ran back up the steps inside again to emerge only seconds later with an old box camera for portraits, attached to what looked like an incredibly heavy tripod made of wood and brass, which couldn't be carried by one man alone, surely. – SS Pastor Meinheit seemed to manage just fine. He was enormous and looked very strong!

On top of his booming voice, a lethal combination producing a show of strength so intimidating, one might want to swiftly reconsider any disagreement with him, just in case of any theoretically arising, silly disputes, as also his right hand on its own seemed large enough to wrap itself safely around one's entire head whilst still writing a complicated letter to God.

Frau Kellergeister was standing in the shadows of the chestnut. She, like Brechwitz, had her hands folded in front of her. Brechwitz looked nervous out of the safe environment of her office domain. Kellergeister didn't. Kellergeister was watching! Carefully.

Her children were now ready to be photographed. She asked Brechwitz to go inside, as it was too hot for her condition. Brechwitz walked off gratefully and disappeared in the main building where her realm was, her safe Reich.

SS Pastor Meinheit had erected the camera and tripod and was now waiting for Frau Kellergeister's sign. Kellergeister walked up and down the line of sitting girls and standing boys. *Mädels und Buben!*

Twice did Kellergeister make the pass, twice did her inspection stop briefly at Fergal. The third time she marched towards where Meinheit and his camera were waiting like a hot mammoth who had just rid himself of his strange triple-tusks. She stopped. Faced heavily perspiring Meinheit.

"Herr Pastor, what, in your considered opinion, is wrong with this picture?"

"Nothing, Frau Direktorin! All looks fine to me." Meinheit could obviously not be bothered.

A pause.

A smile.

Frau Kellergeister's quiet, trained voice, audible enough for anyone in range to hear clearly from Africa to Australia, "Ferkel!"

As if on cue everyone started laughing. Everyone knew *who* was called *piglet* for real! Foreigners were strange! How could parents possibly call their poor child *Ferkel?*

Frau Kellergeister's right hand released itself from its resting place and went up to command silence, "Achtung! Ruhe! Sofort!"

Everyone was quiet in an instant. Kellergeister didn't need to shout to Africans and Australians anymore, "Ferkel!"

"Ja?" Fergal. Very quiet. Invisibility would have been great at this moment!

"Ferkel, come forward! All others keep smiling, and don't stop, or else!"

Fergal walked round the line of chairs and went up to Frau Kellergeister. Halfway she approached him. Before he knew what had happened, did he find himself lying in the dust. She had slapped his face so hard and quick the pain and realization hadn't even kicked in yet, the shear physical force from above though had been of real immediacy.

Fergal was tasting Geesterheimer's dusty sand in his mouth and swallowed a bit of grit. Geesterheim's soil became much better further west where the long fields of vines started. Fergal started crying. And he so didn't want to cry in front of his class. Everyone was very careful to keep smiling. It would be very hard now to make any real friends. He was a crybaby!

Kellergeister took him by the scruff of his neck and picked him up as if he weighed next to nothing. Fergal's feet lifted off the dust. A dangling, naughty, runty puppy, she was contemplating to drown in a sack.

"What's wrong with this picture, Herr Pastor?" she asked Fergal quietly.

"I'm afraid, I don't know, Frau Kellergeister."

"I will tell you! The child is wasting everybody's time, hence everybody's *precious* time at being educated. Do you know why?"

"No," said Meinheit looking at the clear blue sky. Strange. He seemed quite a soft man. Not like some hard SS hero.

"No," whimpered Fergal.

"The child didn't smile when asked *nicely* to smile. Whosoever does not respond to a polite request will be given another request more severe." Frau Kellergeister did not have to raise her voice even a little bit. Fergal understood perfectly well, even though he had found it hard to follow her, as his left ear was hurting badly. She put the runt down. Either Fergal was incredibly light, or she was an enormously strong woman to have kept him up in the air like that!

"Now, let's clean you up." She patted the dust off his grey shorts, blue shirt and linen summer jacket. From a concealed pocket in her black wool skirt she pulled a tortoise shell comb. She combed Fergal's hair. "There, Ferkel! A parting looks much better on you than this modern, antiauthoritarian hippy hair." She gave him a little push, "Off you go! And don't forget to smile!"

There was a first time for everything.

This was the first time in his life Fergal smiled without meaning it.

When Fergal was back standing in line behind the girls, Kellergeister raised her index finger. The endemic German index finger. A phrase Dad had coined. With Kellergeister it was more than endemic. It could mean *or else* or *attention* or *listen.* Generally, it was meant as a threat. In Kellergeister's case it meant everything a raised index finger could, plus pain. Unspeakable pain!

"Everybody! Keep smiling! Say, *Thank you, Frau Kellergeister.*"

With a smile, a choir of friendly voices chirped, "Thank you, Frau Kellergeister!"

"Because," Frau Kellergeister chirped happily, "today is our first day at school, and Frau Kellergeister has just demonstrated … with Ferkel's help," she nodded at Fergal, "thank you, Ferkel, … that disobeying is undisciplined and *will* be punished!"

Without prompting, the choir repeated its, "Thank you, Frau Kellergeister!" with a smile.

"Keep smiling! Girls, close your legs and put your hands flat on your knees! Boys stand straight! Smile and look at the camera! Herr Pastor …!"

Two weeks later, when the photographs had been developed Mutti said "How wonderful!" to Fergal, and later in the evening, when Dad had come home, Fergal overheard Dad say, he had never seen cheery-happy Fergal so sad in his whole life! – Dad said, he was going to put an end to the beatings. Mutti said, it wasn't as bad as it had been back in their own days. Dad agreed but said, Fergal looked much too unhappy, and that way the only thing their son would ever learn was to associate learning with pain and idiots in authority. – Johanna-Frances had never been hit in her life.

Never mind! Discipline hurt, Fergal thought philosophically. All his classmates were really in the same boat as he.

After the didactic photo shoot in the cooling shade of the chestnut tree another surprise was waiting inside their ever first classroom for every first-year.

No one was exempt this time!

Another surprise so special to Kellergeister, it had been kept a secret since 1936 every Geesterheimer grownup knew of.

All children were ordered to choose a desk partner. Boy had to find girl, and girl boy. Strictly mixed.

The tiny desks seated two.

There was a lot of commotion and *Yuck, not her!* and *Yuck, not him, he's smelly!* Strangely, Frau Kellergeister let it pass and everyone settled in without any raised fingers.

Frau Kellergeister was writing something on the blackboard. Fergal sat with Gloria right in the middle. Pastor Meinheit stood himself placidly in front of the door, blocking it with his huge frame. He shut his eyes, folded his hands and seemed to pray again.

Soon Frau Kellergeister was finished. She had written a long poem on the blackboard.

"We will sing this every morning! Pick up a copy from my desk when you go back home for the day. Make your parents teach it to you so you can sing it by heart tomorrow or else! Do you understand!?"

A hubbub of children's voice, *Yes!* and *No!* and, "What's she saying!? Is she mad?"

An enormous crash from Frau Kellergeister's desk!

Utter silence in the pit!

Kellergeister was holding a long, wooden ruler aloft like a baton. She smashed it down on her desk again. Everybody flinched! It made the most incredibly loud noise. Fergal thought it sounded a bit like a shot being fired from a pistol. One of Dad's friends at USAF Ramstein had once shown Fergal how loud a pistol was.

"You say *Yes! Thank you, Frau Kellergeister!*"

"Yes! Thank you, Frau Kellergeister!"

"Do you understand?"

"Yes! Thank you, Frau Kellergeister!"

"Good. Very good! – Now, who of you can read this song?"

Gloria and Fergal's arms shot up.

"Anyone else? – Apart from a foreigner and a spast … a girl!"

"No! Frau Kellergeister!"

"Ferkel, come to the blackboard … and … read!"

This was going to be almost exciting! Fergal dashed to the blackboard to read out aloud to his first larger audience. When he got there Frau Kellergeister was already waiting for him. She slapped his face again. "Don't run. Walk!"

Fergal didn't cry although the pain was atrocious, "Sorry, Frau Kellergeister!" He was getting good at this!

"Read. Let's see if it's true then."

Fergal started reading.

Die Fleißigen Handwerker	*Diligent Craftsmen*
Wer will fleißige Handwerker seh'n,	*Who wants to see diligent craftsmen at work*
Der muß zu uns Kindern geh'n	*Then, come, and see us children work*
Stein auf Stein, Stein auf Stein,	*Stone on stone, stone on stone,*
Das Häuschen wird bald fertig sein, ...	*Our little house be ready soon,*
	…

And so it went on for another nine stanzas covering all the crafts and people who went to Hauptschule only, according to J. J, the Doctor! No one was left out. Bricklayers, glaziers, painters, carpenters, shoemakers, tailors, bakers. And two more stanzas, inserted cleverly in-between, got the singer moving and dancing with his hands in the air. Fergal wasn't going to move and dance. He was just going to read. And read he did! Fluently.

When he was finished Frau Kellergeister and even Herr Pastor Meinheit were making really big eyes. They were obviously very proud of him! He was going to be congratulated for having done so well! Frau Kellergeister came over to Fergal with a smile and hit him with the full force of the back of her hand over his right cheek. Fergal flew backwards on the floor. This time the pain had hit instantly! He was not going to cry. And he didn't! Not crying felt like a *huge* success to him. He noticed that she alternated cheeks.

She addressed class with Fergal still lying under the blackboard. Now was the time for the notorious Kellergeister scream, "Ferkel … might be able to *read* … but when one has not been taught *properly* … it makes no *difference*! Ferkel is *not* different. Ferkel is not *special*, you *hear*! Neither is *Gloria*, the *spa* … the *different* girl, who can also *read* … but has some problems with her … body! We are all the same here in *my* class!" She looked at Fergal with a smile of approval, and said quietly, "Thank you, Ferkel! – Now get back to your seat and do *not* run."

Fergal returned to his seat. Not *too* fast. *Not* too slow.

Gloria was very jerky but managed to tell Fergal that his face was really red and there was blood in his ear. Fergal didn't care. Fergal was hard! And then Fergal started sobbing really hard. It was embarrassing. Frau Kellergeister did not reprimand him.

The scream continued, "Now, *children*, to understand my discipline, I shall now teach *you* a very *special* lesson, which I have to say has become a little bit of a tradition over the years. Fergal is exempt from this. – Everyone … stand up!"

She sat down at her desk, opened the class book, which was used for attendance figures, and started calling out names in alphabetical order.

"Armbruster, Gerhardt?"

"Hier, Frau Kellergeister!"

"Komm' zu meinem Pult und stell Dich aufrecht vor mir hin! – Jetzt! *Sofort*!" *Come forward to my desk and stand up straight in front of me! Now, at once!*

Gerhardt went up to her desk, stood straight, and received the notorious and whopping Kellergeister cheek-whistle. The number-one *Backpfeife* in the village!

Poor Gerhardt looked completely befuddled and started crying, "What d'I do!?"

"Nothing. – Go back to your seat. – Next! Ammenheim, Michael. Come forward to my desk and stand up straight in front of me. – Now, at *once*!"

And so it went on and on and on, right down to Webersdorf, Elisabeth.

The whole classroom was filled with sobbing and bawling and weeping and *Why me? What did I do?* Not everyone of Fergal's classmates was crying though! They were the ones who were quite used to this treatment by a grownup. – Pastor Meinheit was still standing by the door, evidently praying with a nod of his head every time he heard Kellergeister's hand slapping a deserving child's face. It was a nod of assent with closed eyes.

At the end of this lesson in smacking, Frau Kellergeister raised her hand again to underline her scream, "Quiet now! – If you are *good* children this will not happen again. Life is *Zuckerbrot und Peitsche*!" *Sugared bread and whip,* another important German saying, and naturally, "Wer nichts lernt, der wird nichts in der Welt!" *Who learns nothing, becomes nothing in this world,* and most importantly and wisely "Wo viel Licht ist, da ist auch viel Schatten!" *Where there's a lot of light, there is much shadow.* "Remember this! You have to *pay* for everything! Everything comes at a *price*! The higher the price the greater the good!" And all of this depended on two people in this small and only world. Frau Kellergeister and her violence, and Pastor Meinheit, praying with eyes shut.

For the rest of the morning the children practised their song about Diligent Craftsmen, *Fleißige Handwerker.*

The stanzas were memorised.

Unlike this morning at church, there was no laughter or screaming when everyone left for home at eleven-ten. Some parents were waiting by the archway to pick up their children.

Those poor souls had yet another moment of embarrassment coming, for as soon as they saw their mothers and fathers, they just broke down crying, yet again, pouring their little hearts out. But to what effect? Frau Kellergeister's great educational tradition was not going to be stopped despite whatever the great legislators of West Germany were saying already then.

Fergal said goodbye to Gloria whose mother was amongst the crowd of weeping children not knowing what was happening. Gloria's mother, Frau Weiler, was from Frankfurt, and she didn't know much of Geesterheim's educational customs as laid down by Frau Kellergeister. Only the next day did she have an eye-to-eye with the Directress to make sure Gloria would *never* be touched like *that* ever again.

Back home, Fergal settled in to eat as many of his sweets from his first-year's cone as possible. *Zuckerbrot und Peitsche!* Today, he was given special dispensation from any special diets prescribed by Mutti. As Chuck in the morning, he ate all the contents of the cone and was violently sick!

From then on, Kellergeister's policy of pain didn't change much, apart from Gloria's being exempt, completely. Every morning children got up from their seats, when Kellergeister entered the classroom, and again, when she left. Every morning, they prayed the Our Father and sang *Diligent Craftsmen.* Every day they got beaten.

Fergal learnt quickly to stop pretending he knew more than the rest of his classmates. If something slipped out, he got slapped, so it should remain inside of him. Fergal became quieter than ever before. It was a different quiet to the muteness during his sulk.

At home he continued reading the books from their own little library, even the forbidden ones, which had been deemed either too grownup or too complicated by Mutti. Possibly because of Prof. Dr. Dr. Eichenraub's librarian advice, Fergal had access all areas.

He loved the non-baby version of Cervantes *Don Quixote* and Boccaccio's *De Camerone. Casanova* was strange, and the real Odysseus made for an even harder read, as did the Iliad and Aeneid.

Mutti kept buying him Preussler and Ende. – They were very good too, and they could put you in a world of your own without having to think too much. *Wind In The Willows*, *Rabbits Rafferty*, *Winnie The Poo.* Worlds of his own. They were stories that went inside of him and he didn't mind them staying there forever.

Although the Kellergeister educational policy of pain became less and less in frequency as Fergal became better and better in shutting up at the right time when her hand was violently deployed, it was still being done unjustly and demonstratively only, every time. It was her only source of power.

The constant fear was such, it was hard to tell whether somewhere beneath her brutal surface there lay a good teacher. In fact, whether or no she was a good teacher was altogether irrelevant. Strictest obedience was being taught. Without doubt!

Pastor Meinheit's lessons weren't all that different. To be raised and uplifted spiritually, his *Schützlinge,* his little protégés, had to be held down and bashed physically. He was a *very* strong man. – Religious education at the Schafshütte was twice a week on Tuesdays and Fridays. All had to learn lots of hymns by heart. It was painful!

As part of West Germany's past-management, *Wiedergutmachung,* the same Jewish song had to be sung in German and Hebrew every Tuesday at the beginning of the lesson.

Pastor Meinheit said, this was very important, as it was an entirely different approach to the *Judenfrage*, the Jewish Question, or *Old Problem,* as he called it now and then.

Mutti later explained that *Judenfrage* was an unfortunate word for Herrn Pastor to have chosen. It was a *horrible, horrible* Nazi term dealing with the devil's own *Endlösung,* the Final Solution.

Mutti described *Endlösung* in detail. – It gave Fergal terrible nightmares with lots of emaciated bodies in heaps being cremated in big ovens or bulldozed into holes. Mutti said that the Nazis had kept this a secret, but Opa had told Oma mid 1944 that a friend of his who had a weekend home on the Lüneburger Heath had smelt something funny near Bergen-Belsen, like … burning meat. At times the sky was black with smoke and there was ash on his terrace. They were doing something *not* right at the Bergen-Belsen KZ crematorium. It was working overtime! – Why? – It could only mean, there was mass-dying going on over there! The news on the BBC World Service was getting worse increasingly! They kept listening to it in spite of dead Otto. – Yes, it was the *Feindsender*, the enemy station, but it sounded truer than the evident lies they were being fed from Berlin. – The BBC spoke of horrible atrocities in the East. Jews, homosexuals, communists, socialists, gypsies, cripples, artists, the contrarily opinionated. All enemies of the *movement*.

Oma: Did you hear what they just said on the BBC!

Opa: Yes. – Keep your voice down!

Oma: And!?

Opa: I don't want to talk about it.

Oma: You're one of them.

Opa: I am *not!* – I'm only doing my duty at work! And these scumbags are finished anyway soon, Frieda! Trust me!

Oma: So where did they go? The Gottschalks. Frau Rosenblatt and Frau Weinreich no longer write to me! Who knows where they all are! And what with your friend Heiner Sonnenfeld. He didn't even look Jewish!

Opa: Heiner … filled in … the race-purity form. They *all* did! All good Germans! We all are. Good! Always obedient. *He* shouldn't have! He should have lied somehow. Just a couple of Jews in the family some time ago. I *told* him to lie. Somehow we could have destroyed the records. But he didn't want to. *Ordnung muß sein,* he said.

Oma: So where are they?

Opa: They had to go *somewhere,* when they were collected for re-homing! You know it's safer just to do what the Nazis tell you. Otherwise you just get shot!

Oma: You helped collect them!

Opa: Oh, Murres! – I did once! It was a difficult case. She said, she wasn't going anywhere. And keep your voice down, Liebling, for God's sake! Remember Otto. Marianne came because she trusted me.

Oma: She was the whore!

Opa: Don't put it like that.

Oma: Have you no idea where they went?

Opa: They went East! – We certainly didn't keep any of them at the prison. They weren't criminals. With the communists … we dealt …

Oma: I don't want to hear it!

Opa: Bodo says, he smelt something funny … down on the Lüneburger Heide … near KZ Bergen-Belsen.

Oma: Have you no idea what's happening East?

Opa: Gollermann came back in this … scheiß-brown uniform and …

Oma: Don't swear, Karl! Martha might hear you.

Opa: If you don't keep your voice down, Martha will *definitely* hear you and denounce us at the BDM[6]. And then it's *good night*!

Oma: How can you say such a thing!? – She'd never do that!

Opa: Unwittingly! I mean unwittingly! – She's young.

Oma: What happened to Gollermann in his scheiß-brown uniform?

Opa: When he came back … last week … he said they were really sorting out the Jews, … communists and all the other Staatsfeinde and Untermenschen[7]. East. I know what that scumbag means by *sorting out*. He was the one who joined from the ranks of the SA and nearly shot me in the head when he cleaned his pistol. Just wanted to make sure I was on his side. You know.

Oma: You be careful of that man!

Opa: He's a bully and should sort himself.

And Pastor Meinheit sang the first line of the Jewish song. Gradually, all children fell in with him.

Hevenu shalom aleichem,
Hevenu shalom aleichem,

---

[6] *Ger.* Hitler Youth, girl section, Bund Deutscher Mädel (Federation Of German Girls)

[7] *Ger.* enemies of the state and subhumans

Hevenu shalom aleichem,
Hevenu shalom, shalom,
Shalom aleichem.

Wir wollen Frieden für alle,	*We want peace for all,*
Wir wollen Frieden für alle,	*We want peace for all,*
Wir wollen Frieden für alle,	*We want peace for all,*
Wir wollen Frieden, Frieden,	*We want peace, peace,*
Frieden für jedermann.	*Peace for everyone.*

Somehow it didn't seem to Fergal that Pastor Meinheit wanted peace for him and his classmates.

After the New Year Fergal decided to develop a cold so he wouldn't have to go back. He had tried to feign illness a lot to get away from school, but Mutti had become a little too Fergal-wise for his taste.

The cough sounded real.

Chuck downstairs had the whooping cough and so did numerous of his classmates. Two weeks of pleasurable pretending went by. And then the real thing hit just after Chuck had been released from his parent's quarantine to play war upstairs at Fergal's.

Fergal's whooping cough went on for eight weeks! Chuck, too, got somehow re-infected with something else. Fergal knew it was the dread of going back. Kellergeister-hell!

When Chuck had turned up at school after having missed the first-year's first day, Frau Kellergeister took him through the same rigmarole. It was horrible! After that Chuck had been coming down with all sorts of great illnesses.

After Easter, Fergal, Chuck, Joachim – back then a new friend – plus five other of their classmates, including Bernhardt, the Pastor's own son, had developed a strange nervous condition.

Every morning before school they would start crying and trembling quite badly. It was also found out that they were playing truant whenever given half a chance. Such a chance would only arise when parents didn't take their children to school personally and made sure they were inside the school building. Everyone was furious! Mutti, Dad, the Noldes, and a contingent of non-Geesterheim parents, excluding Pastor Meinheit, went to Kellergeister. A truce was arranged whereby Kellergeister, the definitive and only first year teacher, would definitely refrain from hitting the children in question.

As to most real Geesterheimer kids, well, … their parents approved of Kellergeister's *traditional* ways.

And as to playing truant? – Well! That wasn't her fault, and if *her* kids persisted in skiving off, they would have to repeat the year and meet her again next year for re-education! Repeating was good practice for uppity kids with attitude. Frau Kellergeister's decision was final!

Fergal stopped playing truant.

Fergal was looking forward frantically to the end of the year!

Letter #4 – Fergal To God Via The Pope

Hello God, and hi, Holy Dad in Rome, Father Paul,

You know me by now! – Dad says, a long time ago his education was a brutal waste of time. Mine is the same, dear God!

Dad hates Catholicism. I don't. I hate Luther! Luther just shuts his eyes!

Please pray for me because I am in pain!

Please pray that this school stops.

Please pray that I can learn in a place where I can really learn.

Don Quixote is nice and sees things. That is because the Don has imagination! Frau Kellergeister is not nice. She is blind. She should go somewhere else.

I nearly had to repeat the year!

I was very scared because then I would have met her again! And she will teach me nothing again and I will still be older then. So I am even more quiet! Mutti and Dad made it so she won't beat me again.

Next year there is a new teacher. He is nice. Everyone says so! After Kellergeister everyone is nice.

But what have I learnt? Dad says I learnt humility at least. Humility is when you are small and someone bigger and stronger makes you feel even smaller and then you shut up. I looked the word up. It means to think little of oneself. Is that good? How can I think a lot of other people like love if I cannot think something good of myself? And I am told by Kellergeister, that I am stupid.

I am pretending to learn at school.

I am not a Roman Catholic but a Lutheran.

As ever, yours faithfully, my dear God!

J. Fergal Bulhof-Murphy

Frankfurt Means Business

Wow! The new showroom at Frankfurt was fantastic! – Dad had opened it in just under two months. Frankfurt was great and modern, and it didn't smell of cows' and pigs' wee-wee like Geesterheim. Fergal would also like to see Munich soon, and the Alps! Mountains! Wow!

Mutti had said, that was too far away for Fergal for the moment, and he shouldn't always ask for more than he was being offered. Being taken to Frankfurt for the day was quite enough! Dad had said they might go to Munich altogether soon in spite of Mutti disliking mountains. Mutti was the sea-type, apparently.

Fergal and Dad had been racing down the Autobahn to Frankfurt doing an almost steady hundred-and-twenty miles per hour in Dad's Stingray convertible. Open! They had taken the top down just outside Geesterheim because Mutti was afraid Fergal would get sucked out by the wind. Dad had also permitted Fergal to sit in the front. The rear was just too cramped and there were no seatbelts. Mutti had specifically asked for Dad not to do more than sixty miles an hour. When they had taken the top down Dad had said, "Sixty is a joke. Let me show you what this car can do, my man!" At one stage Dad had managed to get the Stingray up to one-hundred-and-forty-five. A bit windy!

The showroom was all glass, big, clean mirrors and very high ceilings. Dad had started his car business in Darmstadt. All he had had back then in 1969 had been a tiny office on Kaiser Straße with a huge window and a small showroom. This had been just before he had called Mutti in London and said he had found a nice house, and they could all come over now.

In the old Darmstadt office there had been no cars in the showroom only a circle of square white cement columns no higher than Dad's bellybutton. On top of the columns Dad had placed Corgi Toys of the cars he was selling. Germans had come in and asked what in the name the shop name B&M Automobiles stood for. Where were the cars? Dad would direct them to the columns and show them his favourite toy car collection, adding most seriously with a smile, it was his business to order the real thing. Germans left his shop shaking their heads.

American and English customers came flocking.

The showroom here at Frankfurt was a far cry from Darmstadt, which still existed and delighted people as a curiosity.

Fergal couldn't believe his eyes! It wasn't that huge really, but big enough to hold seven cars. A red, a yellow and a silver E-Type, two green Minis, and two Corvette Stingrays, one red, one yellow.

Fergal went straight for the yellow E-Type, his most favourite car of the minute and looked at himself in the bulging door. Everything about this car was swollen, bulbous, flexed like elegant muscle. Not the kind of brutal muscle you'd get with the Shelby Cobra.

The yellow reflection thrown back at him was that of a squat, fat, little round thing. Fergal laughed. An English sport scar was reflecting him in its door as a Wetchamoonsi. A perfect Wetchamoonsi! The legs were a bit long though as a real Wetchamoonsi's feet were flat, and they had no legs.

Fergal turned to view his body in profile. And that really cracked him up! He was as fat from the side as the front, and he could almost make his head disappear. A new, yellow Wetchamoonsi as seen by an English sports car. He would love to be able to do this for real. Turn himself into a fat ballooning Wetchamoonsi! It would have his friends in stitches.

Fergal was laughing so much he had to burp like Oma, and sit down. Dad was standing with a group of men in dark suits and dark glasses. One of them stood out. He had long hair. Very long, but still not like a hippy, more like a musketeer. His shirt was frilly and white, his trousers black and tight. Dad had a record album at home of Spanish music. The musketeer looked like a flamenco dancer. Where was his wife?

Fergal's time at primary school was much better now. The second year had somehow gone by magically quickly. He had made lots of friends to play with and they were all his age rather than a year younger, which would have been terrible. Playing war was the greatest game in the world. There was a little, thin kid called Tristan who had all the gear.

The third year had just started and was completely different. He was beginning to actually learn new things like maths and real drawing and painting and history and geography and music from sheets. He didn't like the recorder.

Oma and Opa had given him a piano for Christmas just as Prof. Dr. Dr. Eichenraub had recommended, recommended. It was fun, fun! Black musical notes were funny and a different language altogether. You could be angry with music and not say a word.

The pain Kellergeister used to dole out seemed a long time gone. Now and then Fergal might get into a bit of a fight with his friends. But that was different pain. And mostly in perfectly good humour.

Even though, now there were rumours that some *very* foreign Yugoslav *Gastarbeiters*[8] were going to arrive at Geesterheim soon. They all had knives, and they all loved to inflict pain, and they all came in dangerous gangs. That's why another house was going up behind the block catering for the asocials' needs on Mönchsgasse.

They had actually uncovered an ancient Germanic burial site on the asocial land, which stretched well into the grounds of the old monastery. Ancient Germans even took their dogs with them to their grave.

"You must be Fergal, Seán's miraculously healed ex-mute son. Do you always laugh quite as … endearingly?"

"Yes, sir."

"Oh, really!? – You think of your laughter as endearing, do you?"

"No, sir."

"Yes, sir, no, sir. What then?"

"Yes, sir. I am Fergal." Fergal didn't like the man at all! He didn't look Fergal in the eye. In fact, he didn't look at Fergal at all. He looked at somewhere else over Fergal's head. Fergal realised it was at his father with the group of men in dark suits and sunglasses. This tweedy fellow was somehow watching them! Also, he was far too tall and thin to be liked. Flimsy blonde and red hair, and freckles, and an odd, very clipped moustache, over lips that looked strangely crippled. Fergal concluded the man had no lips at all. Someone must have cut his face open to make room for that ugly mouth!

---

[8] *Ger.* guest (i.e. foreign) workers

Fergal was convinced this tweed-bag of bones was the first edition of the Mitschnacker family he had ever met. Was it Peter Ast or Peter File?

"Is your name Peter Ast or Peter File, sir?"

"What? No, it isn't. Now, hop along and don't smudge the cars. There is a lot of money here."

"Dad has allowed me to sit in the cars as long as I am careful." Fergal decided that despite the age difference, and as such the respect he should have invested in this tweed-sack, he was not going to say another word. The man scared him a lot, and he was very happy Dad was about!

Danger-man Peter File, or whatever his name, just walked off.

Fergal went back to looking at his reflection. He didn't feel like laughing anymore. More serious business ahead! – Car after car, even the Minis, he sat in and played Autobahn. Sometimes there were terrible crashes and pileups with lots of blood and dead people lying around all over the place. Sometimes the people were still burning and moving like in Mutti's stories about people burning alive and running around and burning on under the surface of the water or lying on the pavement with their body fat dripping out of them like sunflower oil for cooking.

"Hey, Fergal, where are you now?" It was Dad. Dad knew that Fergal took his driving around the world very seriously. His green Land Rover from almost three years back had seen service even in Antarctica. Fergal got around!

"I'm navigating through Paris traffic, Dad. It's not easy, but I shall manage."

"Navigating, eh, are we! Well, let's navigate over to Marcello's Pizzeria. He's going to cook some special Sicilian pizza for you. – Come on. Let's go!"

Now, apart from fish n chips, sausage rolls, meat pies, shepherd's pie and Yorkshire pud, all of which were hard to come by in Germany, but Mutti thankfully knew how to make all of them, pizza was the best food by leagues. Mutti said English food wasn't so brilliant because it wasn't so good for your health even though it tasted really rather fabulous. German food was better. Schwarzbrot for example. *Yuck!*

Dad and Fergal went in the car.

Peter Ast's or Peter File's name was Bragstone and Bragstone only. He wasn't of the Mitschnacker clan, father assured son. Bragstone had been in the RAF too. A Flight Commodore turned accountant for Dad and all his business affairs. He had been given a dishonourable discharge over something … a little unfortunate! Something about lost funds and women and alcohol. Fergal didn't understand.

"Do you trust him, Dad?"

"Oh, yes."

"Why?"

"He said he had turned a new leaf. I checked his files with some friends back in London. Well, it wasn't a trifle, I can tell you. He's been to prison over this silly affair. But I am giving him a chance. It's the honourable thing to do, and he's ex RAF."

"I see. He was higher than you?"

"Yes. Quite a bit. I didn't have his money or education. But … I had the more interesting job and spoke German fluently."

"What did you do?"

"I opened letters." Dad laughed. He said something different every time you asked him. Licking stamps, delivering letters, doing accounting, listening to enemy conversations.

Dad had taught himself German and spoke it without the slightest trace of an accent. The RAF had further educated him with his language ability. Opening letters though was a new one to Fergal. That wasn't nice, and he didn't probe any further.

Dad turned into a private parking lot. It was the pizzeria's.

Marcello was the most colourful pizza baker Fergal had ever met. Well. Marcello was the *first* pizza baker Fergal had ever met. He was convinced though you couldn't really get any more colourful than Marcello, pizza or no. He had apparently sung at the reception when Dad had opened his showroom here. Marcello had pizzerias in Munich and Frankfurt and just everywhere. And he was just now beginning to start one of his tunes! A Sicilian welcome especially for Fergal. Marcello sang, with his long hair obscuring his face, mysteriously and tragically.

Although Fergal did not understand Italian, it was a beautiful song in a beautiful language. Dad and he stood completely still and silent, and Marcello's other friends in dark suits and sunglasses looked very moved. One took his dark glasses off and wiped away a tear. And, what was even better, despite the darkness in the pizzeria, everybody loved and cuddled Fergal and admired the story of his miraculous recovery which Dad must have told them a hundred times.

Dad seemed on best terms with these men and they liked him a lot and smiled even more. Above all, they waved their arms around more than any normal German and made signs with their hands so frequently, Fergal wanted to be as expressive as they. He imitated them at every step and they loved it. Dad told Fergal off, but they said it was alright and an honour to have Fergal gesticulating like a true Sicilian.

A lot of food was served. And by no means just pizza. There were types of fish and meat Fergal had never tasted.

This was the most fantastic day ever, and everyone talked a lot and laughed loud. At the end of the meal the mood suddenly changed as if at the death of a dear friend.

"Now, Seán! You know we are very fond of you. You know that! There is something we'd like to tell you in complete confidence." Their accents were brilliant. Heavy and rolling along as over soft ground. Fergal imitated, "Dell ya in campleet canfidentsey." All smiled but only very briefly. Fergal was now being ignored.

Dad's smile vanished, "Would you like my kid outside?" Dad had never called Fergal a kid before. Baby, child, munchkin, my man, my lord, or simply Fergal, yes. Kid!? No!

There was something brutal in his voice.

"No. He's family now. He is of you. He's an honorary member of us. Come on, Seán! He's a miracle. He'll listen. But Marcello, you go to the kitchen and sing, ok!"

Marcello disappeared at the back behind the rustic bar muttering something.

"Seán. You like that rat Bragstone much, don't you? You have some history back in the war, right?"

"Well, I'm giving him a chance. No. We have no history." Fergal had never seen Dad pale. Red, even crimson to blue with anger, but not this shade of light grey.

"A chance is a good thing if it not get abused, yes. But a chance comes to an end. You saved my brother Calogero's life here from car accident because that stupid German see not the red light and nearly kill him, yes. Now, you are our close friend. You save a man's life you are family. You are like Calogero to me. Good. Bragstone is not good. As I vowed to help you but I know you won't ask because you a good man, Seán. Very Irish. Commendable. You don't need chance from people. You get chance from God." All made the sign of the cross and kissed their own hand including Dad. And so did Fergal.

"But now … you need help. You can say no. I will not be offended."

Dad inhaled deeply, "Ok."

"Bragstone is cheating with your money. I have my eyes and ears. I am your insurance because you have no insurance here in Germany. We stick together."

"Right."

"Right!" exclaimed Calogero's brother. "Bragstone has so far funnel out of your business twenty-thousand Marks. That is enough to make me sad for you."

Dad was trembling, "How so?"

"Bragstone is a good cheat. A bad man! He will go to hell. If you keep trusting him with accounting you be poor, and Fergal and all you real family too. I don't want that! You see, Seán. I like you. No. No, no!" Calogero's brother slapped himself in the face and put both his hands over his heart, "How could I say it *!?* I *love* you, Seán. I *love* you! We are one! The passion burns in me for you and your misery. Bragstone must go to hell!"

"I see."

Calogero's brother shook his head for what seemed a good minute, "But …" he raised his index finger. This was not the German endemic index way. Slowly index finger and thumb came together describing a circle with the rest of his fingers stretching out in front of him towards Dad. Then suddenly, with the same hand, he made a fist and his face contorted terribly. Calogero's brother went quite red. He seemed to hold his breath. Then he burst forth with deep anger "But, Seán. You do *not* see! You are a *good* man. A good, very successful businessman! That is God's will!" All, bar Calogero's brother and Dad, crossed themselves again. Fergal crossed himself too.

"Bragstone is the Devil's emissary. You understand *that*! Let me send him back where he has come from." He smiled, "With a message for his emissary worth of the Devil himself."

"Good Lord, no! Matteo! – Do you know what you are suggesting?"

"Seán, Seán, Seán!" Matteo shook his head and moved his shoulders as if about to cry. His hand poked his own chest hard emphasising each point, "I" poke, "am", poke, "a", poke, "businessman", three pokes, "myself", two pokes, "I understand!" Four pokes.

"I understand."

"I know you do. – Good! Then let me do what I have to do for Calogero, for me, Matteo, and above all, for *you*. You are part of my heart, my soul, my family!"

"Please, Matteo! I am asking you … from the bottom of my heart …" This was *Dad* talking!? Quite new to Fergal all this. He was frightened.

"What you are asking … is … almost impossible for me, … my dear brother, Seán, you are my brother! And you … asking me not to punish who hurt *you*?"

"Yes. Please, Matteo. Don't"

Matteo did a *conversation-over-all-settled* outward sweeping motion with both of his arms. – "Seán. You ask me to leave the Devil. I will let the Devil and his emissary live. For *you*! You understand. I was just making you polite offer at you. You and your miracle kid must go now. I'm a little sad." The other men nodded. "Now don't be afraid, Seán. I'm not angry! You can come to me whenever you have problem of great size. But I will not come to *you* again!"

"That's perfectly clear, Matteo. Thank you and God bless you." Signs of the cross all-round.

"God bless you too, my brother. I love you. You are part of my body."

Dad and Matteo hugged first and exchanged kisses. Then all the other men hugged Dad too. Marcello stayed in the kitchen throughout.

Matteo came over and took both Fergal's cheeks in his hands. "You are a beautiful boy, Fergal. Keep it that way! Always think of justice all your life. When you grow older protect your Mama and Papa. Here, take this!" He clicked his fingers in the air and said something in Sicilian. Calogero came hobbling over and gave Fergal his Rayban Wayfarers and a golden Zippo.

"Little Fergal, you light of God and path for the good, take this. Remember us! When people say bad things, don't believe them! We are like German *Allianz Versicherung,* just more personal. Now go and look after your father for me."

Fergal said his thank-yous and bowed and made the sign of the cross, when Dad took him by his neck and forced him outside. Fergal thought he could hear Matteo crying just before the door to Marcello's restaurant shut.

The sunglasses and the golden Zippo were fantastic! – Dad said they were going back home, pronto. He would then have to go back to Frankfurt and Darmstadt to check a couple of things. From then on he didn't talk until the moment father and son saw the real accident close to home.

Dad was in no mood to drive fast. He was doing about seventy to eighty. He was a good driver always checking his mirrors.

"Shit! That idiot's going too fast!"

Fergal couldn't see who was going too fast. He was too small and wasn't allowed to stand on the seat when the car was moving.

Ahead of them a lorry was indicating to the left to overtake whatever was in its path. The lorry began pulling out. Fergal could see the obstruction was a slow moving Citroen 2CV, the one the Germans called the duck, *die Ente.*

"He's flashing the lorry. Is he stupid? He's going to …" at that stage a small white Mercedes SL with a young man and woman shot past the Stingray. The lorry didn't move back into its lane. It continued overtaking. Dad braked gently and turned his hazards on.

The SL hit the brakes too late! It went straight under the lorry. Both passengers were decapitated in an instant, as the force of the Mercedes lifted the back of the lorry up in the air and to the side, where briefly it was two-wheeling perfectly balanced, before it crushed the 2CV and its driver who hadn't stopped.

Before Dad pushed Fergal down out of view, Fergal had managed to see two heads rolling along as if in pursuit of their lost bodies in the SL. Dad kept holding Fergal's head down. More cars seemed to pass at high speed. Then for a good minute crash after crash followed. The noise was deafening. There was a thumped explosion up ahead.

Dad had stopped, still holding Fergal down, and drove up the embankment on the right. He stopped at the top and got out.

"Do *not* come after me!" Dad looked at Fergal and knew his son would do exactly the opposite. "If you come after me, I'll … arrrgh … be very … disappointed!" With that he vanished into a cloud of black smoke with tongues of fire spitting at him.

Naturally, Fergal got up from his seat! The vantage point was too great up here on the embankment. An amphitheatre in his illustrated baby-book about the ancient Greeks. He had never seen anyone decapitated for real before. This was a fantastic day!

The fire in the pile-up was spreading fast! Dad and some others had managed to pull some survivors from the jumbled mess of metal. A horn was hooting away at full blast. The Autobahn had come to a complete standstill.

As far as Fergal could see, an immobile line of cars to the horizon on their side, southbound. On the other, northbound, cars were beginning to slow down. Windows were rolled up. Drivers needed to watch the chaos of accident through the two-dimensional safety of their shut windows. The angrily whirling smoke might get into their eyes. This was an accident they had escaped. Flames, bodies burning, somebody was screaming on one side. On the other, the passing spectators were down to a crawl, walking speed, open mouths in shock, hands covering some, wide eyes, even some smiles and astonished laughter. There was a common theme, an underlying tone, Fergal could almost hear. A harmony of excitement and relief.

Was this Damage Fun at its core? The truest form of Schadenfreude, uncontaminated by fear of repercussion, as the ones you were damage-funning at were dead? People seemed almost ecstatic, they weren't afflicted!

And then on the other side of the Autobahn it happened too! Somebody went into the back of a car that had come to a complete standstill. Inside, a ghoul taking photographs. A reporter maybe, one moment. But certainly dead with a broken neck, the next. Lifted up and turned over in under three seconds. Buried and forgotten under a mound of metal in ten.

It was all happening so quickly! Car after car after car went into each other. Crash after crash. The previous harmony replaced by a discord of tearing metal.

Dad and the other helpers were now just standing around impotently. Survivors had been laid down in the grass on the embankment.

A man laying still was howling each breath. When he stopped, it looked to Fergal as if he had sunk into himself. Fergal somehow knew the man had just died.

A woman with no arm. She was gasping for air. She was close by. Bleeding badly. Somebody shouted, "I'm a doctor." About to bend down he shook his head. The gasping had stopped.

Dad was nodding as if he'd seen this sort of thing before. Lots. The doctor and Dad covered the dead with jackets and blankets. There were six of them.

The dead lay amongst the living in a neat line on the embankment.

A young woman came to next to a corpse. She pulled off the blanket. Her eyes and mouth opened. She covered her mouth. She started shaking with grief and put the blanket over herself and her boyfriend or husband. Under the blanket she hugged him, shaking him.

Fergal noticed he was crying. Tears were just running down his cheeks leaving trails in the soot caused by the fire. What strange tears these were! New tears. – When you hit your shin or scraped your knee the tears were different. You could really sob then, especially when Mutti was around.

Fergal was proud of his father! But something beyond the little child in him knew that he didn't really know his father and would possibly never come to him properly.

The crashes on the other side had stopped now. There was no fire over there. But a lot of people were shouting for help or simply just screaming. There too a little army of volunteers was doing its best.

And then, finally, Fergal could hear the sirens.

Letter #8 – Fergal To God Via The Pope

Dear God,

I hope Your Holiness, the Papa in Rome, is sending my letters on to you. I know my Dad, who is also a Papa, is sending them to Rome.

I saw a whopping, big car crash today. There were a lot of dead and burning people there, just like in Mutti's stories. And one woman held her boyfriend under the blanket for the dead.

It was very horrible.

I was very excited.

Later on Mutti said together with Dad I should not feel excited about it, as it was sad and horrible! Brave husbands lost their beautiful wives, little innocent children their parents. – I understand that all of this is very horrible.

But I think what is worse is when Chuck, my neighbour with the poo downstairs and the towels, if Chuck cuts worms to bits or even wasps. I can't explain.

Mutti was still very angry at my lack of compassion. Compassion is important and can be learnt, she says. Dad was compassionate because he forgot about himself and helped others. I want to learn more of that.

One woman's arm was off and she died in the grass with lots of blood. I think Dad cried. I saw somebody going mad when he burnt in the car but then he was quiet and covered by flames. A man was also mad about his car being broken, but he was on the embankment and alive and angry shouting *Sonntagsfahrer* even though it wasn't Sunday, so there couldn't be any Sunday-drivers about. That man was very alive.

Dad knows the Mafia. I am not allowed to tell. After the accident he told me a lot I am not allowed to tell Mutti. Just like Opa. Bragstone is a bad man. The Mafia like you. I like you too.

Please pray for the dead in the pile-up. Do you pray, or do you just take them up in your Kingdom?

Actually, there were two pile-ups. One on each side! South is were we are, north is were Oma and Opa are. Pray for me to understand compassion, but not like Chuck and the insects.

Lots of love from Luther too

J. Fergal Bulhof-Murphy

The Importance Of Knowing What To Listen To Carefully

It was Tuesday, early afternoon, five past one. Holger Herbholz had taken a bit of LSD with some friends the night previous. Not much. He'd done it before and knew what to expect. *Alles cool!*

It was the 6th of November, and for an autumn day, beautifully warm and sunny outside. A real Indian summer.

But this commie nuclear attack alarm-nonsense *really* wasn't supposed to happen on a Tuesday, Herbholz agreed. He looked at his little pupil across from him. One of his favourite pupils! Bright. Cheerful. With the smile of an experienced, almost world-weary grownup. Fergal would one day become a lawyer, Herbholz decided.

Fergal had spent most of this school day, post nuclear-fun exercise gone wrong, in detention, because it hadn't really been an exercise, he had been told.

"It was deadly serious!"

And Fergal's behaviour had been beyond the pale, bordering on incitement. His third year teacher, Herr Herbholz, was writing a long entry inspired by angry movements in the class book. All about Fergal.

Young Herbholz was a fair and longhaired, clean-shaven hippy of the white shirt, tennis shoes and blue jeans variety with a yellow Citroën 2CV, loved by *all* the girls, six years and up. – Handsome Herbholz was a '68 pacifist. Against imperialist Bloody Sundays. Against Mao? No *Little Red Book*? Against Mao! Against atomic energy. Mostly for and a *just a bit* against the ratification of the Extremist Resolution. A tiny bit for but mostly against the Baader-Meinhof Gang. Against killing Israelis at the Olympics. And against a whole lot of other things.

Sexy Herbholz was all for love, children and making children.

The year before had been bad for Herbholz. His girlfriend had left him, and no one had received the Nobel Peace Prize! Could this year, the year of 1973 get any worse, than it had already been? He had a new girlfriend, yes, but you just had to look at the newspapers! OK, so there had been a ceasefire agreement, and the

Ammies[9] had withdrawn their troops from North Vietnam … great … but Papadopoulos was dictator in Greece, the Americans got Pinochet in and killed Allende in Chile by proxy, … well, Allende was so scared, he had apparently committed suicide. Then Egypt and Syria attacked Israel on Yom Kippur! Not a hope against the last Jewish outpost of America, run with money from German reparations. And just last month in October OPEC had decided to increase the oil price by seventy percent, and those Arab desert dwellers were boycotting Israel, the US *and* the Netherlands with an oil embargo! The poor Dutch!

"I agree, Fergal!" Herr Herbholz' pronunciation of Fergal's name was great, "It's all nonsense! There *has* to be more love! I was devastated when The Beatles split up three years ago, but John's better anyway. *Give Peace A Chance*, man!" He continued writing and speaking at the same time, "You are on the right track, Fergal! And I am totally on *your* side. Totally! Don't forget that.

"But today was one of your little steps too far, OK! Bit like Tristan, Bernhardt, Joachim, *and* you weeing against Brechwitz' car. Even though I might like to agree, I can't. Brechwitz shouldn't drive anyway.

"I have to write this report about you, and then we'll have to talk about it. You'd better be very glad that Frau Kellergeister isn't here today."

Fergal nodded emphatically. He liked Herr Herbholz a lot. He was the male version of Anne, the speech therapist of three years back. But today Herr Herbholz was stern, and that made Fergal very uneasy and a bit afraid. His neck was twitching and trembling.

"Love, love, love! We do need more love, of course, but you do understand that today was a *real* defence-situation alarm, don't you? With the oil situation as it stands at the moment the East might think it a great idea to attack us. We are weak and distracted at the moment. When you're weak you'll be taken advantage of. Russia might just nuke us to high heaven!"

Fergal nodded. He did feel bad on account of what he had done today because Herr Herbholz and all the other primary school teachers were angry with him.

---

[9] *Ger.* die Ammies (the Americans)

"Of course! You must not forget to feel love for the Russians *too*! Remember they are only people like us. To a degree."

This was a bit confusing. Herr Herbholz was extremely non-extreme.

Be it the communist USSR and their satellites, or the fascist, imperialist USA and its satellites, "There has to be, … and there is a middle way," Herbholz had told his pupils when he had introduced himself at the beginning of the third year in late August. He drew a line though when it came to any direct threat his little students were under!

Fergal felt genuinely guilty and remorseful, and he *was* ecstatically happy Frau Kellergeister wasn't in today! But still, this wasn't supposed to have happened on a Tuesday. It was supposed to happen on a Friday! Lots of things happened on a Friday.

Most Fridays was fish-day at home. Fish, unless cooked by Marcello the singing Mafia man, was not exactly Fergal's favourite food. It was on a par with eating your own snot after a nose bleed which was still better than eating even your best friend's snot without the blood in it. Sun-dried slugs tasted better.

Friday could also be great-surprise fire-alarm-day at school. But that was irregular as it could happen at great intervals. Sometimes months would go by without the need to play fire alarm. It was supposed to really take you by surprise as if the real thing were happening. It never did. – Frau von Brechwitz was in charge of the red fire alarm button in her domain, and she only ever hit it on Fridays. On any given random fire-alarm Friday she would have that special, dead-giveaway look about her. The metal fragments in her eyes were giving off a tremulous excitement so blatant, squidgy and coated in syrupy madness, everyone, who had said *good morning* to her early on random fire-alarm Friday to receive either no look, a blank stare full of *whys* or just a simple *yes,* knew, she was working herself up into the frenzied anticipation of hitting the red button.

Tristan said, Brechwitz was always playing worldwide nuclear holocaust. Big Bernhardt, Pastor Meinheit's son, knew for a fact she had haemorrhoids in her brain with little creatures in it that guided the secretary's every move like Star Trek which had started on German TV the year before. The haemorrhoid-beings told

Brechwitz to hit the button, and then they had a party that made her even more gaga.

Fergal tended to agree with Tristan on this one, although Big Bernhardt threatened everyone who differed with him with a broken thumb and long-lasting headlock.

Bernhardt really didn't have any friends, and he said and did some very strange things. – He'd foist his presence on people and stay the afternoon. Even if told to go away he'd trail Fergal and his friends all around Geesterheim. He'd pretend he just happened to be going the same way, and then he'd start crying fat tears if the group split up running off in different directions to get rid of him. He couldn't decide whom to follow. It was embarrassing and very sad!

Joachim enjoyed the fact that Bernhardt was being beaten by his pastor father more than he himself was by his deaf grandmother, Hammerich. Joachim said the only sexual excitement Brechwitz got, was from the red knob up in her domain. *Sexual excitement* was the latest buzzword.

But above all, … the war siren! – Every Friday was also without fail nuclear fun exercise day all over Geesterheim.

Every German village, town and city had one day of the week dedicated to ten minutes of siren testing. Everyone was expected to know what the code sequences meant, and somehow everyone did. Mutti said this was because of the war, and this was passed on to the children, and that was called tradition.

Sirens were things that looked like a UFO on a stick on top of either the fire station or the village *Rathaus,* Germany's unfortunate name for town hall, at least from an English speaker's point of view. Sirens made the loudest noise ever, and it was indeed a good thing that asocials didn't have sirens in their dirty government housing estate accommodation because sirens would have been a real weapon in an asocial's hand. On the other hand, it could wake even the most hardened of alcoholic asocials from their sleep.

Mutti would ponder and say, sirens, if used incorrectly, were asocial, so to have an asocial being given an asocial instrument would create something even more antisocial. A terrorist! In the right hands sirens were a great device that told you something bad was about to happen or was already happening. Although, in the war the sirens had been howling all over the place in Hamburg, and it still didn't change a thing. People were ablaze and screaming and running around burning alive, dying, smouldering corpses, cooking oil dripping from their bodies, children and parents as one fused together by the heat in black piles of meat surrounded by glistening puddles of their burnt-off fat, and the nuclear holocaust was a thousand times worse, but, … Mutti thought, … much quicker! That was when Mutti would generally shake her head, close her eyes, and a tear would find its way down her left cheek. Fergal had noticed it was the left cheek, … always.

As the day of the week was set for the siren test to be on Fridays, always, it was completely ignored by all grownups and children alike. If though it happened out of the ordinary, a great panic would ensue with people running out into the street to see where the fire was or where the nuclear bomb had just detonated. Especially, at moments of great physical stress, like Bernhardt's headlock or thumb-breaker or simply J's presence, Fergal often wondered quietly about the likelihood of a disaster occurring at the same time as the siren test. Over time he had noticed that, possibly due to his sister's education of torturing him, there was an easy way of coping with pain … you just thought of something else! Siren tests during times of disaster? How much milk could you drink before it came out of your nose?

Strange, how easily grownups could lie to children and other grownups! The fascination with the obscure, with secrets, the language J was speaking to him when she hurt him without saying a word. Why? Contemplation of such subjects would indeed infuse a great calm in Fergal letting him forget about the pain of headlocks, thumb-breakers, olive oil torture, Tabasco torture, urine-torture, and so on.

With both Bernhardt and J though you had to be careful! You had to wince and writhe a little, so they got a sufficient amount of fun out of it but at the same time knew when to stop.

Fergal would often perceive how this outer, less real Fergal went "Oh, the pain! Bernhardt! I'm dying!" whilst the inner, more tangible Fergal meditated on microscopes and how things never ended even if you looked into them. The more powerful a microscope the more endless the quest into the never-ending.

Fergal thought of the *Incredibly Shrinking Man*. A scary film J had allowed him to watch when Mutti and Dad had been out. Not as bad as *The Time Machine*, or worse, *Journey To the Center Of The Earth*. Johanna had tied him up in the chair and made sure he'd keep his eyes open all the time or else she'd squirt soapy water at his eyes from the flower spray.

Sirens were fun though because they promised real excitement if they went off on any other day than Friday.

In Fergal's case it had been Mutti of course who had passed on the great tradition of understanding the secret language of the siren.

The signals were divided into *Peacetime* and *In Case Of A Defence-Situation Arising*.

"Why doesn't it say *Peacetime* and *Wartime*, Mutti?"

"Because ever since the Nazis the word *war* has been taken out of the German vocabulary. We don't want a war again, Fergal! And if there is one we're only going to defend ourselves."

"Isn't that a bit like lying, Mutti?"

"Ach, Johann! You are so little! Lying is different. This is making an effort to be good, to be better even! And us Germans are very good now at making a greater effort than anyone else in the world."

Fergal knew all the signals.

He saw them as baaing sheep.

Sheep made things easier! Sleep and all. – Very early on Mutti had taught him this trick. If you couldn't sleep you counted sheep … and *it* worked!

As of 1970 Mutti had taught him the simple language of the siren.

Three continuous twelve-second tones with two twelve-second pauses: Fire during peacetime.

Baaaaaaaaaaaa   *Baaaaaaaaaaaa*   *Baaaaaaaaaaaa*

Three laidback sheep around a fire drinking coke.

One-minute uninterrupted howling: Turn on peacetime radio and/or television and wait for announcement.

BaaMooBaaMooBaaMoo
Three cows visiting their three sheep friends to listen to the radio.

Three continuous twelve-second tones with two twelve-second pauses followed by a one-minute continuous tone: A peacetime catastrophe.

Baaa Baaa Baaa Baaaaaaaaaaaa
Three small sheep and one big bully sheep like Bernhardt.
That's a catastrophe.

"What's a catastrophe, Mutti?"

"Something really bad, affecting a whole lot of people."

"Like …?"

"Earthquakes, floods, hurricanes. Biblical things. Like the big wave in East Pakistan in November. Three hundred thousand souls were lost. Or the earthquake in Northern Chile and Peru that killed over sixty thousand. A valley of tears."

"War?"

"I don't know, Johann! But I should think they ought to announce a war with the catastrophe-tone."

"Yes! Then people would just stay at home and duck and cover like we train at school, and there'd be no war! It would be like on strike."

"You are clever." Cuddle. "I love you. We need to wash your hair later."

One-minute uninterrupted howling: Attack from the air during wartime.

BaaMooBaaMooBaaMoo
Three cows visiting their three sheep friends to listen to the radio. The radio is kaput.
They are very sad and watch an RAF film.

"How can you tell the difference between the tone for the radio and the one for an air *Luftangriff*, Mutti?"

"Well, you can't! But normally when there's a war on, you know! Trust me!"

"Why?"

"Because … it's very loud, and you're very afraid when you hear the big planes going over with their *brumm-rumm-rumm* when you get attacked."

"Because of the bombs?"

"Yes, Johann."

"So, you rush to the radio or the television and you die because of the bomb in your living room. So hadn't you rushed all'd've been fine."

"We didn't have television then. We thought, talked and read more. And there was the wireless and the BBC World Service that got Oma into trouble."

Three continuous twelve-second howling tones interspersed with two twelve second pauses. One minute interval. Repeat. ABC-alarm. That's bad.

"ABC-alarm?"

"It means *atomic, biological, chemical.* A slow, rotting death. Disease. Coughing. The apocalypse. Dying lonely in corners, cells and body disintegrating. It's the modern alphabet of war, Johann."

"Or a defence-situation."

Mutti smiled, "Yes. Or a defence-situation."

"And what's atomic and biological and chemical."

"Johanna has three subjects at school called physics, biology and chemistry. They are three of the sciences. Maths is another. In theory the atom is the smallest indivisible particle of everything that is physical." Mutti was breathing heavily, "There is something called the periodic table. There you get all the atoms, which combine to form some … molecules … which is more than one atom. Some very clever of our scientists managed to split the atom, and that was quite unfortunate, as it says in the Bible, something, something, … they are no longer apart, but one flesh like one atom. What therefore God has put together, let man not split!" Mutti was respiring heavily, "You'd better ask Johanna about the rest. I was a *very* bad scientist at school and get asthmatic just thinking about it."

Fergal would ask J. His sister loved telling him things. If he didn't understand, she'd torture him. Not understanding also meant losing precious points. So, ABC was …

Three continuous twelve-second howling tones interspersed with two twelve-second pauses. One-minute interval. Repeat: ABC-alarm. That's really, really, really bad! Duck and cover training! Yippee!

BaaMoo *BaaMoo* *BaaMoo*
(wait a minute)
BaaMoo *BaaMoo* *BaaMoo*
The three cow-and-sheep friends are dancing up and down like mad.
Then they have a breather because the world is turning too fast.
Then they dance again like mad, fall down and rot, coughing in a lonely corner.

A continuous one-minute tone: The all-clear.

Baaaaaaaaaaaa
The big bully sheep is on his own because the other ones separated and ran away to dance and rot, which confused big bully sheep no end, so he's crying now. Poor big bully sheep!

But all of this was supposed to happen on Fridays!
Friday was nuclear-fun-exercise day!
Not Tuesday!
Fergal was watching his third-year teacher very carefully. But today there was something not quite right with the man!
Herbholz had arrived mid-page of the class book in which he was writing the report about Fergal's misconduct. Suddenly, he continued writing on his leather-covered desk instead of starting a new line in the book! When he had arrived at the right edge of the desk he did start a new line. However, it was the far left edge and it was *still* the desk.
"Sometimes, … I feel very small Fergal. At the moment, … I feel very small. I am very small. I should not reprimand you when I am that small. You are absolutely right, of course. It's all nonsense!" – At this stage Herr Herbholz had arrived again at the class book in the middle of the desk in front of him. He stopped, stared, picked up the book, "For God's sake! Why do they make them so big and bright? Have you ever seen such a lovely, bright

and vibrant colour?" And slowly slid from his seat, slipping under the table. "I'm so sorry, Fergal! I didn't know I was going to shrink today."

Fergal's neck stopped trembling. – This was bizarre, but fun! Teachers were really not supposed to play with you like that. Maybe all was alright now. He looked at Herbholz under the desk. "Are you alright, Herr Herbholz?"

"I'll be fine in a minute, Fergal. I do shrink like this now and then. Not to worry! Just sit back down on your chair and wait."

Fergal did as told. The class book was just over an arm's-length away.

Herbholz was evidently out of it. He hadn't shrunk at all! This wasn't the normal kind of behaviour, play or no, to be expected from a teacher. Herbholz was mad. That was OK because it wasn't dangerous. Frau von Brechwitz was insane and *not* funny, and that was not OK because she exuded menace.

With the class book that close, Fergal could tear out the page and pretend nothing ever happened! After all, Herbholz was still mad and under the table. Maybe he was blind too!?

Fergal reached out for it. He had to get up. He looked at his teacher's writing upside down.

That wasn't writing!

They were just ornamental squiggles!

"Can you hear me up there, Fergal. I am sorry! I'll be disappearing in the carpet for a while. But I'll be back! And don't you think I can't see you! I can. Hey, can you still hear me? Don't touch the class book!"

Fergal sat back down again. The incredible shrinking Herbholz! He really didn't want to mess it up with Herr Herbholz.

All that had happened today was down to the fact that it wasn't Friday. It was Tuesday, and early at eight-fifty the sirens had started blaring out the ABC-attack alarm code like mad.

BaaMoo *BaaMoo* *BaaMoo*
(wait a minute)
BaaMoo *BaaMoo* *BaaMoo*

It was part of every school kid's ABC to know the ABC-sequence. But all of this was supposed to happen on Fridays! Friday was nuclear-fun-exercise day. Not Tuesday!

The panic that had ensued had been well worth it! Fergal had never seen anything like it happen before!

Herr Herbholz had screamed like a piglet stung by a hornet, "Tables forward, tops facing the windows, nowwwwwwww!" Some girls had started crying. Everything had happened very quickly despite the fact that the boys hadn't ever trained for this. "Hide behind the tables! Hide, hide, hide! Away from the window!" Herbholz had been screaming and shouting, helping quickly wherever he had to help with the tables.

Fergal had heard tables hitting the floor throughout the school building. Deep echoes. "Hide! Flat on the floor! Don't look at the window! This is not a drill! I repeat *not a drill!*"

There had been absolute silence!

More children crying. Even some of the boys for their mummies.

Fergal and Tristan had been lying face down on the floor behind one table, Joachim and Chuck behind the next. Chuck had been giggling. Joachim had uttered a quiet, "Shit! Real, good shit!" Herbholz hadn't reprimanded him. He had been calming a group of girls crying terribly behind his desk.

Herbholz had once said the new tables were made especially for the imminent attack expected any second from the commies in the East. You could tip them over easily and they would rest with their tops at such an angle it was perfect to protect you from glass flying around all over the place.

"Wow, Ferkel, this is exciting! War at last!" Tristan's breathing had been fast. Fergal had felt the same. There'd be the biggest nuclear explosion somewhere outside Geesterheim and everything would be flattened and later they could go and have a look at the crater.

"Do you think the Russians will invade, Tristan? I'm sexually excited, man!"

"I don't know. Could be friendly fire. Papa says the Americans get things wrong all the time and shouldn't be given all these weapons."

"Mutti says when the Russians invaded Germany they ate a lot of Germans because they are so hungry all the time. What they couldn't eat they cut up, dried, and carried back to Russia."

"Papa just says it was horrible, and he won't talk about it. But Siegfried told me all women got raped and cut open with their guts hanging out and even little babies coming out of their tummies."

"Wow! – Siegfried really knows!"

"He reads a lot. And he talks a lot to the old guys at his place. You know where."

"Shut up, I'm trying to sleep and be sexually excited, you perverted, sex-starved infants with wasted penises!" Joachim had whispered hard.

Herbholz had screamed panicky, "The all-clear will sound in a minute. – Don't worry!"

Why had he screamed like that? A frightening scream! More reinforced, girly crying. Herbholz had been upsetting everybody with his own fear. All the boys had been whispering.

The all-clear hadn't sounded.

"There hasn't been an explosion yet, Tristan."

"Maybe it's a nerve, bio agent or chemical, or something, and we're going do die a horrible, slow, twitching death, like melting, like hot wax, and then we cough a lot until it's all over."

"Yeah! – Mutti once said you cough yourself to death! Or you rot in a corner! And sometimes you burn and you just can't help it."

"Wow! – I hope Siegfried is getting this!"

Fergal had got up and looked at the window. Everyone including Herbholz had still been lying down, hugging the floor. It had been beautiful outside with the sun still rising.

Fergal loved the expression *Indian summer*. Chief Sexual Excitement and his Penis Warriors were dancing like crazy round the ABC totem pole.

"Herr Herbholz! Herr Herbholz!"

"What is it, Fergal?" Herbholz had looked up from behind his desk, "For God's sake, Fergal! Lie back down behind your desk!"

"I think I feel, … I feel … sick! Very sick!" Fergal had started coughing, "My head feels all strange!" Fergal had fallen to his knees and screamed, "My head is exploding. Oh, the pain! Everyone! Save yourselves, …" cough, cough, … cough harder and harder. "It's a nervous, bio-chemical agent. It causes sexual madness and a bad cough …" cough, cough, choke. Fergal had got up screaming, "I'm dying. The pain is so … terrible! Oh, it's terrible!!!"

"He's right," Tristan had backed his friend up, "I've heard about it! I feel the sexual excitement, too!"

Fergal had run to the door and out the classroom into the big corridor with all the red doors. Door after door he had opened screaming and coughing, "I'm dying! We're all going to die of sexual madness! It's a nervous bio attack! It's invisible, …" cough, cough, choke, retch. "Let's all run home, …" cough, retch, choke, scream, "… the pain, my head, … death, …" he had fallen to his knees again, and gripped his chest, then his throat and his head, "Run, run everyone!"

From his own classroom Herbholz had been screaming at the top of his voice to come back in. By now though, the fear amongst the other children from first to fourth years had been such, teachers had lost all control!

Fergal had run downstairs coughing and spluttering. He had fallen down in the dust right at the centre of the yard to die the nervous bio agent chemical death. Spit had been drivelling from his mouth when finally he had died with some spasmodic last movements of his right leg and left foot.

He had been watching the entrance, carefully! The stampede had started!

Falling over one another children had been pushing and shoving to get out through the door and home to their mummies, even fourth years … and teachers!

Seeing Fergal lie dead in the dust hadn't exactly helped. The panic had increased!

The screaming and screeching of fear had been terrible. Glorious!

The teachers' panic though had been different. They had looked terribly worried!

Fergal had raised his head a little more off the ground. A wave of deep remorse and guilt had gripped him. He had never felt this before. It had made him feel sick and he had wanted to cry.

He had to stop this. He had been responsible for this! He had jumped back on his feet and shouted, "It's all nonsense. All nonsense! All of it! I played! Look … I'm fine!" No one had heard him.

At this moment the *all-clear* had been sounded.

Baaaaaaaaaaaa

The big bully sheep is on his own because the other ones separated and ran away to dance and rot, which confused big bully sheep no end, so he's crying now. Poor big bully sheep!

As if frozen in time everyone without exception had stood stock-still, counting the first thirteen seconds to make absolutely sure everything had been alright and the tone continuous.

Before the minute of the *all-clear* had been over teachers had begun to stare at Fergal. Two had run out into Mönchsgasse to gather in the ones of their flock who had gone astray.

Frau Sturm, the second year teacher, had come over to Fergal without a word and smacked him so hard in the face, he had flown a good two meters sideways back into the dust. She had turned on her heal and gone to the business of controlling her children.

Fergal hadn't cried. He knew he had deserved this most massive of Sturm's own variety of notorious ear-fig, the Sturm *Ohrfeige*. He had got up again.

Order had begun to resume.

Teachers had been marching their children back into the building in twos. Hand-in-hand.

At the top of his voice Fergal had addressed teachers and children alike, "I'm sorry! It was all nonsense! All of it! I was only playing. I am really sorry!"

Herr Herbholz had come over with a very unpleasant frown on his face. He had taken Fergal by the hand squeezing it intentionally so hard, it hurt badly. Fergal had ignored it and thought how strange it had been to see everyone stand so very stock-still to the sound of the *all-clear*.

Instead of taking him upstairs Herbholz had taken him downstairs to the lower ground floor. Despite the door to the room where Anne had taught him how to speak German being open, it had been very dark down there. A real J torture-basement.

"Detention until the end of the day!" had been all Herbholz had said. He had pushed Fergal down in the chair behind Anne's old desk, produced a pen and an A4 exercise book, had opened it and written something on the first page. Open, he had tossed it in front of Fergal. In Herbholz' neat hand it had read, *I nearly caused the death of my fellow pupils today. I will never again endanger the life of my fellow pupils. (100x in clear script. Your best handwriting, or you'll have to do it again! Teachers' Office when you're ready. By ready I mean today).*

It had taken Fergal almost up until the last bell at one o'clock in the afternoon before he had knocked on the door to the Teachers' Office. He had never set foot in there before. You only set foot in there for a *Rüge* or a *Tadel*. A *reproach* or a *rebuke*.

The disciplinary system was simple and was calculated in units. – Three *Rügen* equalled one *Tadel*, three *Tadel* meant a disciplinary conference was going to be held in your honour. At this conference it would be decided whether your parents would have to find another school for you or not. As it would be a little hard for your parents to find another school for you with three *Tadel* and an order of expulsion, a lot of grovelling would have to be done by pupils and parents alike thus afflicted.

"Come in!"

This had not sounded good.

"Sit! – Exercise book!" Herr Herbholz had checked what Fergal had written whilst Fergal had been offering his deepest regrets about the incident caused by him, and how incredibly remorseful he felt and how he was going to write to God via the Pope.

"We don't write to the Pope here! – I have spoken to your mother. She's going to give you another bit of detention until your birthday in late November. Let me write my report on you.

"The staff and I have agreed to keep this from Frau Kellergeister as we're afraid she might hurt you quite badly. Times have changed. I'm giving you two *Tadel* for this. That's a first for me! I don't think this has ever happened at any German school.

"The first *Tadel* is for disobeying my direct request to *hide* so the glass from the nuclear blast wouldn't cut you to shreds. The second is for incitement and causing unrest and a stampede, thereby endangering your fellow pupils' lives. Do you understand what I'm saying, Fergal?"

"Ja, Herr Herbholz. Danke."

"Bitte. – Now, let me write this wretched report, and then we'll talk about what you did today and why I consider it as almost a crime, OK!?"

"Ja, Herr Herbholz. Danke."

"Next year I might take you all to see the Roman wall at Saalburg. It's called the *Limes*. You will enjoy it! And then we can go and see the Iron Curtain. You might understand then."

Herbholz had kept talking. Fergal had been very hungry. At last his teacher had started writing. And then he had continued writing on his leather-covered desk towards the right instead of actually writing in the class book. He had even started a new line on the left of the desk, and then he had shrunk. At least, from Herr Herbholz' own point of view.

Herbholz remained lying hunched up under his desk for about five minutes staring forlorn at the soles of Fergal's trainers with slightly watery eyes, before his hand reached up to touch the underside of the desktop.

"I'm fine again!" Herbholz sat back in his chair. "Now, let me tell you what happens when the atom bomb goes up. It's not nice, Fergal! Listen carefully and remember, because when it happens there is no escape if you're nearby."

"Yes, Herr Herbholz." Fergal was feeling quite good again and he was going to be a good boy now, forever, and he was never going to endanger the lives of his fellow pupils ever again.

"There is a massive, thundering, red-hot explosion. The pressure and wind is such it tears everything down. If you're standing by a window, the glass will tear you into little pieces, and then you're *dead!*

"If you're *not* dead, the pressure and heat will blow you up like a balloon and rip open your skin and burn you all over until you're a black crisp …" Herbholz stopped abruptly and gave Fergal a really odd look. He blinked and shook his head. He coughed covering his mouth, shutting his eyes for a couple of seconds. "Are you alright, Fergal?"

"Yes, Herr Herbholz. Thank you! Mutti would have described that quite differently! Like more burning and screaming, and …"

"You don't look so fine to me!"

"I am. Really! That's a very scary story, but it could do with some …" *embellishing* was the word he was looking for. When he had it Herbholz interrupted him again. This time his eyes were quite wide.

"You are blowing up like a balloon. You look just like … has this ever happened before? You're all puffed up and red."

Fergal looked down at himself. He was absolutely fine!

Herr Herbholz realised he couldn't continue this conversation. The LSD he had taken yesterday had still too much of an effect on him. He would never take this stuff every again. He coughed, "Listen Fergal. I think I feel a little sick. Happens to teachers too, you know. I've asked your mother to tell you all about the atom …" he stopped mid-sentence, staring with grave intensity at Fergal, but this time it was as if he'd seen the most terrible spectre, exactly where Fergal was sitting, "… my God! I have to stop this!" He shut his eyes and covered his face with his hands. "Listen, Fergal! Go home. – I'll give you only one *Tadel.* Goodbye."

"Goodbye, Herr Herbholz."

"Just go!"

Fergal left the Teachers' Office, picked up his satchel in his classroom, and was about to run home as fast as he could, when he realised he couldn't. He felt fat and immobile and in tremendous pain. It reminded him a little of the electroshocks he had once received from J. Slowly he made his way down the staircase and opened the big glass door downstairs that took you out into the dusty yard. When he had passed halfway through the entrance he noticed his own reflection in the door and gasped in horror! It was as if one of J's nightmare stories were being told in there!

He saw himself with a hugely bloated and burnt face covered in bleeding, open sores. His body too was much bigger and wider, almost balloon-like. His arms burnt so badly, they too were black, shiny sticks. He was right out of Herbholz' description of a nuclear burn victim. And then the vision was gone again in the bat of an eyelid. As if nothing had ever happened.

So nightmares could happen in full daylight and you could see them when you were awake.

He ran home as fast as he could. He was starving.

Letter #10 – Fergal To God Via The Pope

Dear God and Your Holiness, Papa in Rome,

I am grounded up until my birthday. That's almost three weeks! I am really very sorry for what I did. *I nearly loused the beds of my mellow loo seats today. I will never again derange my yellow stupids' wives.* I am really sorry. And I wrote it one hundred times!

My class teacher, Herr Herbholz – he is a Lutheran, but a very nice hippy – talked to me about being naughty and why it is not good, because you might kill your friends.

The atom bomb does some terrible things and people have to think about it all the time to be alert all the time, because that makes them safer and happier. Then he thought he was shrinking and lay under his desk for a bit. When he got up he looked at me like I'm the tennis shoe monster from the lagoon court and shuts his eyes. And then in the glass door I see how terrible I really look, and it's a nightmare but then it's gone again. I was very afraid. Worse than J.

Dear God, you did that to show me how not be horrible to people because otherwise you'll look like this when you are always horrible. Mutti says the wind will change. And all I want to be is funny. Sorry.

Please pray for me through your Pope. This must not happen again. I was very ugly in the glass! Please pray that I get my presents for my birthday!

If I become a priest I will teach people how not to look ugly like that and get their presents all the time.

Yours faithfully

J. Fergal Bulhof-Murphy.

Dunkin' Tennis Balls

Steinhöfer's Dump

Steinhöfer's realm was the dump. It was his very own and private property, and he was proud of it. Steinhöfer's left leg had deserted him without leave in Russia in 1943 when he was only twenty-four. So had both his middle fingers and his right ear. To add insult to injury, another bit of entirely unexpected shrapnel had then travelled, only seconds later, across his face at high speed, leaving a neat diagonal from his left cheek to his right forehead surgically cutting through the nose in its path. The nose had healed reasonably well. The red diagonal scar stayed with him for good, as an incomplete *X*. To some outsiders it looked like a perfectly viable though massive duelling scar sustained at one of Heidelberg's fraternity fencing fests without masks. To other outsiders it looked like somebody had tried to cancel him out.

There were no insiders.

Steinhöfer let no one in, dump or life. Anywhere.

At fifty-five his hair was still naturally blonde and kept carefully to agree with the latest style of 1943. Extremely short back and sides, long on top, combed back with a bit of pomade. In spite of his love for mustard yellow silk cravats with an elegant paisley print in azure blue, Steinhöfer looked an extremely angry man.

He had the latest in prosthetic pieces for a leg, and was the proud owner of a black 1952 Mercedes Benz 300 S Cabrio with B-plates. An automobile as enormous as any good American car. The B-registration told everyone he was from Berlin.

Not East-Berlin.

Proper Berlin!

The new Berlin.

In East-Berlin they had kept the old numeric plates. There Berlin was still 1A just as much as those *Kommunistenschweine* hadn't filled in the bullet holes in most of the old buildings there. And that was because the communists wanted to remind the Germans *over there* that they had lost the war. The Americans and Brits weren't like that. They just wanted the Germans back to work a.s.a.p. without all the Nazi nonsense, the reason why most top ranking Nazi officials hadn't been killed like in the Russian zone. Germany was good for business and the Western Allies knew it.

A fervent supporter of the Daz Witch-Awonda, aka *das Wirtschaftswunder*, Steinhöfer had bought the car at the end of 1952, and in spite of being of an overall scummy and grimy appearance himself, the car had always looked like new ever since Fergal could remember.

"A Mercedes looks after itself forever if you look after it a little," Steinhöfer had scowled at Fergal at their first and last ever vis-à-vis meeting. All Fergal had done was stand outside Herrn Dorfgeist's village shop admiring the beautiful car.

"I like you, Ferkel. I have heard about you. Now, piss off, and leave my car alone!"

Apparently, scarred Steinhöfer liked Fergal because he loved the Americans and the English, and somebody like Fergal was heralding the new Europe for Steinhöfer. A new and united Europe meant lots of scrap and rubbish, which could be sold at a profit.

Although an altogether very scary and dirty looking fellow, there was a strange, nigh on hermetic elegance about the owner of the dump, which redeemed him to Fergal. It had to be the sartorial cravat, the high-quality car, and his impeccably crafted shoes. Good shoes! Shoes told you everything you'd ever needed to know about the wearer, J said. J loved good shoes.

Johanna had trained Fergal to understand the art and craft of a well-made shoe, so her future servant could at least be of some use outside of toilet duties. He had described to her Steinhöfer's shoes. J was absolutely certain they were real Budapesters. Possibly cordovan. Certainly not pigskin!

Steinhöfer looked grime-time. Steinhöfer was abusive. Deep down though he had a stylish Mercedes, a sartorial cravat and wore beautifully crafted shoes. However, his greatest pride was to be owner of the dump. From his point of view there wasn't a single location at Geesterheim that could be termed prime property.

The plot of land behind the woods and the little swamp had been with the Steinhöfers for nigh on three hundred years. And, apart from shredding and banging Immelmann, there wasn't a single Geesterheimer who would have objected to Steinhöfer keeping the property for another thousand. It was however unclear to most villagers how Steinhöfer had come by those B-plates of his, as he had never been seen leaving the village for longer than a day or two. Didn't you have to properly live and be officially registered in a place before you were legally permitted to acquire the requisite local plates? There was something not quite legal about this man!

Steinhöfer himself had told Fergal on that one vis-à-vis occasion the *B* stood for Steinhöfer and his family lived in West Berlin. That's why he got it. His family owned wineries in the area and he had turned his vineyard into a dump. So there! *B* also stood for *beißen, bellen, brutal* as in his two *biting, barking, brutal* Dobermans both of which were called Hölle. Those two Devil's own Dobermans out of hell appeared to like Fergal a great deal as they kept trying to lick his face and hands. "My dogs like you, Fergal. They haven't bitten you yet. Don't let anyone see this. Now, go on, piss off! Now!"

Martin's father, Immelmann, was convinced Steinhöfer, in spite of being a true Geesterheimer winemaker from Berlin, had a very shady past as he couldn't prove he had not worked for the Nazis in Berlin. And as everyone knew real Nazis had lost all their documents unless they had gone off to Bolivia or Brazil or Brooklyn or Bollerboe because it started with a *B* as in Berlin.

Immelmann really wanted to buy Steinhöfer's dump which by the laws of nature should have been his in the first place as Immelmann had seen the terror of Ivan advancing from the East. Thus Immelmann kept reporting Steinhöfer in Nazi-style denunciation to the police for a variety of charges he assiduously made up. There was threatening the public peace by driving around in an open-topped car like a criminal pimp with his two Dobermans. There was looking dangerous and up to no good. There was trying to steal Immelmann's own steam roller and belt-driven saw including his precious bell. The man had unlicensed weapons, machineguns! Sold pistols and drugs to children. Was a

Russian rapist. A bayonet swinging maniac. A known Plötzensee communist murderer, escaped from that most notorious of Berlin prisons, now in the East. A spy! Unless he had been at Spandau prison, possibly together with Hess himself! Well, Hess was a known traitor, wasn't he!?

"Yes, thanks again, Herr Immelmann. We'll look into it. – Goodbye now!" Polizei Oberwachtmeister Knopf would say. Kümmerling his underling would nod solemnly. Something to do!

One problem with all of Immelmann's accusations, which he never failed to take to the police as soon as he had made them up, after days of an avid denouncer's difficult plotting in darkness, surrounded by heaps of bits he had neatly cut up and carefully shredded, already anticipating the dump to be his, was the fact that they all rang somewhat true according to the laws of prejudice. The other problem was that the police had to follow up these hunches so as not to appear negligent.

Geesterheim was a very safe and quiet place, and by taking Immelmann seriously they demonstrated there was a need for police at Geesterheim.

Steinhöfer had a real disadvantage in that he'd always quite impulsively tell the police to "Piss off, or I'll get my dogs on to you!"

Every time.

After such despicable and threatening utterance he would have to apologise humbly in the form of wine or beer. The police station's cellar was said to be well-stocked with Geesterheim's own reds and whites and the local beer, Pfungstädter Pilsener, courtesy of Herrn Sebastian Steinhöfer.

It was mostly down to Immelmann's persistent accusations that the proud and cravatted owner of the dump had acquired his reputation of mean mass-murderer type pimp who was so clever he kept forever evading the law. It was Steinhöfer's actual air of *let's shoot the lot of them and have lunch* which scared the living daylights out of Tristan, Chuck, Joachim and Fergal as much as it attracted them in their secret missions to the dump.

And what a paradise of a dump that was! – Row after row of neatly parked and lovingly valeted old cars. Anything from the twenties to the mid sixties. Horch, VW, Mercedes, NSU, Opel,

BMW. About twenty of them. As number and models were changing, it was a fairly safe bet that he had a bit of a car business going on the side. He didn't restore them, he just cleaned them with insanely dedicated eyes! The cars' interior always immaculate, their exterior as battle-bruised and scarred as Steinhöfer himself. All had without a doubt performed their final duty willingly on the Autobahn.

Once Fergal and his friends had even seen a blood-soaked VW with teeth in the footwell! Mutti said it possibly hadn't been teeth. No, most certainly it hadn't been teeth. Fragments of a porcelain cup that had contained a lot of tomato juice.

"So, you've been to the dump again!?"

"Yes."

"Haven't I told you never to go there ever again. It's dangerous! Full of rats and disease. Promise me, you'll never go again! Promise me now!"

"I promise, Mutti."

Fat chance, Mutti.

Mutti also thought Steinhöfer was a very attractive man, with a bit of the rougher Cary Grant about him. It was a shame he didn't like women.

"Why doesn't he like women?"

"Some men do, Johann, others don't. It's nature or absent fathers or bad mothers."

"Why?"

"I can't tell you now! When you're older, you'll understand."

That was the worst and most patronising answer ever! Fergal understood *completely* why Steinhöfer didn't like women! Most women, including girls – apart from Mutti, Oma, Anne, and Gloria, and maybe some others – were whingy, whiney, annoying little creatures who could follow you around for a long time smiling, and then they'd scratch you if you didn't want to play! Although, ... Big Bernhardt could be a bit like that. It was sad about Gloria because she was back with God again. Mutti had cried a little last year. But Fergal had been adamant Gloria would be back soon with a better neck and a new name.

"That's not very Christian, Johann! Gloria is in heaven and that's nice. So let her stay there!"

"Of course, Mutti."

The cars were at the top bit, at the back of the dump. The peak! As were Steinhöfer's twenty barrels of petrol and diesel, all concealed behind ordinary household rubbish and mountains and mountains of tyres.

The dump was arranged like half a hill with its foot by the entrance gate and its highest point up at about thirty odd meters by the cars, overlooking the woods where it fell off steeply to join the swamp in eerie darkness.

Around this paradise property Steinhöfer had set up a perimeter fence, the locals called the *Iron Curtain.* The locals, most of whom had never been out to Steinhöfer's arcadia, also said the fence was four meters high and continued two meters below the ground where it merged with a cement wall.

Fergal knew this wasn't true because he and his friends had dug their secret entrance under the fence at the top by the cars. It was a very steep and dangerous climb, well worth the risk. The fence continued only one meter underground, and there was *no* underground cement wall.

Locals and grownups generally really didn't know what they were talking about! Neither was the fence electrified as advertised on little yellow plastic warning signs all the way round with a red bolt of lightening and a jerky black person falling backwards. *High Voltage! Danger Of Death! Positively No Entry! Danger Of Explosion! Any Playing Most Severely Prohibited! Parents Will Be Held Liable For Their Children!*

Steinhöfer knew his clientele!

What Steinhöfer didn't know was that his signs were adventure balm on a kid's soul. It was the best advertising any place could get! It did promise more of course than the dump could actually offer.

"But that's advertising for you," Tristan said, "the American way. Have rubbish. Will sell."

Still, it was great fun.

Fergal and his friends had carefully spent one afternoon watching the new fence, just a week after the old wooden one had been torn down. If millions of rats didn't mind the new fence and you could have a good long wee against it without dying from electrocution, "or even being castrated" Joachim remarked clinically, it had to be safe!

At night though floodlights came on, and the Dobermans were on guard growling menacingly. And if Steinhöfer was around for a sleepover at his beloved dump, he'd kill you and suck your brains out with a spiky straw. He needed to eat brains because he was a *saudummer*, sow-stupid Neanderthal throwback with unlicensed guns and dead and buried girls in the cellar alongside his Nazi-past, and Immelmann knew! At night the dump was a bad idea, apparently. You could drown in the swamp, get lost in the woods, be bitten by a snake. All sorts of fantastic adventures, all Muttis and Mammis just didn't understand.

Fergal and his friends had stayed out well beyond nightfall only once. All Muttis, Mamas, Mammis united had called the police, who couldn't make it as Polizei Oberwachtmeister Knopf and his underling Kümmerling were desperately busy repairing a major leak in the cellar, and it was impossible to hear the telephone from down there. All Muttis had then resolved to sit down their little sons to give them a good talking-to. It was just too dangerous to stay out after nightfall because it made the Muttis scared and angry. No one was grounded this time round. But never to do it again, also on account of the roaming Peter Files and Peter Asts of the Mitschnacker family.

"Steinhöfer's new fence is now electrified, Johann! Like the Iron Curtain. Now, promise me never to go there ever again!"

"Of course, Mutti! Yes, Mutti! Sorry!" Bruised and humiliated on the outside, otherwise you'd get grounded for being too cocky. A loud *don't care* and *fat chance* on the inside, otherwise you'd lose all self-respect. Interior and exterior. A bit like Steinhöfer's cars.

Fergal had never seen the Iron Curtain but last year his teacher, Herr Herbholz, had promised he was going to take class to see it *and* the Roman Wall outside Frankfurt. By the end of year three nothing had happened.

Yes, ... well, ... a few new developments, not all of them bad, had taken place in the Bulhof-Murphy household during the first half of 1974. – Fergal's parents had become so tight-lipped they hardly talked with each other anymore. Their lips were *actually* thinner.

The business of B&M Automobiles was seriously in the red and the reserve was gone. It kept ticking over only because the family savings were being used up, or rather *wasted* on it, according to Mutti via J. This meant Fergal was not going to get his very own room in the near future, and the Black Forest peasant hut in the neo-American pig-sty style was completely out of the question because it cost over three-hundred-thousand DMs. That was a lot of money. This was bad!

However, J had become much quieter and hadn't tortured Fergal for some months. The bathroom electrocution had been the last, proper torture session so far. Fingers crossed. Mutti talked to J a lot behind the closed living room door. J, now closing in on sixteen and adulthood, always emerged very down in the mouth from the pit of these one-sided conversations. Her lips too were becoming thinner.

Fergal was now actually living in her room full-time and went to bed as late as his sister. He felt terribly grown-up and responsible, and his performance at school hadn't suffered one little bit. J said she was fine with him staying in her room because Mutti and Dad had to sort out their grown-up problems.

J seemed quite the grownup herself these days. This was good. Her teeth-grinding though was getting louder and louder when she was asleep, and sometimes she'd wake herself with a scream because she had bitten herself bloody.

It was the summer holidays now, and Mutti and Dad had sent J up to Oma and Opa in Hamburg. What a relief that was for Fergal! Although, he wouldn't have minded going up to the Baltic and hiring a *Strandkorb* to watch Opa build a sand-wall round it, swim whenever you like, listen to Opa's stories about the war in the shade of the Strandkorb canopy!

That holiest of holy sanctuaries! The Strandkorb! The beach-basket! A very big basket seating two people. The male of the variety preferably donning a captain's cap on top of an angry look, the female guarding the towels furiously. A German institution with pull-out leg rests to complete any Baltic holiday bliss, to stake your own claim on the short stretch of rough sand, to stare at the dead calm of the fishy azure grey waters of the Ostsee, the East Sea as it is called, waiting for another exciting twenty centimetre wave to make its oily way like a staggering inebriant of the night slowly through seaweed and jellyfish, dead or alive, towards the beach within the next hour or so, rolling like unstoppable liquid slime to eventually burp itself onto the shores before the expectant eyes of angrily excited onlookers, who never for a moment forget about their inherent duty to guard their Strandkorb territory vigilantly, surrounded by a perfect circle of sand, piled up to fifty centimetres high, demarcating up to four meters in diameter. God help anyone who oversteps the line!

But wait, Fergal's quiet inner voice demanded, *consider J for just a moment! She would feed you those horrible jellyfish again and make you swallow without Opa seeing, and then Oma and Opa wouldn't believe you because J is the all-good girl!*

True. – On second thoughts, staying behind was a good idea! Individually, Mutti or Dad might do something with him.

Maybe they'd even do something as a family.

Family? Now what was that exactly? – A man and a woman who had made a girl and a boy before they had gone to sleep!

Family was beginning to appear like a vague memory, the definition for which escaped Fergal every time he tried to pin the word *family* itself down.

Family unit.

Family disunity.

When had this started?

Never mind!

He'd find something to do during the summer holidays!

Granny Hammerich, Tennis & Dope

This was going to be yet another scorcher of a day! Fergal went downstairs to see if Chuck was up for anything.

Chuck, Joachim, Tristan and Fergal had since the beginning of the summer holidays founded the Double-Bubble Gang. On the last day of school Herr Herbholz had announced, year fours would see some new arrivals to their class. Two Gastarbeiter kids from Yugoslavia!

Mighty Micky, the fat butcher's son, who always kept chewing on bits of meat when teacher wasn't looking, had actually seen the foreign tribe of Yugoslavs already! They lived in new government housing just outside Geesterheim by the new tennis courts and football field.

The council had abandoned the Gastarbeiter housing project behind the asocials' block down Mönchsgasse because archaeologists were still busily digging up the ever more extensive Germanic necropolis and remains of a village. A fence had gone up and no one was allowed in. There was a rumour of vast treasure having been uncovered. As the diggings partly extended into school and church property, Pastor Meinheit knew exactly what was going on! Just lots of very old, brittle bones and necklaces.

Mighty Micky had said all Yugoslavs sounded like *chick-chack-vatch-vitch,* with names like Vladimir or Kasimir, and all had tiny black raisin eyes, crooked noses, clawlike fingers, looked like a hungry bunch of emaciated rats, and the lot of them came with long flick knives. – Micky had it on the best of intelligence, the two new arrivals were a gang of real *Messerstecher,* knife-wielding stabbers, and they had, in point of fact, formed a dangerous gang already increasing in notoriety locally.

The Stab Gang!

Mighty Micky had gone on to relate how he and Great Gerhard, the fat baker's son, who shared Micky's secretive, recreational meat-chewing, had in turn formed the Blood & Bone Band, because this was after all a serious and official Defence-Situation, and the siren should sound the Catastrophe Alarm daily and … at this stage an open-mouthed Herbholz had interrupted Mighty Micky, whose cud of white-chewed pork fell out of his mouth to the vinyl floor, only to be picked up and reinserted inside his cheek again, and told him about *Love, love, love! Love is all you need!*

Boring!

The Double Bubble Gang had come to an understanding with the Blood & Bone Band. Despite a variety of traditional differences, like fights to the death in the schoolyard, a truce had to be called for this infighting to stop, so the standard of union could be raised against the new enemy.

This historic concord was referred to as the Blood Bubble Pact. – If gang members of both gang and band fought alongside each other, they were to refer to themselves as either the Blood Bubble Brotherhood or the Blood Blisters, which was snappier.

Joachim and Chuck had come up with the Double Bubble Gang's name as Fergal was plying everybody with chewing gum from the Frankfurt PX.

Today would be another glorious day in the historic pursuits of the Double Bubble Gang!

Fergal knocked on Chuck's door downstairs.

There was some movement behind the door. Fergal knew it was Frau Nolde, Chuck's mother. The door remained shut.

"Is Chuck in?"

"Yes," came a tired voice. And that was all. The door remained shut.

"Will he come out and play?"

There was no answer. Fergal could hear Frau Nolde moving away from the door. Then he heard the living room being shut.

Strange people!

Fergal turned to leave. He would wait in the sandbox at the front of the house. It should still be in the shade. Just about! Chuck *would* turn up.

It only took a couple of minutes, and there he was! Tennis racket in hand. Two tennis balls stuffed into each of his short's pockets.

"Mutti is having her depression today. Let's go get Joachim. Play Double Bubble. We could burn some shit." Chuck liked burning things, or *shit* as he called it. Everybody liked burning things.

Chuck was alright, apart from his fascination with killing things like insects and stuff … or shit. He'd kill a single ant and watch what its mates would do. It was always the same. The squashed ant, or its bits, was carried off just like all the other stuff ants kept carrying about all over the place.

"Or, … how about we go for a swim in the Frog Pond. We might catch a snake!"

"Could do. Let's just go. Ma's very depressed. I think she's still angry because of the towels yesterday." Chuck took his willy out and weed in the sandbox.

"You're going to be ten this year, Chuck! And you got to stop asking your mum for wipies, man!"

Chuck boxed Fergal on the arm, "I don't! I just like the soft towels, and Ma's gonna get me some flannels she promised like a century ago. She always forgets!"

"Chuck, …"Fergal hesitated, "… loo paper?"

"Na. Itches like shit!"

"OK."

Chuck was right about the loo paper! Fergal told him that Arabs also liked it the soft way. They used water. Dad had witnessed all this in Egypt and Yemen. Paper was more practical. OK. Arabs used water because they honoured their paper Koran which was their Bible, and they squatted and pooed in a hole.

"Arabs do their duty in a hole, and then they wash it off with water with their left hand because they use the right hand for saying *hello* or cutting your throat from behind."

The left side of Chuck's upper lip went up as he was stirring the cement of wee and sand, "It's all fucking desert there."

"Hm. Maybe they carry a canteen around with them wherever they go."

"Arabs and their arse canteens. Fuck all Arabs."

"Or they wait until they get to their river … or beach?"

"Do they have rivers? Arse rivers!"

"Must have. In my book it says they're called wadi. Dad says so too."

"Wadis are dry."

"Except when it rains."

"Wadi arse wash. Fuck it!"

Chuck and Fergal were going to start year four as of the end of August. That was another four weeks to go. And then another year and then Big School!

From the protective, cool shade of the sandbox the friends stepped forward into the heat. Immediately, the shade behind them was denser and darker.

"Is the shade darker for you too now."

"Arse shade wash. Fuck the shade!"

Joachim's house was just across. – His parents had left him behind at home with his grandmother yet again. The LeBatards had gone on holiday, diving in the Maldives. The LeBatards hadn't forgotten their son! They had just left him behind because it was safer for Joachim. And the little LeBatard should not complain! He had all the toys in the world and the latest techno-gadgets.

Joachim was the only kid in the village with a tennis and football video game. He played on his own a lot, and if you wanted to touch one of his toys, he'd kick you hard. Joachim mostly played video-tennis with himself.

Whenever the LeBatards came back from their sonless holidays, they brought lots of stuff for their little LeBatard. Photographs and slides. Yeah. Great. After this year's diving tour Joachim knew they'd return with a six-hundred shot super-scuba underwater slideshow for him to cheer up at the beautifully coloured flora and Joachim would really want to shoot them.

During school, one of the more frequent early morning scenes, when his parents went to leave for Opel GM at Rüsselsheim, was Joachim chasing their car begging and pleading not to leave him behind. This was possibly Joachim at his most emotional. Sometimes he'd break down in the middle of the road just lying there until his granny came to tear him into a standing position and reprimand him with a good whack about the head.

Today though, across at Joachim's house something different and new was astir in the heat. There were a number of frustrated, hollow screams from behind the house. His grandmother!

Both Chuck and Fergal hid behind their wall with just their eyes showing. Out of view seemed a better idea at the moment!

Joachim appeared running into view. He stopped on the front lawn looking over at Chuck's and Fergal's house. He was smoking a fat, long cigarette, inhaling the smoke proficiently. He was the only one of Fergal's friends who smoked regularly and knew how to inhale. Then Joachim saw them.

"Hey kids, it's granny-race today! I've got a new name for her. Unorgasmic saggy testicle face arsehole piss mouth." Granny appeared around the corner at a stiff walking pace, letting off another of her frustrated hollow death screams. She was closing in quickly with her hand raised to put an end to her grievance.

Fergal and Chuck couldn't let this happen. "Joachim! Behind you! Watch out! Testicle face! Run!"

Joachim grinned at his grandmother, gave her the trendy American finger with his free hand and ran behind the house again screeching *testicle face* three times. Frau Hammerich, Joachim's grandmother, for that was what she was known as by grownups and feared for by Joachim, thankfully hadn't spotted Fergal and Chuck! In any case, she was too deaf to have heard them. Had she seen who had warned her grandson, she wouldn't have hesitated to come over and teach them some respect! She disappeared from view, striding after Joachim. She would of course get him eventually, as he, like any other living being, required food and water.

Joachim appeared back on the front lawn taking a deep inhalation from his big cigarette. But his grandmother was a clever and wicked woman right out of Grimm's *Hänsel und Gretel!* She had only pretended to walk to the back of the house! Around the same corner, where she had just vanished, her head moved in catlike confidence. Her head went down a little, her back arched. She was ready to pounce! This old lady couldn't jump, or could she? Or was she that old, actually? Mutti said she was only fifty. To Fergal that might sound ancient but in actual fact it was still quite young these days, Opa said.

The distance between Granny Hammerich and Joachim was a good five meters. Joachim was nodding over at his friends and called, "I know, kids! I'm not stupid! Penis nose is back!" He took another massive drag and left the fat fag dangling from his mouth, blowing thick smoke out through his nostrils with poise.

Mistake!

Big mistake!

"Big fuckin' mistake!" Chuck commented.

In a flash granny Hammerich had shot forward, pushed Joachim over and sat on top of him, her knees on his arms, restraining his every move. His legs were kicking, but to no avail! She had him pinned down! He wasn't screaming or shouting abuse. Joachim was scared!

Slowly did she take his big cigarette from his mouth and threw it with a most elegant movement into the street. How strange this was though! Joachim hadn't moved, hadn't run. He could have! He was normally very quick to react! What had happened? It was as if he'd been trapped in something sticky! A fly's nightmare of flypaper. Joachim was on the flypaper! And now, Granny Hammerich was beginning to lay into Joachim. Neither Chuck nor Fergal had ever seen such a thing.

At first slowly. Left cheek … smack … right cheek … smack … and then faster … left, right, left, right, left, right. Joachim wasn't crying … he was whinging like a puppy!

"This is fucking terrible, Ferkel!"

"We've got to do something! Like … now!"

The first tennis ball swished closely over Granny Hammerich's silvery topknot.

Left, right, left, right. Smack, smack, smack.

Chuck shut his eyes and concentrated. The second ball appeared from his shorts' pocket. He probed it with his hand.

Smack, smack, smack.

Chuck squeezed the ball.

Smack, smack, smack. Smack, smack, smack!

Bounced it.

"Do something!"

Smack, smack, smack.

Caught it. He nodded, then spat on it.

Left, right, left, right. Smack, smack, smack.

He threw it up in the air and with a vast volley bashed it with all his might over at Granny Hammerich!

Fergal always wondered where Chuck got this power from!? He was unbeatable on the court! If you fought with him on the lawn, he was totally weak and gave up quickly. Arm wrestling too. But tennis!? Wow! You really had to get out of the way, and his serve was never long.

Chuck's ball was describing a gentle arch, shooting across at the LeBatard lawn at high speed.

Left, right. Smack! Smack, smack, smack. Left, right, left, right.

Another thing, which could only be described as awesome, was Chuck's ability to win at target tennis. No hope for Fergal or his friends or anyone! Put up a row of empty tins on the ground or on a wall and Chuck would shoot them right down with his tennis balls, one by one.

They had once put Chuck to the distance test. Chuck's accuracy decreased ever so slightly under half a football field. His farthest hit – whack ball, see where it first touches the ground – had thus far been one football field and a good bit. Accuracy really suffered after three quarters of a football field though.

Granny Hammerich was about twenty meters across. That was about a fifth of a football field from Chuck's and Fergal's point of current view. The tennis ball's point of view in this case had improved no end! From Chuck's dark pocket via very brief stop-over whack on Granny Hammerich's temple straight into the soft green of the incredibly well cared-for LeBatard lawn under blue sky. A tennis ball holiday for any ball that had experienced even only a short service under Chuck's reign.

Granny Hammerich was restfully lying on her side in the grass.

Joachim moved off her leg, got up and looked at his grandmother.

"She looks quite peaceful now! She should sleep more. Vicious testicle rat!"

Joachim was beginning the short walk over to Chuck and Fergal's. Very, very slowly! It was as if Joachim were in a different time zone altogether.

Fergal just hoped none of the grownup Muttis or Mamas were looking out of windows at this moment! Pas and Dads and Dadas were at work.

But what the …! What was *wrong* with Joachim?

Their friend picked up the smouldering cigarette from the middle of the road.

Chuck made a face of distaste. Joachim would never be a sportsman.

Joachim looked up and smiled weirdly, "Thanks, kids! Good shot, Chuck! David and Goliath. Full on!"

Chuck shook his head, "Are you fucking drunk or what?"

"Noooooo. I just found this really dark dope at the back of my mum's drawer in the bedroom with all the dildoes and stuff in it. It's really relaxing. I rolled the joint myself, kids."

Chuck rubbed his nose. Fergal grinned. Joachim was like a sad grownup trapped in a little body. He was *very* cool!

"Where're we going?" He certainly seemed much calmer than usual and so far not a single swearword in his friends' direction had left his lips.

Lt Hardy had told Fergal they had all been smoking dope in Vietnam all the time and their Coca Cola still had real coke in it to cheer everyone up a bit. When Fergal had last seen Lt Hardy in April, he hadn't reminded him that he had promised to get them a 1911 Colt each after they had played Hitler Youth in Geesterheim's drainage ditch last November. Maybe Tristan was right!? It was all bullshit and Hardy should go to Bollerboe!

Chuck looked over Joachim's shoulder. His eyes opened wide, "We're not going anywhere, guys! We're fuckin' runnin'! You're granny's woken up!"

It was evidently very hard to run for Joachim. He staggered fast, but as such it didn't matter much, as Granny Hammerich was too disoriented.

When they'd reached the big car park at the back of the LeBatard property they stopped their hurried escape and waited for Joachim to catch up.

Just over eight months ago there had been a terrible accident in the field over there. Lt Hardy said the soldier had died there and then. Now the field was covered in fresh, green maize already grown higher than Fergal in a short time.

Joachim had caught up with them. "Do you wanna a puff?"

"No thanks!" both Fergal and Chuck said at the same time.

Joachim dropped the joint, "Where's our KZ victim, Tristan?"

"Don't call him that, thickhead! You know he's having a bad time with his brother." Fergal had come to dislike Joachim more and more over the past four months. His language was getting worse and worse. It seemed the more he was being beaten the more abusive he became himself.

"Shit! So? Still doesn't answer my question. Where is *thin* Tristan?"

Chuck shook his head. Fergal answered, "I don't know. When I called him earlier his Mama said he was playing in the trenches. I don't think so! I bet he's roaming the fields playing Afrikakorps, and then he'll die of thirst. He's really good at that!"

"So? Who gives a runny shit!? And I think …" Joachim stopped mid-sentence as if he couldn't be bothered to ever say a word again. He looked asleep on his feet.

Fergal shrugged, "I think we'll meet him."

With his eyes shut Joachim commented, unbelievably slowly, "Fucking boring. Stupid kid. Stupid kiddie games. He's down to his fucking skeleton. He'll die for real soon, he's so fucking sorry for his fucking waster of a brother."

Fergal had to shake his head, "You're getting worse, Joachim. If you want to join us, smoke some more dope and calm the fuck down! This is a tour of duty … for the Double Bubble Gang!"

Joachim went back in the car park a bit and picked up his joint. It was still going. He gave it a drag and held it up to the hot morning sun, "Tristan's burning up like this."

Chuck nodded, "So are you, Joachim!"

The three friends took the dirt paths. This was the long way to the swamp and woods. They were careful not to cross the fields haphazardly destroying the crops as it would get you into too much trouble with the farmers. Trouble as in a clip around the ears and a hefty fine for your parents if you were too lippy. The LeBatards had been fined six times already!

Joachim was right though, Tristan was much too thin at the moment. He was naturally quite gaunt and anaemic looking. His sallow skin, hollow cheeks, and dark eyes in deep sockets hadn't improved much ever since Fergal had come to know him.

At the beginning of the summer holidays Tristan's brother Siegfried had been sent to a psychiatric hospital for re-evaluation, yet again. Nothing ever changed with Siegfried! This time Siegfried had attacked an American tank.

The tank had been slowly rolling through Geesterheim, pointing its small calibre cannon at windows now and then, with the machine-gunner taking out people, cars, houses, kids, making machine-gunning sounds with his mouth.

There hadn't been much Siegfried had to do as he was fully geared up in his trench outside at home in the garden already. In SS Sturmmann battledress he had been waiting for something important to happen, any second! Then he had heard the American tank with the loud Chrysler diesel, had done up his *Koppel* belt with the leather pouches for the sub-machine gun clips already attached, had put on his helmet, slung his Schmeisser over his shoulder, had considered for a moment, then stuck two potato masher grenades in his belt and had left the security of his trench to face off the enemy.

Siegfried's Schmeisser had had the pin removed, his cartridges were fake, the grenades had been empty on this occasion. All part of the American and English memorabilia market, and Siegfried's own collection of stuff. Stuff he had found on the old WWII battlefields in the area. Everywhere around Geesterheim was still littered with the debris from the last war. You just needed to know where to look!

The only majorly illegal bits about Siegfried were his helmet, tunic and collar as they bore the skull and crossbones, eagle, swastika, and SS insignia. Everything well looked after and original. Very illegal in Germany, especially when worn outside your closest circle of friends in public. You just didn't do such a thing, especially to outsiders!

Siegfried had been following in the tank's wake for a bit watching the young machine-gunner do shooting sounds when he had grabbed the rear handle to heave himself up, and had put the Schmeisser to the mouth-shooter's neck. Then he had dropped the grenade in, made an apt explosion sound for the grenade with his own mouth, and had asked the driver to "Shtopp zer vehicle end get out!" Everyone of the tank crew had been very scared and shouted, "Rock n roll! It's Zigziggy!" and surrendered.

Siegfried had lined up the crew at the back of the tank, had taken their weapons and then something quite unforeseen had happened. Zigziggy had driven off with the tank!

What Siegfried hadn't known was that the tank crew had come to Geesterheim especially for Sick Siggy aka Zigziggy, the very reason why they had been cruising around the village for half an hour.

All a big lure!

Siegfried wasn't just known as *that mad Nazi* but also as somebody who could procure medals, rifles, sub-machine guns, uniforms, machine guns, … the lot. With or without pin, and with loads of swastikas. Active or deactivated. All original. In good working order! It was only when he was in trench-mode that he wasn't in one of his bartering moods. Simple really.

But you had to know. About his moods.

Up until the moment when the rear gate had shut, and the bit, where the crew realised Zigziggy could actually drive the damn thing, "Motherfucker can drive!?" in spite of the rumours that he was totally gone in the head, there had only been friendly words of surrender, "It's cool, dude! Chill, man! We're just tourists!" Then they had started shouting their "Eh, eh! Ehhhhhhh! Hold up right there! Son of a bitch!" when the tank had disappeared.

They had been stranded in Geesterheim.

Helpless in enemy territory!

The crew had traipsed over to Herrn Dr. Neussler', Siegfried's father, where they had got some coffee and cake after which they might have to discuss a rather more serious matter. As politely as possibly had it then been revealed to Dr. Neussler that his son had nicked a US tank, dressed in an SS uniform, armed with a Schmeisser sub-machine gun and grenades, and, that he had thrown one of said grenades into the tank, etc., and would it be possible to buy the grenade off him.

Dr. Neussler knew exactly what to do!

He had taken all of the American soldiers down Siegfried's trench system at the back of his garden and had led them to the specially fortified comms dugout. There the Second Lieutenant had managed to establish a radio link with his tank and had told Zigziggy to fucking stop or else he'd destroy his goddam fucking trench system.

In the meantime however Siegfried had managed to pick up Fergal, Tristan and Joachim down by the gravel pit to *really* play war. The tank had had *real* ammo inside, and Siegfried had had the time of his life shooting at just everything in the gravel pit. He had even made one of the grassed overhangs collapse!

And shots into water looked great like a chaotic fountain.

It had been fantastic and was going to be kept a secret forever. At the same time as the Second Lieutenant's voice had come over the radio, the tank had stalled and Siegfried couldn't get it started again. The diesel gauge had still been at half full. Siegfried had told his little friends to scarper. Close to the woods, only three kilometres outside Geesterheim, they could hear the siren blaring out the fire signal.

The things that had happened later that day at the beginning of July hadn't been so brilliant. Certainly not for the tank crew who had been forced to explain to their superior why they had gone to Geesterheim at all, instead of Griesheim near Darmstadt, as ordered.

Siegfried would take two helmets to the psychiatric hospital this time. He knew he would be in for a longer stay.

So far the summer holidays had been OK.

Fergal looked over his shoulder. Joachim was a way away puffing on his joint. Last drag. He stamped it out like a real man, and then he fell over.

"This is getting really boring!" – Chuck was right. They went back over to Joachim who was just lying there in the dust of the dirt path giggling quietly. They picked him up and continued walking, drag-carrying Joachim along with his arms around their shoulders.

In this heat they'd need water soon, and Joachim even sooner. The only water point was in the old clubhouse of Geesterheimer F.C., the *Sportplatz* outside the woods. It had been built by Hitler for the physical edification of his Youths thirty-five years ago and was now completely derelict. Because of the HJ's[10]

---

[10] *Ger.* Hitler Jugend (HJ)

historic last stand and the fact that the war had been lost, Geesterheimers wanted no more to do with that bit of their past. So they ignored Hitler's *Sportplatz* and built a brand new football field after the war. There was an even newer one now.

Of course, the old Hitler field was still being used, but only after exploits to the woods, the swamp, the Frog Pond, and best of all … the dump!

Hitler's water point was another kilometre before they'd get there, and with having to drag-carry deadweight Joachim it might take another half hour.

"Why don't we leave him here to die?" Chuck said with a wink.

"Good idea!"

Both pushed Joachim's arms off their shoulders to see what would happen. Well … he was still standing. Joachim stopped giggling. "You two arseholes would do that, eh? Stupid swine dick cunts."

"No!" both said, and Chuck added, "But you'd believe we'd do that!? And you'd call us arseholes and swine dick cunts anyway. – Who's the bad friend, eh!?"

The mood wasn't right for talking at the moment. They just kept walking. Dehydrated and angry. Joachim kept repeating he hadn't had breakfast and was extremely thirsty, which really didn't help.

Only quarter of an hour later and Joachim was the first at the tap. The ice-cold groundwater was lovely! They should have brought canteens! And they still hadn't come across Tristan who should be around.

Even if Tristan did play Afrikakorps desert rat dying horribly from thirst on his own, he'd have his original German Wehrmacht felt-covered canteen on him.

In Paradisum

The woods ahead of them looked dark and foreboding. Terrible adventures were awaiting them in there!

Chuck raised his racket like a sword just before they entered the wet, gloomy hell of this green kingdom via their own secret and well-trodden path in. "That we may survive and live to tell the tale! Long live the Double Bubble Gang! Down with the Stab Gang!"

"Down, down, down!" cried Joachim and Fergal.

After ten slow minutes, they had passed the little pond everyone knew was the most deadly of dangerous swamps. Another five minutes, and the steep, overgrown wall to the well protected Castle of Dump, built on the rubbish of the ancients, arose before them blotting out the sky above.

You had to crick your neck to see the top where the fence had been built close to the precipice. The ascent was strenuous and unforgiving, but they encountered neither enemy forces nor members of the Blood & Bone Band who were known to chew their cud around here. Mighty Micky and Great Gerhard had said, sometimes they came to the woods to smoke cigarettes.

Wow!

What an exciting life they had outside the bakery and the butcher's, being fat and cuddy and all!

They had just about reached the top when Joachim slid all the way back down on his front again. It looked ridiculous, as Joachim made absolutely no effort in stopping his slide. So, face down he slid. It took him another five minutes to get back up again. He was covered in mud from top to bottom. He even had mud and little roots stuck in his teeth and coming out of his nostrils.

"You look a very scary mess, Joachim!" Fergal smirked.

"I know. – That's why I did it."

"Yeah, yeah, yeah! Get out of it! You're just full of kif, man! If you wanna fuck off, be our guest!" Chuck was serious. Fergal agreed quietly.

All the cars were there! Steinhöfer hadn't sold a thing this quarter. – The nice thing was that Steinhöfer had all the keys in his shack by the entrance. When he wasn't in, all you had to do was push the door in a certain way, and suddenly you stood in the shack, and there were the keys! At one time or another, they had all started and even driven a car here. Tristan was too small to drive, but he had sat on the passenger seat every time and that counted too! – "I know know how to drive with the gears and brake!" Tristan would say, quivering.

They went left at the fence, and after fifteen paces they reached the tunnel they had dug. The camouflage used to cover it was gone. Either Steinhöfer had found it and he'd be waiting for them hiding behind one of his barrels with a machine gun and flame thrower, or …

… *there* was Tristan! In an enormous *Wehrmacht* helmet and something closely resembling an old German uniform, which his Mammi had made for him.

Tristan had noticed his friends but was ignoring them. He was much too busy doing something by the petrol barrels. With a huge amount of effort he was pushing down a big, strange tool he had stuck into the middle of the barrel.

Chuck, Joachim, then Fergal crawled through their tunnel under the fence and, ducking down to avoid any possible enemy fire, made their way over to Tristan.

"You look terrible, Joachim!" was Tristan's only greeting. Tristan himself really looked in quite a state.

"Joachim slid all the way down the hill like a dead person. It looked great! He's smoked some kif like his parents with their dildos. – Let's burn a car today, guys!" Now Chuck made it sound all so adventurous.

"I'm not interested." Tristan looked sad and tiny today. He kept pushing the tool down.

"What do you have in your rucksack?"

"Two stick grenades. They're real and *full*. I'm going to set fire to the rubbish as a diversion, and then I'll leave the hand grenades attached to the barrels, run, and they'll blow up, and then the petrol will explode so the cars get covered, and then we'll make our getaway. It'll be the biggest fire ever!"

Joachim turned round and walked off towards the tunnel behind the cars, "I'm going home. This is too dangerous!" And with that he was off.

Chuck and Fergal had to admit, throwing a hand grenade into the clubhouse or the ditch, as they were wont to, was something quite different to what Tristan had planned here! Yes, it was exciting, … but Tristan really didn't look as if he were playing. His uniform looked too serious!

Besides, there would be huge amounts of smoke and noise! With a hand grenade just let off now and then, Geesterheimers would put it down to the Americans. With *two* detonations followed by a *massive* fire … actually, … who was to say what would happen? Maybe the barrels would explode too with a loud bang!?

"I didn't know you had any grenades left!!!?" Fergal and Tristan knew how to let them off. Tristan had always told Fergal how many there were left in Siegfried's cache.

"These are my brother's last two. He asked me to look after them. Not like the other two. They're just empty toys. These are *real!* I now also have his map of where to find all the weapons and ammo we'll ever need!"

"Is Steinhöfer in?" Chuck was beginning to move back towards the fence too.

"Yes. Last time I looked he was in his shack, reading."

"When was the last time."

"Five minutes."

"OK! – What are you doing with the wrench?"

"I'll open the screw, and then the petrol will come out. Then I'll set fire to the rubbish with the crates and paper at the bottom and run back up and put the grenade in the puddle of petrol. Then we run."

"Phew!" Chuck came back over and watched Tristan pushing away at the tool. Tristan was too weak. He'd never get it open. Neither would Chuck. "You try, Fergal!"

Fergal scratched his head. Was this such a good idea? Well … "OK. – Leave the tool in!"

One push and the nut came lose.

"You're good, Fergal!" Tristan looked alive and very excited. "Now just undo the other ones but not fully. Then, whilst I start the fire down at the bottom, you open them up fully. And when I'm back we'll do the grenades and run."

Fergal looked at Chuck, who only shrugged his shoulders and started moving about. You could always find something interesting up here! But what exactly was happening with Tristan?

Fergal knew this wasn't good. It wasn't like playing, even with real Nazi grenades in the clubhouse down on the old football field. This was what Opa called a crime! It was doing something against somebody else.

The clubhouse was no one's and derelict. One more grenade in there hurt no one. Up here it was all Steinhöfer's, and Steinhöfer was not going to like it if the Double Bubble Gang destroyed it.

"Listen, Tristan! I'm not doing this. This is a crime! I know. Opa used to be in the police." Fergal tightened the nut again. Petrol had already started dripping from the barrel. "Let's go down and throw the grenades in the football field. We can watch from behind a tree."

"No! You foreign traitor! You *Scheißferkel*, you! I kill you!" Tristan was trembling. He looked very weak as if he hadn't eaten for some time.

"Oh, look what I've found!" Chuck came out from behind the barrels dragging a big cardboard box, "It's filled with old tennis balls."

Tristan had sat down crying. His massive helmet had come off. A wonder really that it had stayed on all the time, that he hadn't taken it off in the heat. He was clutching his rucksack like a mother might protect her dying baby.

"Look, Tristan! This is too dangerous! Let's go play war in the swamp."

"Piss off, both of you! Traitors!" He cried the sort of tears you really don't want to cry in front of your friends but can't help crying. It sounded awful, and somehow both Fergal and Chuck felt that they were letting their friend down.

"I have a great idea, Tristan!" Chuck did his *light-bulb-over-head* impression with his right hand, "Pling!"

"What?" Fergal was a bit dubious. After all, the day had started with Chuck knocking out Granny Hammerich, and it certainly was going to end for Joachim with a great massive wallop.

"Fergal, … hang on!" Chuck was off again behind the barrels. A couple of minutes went by. Tristan stopped crying. When Chuck returned he was holding an old steel bucket. "Please, let the petrol run for a bit."

"Why? It's dangerous!"

"Don't be a coward now, Ferkel!"

"OK." He opened the valve just a little but nothing came.

"Open it more, Ferkel!" Tristan was getting excited again.

And all of a sudden the nut shot out, and out gushed the petrol.

"The barrel's having a piss," Chuck laughed. He took the bucket and filled it halfway. "Let's move away. I don't want to blow up!"

The friends moved over to where they could see Steinhöfer's little shack. It was about the length of a football field away. Chuck was dragging the box with the tennis balls, Fergal was carrying the bucket filled with petrol, and Tristan his rucksack and helmet.

Steinhöfer's Mercedes was parked outside his shack, and he was merrily singing inside. The car's top was down.

Chuck started dunking the tennis balls in the petrol. After he had done about twenty of them he asked, "Who's got a lighter."

"I'm not allowed lighters," blushed Tristan.

Fergal and Chuck looked at each other in utter surprise. – Here was their little friend with two potato masher hand grenades in his rucksack! Their little friend, who loved wearing uniforms, who knew how to let off grenades, fire all sorts of guns, … and he wasn't allowed lighters!?

"I have my Zippo." It was the Zippo given to Fergal together with the Raybans by Dad's friends, Matteo and Calogero, the Mafia brothers. He had given the Raybans to J. Well, she had taken them from him, … *or else!* But the Zippo lighter he had been hiding for three years outside the house in the crack by the cellar windows, refilling it occasionally with Dad's own petrol from the garage. It had become reflex to him to pick it up whenever he went out with his friends. "Let's get rid of the bucket first or else we'll really blow. I've seen how petrol goes up. Dad showed me on the barbeque."

"Yeah! Wow!" Chuck nodded, "I was there! Your dad's fun!" – He took the bucket and carried it back to the barrel which was still gushing its contents happily, but because of the incline up here it was flowing away behind the barrels. When he was back he said, "Now, here's what we'll do! I'll put myself over there with the racket. You, Fergal, pick one up, light it and toss it over to me, and I'll hit them over to the paper and wood pile."

"And that'll work?"

"It should. Just keep your distance from the pile of soaked balls and don't set fire to yourself."

Tristan was trembling with excitement. Chuck took up position. Tristan put himself just behind Chuck. If Steinhöfer came out of his shack and looked up here, he'd see them!

Fergal lit the first ball. It caught fire immediately and he tossed it over to Tristan who whacked it as hard as he could. Fergal's fingers were burning. How strange it looked and it didn't hurt at first! Then it did and he managed to blow it out. He'd be more prepared for this with the second ball.

He lit the second ball. The same thing happened again! But it was easy to blow it out.

The third, fourth, fifth … the fifteenth, sixteenth. His fingers hurt and he indicated this over to his friends. From where he was standing he couldn't see what Tristan and Chuck were seeing.

Suddenly, Tristan and Chuck moved backwards quickly, ducking! They were laughing. Then they came running over to Fergal, "Let's get out of here whilst we're still alive! Steinhöfer's outside his shack scratching his head."

"What? What happened? I couldn't see a thing."

Tristan and Chuck were cringing with stifled laughter. Both were holding their sides. Tristan lost his helmet yet again before Chuck could say, "We really have to get out of here! I'll tell you at the bottom. Let's! Now!"

Smallest friend first, then Chuck followed by Fergal.

Getting down the hill was always fantastic fun!

Chuck had been to the great dune at Arcachon in France last year. The dump wasn't as good, but, well, … almost as good, he said. – Because it was so steep and the ground relatively soft, it almost felt like floating down! Step upon step you took down on the descent seemed like meters long.

At the bottom Fergal grabbed Tristan's helmet and the friends just ran!

When they had just about arrived at the swamp a strange scene foisted itself on them from the near distance. – There was Joachim, but there was also Big Bernhardt!

Joachim was being held with his arms sticking out at his sides by Big Bernhardt from behind in a full nelson! Joachim's eyes were shut, and he didn't look like he'd been breathing much for some time.

Big Bernhardt was dressed in his Y-fronts and sandals only. His fat, wobbling body was covered in gooey, black, swampy stuff, and quite a few black and blue bumps which his father was known to inflict. His mouth was shouting, "Who are the Double Bubble Gang? Tell me, tell me! I"ll break your neck! Tell …" he was interrupted by the remaining members of the Double Bubble Gang appearing on this strange choice of a stage for one of Bernhardt's bullying sessions. – Bernhardt must have followed them! The sad bastard had definitely followed them!

Joachim's head looked intensely red and he wasn't saying much, nor was he moving by himself. His movements were entirely directed by Big Bernhardt.

Chuck stepped forward, "We know who the Double Bubble Gang are, and if you don't let go of Joachim, one of our many friends and members, we will, … we will …" Chuck looked behind him. Tristan stepped forward boldly although the marks of his earlier tears were still visible, "… we will kill you dead, you fat, shit frog!"

Big Bernhardt didn't let go off Joachim who was now but dangling as dead from the maniac's grip. He smiled at Tristan and barked, "Woof!" Tristan repositioned himself behind Fergal.

Now it was up to Fergal to say something, "Bernie! If you don't let go of Joachim now, we'll drown you like the fat, sad runt you are, and you'll never know who the famed Double Bubble members are. Nor will you *ever* be admitted to the gang!"

"Because you'll be killed dead," piped up Tristan who seemed altogether much perkier behind Fergal.

"Yes, exactly! Quite dead!" added Chuck.

Big Bernhardt let go off Joachim who just fell to the soft, mossy floor of the wood.

"If you have killed …" but Chuck was interrupted by Joachim's weak voice, "I'm just kiffed out. Don't worry 'bout me!" He then appeared to fall asleep again.

Big Bernhardt rolled his shoulders, "Gerhard and Micky are members of the Brave Blood Bubble Blister Brotherhood Band. And they tell me that there's a gang called Double Bubble who want to kill me, and Joachim is the leader!"

"Joachim is not the leader. We have no leaders." Chuck was most indignant.

Bernhardt grinned an evil grin, "You are the Double Bubbles! Gotcha!"

Fergal laughed, "Stop your stupid games, Bernhardt! You were following us *again,* and you knew we're the Double Bubble! Has your father beaten you again."

Bernhardt looked at his sandaled feet, "I came here to play Vietnam swamp soldier." He pointed at Joachim, "Ask him! I was in the pond and all. It's not deep!"

"Your father's beaten you again! He has, hasn't he!? What've you done this time? Looked at the Holy Cross the wrong way?"

"If I tell you, will you make me a member?"

"No!" both Fergal and Chuck shouted in disgust simultaneously, and a fraction of a second later came Joachim's "No!" and then Tristan's "No?"

Fergal asserted himself, "You tell us what you did, and then we'll make you a member of our gang!"

"Oh, what!?" interrupted Chuck, "No way!"

"We'll make you a member of our gang … after … and only *after* you have passed the *secret* admission test!" Fergal would have to make up the secret admission test pretty quickly.

In his approach to questions Chuck was as direct as his tennis game, "What admission test, Ferkel?"

"The *secret* admission test, Chuck!" As Fergal had put enough intensity into his voice and also kicked Chuck in the shin, not hard, but hard enough, Chuck got the gist of how matters were going to proceed.

"Ah, the *secret admission test*! Horrible!"

"You are really quite thick, Tennis Star!" chimed Tristan from the back.

Bernhardt's eyes went up at something over Fergal's head, then his fat hand pointed at the sky, "Did you do that? You've just come from up there!"

At once the three friends turned round. A huge cloud of dense black smoke was rising high in the sky over the dump. The fire must have reached the tyres! Once the tyres were burning it was only a very short distance to the massive barrels of petrol, and then … the cars. – At this point there was a sequence of five deep, thudding explosions. Not the sort of explosion the Double Bubble Gang would be afraid of! Everyone just made a face. A sound like that was just such a nuisance. But nuisance or no, even from down here you could now see flames shooting up into the black clouds at nervous intervals. The cars had been reached! Somehow.

Incredible how quickly fire could spread!

What was even more amazing is that Geesterheim's siren hadn't started yet!

Suddenly there was an horrific scream from high up at the dump! The fact that it carried as well as the explosions was disconcerting and denoted a lot of anger! Real Steinhöfer anger!

Somehow the friends felt that the scream was being directed down at them in the woods.

Steinhöfer had awoken!

His private property being eaten by flames!

Another terrible and long scream!

Steinhöfer really didn't like the conflagration.

Steinhöfer was pissed!!!

Chuck giggled, "We better get out of here now! – I didn't tell you. Some of the balls went out when they flew, and some didn't. And some also didn't land in the paper bit. I'm not that good a shot! Two landed in Steinhöfer's Mercedes. One of them went out. Definitely! The other might not have gone out, you understand!?"

"Shit!" Fergal didn't swear much normally. "Let's hide in the woods by the Frog Pond!" – And so they did. And Bernhardt ran all the way with them as fast as he could, carrying Joachim piggyback with a broad smile on his fat face! This was the happiest day in Bernhardt's life!

Out of the woods, across the football field, past the old clubhouse, where they all drank serious amounts of water. Tristan did have his canteen. And if indeed they'd be dying of thirst again by the Frog Pond they could drink from the little stream that kept the pond topped up. It was clean and tasted great.

Water wasn't the problem now. The kilometre high column of thick black smoke from the dump was! The friends could still hear the roar of the fire inside the clubhouse. That wasn't a good sign! It must be a fairly big fire.

For a brief moment Fergal felt sick to his stomach. Then, although a trifle late, the Geesterheimer sirens started blasting away through the hot ether of this great summer day.

Baaa *Baaa* *Baaa* *Baaaaaaaaaaaa*
Three small sheep and one big bully sheep like Bernhardt.

"That's the catastrophe alarm."

"Yeah. We know, Fergal."

"I know it because of three small sheep and one big bully sheep."

"Yeah. Who cares!?"

"Shouldn't it be the fire alarm?"

"Maybe Steinhöfer's got poison up there."

"And!?"

It was very close to noon.

"Let's move out, men!" Tristan commanded looking proudly at the flames. "We don't want the enemy to catch wind of our whereabouts!"

Out the back of the clubhouse, through a long field of maize – the perfect cover – into another and even bigger wood further away than Muttis and Mamas would ever want to know!

The Frog Pond had an open bit on one side with little beaches. The other side was shut off by the woods. You could sit on the grass verge and just dangle your feet, or if you felt like it, jump in and float around. And if you couldn't swim, like Tristan, there were enough shallow bits to play battleship in ferociously! – It was beautiful and almost cool even on the hottest of days.

Mutti called it *totally tranquil* and didn't want to know how Fergal had found it. – Fergal had found it with Chuck roaming the countryside with their bikes.

Just before the sun set, the frogs would start, hence the name they had given it. Their concert here was incredible, almost deafening. The strange thing was that it wasn't even on the area's ordnance survey map.

The five boys sat on the grassy bank on the wood side. Bernhardt was still only in his Y-fronts. For a while everyone was just enjoying the quiet, forgetting about the smoke at their backs. Then Bernhardt took off his Y-fronts and jumped in the water. There was an uproar of protest.

"Yuck! – Did fat-arse have to do *that?* Nightmares from now on!" But no one meant it. They all knew what they looked like from PE. "Fat-arse has the smallest willy because he's always scared of his SS daddy."

"If you say that again I'll break your neck, Chuck, you stupid tennis snob! Daddy is a good man. He did his duty. And your family buggered off to America with the Vikings. Cowards!" – Everyone stripped off and jumped in the water.

Fergal and Chuck showed Tristan how to float on his back for a bit. Tristan was more interested in playing half-dead-soldier just about making it to the eastern banks of the Volga Frog Pond after his landing craft had been hit by enemy fire. This involved Tristan just lying there panting with rasping breath, because he'd lost a lung to shrapnel, and pretending to throw up blood. Now and then his limbs would twitch because his nervous system had also been affected. – Tristan did put a great deal of effort in it, and mostly the symptoms could have been backed up by his father, Dr. Neussler, had he been there.

Eventually, one by one, they got out of the water again, drying up in the grass under the shady willows. Bernhardt remained in until last, paddling about.

"Why are you still in, *Fettsack*?" Chuck felt no need to be polite due to the pain this *fat-sack* tended to put everyone through quite regularly.

“I’m a bit embarrassed.”

“You!?” Everyone laughed. – Yes, they had seen Big Bernhardt cry, but embarrassment was not something that sprang to mind when thinking of *Fettsack*.

Finally, he heaved himself out of the water to join the others on the grass. All the black muck from the swamp had washed off now. Thankfully he had no leeches clinging to him. But the rest of his body was a battlefield mess! Tristan gasped, “Fantastic! – Does it hurt!!!?”

“Not anymore. It did! Two weeks ago. I couldn’t walk.” Neck to toe, front to back Bernhardt was one contused mass of uneven flesh. In fact, there were only very few detectable flesh-coloured patches of skin left untouched.

What Fergal had earlier thought to be mostly swamp mud and slime, were indeed shiny welts and bruises, ranging from black through the entire spectrum of the rainbow here represented as Bernhardt’s pain.

“Why does he beat you like this?”

“Because I’m a bad child.”

“How bad?”

“Last time, I dug up a war grave in the cemetery at the back of his church. I got out some medals, a helmet and a thigh bone. The rest was rot.”

Tristan’s mouth fell open, “Wow!!!”

Chuck stuck his chin out and shook his head at Joachim, who had fallen asleep.

Fergal had a little trouble believing you could just dig up a war grave, but then again Tristan had two hand grenades in his rucksack and they had just set fire to Steinhöfer’s dump. And besides, Bernhardt looked perfectly capable of digging a hole even four meters deep in one day! He was only nine, the same age as everyone else here but … big but … Bernhardt was very strong!

In year one, when Bernhardt had eventually joined class after his stint at hospital, he had hit Frau Kellergeister back, when she had hit him! Kellergeister hadn’t hit back! The next day Bernhardt had to stay at home for a week. Pastor Meinheit had evidently been instructed accordingly. SS father’s flagellation of son must have followed.

Fergal remembered that it had been after the *Kellergeister-Incident* that Bernhardt had kept missing out on Kellergeister's schooling input quite regularly, because he was being re-educated by his pastor-father at home. Fergal found it hard to understand what this re-education was all about. Surely, saying *you shall not hit another person, it's bad,* was silly if you imparted this teaching by hitting the person you were trying to re-educate? Nevertheless, Kellergeister had never hit Bernhardt again! Neither did he raise his voice or even fist at her. Kellergeister had left it up to SS Pastor Meinheit. Pastor Meinheit was better at it! Come what may, Bernhardt was the strongest individual Fergal had ever met.

Bernhardt started crying.

It was embarrassing!

Tristan leant forward and started stroking Bernhardt's head. This made it only worse! Bernhardt sagged into himself covering his head with his hands as if to avoid the blows of his father standing by invisibly.

Chuck huffed, "We'll make you a member of our gang! Come on, Bernhardt! Cheer up! I'm going to start crying here myself in a minute if you don't stop. One is supposed to be afraid of you, not feel pity! Have some shame!" For a future tennis star Chuck was most talkative today, "Pull yourself together! You should play tennis more. You'll lose some of the flab, man!"

But Bernhardt kept crying for a bit longer with his hands over the back of his head. It looked pitiful!

All tears come to an end sooner or later, and a sniffling Bernhardt asked, "What's the secret admission test to your Double Bubble Gang. And I'll promise I'll never tell anyone! Not even about the fire!"

"The secret admission is simple, Bernie. It is …" Tristan looked at Fergal.

"You have to eat something so incredibly …" Fergal looked at Chuck.

"… adventurous. I can hardly describe it! It is …" Chuck looked back at Tristan who shrugged his shoulders.

The apparently fast-asleep Joachim clearly and loudly said, "A length of turd from each member has to be eaten by each new member. And that's final! Especially, when new members are enemies from the past."

Without a single moment's hesitation Bernhardt said, "I'll do it!"

Joachim continued his pretend-sleep with a broad smile. The other three found themselves in a bit of a quandary! – Whilst somehow, in an instant, Joachim had become an unwanted member, they had started liking Bernhardt quite a great deal. Whilst they were only Bubbles next to Bernhardt, the latter really looked like a larger than life Double Bubble. Maybe because of his bruised body? Maybe because of digging up a war grave and actually nicking stuff from it? Maybe because he had promised never to breathe a word about the fire on the dump? Maybe because he had so willingly consented to eating their shit!?

Fergal recovered his speech, "Well done, Bernhardt! Bernie, you're in. You are definitely in! Matter of fact is, it's enough to say you're willing to eat our turds! That's all. Welcome! You passed."

Bernhardt started crying again for a bit. Happy tears this time! – It was strange to see such a big fellow, who could have easily passed for a sixteen-year-old, cry like this twice in a row. Tristan put his arm over Bernie's bruised whale-back. It just about reached three quarters over. "Bernie, I have a surprise for you! I've got real grenades in my rucksack and *you* … *you* can let one off!"

Bernie stopped crying instantly! He looked up. Tears made their final run, "Really?" He wiped his wet cheeks tear-free excitedly, "You're not making fun of me again!? You won't run away again?"

"No!" Tristan grabbed his rucksack and pulled the two stick grenades out, … just for Bernhardt. "Fergal told us, his Tommies and Ammies call our stick grenades potato mashers. That is really so funny! Mashing up your enemies!"

How harmless they looked! A small grey tin on top of a nice, thick wooden stick. It looked more like a very secret gardening tool in Opa's shed.

Chuck and Fergal now began watching how Tristan took Bernie through the same grenade education as they had received from him, and Tristan in turn from his brother Siegfried. – Chuck had never touched them even once!

It was slightly worrying though that Tristan had already inserted the detonators at home in the trench.

"Now watch carefully! – Unscrew the cap at the bottom. There's a string called the lanyard. Pull hard with your left whilst already moving your right over your head to throw the grenade away as quickly as possible, because sometimes they explode too fast. They're a bit old, see! Normally the fuse will give you five seconds."

Bernie was quick on the uptake! He threw one over the other side. That was quite a distance!

The explosion was fantastic!

Tristan was so awed by Bernie's throw, he gave him the second one also. It fell short and landed in the pond without exploding. And that was fine by everyone, … otherwise all fish and some of the frogs would have been killed by the shock wave.

"What's this, Tristan?" Chuck pulled out an ordnance survey map from Tristan's rucksack.

"It's the map I told you about earlier."

"What map?"

"Siegfried's map!"

"I can see *that!* It has lots of swastikas drawn on it. – What's it for?"

"It's a secret. But I told you earlier! I'm not telling you again, Chuck."

"Ah! – It's where your brother gets his stuff from!" He grabbed it away from Tristan, "I'm going to keep it. It's too dangerous!"

A massive fight ensued. – Joachim was grinning.

Fergal didn't manage to separate the two. Tristan was a fierce fighter! He scratched, bit, spat, kicked, tore, poked at an incredible speed.

It was perfect having Bernhardt around! He just took Tristan by his neck and pulled him away from Chuck. But Chuck still hadn't relinquished the map! Tristan couldn't have the map back, because … "Where shall I start!?" … his brother wasn't with it, and they had seen what Tristan wanted to do with the grenades at

Steinhöfer's dump earlier, Tristan needed to calm down a bit or go to the mental home himself!

It was finally agreed to leave the map in Bernhardt's safekeeping. – Bernhardt was very big and strong. He seemed very trustworthy and loyal, and he had to prove himself as a new member of the Double Bubble Gang. The map would only be used if they would come under *serious* threat from the Stab Gang. A *really* serious defence-situation had to arise before anyone was allowed to pick up any machine guns, pistols, and grenades!

The map even told of a location where grenade launchers could be picked up! And all of this was for *free!* And very, *very* secret, with lots of swastikas on the boxes, Tristan said.

Tristan had calmed down a bit and admitted that he felt terrible about what they were doing to his brother Siegfried. Maybe they could all cycle over there soon. Pack some sandwiches, make a day of it! The Rhine area around Oppenheim was just so lovely! – Tristan sounded like mother hen!

Bernhardt raised a finger to be allowed to speak.

"You don't have to do *that* here, Bernie!"

"It's only polite now that we're a gang of friends." – A gentle giant.

"Hm." – Everyone apart from Chuck nodded. Chuck was shaking his head vehemently, "That's too authoritarian for me! Antiauthoritarianism brings out the real child, so it can develop into a real grownup."

"And still has his arse wiped by Mammi," Fergal joked.

Now it was Chuck's turn to hurl himself at Fergal and fight to the death. Again Bernhardt came to the rescue.

Once everything had calmed down again Bernhardt said, this time without raising his finger, "My grandmother has an old farm over in Oppenheim. It's a massive house. She thinks it's seven hundred years old. Papa hates her! We can stay with her. She is sure, she's Napoleon's grandchild. She doesn't ever hit you and bakes cakes all day."

That was agreed then! – All that had to be done was repair the puncture in Tristan's bike, be nice to parents for a while, prepare them gently, and off to the Rhine they would go to at least have a look at Siegfried's cache. About a week! Parents were a bit slow when you were being gentle and nice and lovely. So, ten days maybe! Ten days!

Letter #24 – Fergal To God Via The Pope

My Dear God, Dear Most Holy Papa,

I have calmed down a lot about J because she has calmed down about me! She is not altogether herself, a grownup would say.

I am very sorry about all the horrible things I have been writing about her of late. The electricity hurt a lot, but since then she hasn't actually done anything. She found a dead dry wasp in the cellar and wanted to see if it still stung. It did! It hurt. But now we're both wiser. Dry wasps still sting!

We've burnt the dump to the ground! It was just rubbish. It's amazing to see now. It's all flat and charred, and before there were mountains there!

I don't though think Tristan is all that well in the head. Maybe he is going the way of his brother.

Bernhardt, who is now a member of our gang, is the safe keeper of Tristan's map for all the ammunition. Please ask the Pope he pray for Tristan that he won't go bonkers! Let him pray also, please, for Bernhardt, whose father is a disoriented Lutheran Pastor who used to work for the SS in the olden days.

I found out that in the olden days he was a Roman Catholic, so there still is hope! And don't worry about me! I am getting there! – The teaching is relatively similar apart from the sacraments, I think.

Pastor Meinheit says I should wash my mouth out when I mention your Holy Name or that of your Pope, because the Catholic Church is founded on lies, lies, lies, and those are its foundations. I said, sometimes a bad beginning can develop into something good like Catholicism, and at other times a good beginning can develop into something bad, like the Lutherans. The Pastor boxed my ears quite hard, and it hurt. But Bernhardt said that was nothing.

I said to Pastor Meinheit if he had to respond to what I said like that, he only showed his ignorance and inferiority and demonstrated that he was in the wrong! Frau Nolde told me that! Pastor Meinheit absolutely flipped. He hit me around the face, which is rare in year three, but then the holidays started and its fine now!

Mutti went to see him and said that if he ever did that again she would take him to court. He grew into a very small man then, Mutti said. I was proud of Mutti standing up for me like that! It was a bit like Dad when he still had some time for us three years ago.

Anyway, the good thing is, I don't want to see J dead anymore! Oh, and do please forgive Big Bernhardt for digging up the war grave! He did put the things back. Please do not forgive Pastor Meinheit because he is a bad man and needs to learn his lesson here the hard way.

I suppose the Catholic Church and Lutheran Catholicism is a bit like East and West or Mutti and Dad. Luther took a rotten apple with good seeds and got rid of the rot. But then he started splitting the seeds around a bit and that's a bit like splitting the atom and Mutti says in the Bible it says you should not split atoms or hairs.

Please forgive all of us for the dump because even the dump was someone's property. I haven't told anyone and never will!

Why do you have to call yourself anything like Lutheran or Roman or East and West if You are everywhere and all powerful and in everything and everybody? Isn't that like splitting things too? Is it like me Fergal and J and Mutti and Dad?

My dear God and especially my good Pope, you guys do have to tell me these things as, after all, you, dear Pope, are God's representative on Earth! I haven't received a SINGLE letter from you since I started writing to you some four years ago! I am a patient boy as you can see. An answer in time would save nine. At the moment I would like to be a soldier because explosions are really nice.

Yours faithfully, I believe in your wisdom
Your future priest and forgive me and thank you in advance

J. Fergal Bulhof-Murphy

Enter The Devil Diabolo

Violation By Rights His

The Double Bubble Gang never went down to the Rhine that summer.

One day, after the fire had destroyed Steinhöfer's dump and car collection completely, Tristan came down with a strange summer cold and had to stay inside for the remainder of the holidays. His Mammi called all the other Muttis and Mamas and Pastor Meinheit. No one was allowed to visit him!

Two days after the fire, Chuck went on a surprise holiday to the south of Italy with his mother. Herr Nolde had to stay behind because of clients he was building a Black Forest Peasant Hut on the Rhine for.

Three days after the fire, Joachim had a go at his first suicide attempt in the LeBatard's garage. He had found the keys to the Opel Commodore, knew how to start the engine, and left it running with garage door down.

Four days after the fire, Immelmann was found sitting expired in front of his saw on a pile of metal fragments he must have cut prior to his death. The saw was still switched on. It was rumoured he had been murdered, as Martin had found him with a smile on his face. Immelmann hadn't been known for natural ebullience. This was just unnatural! – It was commonly agreed, the smile had been *terrible*! Steinhöfer had a solid alibi. He had been to see a psychologist in Frankfurt.

Five days after the fire, the LeBatards returned from their interrupted diving holiday in the Maldives. Neighbours related what had happened. Granny Hammerich had really laid into Joachim, beating him black and blue and bloody. There was a lot of screaming and shouting at Granny Hammerich. Frau LeBatard decided, loudly, to send her mother back to Nierstein where she had her own house. Frau LeBatard resolved, loudly, never to leave her son ever again! She was actually going to stop working.

Six days after the fire, J returned home from Oma's and Opa's, and J said nothing.

And on the seventh day, Fergal's Dad came home in an old, white VW Beetle 1200, a bit like Anne's, the speech therapist's, just vibrating harder, sounding much louder with more backfiring going on. Fantastic! But no one else seemed to think so.

The yellow Thunderbird, red E-Type, green Chrysler Town & Country, and even Dad's beloved and own white BMW were gone! Mutti and J spent a lot of time crying and whispering behind closed doors in the living room. Dad was in the bedroom. He wasn't singing or whistling.

This was the first time ever that Dad wasn't whistling or singing! At least, he still coughed a lot!

Fergal himself was in J's room reading *Asterix In Britain* for the third time. VW Beetles couldn't be *that* bad!

In the evening, a totally exhausted J shut the door to her bedroom behind her. Her eyes were sunken in. She had definitely cried a lot. What about!? – Fergal had seen her cry before but not like this! This wasn't about shoes or perfume or the right leather or type of fabric. This was a new, basic J, threatened to the core, knowing she could do nothing about whatever the situation out there was!

A VW Beetle!?

J curled her lip in disgust and fell down on her bed, "Well, … little brother, … I think *I* have to look after you now!"

This came as a grave shock to Fergal! Living in the same room as his sister was just about enough, but having her pretend to look after *him?*

J continued, "A lot of things have been happening of late. Mutti and I have tried to keep it from you to protect you. But now the disaster is out there, …" she pointed at the window, "… in the driveway … for *all* to see. You might as well know! Everyone will be having quite a laugh at our expense!"

"What disaster, J?"

"We are *poor*, Johann. Very poor! We have nothing! – Oma and Opa are supporting us so we don't have to starve, go asocial and die in the gutter. And you can do me a favour right now and never ever refer to me ever as Frances again!"

"I never have! You're J to me!"

"Means nothing to me! – The name *Frances* has been struck off the register of my inner self, and so has the name *Murphy*, you understand? Our father is the *Devil!* He is dangerous *and* mad. From now on, we'll have to keep our door shut, and we'll have to hope that he doesn't break in! Killing us in the middle of the night! He might pour petrol over us and then we'll burn! Living torches of hell, screaming in the night, dying a *horrible* death!"

"What do you mean!?"

"Your father, Fergal, … your father … he … is an idiot! – He gave Bragstone access to our money some time ago. And Bragstone has disappeared with almost three-hundred-thousand marks! *All* of Mutti's and Dad's savings! Your father also hasn't paid any tax in West Germany … ever … on the advice of Bragstone who … who also took the tax reserve with him. Everything! Interesting … interesting … that the bank didn't at least *call* when Bragstone drew the money! But then *your* father had taken Bragstone personally to the bank to introduce him as an equal signatory. Total idiot! All his cars had to be sold. He no longer has any showrooms anywhere. All assets are gone!"

"What are assets and signatory?"

J explained what these words meant. – There was a first time for everything and this was a first for J explaining something calmly to Fergal without driving it home with a bit of pain or more. J also said that all Fergal's and her own savings accounts had been dissolved. There was *absolutely* nothing left! – It was the end of the world as they knew it. The end of Fergal's own room!

"What's so bad about being poor and having nothing?"

"People treat you like shit! – It's like … we're asocials now!"

After that J was quiet. – The sun went down and she went to sleep straight away. She seemed completely exhausted. Fergal could smell her perspiration from his sofa bed. There were hundreds of midges humming away in the darkness of the room. J didn't stir. Her teeth-grinding was very loud and kept making Fergal shudder. He couldn't sleep.

Towards midnight Johanna started sighing terribly in her sleep. Fergal saw that the light in the hallway went out. Mutti was going to bed. Dad had been in the bedroom all day. Only seconds later there was a terrible commotion next door. Something banged against the wardrobe. Fergal knew the sounds the wardrobe could make very well. There was a short scream. Fergal ran to the door. It was locked. Another scream. Mutti was screaming! These were new screams. They were terrible and deep!

Fergal's body started quivering and trembling. He couldn't help himself. His body had taken over. He wetted himself. He was not going to stop trying to open the door. Up and down and up and down he pressed the door handle. Faster and faster in time with his trembling arms and neck and back and legs. Even his bottom was jittering. The commotion next door kept going on and on and on.

Suddenly an ice-cold hand gripped Fergal's shoulder from behind, "Be quiet and go to bed." Fergal obeyed his sister. A chilling calm in her voice. It made him calmer. His body though didn't stop trembling. It was so embarrassing! Her hand felt so cold. It felt like dead.

"Why aren't you doing something!? We have to do something, Johanna Frances!" Why call her by her full name?

"I told you not to call me Frances! Call me J if you must."

"Answer me, J! – We must do something! What are they doing next door?"

"They are fucking! *Dad* is fucking. It's a male outlet for the idiot to reassure himself that he's not gone completely impotent."

Fergal knew that his sister was looking closely at him in the dark. In the little moonlight there was, her eyes were glittering. She was crying again. The reservoir of her tears had been restored.

Fergal remembered that once *fucking* had been explained to him as *more than love.* But later it had turned into almost the opposite. There had been Anne. Mutti's evasiveness. Then Johanna had explained, much, much later, almost two years after Joachim had explained what it meant. It made no sense. Her eyes were quietly resting on him.

"Welcome to life, little Fergal! Life sucks whether you're English or German. I'm going to get the nationality with Mutti's help."

"What are they doing?"

"I told you, … they're fucking!"

"Is he throwing her around the room or what?"

"It's been like this for some time, … but you sleep rather well."

"You grind your teeth in your sleep."

"Do I?"

"Yes!"

"Ah well. Mutti goes in at the last moment. He's waiting. He's saying, if they can't do it now, what's it all been good for. She says, no, I don't want to. You disgust me. And he takes what is his, as it stands written or some such bollocks. She might struggle for a bit. But your father is strong. Very strong!"

"What do you mean?"

"I told you he is evil."

"J, … I don't understand."

"He is raping Mutti every night. Spoils of his war. Get it, twerp? And you wanna be English, eh?"

"Dad's Irish. I *am* English. What's raping?"

"Oh, fuck off! – You must know that!"

"No!"

"It's taking by force what isn't yours to have. It's violation."

"What?"

"Fucking somebody who doesn't want to be fucked."

"Horrible!"

"Yes!"

"Like fighting!?"

"Yes!"

At that moment Dad started panting loudly.

"He's coming. The Devil is jerkin' off in a human! He's coming!" Johanna pressed her hands against her ears.

Dad gave a brief shout. Then it was completely quiet.

J gave her brother a strange look. Somehow Fergal understood. He nodded. She took the palms of her hands off her ears and wiped her eyes dry.

"What's coming?"

"Orgasm."

"What's orgasm?"

"Climax. Sexual climax. You'll understand soon! Men have no trouble understanding. They just come and do it wherever. Tree trunks. A hole in the fucking ground. Exhaust pipes. Stupid arse fucking fuckers the whole fucking arse fucking wanking lot of them!" She ground her teeth.

"There!"

"What?"

"You just ground your teeth! Like that. In the middle of the night."

"Shit! And you say you haven't ever heard them do this before like at least over the past three four months?"

"No."

Johanna just turned round and sobbed.

And so it went on for two weeks.

There were another ten days left until year four for Fergal, year ten for Johanna. Four years to go until university for her, ten for Fergal.

Dad spent most of the day on camp drinking with his American friends at Frankfurt, Darmstadt or Geesterheim Officers' Club, trying to tell them he was still there. In the evening he could hardly climb back up the stairs, he was so pissed. He had devised a way, which made it dead safe to drive when completely sloshed. You just had to shut the eye where the image was drifting most.

Matteo had apparently told Dad he knew where Bragstone was. He would get rid of Bragstone for Dad, and Dad would get his money back into an English bank account minus ten percent.

Fair deal.

Dad had declined.

Matteo couldn't believe it! "We're quits now, Seán!" The day at the Officers' Club was the last time Dad ever saw Matteo.

"So, Mutti and Dad are still talking? If she's told you about Matteo, …" Fergal asked hesitantly.

"Yes!?"

"… then it can't be quite as bad, J! The way you put it always sounds terrible." Fergal thought of his Zippo hiding in the gap of the cellar window outside.

"It is bad! I'm telling you! Dad is close to *killing* Mutti! She told me so! Every night! And last time, last night, he threw her against the wardrobe and then the wall. She told me so! Her hip is bruised and her back looks bad. Black and blue! Dad is the Devil!"

So, that was what those funny sounds meant!

"You're not a Catholic. Only Catholics believe in the Devil!"

"Fuck off, Fergal! You're not a fucking Catholic either! You're a German Lutheran!"

"I *am* English! I want to go back to England! Wetchamoonis sucks!!!"

Now knowing what the sounds meant, the first time round, when he had heard them with his new knowledge, and the other noises coming from next door, Fergal resolved he wasn't going to cry!

For two weeks he and J had been crying together every night. He was fed up with crying! Their door was always locked. Being fed up with crying didn't always mean it wouldn't come anyway. Dad would kill them one day if he could. Petrol. Burning. Screaming. Inhaling the heat. Suffocation. He was killing Mutti slowly!

Mutti's face was never bruised, only the parts other people couldn't see. A bit like Bernhardt, Fergal thought. With eyes red and swollen from crying Mutti put on a very brave face behind Matteo's and Calogero's dark Raybans at Herrn Dorfgeist's.

Matteo had given them to Fergal together with the golden Zippo four years ago. Apparently Marcello was now in disgrace with Matteo because he had insulted his brother Calogero over an old family recipe for Pizza. It was safer not to know these people, Mutti and Dad agreed, but for different reasons. Mutti, for reasons of the Damage Fun society around her in her own world. Dad for mortality's sake!

The Raybans hadn't stayed with Fergal long. Johanna had taken them away from him, "Can I have them, please. Thank you! They're too big for you anyway."

"No!"

"Thank you!!!"

"Ouch. Owaaaa! That hurt!"

"So, … what are you going to do about it?" Johanna had bequeathed them to Mutti, renowned for her dislike of sunglasses, to look like Jackie Onassis, to hide her tear-sore eyes behind. Matteo was no longer there to help.

"If Matteo kills Bragstone, everything will be fine again, J! That's right isn't it!?"

"I doubt that. Too much is wrong!"

This evening things went slightly different. – Dad came home at two in the morning. He was signing and whistling Sinatra's *Strangers In The Night.* Nolde downstairs had one of his sleepless nights and shouted an asthmatic *shut up, stupid foreigner!*

With all the wet summer heat, without wife and child around, and with his allergic bronchial condition Nolde had gone a bit sour and very tense.

Dad shut up. – When he came in through the door Fergal heard him say in an American accent, "I'm gonna kill y'all dead!" He resumed singing loudly.

On his way to the bedroom Dad fell over twice knocking telephone table and flower stand flying. Fergal and J were holding on to each other tightly. So far, brother and sister, though in the same room and crying together, had never been physically as close as this early morning. Not even when J had tortured her little brother.

Their bodies were pressing into each other now. J was cuddling him.

Fergal was huddled up on her lap. Both sitting on the floor with their ears pressed against the wooden door listening to Dad's noise. His singing sounded terrible. There was something very off!

"Where are you, my German war whore!? I need a screw!" He continued stumbling around the flat. Eventually he found her in the living room, "Sit on me, like you sit on Meinheit and LeBatard and all your other fucking fuck suitors."

Mutti's voice was hardly audible.

"You think you could do that?" He laughed, "I'd crush you with my left hand and still have you. It's your choice!"

Another hushed few words from Mutti.

"You stupid bitch! Come here! I killed more people in my life than you want to know. I need *you* and your wet cunt now! Nowwwwwwww!!!"

Now, Mutti was screaming back at the top of her voice, fast, "You're nothing! You never killed anyone, you sad man, you think you can kill me, threaten me with death, you complete *Verlierer*[11], if that's the only way you can get me. You were an RAF postal clerk! Nothing else! You opened letters. You fucked about in Yemen. Come on, tell me your secrets! You fucked Lydia tonight. You live in a world of lies. Had I looked beyond your uniform and stories of heroism and glamour, I should have never married you. You're a quivering loser! You can't even take a model plane

---

[11] *Ger.* loser

off the ground. You'll never amount to anything without either me or my parents or our money, you badly self-taught working class scum bag from the gutter of asocialism! You want it, don't you …!? – Oh yes! With your mad Irish eyes and mad *Ausländer* friends … oh, oh and those scary eyes of yours! You want to kill me and fuck me, don't you!? You can't cope with the truth! We were on our knees, all of us, and scum like you came along in your uniforms. The winners! What a joke! You want it!? Come here! Get me! Oh! I'm still young! I can have anyone I like! But you are at the end! Yes come here! Try and get me, you stupid little impotent …" there was a terrible clang like a heavy but soft weight dropping on the glass table in the living room, then Mutti screamed briefly. Her scream was stifled. It sounded as if Dad had her by the throat.

With Fergal on her lap J crawled backwards into the corner by the door. Her whole body was shaking violently. She was sobbing hard and trying not to breathe, not to make a sound at all cost, as though not wanting to give away her whereabouts to the Devil outside. Fergal on the other hand found he was immensely calm. He was stroking his sister's hair.

There was a thud in the hallway now. Rustling. Hard breathing. More stifled screaming. Fergal released himself from J's grip, got to his feet and looked through the keyhole into the hallway. The sight he found presenting itself beyond the keyhole was so grotesque and new to him, he couldn't believe his eyes! He had to be out there and see the keyhole vision manifested for himself without any distortion!

He took the key from J's desk and opened the door. His sister was too weak and afraid to object. He stepped through the door approaching his mother and father lying in the middle of the hallway. Mutti was not moving. She had her legs spread to the side. In-between her legs his father was rabbit-hammering away with his lower body into her lower body like mad. His tongue was hanging out as a panting dog's might in the heat of summer. But there was nothing doglike, harmless, naïve about Dad. This man. His eyes were wide staring ahead of him at something on the wall. He didn't see Fergal. His son. He had a woman by the throat with one hand pressing down hard, with the other he was holding both her hands.

How strange this woman looked!

It was as if she had given over and was ready to die although she was gasping for breath. Her head was violet.

The man looked at Fergal and smiled as an addict might smile about to inject. A weak and terrified smile of apology for such grave helplessness, yet unwilling to give up before the imminent hit. Every time.

Welcome to life, little Fergal!

A type of life.

This wasn't an image of Fergal's belonging to his own mind. It was as one of Lt Hardy's or Colonel Brechner's images from some of their Vietnam stories Fergal hadn't been able to place and put into his own mind's movie. Up until now. The Colonel's wife was called Lydia.

Life sucks.

This man was his father.

Dad.

Not his smile.

This was not a smile.

It was the worst thing Fergal had ever seen.

His mother had given up this very moment.

His father was going to rape her to death, whatever came afterwards.

Up until now everything had been happening as in slow motion.

The kick Fergal placed with all his power directly on his father's throat happened in time-lapse. He hardly saw it.

He looked at his bare feet. He had kicked with his left. He always kicked with the right. His toe hurt. It was broken. The pain was without meaning.

Dad was lying on the floor, under the coat stand, gripping his throat and chest, fighting for air, rolling his head and eyes. There were strange gurgling, swallowing sounds. Fergal looked down at Mutti. She too was gripping her throat. She couldn't look at him. Her son. She kept her eyes shut, shaking her head hard from left to right.

He went over to his father and looked straight at him. Without anger he said, “Don’t ever scare us like that again! Don’t ever touch Mutti like that again! I love you. But there is an end to love too.”

Had he said that?

Fergal was only nine and a half.

Mutti opened her eyes. She kept shaking her head wildly. Her little son. She croaked, “Don’t! He’ll kill you! Run as fast as you can, Johann! Run! Lock the door!”

Dad had become very quiet. – His mad eyes had given way to a deep sadness. Fergal could see he was very drunk und uncoordinated. Dad reached out a hand as if to stroke Fergal but missed. He had to keep shutting one eye so that Fergal’s image wouldn’t drift away completely.

Fergal moved back.

“Promise you’ll never rape Mutti again! J and I have been thinking that you are going to kill us soon. We’re going to leave the door open this evening. I know you’re not a bad man, Dad. You just lost one game. There are more to come. Good luck!”

Yes, Fergal had just said that. It had been *his* voice!

Dad nodded.

Fergal went back into J’s room without a limp although his left big toe hurt like hell. He turned in the doorway.

Both Mutti and Dad were lying on the hallway floor, crying. Dad suddenly turned and threw up on the runner.

In a way, this was some kind of battlefield.

There were too many tears in this life. And not enough was being done to stop them.

Fergal shut the door behind him.

J was still sitting in the corner behind the door, crying. She too was shaking her head. Slowly. Not like Mutti. At whom? Fergal sensed after a while it was directed at him.

“I did the right thing.”

Her tearful voice echoed quietly as though from deep underground, “Little brother. Very brave. Too small for this!”

“Small is not what counts.”

“Can’t change nature. Remember that. He is Irish. He is a Catholic. He might feel remorseful now after your little spectacle out there. But he's been hurt too much himself not to hurt back. Next time he's drunk he'll have forgotten."

Fergal looked down at his sweat and tear soaked sister. Her men's pyjamas looked as if she'd just spent some time in a tropical shower.

The humid night heat outside kept people awake at this time of year. Neighbours must have heard what had been going on. J looked old but at least the irritating midges had given up on her! Maybe it had something to do with what grownups kept referring to as puberty, "So who hurt you, J?"

"What do you mean?"

"You said Dad's been hurt too much not to hurt back himself."

"Yes."

"Well, who hurt you? You had me to hurt back and take out on whatever."

"I have no idea what you're talking about."

Both of them went to bed and slept deeply.

To any onlooker even peacefully.

Inside their minds both went into a labyrinth of nightmare visions every which way they turned.

Vicomte Monroe Lombard & Father Martin O'Brady

"We're going to stick together from now on!" J decided the next morning.

"Does that mean you're still going to look after me?"

"No! We're almost equals now."

"And you're not going to torture me again?"

"Oh, come off it, Fergal! I never tortured you! And if I did, you liked it. You were always so … quiet."

Well, one thing hadn't changed. J was still mad!

"OK, Fergal. – Now listen! I'm Vicomte Monroe Lombard. I'm chasing the dreaded Devil, Diabolo from Bolivia. Who do you want to be?"

"Fergal Murphy."

"No! – Try again."

Fergal sighed, "What *are* you on about?"

"We're going to play! – I've never played like this, and recently I read on the loo …"

Fergal interrupted, "You read the Reader's Digest! You poor, little mental home to your brain cells."

"Who taught you that expression?"

"I just came up with it myself! It fits."

"You're only nine."

"Almost ten."

"In half a year."

"In November. That's under four months."

"Aren't you clever!?"

"Anyway, … don't read the Reader's Digest. It's rubbish in short sentences. Anyway …"

J did a strange thing with her eyebrows, and suddenly Fergal realised why all boys kept referring to her as elegant, great and sexy and just … ahhhhhhh! Even Joachim!

She was beautiful. She was no longer a girl.

J continued, "*Anyway* yourself. So, … apparently, it's good to role-play."

"So?"

"Do you ever role-play?"

"What for!? You are mad, J! – Go back to that single brain cell you just came from."

"You never play?"

"Oh, go to Bollerboe, J! Of course, we do."

"Bollerboe yourself. So you role play!?"

"No! We have no roles. We just play, OK!?"

"OK. So, … let's play! – I'm Vicomte Monroe Lombard. I'm chasing evil Diabolo from Bolivia, and you are …?"

"Why Bolivia?"

"*I* don't know! I just made it up."

"Bollerboe! – Why not Ireland?"

J looked sick for a moment, then she laughed out loud, "That would be the Diarmaid Bolokrooney from down there in Bray." She looked seriously at Fergal, "T'at, … my little friend, would be defeatin the porpus, now, wouldn't it, … of the role-playin, Oy mean!"

"Is that Irish? That's Oyrish Oy t'ink."

"I think so!"

"Dad doesn't talk like that."

"Dad doesn't want to be Irish. But he is!"

"I don't want to be German. – I'm English!"

"If you'll say you want to be German, that'll make things a darn sight easier for Mutti and me and the whole world."

"I am English!"

"Fergal, I'm getting the German nationality."

"What for?"

"Because I'm German! I think and dream in German."

"Frightening! – I don't."

"You must!?"

"I dream in German, English and Chamoonian."

"Really?"

"Yes, J!"

"I don't believe you!"

"That's your problem. But you're not German."

"I'm half German! And I'm going to make the best of it! So now … what do you want to call yourself?"

Fergal thought for a moment, "You're actually going to play with me? Not teach me or torture me?"

"I promise, I'll role-play with you!"

"I'll be … Father Martin O'Brady then."

J made a face, "Irish, Catholic, Brady Bunch. Alright."

"What shall I call you, J?"

"You may call me Sir or Vicomte Monroe if you like."

"What's *Vicomte*?"

"An aristocratic title like viscount."

"OK. – You can either call me Your Holiness or Your Grace."

"I'm not."

"Then I call you *turd-girl*."

"I'll call you *Martin*, Fergal, or *Father*."

"Just call me *Father Martin*. I'll be fine with that!"

J made another face but said, "Nice to meet you Father Martin. Enchanté!"

"Pleasure's all mine Vicomte Monroe."

"Have you seen Diabolo lately, Father Martin?"

"Just this morning. He still seemed quite drunk when he left."

"Yes, Father! He drinks because he's scared of life and us. We'll have to find him and kill him, otherwise … he will kill *us*!"

"I know just the place where we can watch him from, my dear Vicomte Monroe."

"Do you indeed, Father?"

"I do indeed, Vicomte."

"Then take me to it."

Fergal got a rucksack ready with some apples and two bottles of water. J prepared some sandwiches. Fergal had never seen his sister do anything in the kitchen in his life! Mutti was nowhere to be seen, which meant she had gone shopping to Herrn Dorfgeist's.

Then J had the best of ideas! She ripped the page with Bolivia out of the atlas so they could find their way around the place, and out into the fields beyond the big car park at the back of the quiet LeBatard property they went!

Maybe J wasn't that bad after all!? – Still, Fergal had to be careful! He had never roamed the wilds of Bolivia with *her*. It was exciting, though! He even managed to forget about the pain from his broken big left toe. He was not going to limp!

"What am I looking at here? Where are we."

"That's … a *field*, J! And I know exactly where we are!"

"Don't be a smartarse, Fergal. I know what a field looks like! Remember I study more, and you get out more. And it'll be *study, study, study, only study* for you soon, too! – So, Father Martin, where are we?"

Fergal looked at the map, "My dear Vicomte Monroe! We're on the right track. This is Oruro behind us over there. Lago Poopó is just down there."

"You're making that up, Father! Give me the map." Vicomte Monroe Lombard ripped the map away from Father Martin O'Brady, "Oh! It's true. There is a Lago Poopó. I'm terribly …" The Vicomte didn't get much further. Being Irish, and, although a Jesuit, Father Martin was not a patient man at all! His reaction was instant enough to be considered perfectly natural. He kicked the Vicomte in the shin. He placed a firm and hard old kick on him and grabbed the map back immediately. The Vicomte's swift reaction was just as natural, and as such beyond reproach. He slapped the Father's face with such force he fell backwards into the dust.

But what was that?

The Vicomte seemed to be sorry!

He stepped forward and immediately apologised to Father Martin, "I am so sorry, Father! – I should have never done that! Would you accept my apology, please!? And here I stand before you, brought up to respect the Church of God and her soldiers, guilty of having offended you most deeply. To underline my sense of deep shame and guilt, I offer to you to kick me again in the other shin, so there may again be a balance."

Fergal couldn't believe his ears! *J* had apologised! A first. A world first! Then again, she was the Vicomte now and he a Father of his beloved Church.

"You are very much forgiven, my man."

"You don't say *my man,* Father. We're in Bolivia now. You say *my child* when you speak on behalf of the Church."

"Right, my child."

"Give it some *dignity*, Fergal. Father Martin wouldn't say *right!* He would say *yes* or *of course* or *naturally, my child*."

"Yes, of course, my child, naturally."

"And if you try and kick me in the other shin I will break your arm, Father Martin."

This was scary Vicomte J! "Yes, of course, Vicomte Monroe. I'm the keeper of the map, naturally."

"Father, do please be polite and slightly more aloof despite your condition of being Irish, which, evidently, cannot be healed entirely. Do say, *My dear Vicomte Monroe, honoured friend and companion in this our hair-raising and most adventurous chase after Diabolo, enemy of the Church and mankind, please, let me have the map as I have great knowledge of this terrain due to my previous disposition of having resided in the land and a great many of its monasteries. Indeed, I was a teacher of the poor and ...*"

Father Martin interrupted, "Yes! Thank you! Vicomte, over there is Lago Poopó. You can't see it. It's hidden behind trees."

"I am hungry. I need rest. What about the bush over there, Father? It should afford us some shade. Do you know it?"

" '*Afford us some shade?* ' Course I know the damn bush! Tristan, Chuck and I have dug a damn trench in it."

"Don't swear! It sounds American. Who are these people you speak of, Father?"

"Never mind! Let's go and afford shade."

In actual fact, Tristan at one stage, two years ago, had got everyone to dig trenches all around Geesterheim. It had been great fun but very hard work! Had they back then enlisted the help of Bernhardt it would have certainly been a lot quicker!

Each trench, considering depth, width, length and tenacious roots, had taken them about a week. Three meters wide, one meter long and deep, and ever more roots. All in all they had dug ten trenches encircling Geesterheim as part of its defences. Their favourite ones had become the two in the drainage ditch as the soft soil had allowed them to dig deeper, and they were open at the back. One was under the old hawthorn bush from where they had attacked the American tanks last November. The other trench was concealed beneath the dense pussy willow Vicomte Monroe had just pointed at. Whilst the hawthorn trench was part of the circular drainage system surrounding Geesterheim, the pussy willow trench was about a kilometre outside Geesterheim serving to catch rainwater and nourish the surrounding fields.

Vicomte Monroe and Father Martin were outside the pussy willow.

"Do you spend quite a lot of your time in ditches and bushes, Father Martin?"

"Yes. We *have* to hide. There is a war on, you know! We have dug trenches all over Bolivia."

"How do I get in there?"

"Follow me. It's down, down, down!" – Father Martin walked sideways down into the ditch. The embankment wasn't as steep here but, all in all, the ditch must have been two meters deep from ground level.

At the bottom you had to get on your knees and crawl in through an opening in the bush Joachim had cut in angrily to make it more accessible. It was a little overgrown now because they hadn't been back in some months.

Vicomte Monroe followed but seemed quite indignant at having to crawl in on hands and knees. When the aristocrat got up again he found himself standing under a dome of green leaves. The summer light was shimmering in a thousand radiant colours. He looked at the iridescent light on his arms. It was as if his entire body would dissolve in light at any moment. His mouth parted slowly in wonder, "This is a wonderful place, Fergal, Father."

"In summer and autumn it is. After that it's really quite useless from a military point of view. Too open, Vicomte. Snipers can pick you out easily!"

"I see!" the Vicomte frowned. "There's quite a war on in Bolivia, isn't there?"

"Yes, it's quite terrible. But our courage and love helps us."

"I see. – Are you in the war a lot, Father?"

"Yes, Vicomte Monroe! – Everywhere I leave, I leave to go to war, … but I leave peace behind."

"How tragic! – But … you are quite eloquent for your age, Father."

"Please! No flattery! I am thirty-five, Vicomte."

"Twenty-six, and very thirsty!"

"Then it really is better that I lead. Have some water!" He handed the effeminate Vicomte a bottle of Apollinaris. The spoilt aristocrat drank too hastily. The water was too fizzy, and, embarrassingly, he burped up half of it, and it shot out through his nostrils.

"Sorry!"

"Well, Vicomte! You don't drink from bottles much, … I can see that. Here in the trenches of Bolivia, where the war with Diabolo isn't going all that well at the moment, we have no space for cups."

"I see! – You really are quite eloquent, Father. At home … in my castle, when you are around, I rarely find you … your Grace … talk as much. Can you explain that?"

"No."

"That's it? Just … *No?*"

"Yes."

"That's more like it! I like an answer in the positive!"

"Do remember, dear Vicomte Monroe! At your castle I was the enemy up until recently and tortured in your cellars. Quite a lot! Had I talked too much, I should have lost my friends and my life."

"I do get your point, Father. – What luck I found you, eh!"

"We'll have to see, as still I feel a certain discomfort due to our historic connection and disposition."

"What!? – Where do you get all these words from, … *Father!?*"

"I was permitted free use of your library and the Vatican helped a bit."

The Vicomte laughed out loud, "And so it would!"

"Tell me, my child! Is Diabolo one of us or a dreaded protestant Lutheran?"

"He wouldn't know his left Luther from his right testicle! He is an atheist, I'm afraid. – No … I give a … I don't care!"

"How sad! How empty! How alone! – Tell me more about this disease, Vicomte. Please! I have never heard of it."

"*Ha!* – You do not know the word, Ferg … Father! It's somebody who doesn't believe in God!"

"That really is tragic. – Do you believe in God, Vicomte?"

“ ‘fraid not, Father. Love is *what* I believe in!”

“OK! – Will you excuse me please, Vicomte! I need to teach some Chinese how to swim.”

“What?”

“I need a wee.”

“Go right ahead!”

“Go away! You’re my, sister … Vicomte!”

“No! Let’s have a look at you, Father.”

“I can’t do it if you watch.”

“Bet you can do it with your friends.”

“Of course!”

“I’m your friend.”

“Hm …!?” Father Martin turned away from the Vicomte. – The Vicomte had just asked something rather strange!

The churchman started weeing when he heard the Vicomte creep up quietly from behind.

“I warn you, Vicomte! I’ll turn round and my Chinese will leave a patch on your jeans!”

“No! You wouldn’t dare!”

“I would!”

The Vicomte was too close for comfort! Father Martin turned round and weed in the direction of his friend who jumped back instantly but with a massive smile on his face.

“I’ve seen it! I’ve seen Father Martin’s Martin. It’s more like a Martini. How tiny and harmless and as yet without impact. Surely, if I cut if off it would never do any harm, … ever! All the damage that could be avoided!”

Father Martin felt a familiar fear rising up from his feet. It was like weak electricity. A battery discharging. He had seen too much in the cellars of the Vicomte’s palace! Too many of his friends had he seen being put to a slow death by torture down there. Even he himself had endured almost nine years of it. But then the Vicomte’s castle had been destroyed, burnt to the ground, and he, Father Martin O’Brady, had saved the Vicomte’s life. – No! The Vicomte *had* changed! One had to believe in such change. One *had* to trust! Otherwise the world was a place that lacked, a place like that of the Atheist Diabolo.

"… but, alas, I have no knife." The Vicomte laughed. "In any case, I require some release from the … Chinese? … what a strange thought! A yellow, perilous pee, eh!? Your friends teach you some weird ideas, Father."

"The other thing, we call *abseiling a negro.*"

"Oh, my goodness! I know *that!* But I'd never use those words! How disgusting! You're a bunch of little racists, really, aren't you!? Your friends from the seminary?"

"What's seminary?"

"Where they train priests like yourself. That's the seminary. Don't tell me you haven't heard that one yet!? With your display of the Father's earlier vocabulary."

"No! Thank you. – An important word in my line of work, naturally."

"Quite. – Anyway, … turn round! I need a wee."

"No! You saw mine. I see yours!" Father Martin had never seen a Vicomte's aristocratic thingy before.

"I'll break your fingers if you watch."

"Only Bernhardt breaks fingers. Vicomtes don't talk like that!"

"OK! A quick peek but not whilst I pee."

"OK." Father Martin made a solemn promise and crossed himself.

"Oh, my goodness, Father! You really are a little Catholic. Turn round now!"

Vicomte Monroe took his trousers down. This aristocrat really was a bit like a girl!

"Turn round!!!"

"OK."

And the noise he made … more like a horse.

"You piss like a horse!"

"Watch your mouth, Father! You're still a lot smaller than I."

But it continued for much longer than Father Martin's wee. Maybe that was because Vicomte Monroe had called it pee. How funny! He really didn't know the Vicomte well at all. Then again, the Vicomte didn't know him either.

"That took a long time. Now, let me have a look."

"No!"

"You promised!"

"You could have peeked."

"I shouldn't do that."

The Vicomte gave him such a sad look, Father Martin took a step back.

"Sorry! Of *course*, you wouldn't! Anyway, where're we going now?"

"Lago Poopó. – It's also called Lago Poopó Frogo Pondo. It's very secret!"

"How far is it?"

"About thirty kilometres from here."

"I mean in real terms."

"About three, … I think."

"That's quite far! Have you ever told anyone … like Mutti, what you get up to?"

"Who is this Mutti? No. Never!"

"Good. I think that would make *anyone* quite unhappy."

"I know. It makes no sense telling anyone."

"Do you mind showing me all your secrets?"

"No, Vicomte! We have to find *and* get rid of Diabolo."

"How very true, Father. Very true!"

The Vicomte really appeared to love the walk over to Lago Poopó Frogo Pondo. – Never before had the effeminate prince chatted away quite like this! The terrible scenes of his castle's destruction, just last night, seemed to weigh on his mind no longer.

When they had arrived at the Frog Pond, Father Martin chose an especially secret bit of his most favourite pond in the world. It was very soft and grassy right on the water's edge with a lot of shade from his friend Hotzenplotz, the laughing willow.

Father Martin called it his friend Hotzenplotz because of *Räuber Hotzenplotz* in Preussler's book of the same name. He was his favourite character ever. The film was out. It had the German actor Gert *Goldfinger* Fröbe in it. *He* was perfect!

Father Martin had been promised a visit to the movies in Darmstadt or even Frankfurt. Well, at the moment things were a bit busy back at the castle. The laughing willow looked like a laughing Hotzenplotz with *very* wild hair.

Vicomte Monroe and Father Martin sat down in the soft grass.

"You have chosen well, Father! It is a very remote little spot, this. And we can see the entire pond, and the other side. I doubt anyone can see us here!"

"No one can see you here, my child. – It is very peaceful."

"I have no doubt. – I'm sure Diabolo will come along in a minute."

"Let's hope so!"

The Vicomte had another swig from the Apollinaris bottle, but far more carefully this time!

"Do you promise not to say anything about Martini, Vicomte?"

The Vicomte drew his breath in and stuck his bottom lip out, "Hmm! Depends. As long as he doesn't throw any Chinese at me. – Why?"

"He won't! The Chinese will join some of their friends for the big swim in the pond."

"Yuck! – I didn't need to know that! I wanted to go for a swim myself, Father."

"Well, … then I won't teach them how to swim."

Father Martin took off his clothes. The heat and the grass felt wonderful on the skin. No shame about his nakedness in front of the Vicomte. A strange sensation! Father Martin knew something was happening here that was making him older.

"You have seen me naked before?"

"Yes. When you were tiny, Father. Still, … not much of a difference."

"*You* take your clothes off then!"

The Vicomte tilted his head to the side and gave Father Martin a strange look. An intense look! It was the longest look Father Martin had *ever* received. And then the effeminate aristocrat got up and began undressing. Slowly. No man undressed like this, *ever!* It was *too* careful. You didn't have time to undress like this in a war of so many defence-situations!

The Vicomte was a strange sort really! With his wide hips, he had the skin of a baby. Not a hair insight! He had no beard! Could he be an impostor … a *woman* in fact? Perish the thought!

"Vicomte, you have rather large …"

The Vicomte violently moved his finger over his lips. A perfectly aristocratic *shut up!* The nobleman continued undressing.

Father Martin was not to be deterred, "… like, have you noticed them, they are … like breasts … just there … where your … chest is …"

The Vicomte looked down at them and shook his head in disbelief.

"…almost like Sister Anne's! When I was very young she taught me how to cough and spit German, and then she …"

The Vicomte did the *shut up* finger again. He was for some reason watching Father Martin's lower body intently all the time he was undressing. When he was finally naked his eyes went up to meet the Father's again.

And again, a long stare!

Longer than last time.

"That's me!"

"Yes, my child! You have hairs down there. You're grown-up."

"So?"

"Where is your Monroe, Vicomte?"

"Mine is different to yours, but … it is there! I just draw it in so it doesn't get in the way like yours when I'm riding."

"Can you push it out again?"

"Not in the mood, Father."

"Now, Monroe! What I always wanted to ask you … are you a woman!?"

At this, the Vicomte gave Father Martin such a ferocious look, the wise cleric was not going to pursue this line of inquisition any further. Obviously, Vicomte Monroe was quite aware of the fact that he was deficient as a man without a beard, who had the kind of *very* fat chest, only to be found in gluttons, and *very* fat hips, only to be found in sloths. Yes! Father Martin was quite aware of the seven deadly sins, because he had been taught well at the seminary … *ha-ha*, the seminary … taught by Father Seán, before the latter went mad. He didn't understand all of the Deadlies, but he'd learn!

"Sandwich?"

"Yes, please!"

They finished the cucumber and cheese sandwiches quickly and had an apple each.

"Can I have a look at your willy please, … Vicomte?"

Without hesitating Vicomte Monroe turned to Father Martin and opened his legs, cocking his head quizzically.

What Father Martin saw there astounded him a great deal! It wasn't like in the book from the castle library at all, where four drawings showed how a child was gradually emerging. This was completely different! It was hairier, and there simply wasn't *anything* there!

"There's nothing there! It's not like in the picture with the head coming out."

"Yes, it is. It's nicer! And you are the first *ever* Father to see this!"

"I've seen lots before."

"Yeah, yeah, yeah! Of course you have."

"So, that's all!? Flat, crinkled, and hairy."

The Vicomte sneered, "That's by no means *all*, Father!" and instantly turned the sneer into a smile, "There is so much more, … if … and only *if* you know what to look for in a man like me!"

"How do you wee?"

The Vicomte parted two bits of skin and pulled them out slightly. It all looked far more complicated than Father Martin had ever thought possible. That's exactly why it was good not to get involved with those little pests. Girls were difficult. Of course, the Vicomte wasn't a girl!

"Here is where you came from when Mutti gave birth to you."

Father Martin had another shock! Although he accepted completely the fact that he might one day grow into something equating his father, Mutti just couldn't look like *that* down there! Also, … it was *much* too small! You couldn't *possibly* get a head through there!

"You are lying, Vicomte!"

"No, I'm not! Cross my heart."

"You came from there too!? – Uargh! Yuck!"

"Don't make that noise! Yes, I came from there too, but before you."

"Do you wee from there?"

"No." The Vicomte's index finger went up to a little arch with a knobbly thing in it. He pointed at it. "Here, … just underneath."

"There's nothing there!"

"Yes, there is! And just a tiny millimetre further up is what is like your … willy." The Vicomte made a face at the mention of *willy*. Father Martin didn't understand what the face meant, but considering the earlier suggestion to cut it off, he put *willy* between his legs and closed them.

"So, … you have a really tiny willy and it won't grow."

"Well it does grow a bit but you have to rub it a little."

"Why?"

"Because it feels nice. And that's exactly where this conversation stops!"

"Mine doesn't feel nice if I rub it! – Well!? A little … maybe …before I have to go to the loo."

"Oh, good Lord! *Too* much information! You are *too* young … Father … and you're a priest. You're not allowed!"

"I'm not allowed to rub myself? Why not? You're talking Bollerboe! All of it. All Bollerboe nonsense! I rub myself whenever I want to."

"And you're not allowed to rub or lick women, Father. No man should!"

"Uaaaaargh, yuck! – Too much information, Vicomte!" Fergal rolled on his back from his crouching position and clutched his throat with both hands. Pretending a wheeze, he said, "I think I'm going to be sick." He turned on his side away from the Vicomte and got on all fours starting to retch. What a gross thought the Vicomte had put into his head. He spat out the thought to get rid of it.

"Yuck, Father! Stop spitting. That's gross!"

"Don't ever say such a thing again."

"I promise."

"Good!" Father Martin lay on his side resting on his elbow, "You do look like a man who looks like a very beautiful woman, Vicomte."

The Vicomte smiled down at his slender, feminine feet, "Thank you! – This is why the world keeps moving, Father. Why there are people and everything, and why …" his face darkened, "I don't want to be a woman ever! The scenes at the castle yesterday were horrific! You were *very* brave! But you and I have to rise above this now." With that the Vicomte got up and jumped headfirst into the pond, disappearing under the water. The effeminate aristocrat hardly caused a wave on the shimmering gold of the surface.

Father Martin followed the wake of u-shaped ripples that followed the accomplished swimmer like a pair of hands folded in protection over him. A prayer for the swimmer to find a new and peaceful life when he came back up again, leaving behind at the deepest point of the pond all that would otherwise cause him to drown forever and ever, never ceasing to descend to lower depths of desperation in his mind.

The destruction of the castle had taken its toll.

Here and now, though, paradise.

Father Martin was searching his mind for a word that could possibly describe this wish for the Vicomte as much as for himself. It was like children being photographed in the schoolyard in summer in the shade of the old chestnut tree by the Schafshütte. A word that described children who hadn't been asked to smile, but smiled. A word that described the absence of being hit for not smiling. Maybe there wasn't such a word!? Father Martin couldn't think of it. He hoped he'd find it one day! For the Vicomte, and, yes, for himself too, although that might have been selfish.

The word he was looking for and couldn't find at that moment was *innocence*. He knew it. He had read it. But it didn't come. The feeling though was there.

Then from the middle of the pond a waving hand directed at him. A face with an effervescent smile, and long, blonde, wet hair flowing down over Vicomte Monroe's shoulders as delicious honey.

"Come in! It's like bath water." The Vicomte turned and crawled fast to the other side. He was a magnificent athlete.

When the castle had still stood his sleeping chamber bore copious witness to his physical prowess. Medals, trophies, certificates for two national and uncountable regional championships. First and second place. Not a third in sight! The Vicomte could jump almost five meters!

Father Martin had to admit, he did feel proud to know this man and maybe even call him a friend. And, *Good Lord!* There! He was already back on Father Martin's side, quickly, to beckon him in again, "Come in! Lago Poopó is absolutely lovely at this time of year!" and off he was again.

Father Martin was an OK swimmer. A lot of the fellows at his seminary couldn't swim. Most of his closest friends though could. Father Tristan couldn't. But Father Tristan was a great floater unless he wanted to play *dead-on-the-beach*, which was more frequently than not the case.

Father Martin's swimming education had been quick and simple. – Back in London there had been a lido at Gospel Oak. His father had thrown him in. No looking back after that! Diving in headfirst was still an accomplishment left to the likes of Mark Spitz, David Wilkie, and Vicomte Monroe Lombard! The famous *A-Bomb* aka *arse bomb* on the other hand was Father Martin's prerogative.

"Come in, you coward!" Vicomte Monroe laughed from the other side. Too fast for Father Martin! The Vicomte seemed a little impatient.

Father Martin took a running jump, went up high in the air over the water, and came down on it like a flat rock. He went deep under the surface. The water made a great bubbling noise around him. His bottom and testicles hurt like mad. The most successful *Arschbombe* had been completed!

Back up at the surface the Vicomte was swimming like mad towards him. Had he seen the great tidal arse-wave? What was he shouting?

"... get you, and then ..." it was lost amongst the strokes. Then his face was back up again and the Vicomte changed to a swift breaststroke. His eyes were mad with fury. What was going on!!!? His hair had lost all the earlier lustre. It covered his face in strands like gashes. He was cutting through the water with such anger! How could any person change like this!?

" ... and drown you. You'll rest forever in this pond. I have you now!"

Father Martin turned round to swim back to the grassy outcrop as fast as he possibly could, but he knew he wouldn't be fast enough! He felt his kicking leg being gripped and pulled back hard. His head went underwater briefly but he managed to get back up quickly. J was gripping both of his legs now, pulling back. He heard her voice clearly, deep and terrifying, "... got you now. I'll drown you."

Fergal had not seen his sister like this before! He was deadly afraid! – Drobat had always been performed with a calm so clinical, she had appeared like a doctor performing what was strictly necessary only.

Fergal's head went under again. She tried to get hold of his head but failed as the deep water didn't allow for enough stability. He was back up again. He knew, one more, maybe two attempts and his strong sister would have him in a stranglehold so tight he wouldn't be able to move. He tried swimming away again as she had fallen back a little. He pounded the water screaming, "This isn't funny, J."

J gave a deep laugh. Like a man. Fergal knew his bladder was giving way. He was afraid for his life. J howled a victory, "I am Diabolo. I have come to destroy you and the Vicomte. I have you now, Father!"

Fergal was close enough to the warm and safe grassy verge to get hold of the little outcrop. You could almost stand here. J was still playing some insane game. He turned round and looked straight at his furious sister. Whatever it was, *that* wasn't his sister in there! It was a dark-faced monster from the depth of this slimy pond come to get him and pull him back down with it.

He screamed desperately, "Not playing anymore! Go away!" But this vision of dark corners and nightmares did not go away!

Fergal tried to get up onto safe land. He was almost there! He could feel his tummy on the grass, his hands tearing away at it, trying to claw himself forward into safety with all his might. His feet were now in the air. Just one more second and … Diabolo grabbed him painfully by his ankles and pulled him back into the wet. Fergal's grave!

A fraction of a terrible second later and J had him in a stranglehold. No! This wasn't J! This was Diabolo! The one they had to find and destroy. This wasn't supposed to happen. He didn't want to die. Not in water. His head went under and a terrible orchestra of simple watery sounds engulfed him. Bubbles of his voice bursting up on the surface. He felt his body fighting. Kicking. Boxing.

And then, suddenly, it all stopped! – Diabolo's stranglehold was still as tight and painful. Fergal though relaxed completely as he had always done when J had tortured him. His legs and arms went limp. He had wasted a lot of air, yet he sensed he could almost breathe underwater, respiring within himself. He thought of air going in and out, in and out, but knew he wasn't really breathing. The movement of exhalation, inhalation was of his mind only. The sensation of calm was overpowering as though he had suddenly emerged in another country, beamed there by Scottie in Star Trek.

What this calm had always brought with it in the past, it was bringing with it now, yet more intensely. Problems that offered questions seeking answers for their solution. Fergal was in a state of infinity. He felt his body and his fear of death dissolving. He was infinity. Looking into Mutti's triptych mirror. How could this sense compact itself to form a body like the one he was losing now? What a strange question this was. How very peaceful he felt! To spend forever asking this question would be enough. To spend forever thinking about this one moment when his sister had become the Devil Diabolo would be sufficient. Of itself it would create an infinity of questions. Forever.

Fergal felt himself being yanked up roughly and held in Diabolo's arms above the water. He heard his sister's voice talking loudly.

He hadn't drowned! He was not dead! He coughed water up hard. His neck hurt. She had tried to kill him.

What was she saying? Whom was she talking to?

"He's OK. We were just playing. We do that. His my little brother."

From across the pond a male American voice shouted back angrily, "Damn! That didn't look like playing to me, young lady! His just hanging there. He looks dead."

Fergal heard his sister say, "Wake up, Fergal. Wave at the man!" He felt himself cough. He heard the man shout, "Great! – He's alive."

Fergal felt himself raise his hand to say he was alright. Not dead!

"Right. Now. The two of you, if you don't mind, I want to do a bit of fishing here. And fish don't like their water disturbed."

"Yes, sorry! We're getting out," J shouted back. "Would you mind turning round. We're not dressed."

"Right. Paradise, right!?" The man waved and turned round. J pushed her little brother up on the grass and followed herself. Shaking, Fergal watched the man's back whilst J got dressed quickly. He was wearing a big triangular sun hat. In his right hand a fishing rod and net, in his left a green box. They wore hats like that in Vietnam. Lt Hardy had one. Dad had got one from Col. Brechner recently. They looked great!

"Thank you! – You can turn round again."

The man had been good.

J had tried to kill Fergal.

The man began setting up his fishing gear. His car had to be somewhere. Geesterheim was about five kilometres away. Grownups didn't walk that far.

Fergal got dressed, picked up his rucksack without a word and left. He knew the circuitous way back home off by heart. If Vicomte Monroe Lombard Diabolo J wanted to come … fine … if he went back to hell … possibly a better place!

Fergal was going to take the route back through the woods. Woods, football field, swamp, woods, and fields. Today he was going to go straight through the maize field.

"Where're you going, Father Martin?"

Fergal didn't bother turning round. He continued walking. "Home J."

"We don't have a home. The castle's gone, remember!?"

"I'm never going to play with you again, J. You wanted to kill me. I'm not going to talk to you ever again. You're insane!"

"Diabolo took over my body. I couldn't help it! Diabolo is like that. He's invisible. He takes over whomever he likes. That's why we have to kill him!"

"He tried to kill *me*."

"That's why he is dangerous!"

"I'm not playing with you anymore. Bye."

"Hey, wait! I'm coming to."

"I really don't care!"

But there she was by his side again, "Why are you walking back this way?"

"Because."

"The light's lovely!"

That had sounded just like Mutti. Festive moods, nice decorations, and all. Shit!

Transformation

Although Fergal had intended to walk as quickly as possible, the thought of being back home wasn't a comfortable one. He started ambling, and soon did he break his vow never to talk to his sister again.

"Why did you do it? I was beginning to like you."

J looked up at the canopy and stopped, "I was Diabolo."

"Oma would say *Nonsense! All nonsense!* And I'm saying, go to Bollerboe, J! As in take a running jump!"

J was quiet.

"You really don't like me, J."

"Yes, I do! I love you. But you're a pain in the arse, Johann."

"Don't call me *Johann.* Or I'll call you *Frances.*"

"OK."

They had arrived at the old football field.

"And from here, Fergal?"

"You *really* don't know your way around, do you?"

"No. Remember I was eleven when we moved. And, with school and all, that kind of playing stopped."

"We're going to cross into the swamp wood. Can you see the mountain on the left over there?"

"Yes."

"That's the dump. It's a great place with old cars. It burnt down."

"Right."

"Why can't we walk on the little dirt road?"

"Because."

Twenty minutes later they entered the maize field.

"When I was Diabolo you could have defended yourself, Fergal. But you just hung there."

Fergal sighed, "You are very strong, J."

"You are very strong too."

"Not like that. You're angry strong."

"When you were under the water in my arms there was a moment, like you had disappeared. You weren't there and my arms grabbed thin air."

"Bollerboe nonsense! All nonsense!"

J stopped to drive home some point, which Fergal didn't know what it was all about, "I'm telling you the truth. It was very strange. I was frightened!"

"You are *not* frightened! You *play* frightened."

"It's *true*!" She stamped her foot like a baby, "I could still see you but it was like you were water."

Fergal kept on walking. Maybe he had gone invisible just as in Opa's invisibility training. – No! That was playing. Not real. Walking was real. Walking was good even if you had no real home to go back to. The high maize was his home. The cooling green, almost blue comfort. A never-ending field of maize. A maze of maize. He laughed. English was great. In German that was *ein Irrgarten aus Mais*. It didn't sound as nice. This labyrinth felt safe. Home.

"I'll never be German."

"What?" J had fallen behind a little trapped in her own thoughts. She caught up, "What, Fergal?"

"I can't be German. It would be like pretending to be something else. Like a … I don't know … a shopping bag."

"You think strange thoughts. And you did disappear. Never mind. I really don't care."

They came to the end of the field. The magical atmosphere of the maize stopped abruptly. A clear border. Another reality. Brother and sister stepped out on the dirt path the tractors used. Geesterheim lay about half a kilometre ahead of them. Halfway, in the distance, as tiny as a pebble, there was somebody crouching in the dust.

"Do you know what the time is, J?"

"You know I don't like wearing cheap watches. When I can afford one I'll get a Rolex and Jaeger, or I'll get my husband to buy me a whole collection. – Where's your watch, Fergal?"

"My Mickey Mouse watch broke a long time ago. But you wouldn't know because you don't notice me."

"A cheap watch evidently."

"What do you think that man is doing?"

"That's a kid like you, Fergal."

"How can you tell?"

"I just can. Maybe he has a watch."

They came up to the boy who was watching something on the ground. He had a toy pistol sticking out of his back pocket.

"What are you doing?" Fergal asked the boy. The boy didn't move or answer. His face was turned away, very close to the ground. He was carefully examining something under him that he was protecting from view with his hands. Fergal realised the boy was blowing at his hands. Dressed in blue jeans and a striped t-shirt just like everybody. What set him apart was his lack of trainers. He was barefoot.

"Hey, hello! I'm Fergal and this is my sister, J. What are you doing!?"

Now the boy's face turned with a smile. J drew in her breath. The boy wasn't exactly made of the fabric she'd expect her future husband to show off himself in childhood photographs to her. – His shining blue eyes were too close together, his nose a hook long enough to touch his thin upper lip, his ears as big as his hands. Everything about him said *desiccated* like some packets in Mutti's kitchen. Fergal had never seen him before. He wasn't a Geesterheimer.

"Maus kaputt. Nix gut!" the answered in broken German. He smiled with his lips only. His voice was full of fine sand, he was about to cough up at any moment.

"Why?"

"Field, then halt, and *Aus-Schluß kaput*, nix more life. Kaput, kaput! I home mouse my hands and phu-phu!" He blew air at what was lying down there protected by his hands, "Lucky, lucky mouse live with phu-phu. But nix! Too much food. Heat, heat! Mouse kaput! I blow more phu-phu, mouse live and food for family."

"Can I have a look?"

The boy shook his head but said, "Vladimir."

"Hi, Vladimir!"

Vladimir went back to blowing on the mouse with heatstroke.

"Do you think it'll survive?"

"Quiet, or die!"

Fascinated, both Fergal and J watched Vladimir do his kiss-of-life phu-phu on the mouse. After a while the resuscitator was slowly beginning to shake his head. He raised his upper body slightly, his head now drooping. He opened the protective circle of his hands to reveal the evidently expired mouse. Legs in the air, mouth open wide, exposing its yellow rodent teeth, its eyes were gone, tiny ants crawling all over it, inside and out.

J bent down over Vladimir and put her hand on his back tenderly trying to comfort this boy who had just managed to look more dejected than she hoped she could ever feel, even now without a home, "Vladimir. That's more than rigor mortis. That mouse has been dead for a while. In fact, it is *so* dead, you couldn't even use it for a nose-n-face-hat to cover that … thing …" J circled her face with her middle finger.

"Mouse phu-phu. Mouse live! Papa do phu-phu insect. Insect alive! I see Papa. You here mouse nix help soul you mouse fear nix come back now!" Vladimir looked very angry! And all at once Fergal found himself lying on his back with Vladimir on top hitting him in the face. Vladimir was thin and not strong but this was a bit much.

In disappointed shock, Fergal noticed J walking off. Just like that! She just walked off! Leaving him to be beaten up by this sandy fruitcake!? This … Vladimir!? – Nix good!

Fergal felt his head exploding. Vladimir had used his fist and bashed it straight down on his nose. The pain was instant and excruciating! Fergal screamed and pushed Vladimir off hard. Vladimir ran off in J's direction. The pain was blinding! His nose was bleeding badly. He had to pull himself together and save J, however much he hated her. – No! He didn't hate her! He only disliked her. But she needed to be protected!

Fergal got to his feet and started running after Vladimir. His broken big left toe was back. It hurt like hell. Everything hurt like hell!

By now Vladimir had arrived at J's back waving his pistol at her like a maniac. J didn't even turn round. Vladimir overtook J and stopped her in her tracks. She started laughing and was making to push him out of her way, but Vladimir was shooting at her.

"Ow, stop it! Or I'll put you over my knee."

Vladimir screamed, "You mouse kaput whore stink arse shit!" He kept shooting at her. Little pellets were flying out of the gun. Fergal had managed to catch up with them. J was protecting her face, now angrily hissing, "Stop it, you little rat! Or …"

Valiantly Fergal threw himself at Vladimir, knocked the plastic gun out of his hand and boxed him on the nose. Vladimir winced but didn't falter! In quick succession he boxed Fergal on the solar plexus, kicked him in the groin and broke Fergal's nose completely with a loud explosion going off in the latter's head. Fergal doubled up and fell to the ground. Vladimir picked up his gun and just walked off back towards the maize field saying, "Schweinehund, sow, arse, whore, cunt, shit, arse, stink, piss, arse, fuck. Mouse kaput, find new mouse!"

J was cringing with laughter.

The blitz of pain invading all areas of his body was new to Fergal. He couldn't breathe. His head was filled with a thousand spikes and splinters. His nose at a centre of a throbbing heat so violent, although he was on the ground, the world kept tilting in chaotic tremors without direction lifting him up and down, tossing him to and fro. A poisonous sickness so tremendous was reaching up from his groin where a mace must have hit a million times, he needed to retch but found no air to put into his lungs. He saw his own blood in the sand. His throbbing toe complemented this recipe of pain perfectly. The toe he had kicked Dad with yesterday.

He lay in the dirt.

How long had he lain there?

He didn't know. – When he finally managed to get up, self-pity kicked in at the same time as he saw Vladimir's bullets in the sand. They were peas! Vladimir had a pea-gun! Vladimir was the worst and meanest fighter Fergal had ever come across! And he wasn't even strong!? Heap of dry skin and sand bones finished off with a lingering smell of garlic and something else very foreign.

The first member of the Stab Gang had attacked!

Fergal started crying.

J had walked off home!

He couldn't even see her anymore.

How could she!

She could have easily defended him against that Barbarian Yugoslav Gastarbeiter kid.

No! Defending him wouldn't have been good. It would have been worse. He would have lost face in front of himself.

But he had wanted *and* had tried bravely to defend her against the Stab Gang! Come what may! Though, J didn't deserve it. His own life he would have laid down without question. Even for her!

The audacity.

A pea gun!?

Never would he ever speak to his diabolic sister again! – He had been silent for a year when he was little. With J he would be silent for the rest of his life!

Fergal sat down on the dirt path and cried bitterly. He felt so small, so tiny, and this feeling was not subsiding. It grew and grew the tinier he felt. It was crushing him. His life wasn't worth a pea! He felt himself falling, becoming tinier and tinier. He disappeared in the dirt. Particles of sand surrounding him as huge rocks at first, then mountains, until finally they became worlds. He was drifting in darkness.

When he finally limped home, the sun had already set. He staggered through the door, but Mutti wouldn't let him go to bed straight away. He had to wash! Mutti was very understanding. She even mentioned that J had just told her how her little brother had tried to defend her against this weakling who had then defeated Fergal. This was the moment when Fergal had to cry again in the bathtub.

Why hadn't Mutti come to pick him up?

"Because I've just come home from … myself."

From who?

"It's *whom.* And never you mind that."

When Heinrich The Vegetable Man came over to have a look at Fergal's nose and general state he gave Fergal a big hug. It helped a little. His big toe was only sprained. His nose though was broken. And above all, his pride had been scratched a little!? *No! Not just a little!* – Neither toe nor nose nor pride would have to be put into a plaster cast but all would hurt a little for a while.

Fergal's pride though certainly deserved another hug from Mutti. He had to cry again but managed to retell his adventure with The Stab Gang, adding completely new twists! Of long knives and machine guns and flame throwers and mines. The Stab Gang *were* a threat to society! The Blood Bubble Blister Bone Brotherhood would save Geesterheim! - And J was not just mad. J was insane!

"Time for bed, Johann."

Mutti just didn't get it! "It's Fergal!"

"Of course it is, Ferkel." She tucked him in when it had gone ten o'clock. The tucking-in felt not true, like theatre of the past. It was nice, … but! Mutti was in a different world. Dad was in a different world. And so were J and Fergal. Were there right and wrong worlds?

J was tired too, and lights went out. Both brother and sister went to sleep almost straight away.

Fergal had a strange dream.

When he was almost asleep he thought J got up and came over to his sofa bed. There she remained standing for a long time staring down at the wreck of pain her brother was.

In his dream Fergal could see the reflection in her eyes. She picked him up as Mutti used to and went over to the window opening it fully with Fergal still curled up in her arms, his head on her shoulder, sucking his thumb.

J then threw him out the window.

At first Fergal was falling fast, but his fall became slower the further he fell, until, finally, he was hovering there just a finger's breadth over the ground.

Presently, he floated back up again.

Slowly, without wanting to hurry. He observed the whitewashed render on the outside wall of their house clearly and without haste. The window ledge came into view. Then the open window itself. Fergal was being lifted up as in a slow elevator. And there was his sister standing staring at him in disbelief with her hands covering her nose and mouth as if she'd stifled a scream! Fergal floated past her back to his sofa bed and slept soundly.

That night Dad didn't come home at all.

Fergal was completely on his own.

Letter #25 – Fergal To God Via The Pope

My Dear Most Holy Pure Clean Good Papa with the Holy Spirit (as ever, this must go to God, your employer)! – Dear God!

You know by now that my sister is not entirely with it. She tried to drown me yesterday. Then she walked away when I tried to save her from The Stab Gang. Then Heinrich The Vegetable Man said my toe is just sprained and Mr. Nose is fine but broken, and it might look great when I grow up. It hurts badly! Some women like men with a broken nose. That's very strange. J never wants to like men ever again because we saw something terrible between Mutti and Dad, and I don't want to talk about it. We call it the destroyed palace now. That was really her idea. She also wants to continue a game she calls role-playing because it makes her life easier. I don't know whether I want to do that. Even though, I do like playing Father Martin O'Brady. So, I'm almost like one of your chaps. I don't like women and men like Mutti, Dad and J much. They all live in different worlds of anger!

J and I found out that we had the same dream or nightmare last night. She threw me out the window, but I floated back, and she looked quite astonished. J says in her dream she threw me out, and as she was about to shut the window, because of the midges, she sees me standing in the air, and my body is all stretched, and I have fast flapping wings like a hummingbird angel, but I look like a complete monster zombie. She says, I looked furious. Fury is anger but worse! I didn't see myself. We agreed though that I floated back to bed and slept.

J says it was a nightmare. For me it was just a dream. If two people have the same dream or nightmare then it is no longer a dream, is it?

She looked very scared this morning. She said she would try and be nicer to me now.

I do have to say I like being called Father Martin! It makes me feel closer to you. And that makes me feel closer to the answer to all the problems, and the one question I have in my mind always is. You know exactly what I mean! You read thoughts.

Please, pray for Dad, our father! That's funny! An Our Father for our father! There should be an Our Mother and Our Sister too. Please pray for Dad because J and Mutti are very sure he is the Devil. And that is not good, is it? Please pray for Mutti and J because thinking Dad is the Devil is not good. If someone is the Devil is there a special prayer I could say? Please, Dear God and Holy Papa, tell me what to do!

I am completely on my own. Dad used to say no man is an island. He made me learn a section. It's not Hemingway, who only used it in *For Whom The Bell Tolls*, which is a great war story set in Spain with a very boring love story in it. I was not supposed to read it, as I am too little, but I did anyway, and I was only eight, and I asked him, and Dad said it had been written by a chap called John Donne[12]. He made me learn it. This is how it goes.

No man is an island entire of itself, every man is a piece of the continent, a part of the main, if a clod be washed away by the sea, Europe is less, as well as if a promontory were, as well as if a manor of thy friend's or of thine own were, any man's death diminishes me, because I am involved in mankind, and therefore never send to know for whom the bell tolls, it tolls for thee.

It's nice, but I still haven't understood it fully. I'm not a clod! There are lots of images in there. Dad explained long and hard what it meant. I didn't understand fully. But one explanation was beautiful. That we are all of the same book.

I am out of that book. I am no longer in it. I am a cast away island with nobody on it. No Friday, no Robinson. I am the island.

No man is an island sounds nice, but it is not true.

It is a very difficult situation. The question is as clear and pure and true as you are. What is the answer?

Yours faithfully

J. Fergal Bulhof-Murphy

---

[12] 1624, Devotions upon Emergent Occasions, No. 17.

Party Time

Preparation

The atmosphere at home should have improved vastly with Dad finding work!

It didn't.

Dad had been out of work for over a year before he had found a job with a BMW dealership in Frankfurt. He was selling well.

As a businessman Dad had never worked for anyone but himself, apart from the RAF, but that hadn't been business. He was constantly complaining about the other salesmen at BMW there. They were Germans and just didn't know how to sell!

This might have been right, as he had become the best performing car salesman at the dealership within half a year. He wasn't liked, but he enjoyed the security of a good base-salary and the fact that it was BMW.

J and Mutti still saw in him the Devil! And Mutti had secret conferences with her daughter almost daily. Tears behind closed doors always! What J would relate at the end of the day sounded ever more horrific! Fergal didn't want to hear it but J would wait until her brother had stopped pressing his palms to his ears just before he was about to fall asleep, and then she would start relating the stories she had earlier picked up in Mutti's rounds of frequent confession. – Dad was still violating Mutti whenever he felt like it, and that was almost every night! He would do it quietly, so no one could tell he was doing it, but he was becoming ever more brutal, and surely Mutti would die soon!

His alcoholism was getting worse. Apparently he was on a bottle of whiskey a day! His breath certainly smelt of the water of life and tobacco smoke always. He would easily smoke his way through four packets of Senior Service a day, topped off with a Havana. Marlboro, Player's Navy Cut were second choice. Tullamore Dew the only choice for the drink. It was Dad's plan to destroy Mutti slowly, because according to him she hadn't stood by him through the bad time. If this wasn't going to work he would just kill her!

Mutti had explained all this very carefully to J so she could understand the *real* danger!

Fergal certainly noticed that Dad was hardly ever in. He spent a lot of time with his friends at the Officers' Club in Frankfurt or Darmstadt.

Weekend outings, Sunday lunches, happy smiles, … no more. But when had things like that happened anyway!? A long time ago in the past!

Whenever Dad looked at any of them, he did so with a distant frown. His eyes would be half-closed, his mouth pulled down. Fergal knew it was an attempt at grinning, but it failed miserably every time. It was a huge effort to smile at Dad, but Fergal did so *every* time he saw him. Mostly Dad just rushed past him.

Mutti and J were avoiding Dad actively.

It was a mystery what Dad was doing with all the money he earned. Mutti no longer knew. That he did earn good money was clear from his suits, shirts and shoes, J said. Dad still paid for their rent and some basic contribution for food. That was it. – If Mutti wanted to get anything new to wear for either her children or herself, she had to call Oma and Opa. Opa had apparently said he knew exactly what was going on, and *that man* ought to be shot like a dirty mongrel.

The silence in the flat, whenever Dad was around, was complete! – Mutti and J were rigid with fear, and Fergal just felt it wasn't right to sing or play anymore. Reading was the best, as you just disappeared into another world. The atmosphere at home was that of a perpetual funeral, J said. J was waiting for the Devil to die. Her performance at school was suffering badly, but not enough to make her give up her aim to become a doctor. She said, that now and then she was very afraid this aim would just become a pipedream. All dreams were close to nightmares now.

At the end of May the Noldes moved out, taking Chuck with them to their new, self-designed, modern style Black Forest peasant hut outside Munich. Chuck cried. He wanted Fergal to come with them. Fergal said, "I'd love to!" and ran upstairs to ask

Mutti if he could go with the Noldes, as there was no need of him with his own family, as there was no family left. Mutti was so baffled, she couldn't get out a word. She just sat down at the kitchen table and started sobbing.

Suddenly, Herr and Frau Nolde were standing in the kitchen door nodding. Frau Nolde hugged Mutti and gave her a kiss, "We know, Martha! It's hardly been quiet. Just get a divorce."

Mutti promised she'd keep writing to Frau Nolde how things went, but divorce was not an option. Only God could do a divorce, and Dad was a Catholic who thought along similar lines, just more strictly. Frau Nolde just kept shaking her head and said "Religion is poison!" Mutti nodded. And then the Noldes were gone. That's when Fergal cried.

This was 1975, the second half of year four at school.

Fergal was a good student. – Big School was going to be next. And then, university!

Although his reports always stated *too quiet,* teachers were very happy with his written performance. And, after all, didn't Opa always say *silence is golden*? He *had* to be right, because whenever people said something to each other, it was vile, and then the Devil was created by one or the other. Fergal wondered, if Dad thought J, Mutti and he were Devils!?

The beginning of year four had seen three additions to class. The Stab Gang, and a tiny, thin girl called Julia Ronstein. The Stab Gang were by now quite able to speak German with a most eloquent well of swearwords that they were drawing from constantly. They had been amalgamated into the Blood & Bone Band. The Blood Bubble Pact had been dissolved! No more Blood Bubble Brotherhood or Blood Blisters!

The Double Bubble Gang still went from strength to strength as Bernhardt's presence secured fear all-round! – Joachim was a member in name only. He was no longer talking to anyone bar Julia. They were the best of friends now.

Pastor Meinheit had let it slip to his son that Julia too had tried to commit suicide, just like Joachim. Bernhardt knew that Julia and Joachim were going to get married and then throw themselves out of a nice window with a fine view. – No one really thought that was funny, but Bernhardt would mention this about twice a week and then crack up with laughter.

The Vietnam War had come to a complete end on the 30th April.

"Wasn't there a complete end before, Mutti?"

"No, Ferkelchen! – Just a ceasefire and all soldiers were withdrawn."

"Wasn't that a complete end?"

"No. – Now the South-Vietnamese have capitulated, and the Americans have had to flee Saigon."

"The Americans? Flee!?"

"Yes."

"What's *capitulate*?"

"Surrender."

"Ouch. – Have the communists won?"

"Yes."

"That's bad!!!"

"It depends on the viewpoint entirely. – The world is a valley of tears, little man! Pol Pot's Khmer Rouge! The Lebanon is exploding! It never ends! – All war and selling arms."

"But there's also peace, Mutti."

"Yes, of course there is! – Let me do our lunch now."

"Who's Pol Pot? Is he potty-trained and potty?"

Mutti laughed, "Yes, he's potty-trained *and* potty. He's like Hitler. – Now, run along! There's a good boy!"

"J's told me that she'll now be a full grownup at eighteen, because it used to be twenty-one."

"Yes. They changed the law in January."

"But she is potty! And she shouldn't be allowed to be a grownup!?"

Mutti raised her endemic German index finger *and* her voice, "Don't ever say that about your sister, Johann! Do you hear me!? She is a *very* responsible young woman. You can only learn from her. Now, let me get on with it!"

"*My* name is Fergal!"

A week later Mutti announced behind closed doors to J that it was likely the Bulhof-Murphys were going to move up to somewhere in or around Hamburg where Oma and Opa were, because Dad might get his own showroom up there. He was still going to work for BMW, but at least he would be his own boss again. Not entirely his own boss as before, of course! This was quite good, because it was a little safer and more secure.

"*We* own the north of Germany, don't we, J?"

"What do you mean?"

"It's called the British Zone. – It's ours!"

"No, Fergal! We are German now! It is the British Occupied Military Zone. Great Britain is up there because *we* are the enemy. Just as much as the Ammies are down here."

"I'm English! – I cannot be my own enemy!?"

"Stop insisting you are English, Fergal! You'll get the German nationality as soon as Mutti has some more breathing space. *I* have it now! Johanna Bulhof."

"Murphy."

"Bulhof."

"Murphy."

"Bulhof infinity."

"Murphy mubble … double infinity!"

"Bulhof infinity to the power of infinity. So there!"

Yet another week later, Mutti announced with a sad, disbelieving frown to J, who in turn announced it to Fergal in the middle of the night, that it was now extremely likely they were going to move up to North Germany, unless Dad killed them beforehand, of course! It was going to be very, *very* north and almost three hours away from Oma and Opa. It was also a surprise! And she didn't *even* tell J, who couldn't tell Fergal where they were going.

Fergal and J were going to finish school first, and the move was going to happen during the summer holidays. Above all, there was going to be a party first! Dad was going to invite all *his* … well, … their friends.

"Mutti doesn't have any friends, J."

"Up there she has. – Remember, Fergal, … that's where she's from. Originally."

"Are we going to have a party to say goodbye too?"

"Mutti didn't say so. That's a nice idea though. I'll check tomorrow."

"Is Dad still the Devil?"

"Oh, yes he is! I hope they'll get a divorce! – Up there it's safer because we're all closer to home up there."

"I am not! I like it here! But I'm at home in London. Oxford a little bit. But I can't remember it."

"You're at home where your family is! We haven't met any of Dad's relatives in either England or Ireland, little runt!"

"No."

"So, you're at home with *us!*"

"No!"

"Oh, stop being awkward and contrary! Look forward to the party! Brechner and Hardy and the Greiffhorns are going to be there. They are *all* foreigners you *really* like!"

"Yes! They are not foreign! And I don't like the Greiffhorns. Philip tried to put that alligator down my throat."

"Alligator?" J smiled wistfully.

"It was a toy because they're from Florida. They also have a real stuffed alligator. It hurt."

"Mmh. – I'll go to Florida soon!"

"Of course you will. – Do we have lots of family in England and Ireland."

"Yes. Millions! They're not *my* family though. – Go to sleep now. You are annoying me!"

Americans & Surprise Gifts

The party was at the beginning of June, Saturday the 7th. This didn't mean Mutti and Dad had to talk to each other! They just prepared together, unsmilingly, tight-lipped.

Guests started appearing at two o'clock in the afternoon. Fergal and J were allowed to stay up until they fell asleep. That was a very antiauthoritarian Nolde-thing to do for Mutti!

The whole length of Georg-Büchner-Straße and Mönchsgasse was lined with American cars, mostly with green American military plates. Fergal also discovered one with white Texas plates and one with blue plates from Maryland. He counted sixty-five vehicles in all and felt a certain amount of pride at the fact that he knew all the makes. Dad had kept the VW in the drive for Fergal to play with, but Fergal never did. Dad was now driving a BMW 3-series, which wasn't even out yet, he claimed. Small, but very nice!

Everyone was there apart from Dad's black friends. The American Spaniards were also missing. Lt. Hardy had brought Fergal a massive NBC gas mask in army green that gave you a completely new head with humongous eyes and really made you look like a lagoon monster with a pig's face. Putting it on Fergal discovered it instilled a grave terror of tight spaces. He quickly took it off again, panting.

After J had tried to drown him the year before, Fergal had developed a bit of claustrophobia, Mutti said. But she still didn't believe his drowning-story.

The gas mask smelt just like everything military. There wasn't another smell like it on earth. It was a completely fantastic! A distinctly military whiff.

"Thank you, Lieutenant Hardy, sir! That's a great mask!"

"Fergal, come on! Old Buddies. I keep telling ya, call me Jon!"

"Sir! Yes, sir! What do you wash the army with?"

"Is that a joke question, buddy!?"

"No! – All the gear smells the same."

"Oh, yeah. Know what you mean. Really couldn't tell you. General Issue soap, I guess."

"Do you remember the 1911 Colt you wanted to get me?"

"Course I do, little buddy! Your dad gave it back to me. Saying, no offence, but your mum would go ape even though it was just a toy. I can understand that, considering the thing you pulled last year."

"It was the year before, Jon."

"Right. Time, eh. Age! How's your friend Zigziggy?"

"He's out of hospital at the moment. He's fine! He's no longer dressing up for the moment. And Tristan says they're only keeping the trenches in the garden for him to play in. That's really great!"

"That's one hell of a strange family!" Jon shook his head.

"Why haven't you been promoted to Major or at least Captain yet, Jon?"

"Well, … things don't always happen that quickly!"

Suddenly, Big-Eye Nathan appeared on the scene. He was holding his ten-speed under his arm. He stared around the garden for a bit, gave Fergal a wild smile, and when he'd spotted Dad by the barbeque, he jogged over, shook his hand and disappeared again.

"Who the *hell* was that? He was kinda nice lookin'!" Fergal heard a lady squeak. No one answered. – Men and women at these parties were always strictly segregated. There were groups of men and groups of women. They rarely intermingled unless of course some husband would shout, "Gemme a beer, Sam, I'm dryin out!" The good wife would go and fetch a beer from inside the garage to come back to a laughing crowd of men only to hear, "Damn, Sam! You are slow! I had to help maself as ever. There was some beer right here by Seán's barbie."

"Yeah, you too, Rick. Ha-ha. Very funny!" The wife might then shake the can, open it, and empty the contents over Rick, saying, "Sorry, darl! Couldn't hold it, had to, all over you."

"Damn you, little bitch!" Rick might make a fist but smile and say, "Well, darling! I'll tell you later when we're all alone what I thought about your performance!"

Then all men would laugh like crazy and pat Rick's shoulder.

No one had brought any of their kids today because it was strictly grownups! – J said, Dad had sent out these tasteless, *naughty* invitation cards advertising the #1 piss-up of the year. She had filched one from Dad's office corner in the living room. It was postcard size. Orange with three bits to it which you had to unfold. On the front it said *What to do if pussy's stuck up* …, then, you turned to the second page, where there was a little window, offering a preview of what one might see on the last centre page. The triangle of a woman's pubes and a section of her thighs underneath.

Fergal wasn't all that keen to see the rest, but J insisted. – The picture behind the little cut-out window was that of a black cat sitting in a tree. Its tail was the woman's pubes. Her thighs the tree trunk. At the top it said *If she's stuck up a tree, call the fire department, and get her wet a little.*

Fergal didn't get it.

J said, it was a base joke and she was so totally embarrassed that this person was *her* father.

He was the Devil, and a perv, and just … yuck! Sick!

Underneath it continued *If she's just stuck up, be a red-hot fireman for your girl at the hottest, wettest Pussy Ball of 75.*

J said, it told you everything about the kinds of people, foreigners, pervs, American friends Dad had invited! She doubted, any of the men had shown their wives the invitation.

By ten thirty it was completely dark and everyone was thoroughly pissed! Fergal noticed that the earlier gender clusters distributed their members far more liberally now. Everyone was just standing around, chatting and swaying. Two women were having a private puke get-together by the wall in the hedgerow.

"He invited all the neighbours so they wouldn't complain about the noise!" J had said.

"What noise?"

"There's going to be lots of people there! More than a hundred! That's noise! And he's going to have two Californian guitarists playing music."

"Yeah? – Cool!"

None of the neighbours had joined Seán's *Pussy Ball*. A *Pussy Ball* didn't appeal to the kind of nice German neighbours they had here at Geesterheim, Mutti said.

"I give a friggin', flyin' shit about my *German* neighbours!" Dad had said earlier, turning yet another gigantic American-cut beefsteak on the Barbie. "Bunch o' Nazis the lot o' them! Great sausages they make though! But I had to send out invitations so they can't complain. – So, guys, if you see anyone joining our little party with a raised arm going *rat-pack-tsack-attack*, it's one o' my neighbours!"

"Hey, what'ja wannus do widdem, Seán? My *Sieg Heil*'s a bit rusty but I can still pull it off!" All-male clusters, huddling around the barbie, laughed loud.

Somebody else shouted, "I got my gun in the car!"

"Yeah! Me too!"

The music the two Californian hippies were playing sounded great! – J was hanging round them for a while before she disappeared. Mutti said just to leave her by herself. She was just shy. Fergal didn't believe that. Shy wasn't what came to mind with his sister. Now and then one particular soldier, Fergal had never seen before, would put himself up in front of the long-haired guitar duo and say, "Now, … when are ye gonna learn how to play summin good then!? I like *Moon River*. Everyone likes *Moon River*!"

Their names were Matt and Dan from San Francisco. Fergal found out that they especially loved David Grisman and his Dawg, and the Rolling Stones. Maria Muldaur, Captain & Tenille weren't so bad for playing at these kinda garden parties either. Captain Beefheart, Wildman Fisher, Zappa? And Hirth Martinez? Now, that was more like the real thing, they said.

"Cool!"

"Hey, Dan! – Our little friend here digs our music! Cool! – Pass me some!"

"I dig!"

"What in the name are you doing in a crowd like this with a fascist dad like that!? I had a dad like that. Looo-zeeeerr! Left him drunk at home when I was only four, Matt." – Matt and Dan did a thing with their hands and fists.

"He's my father! He's a little disoriented at the moment."

"Uoah! – Dis-dis-what in the orient? You are way-out, dude!"

"Express!"

"Orient!"

"I dig you."

Fergal thought for a moment, before he said, "The people here don't like your music much. Why are you playing here?"

"Friend of a friend kinda thing. It's moneyyyyyy! And I can tell ya it ain't just the music they not likin!"

"I see. – I love your music!"

"Thanks, dude! – Why you think they talkin' so loud?" Matt & Dan did another thing with their hands.

Mutti called Fergal over to introduce him to some new soldier's depressed looking wife. Matt & Dan's music was drowned out completely by the din the party voices created. And then at ten thirty in the evening Fergal found the duo sitting at the centre of the triangle of apricot trees, smoking a joint away from the loud crowd.

He hid in the darkness of the shade and eavesdropped in professional Opa-fashion. The point, Opa had taught him, was not just to hide well, but also to think you *were* in fact totally invisible. Your breathing changed and all! It *really* worked!

Matt & Dan's joint was bigger than Joachim's, and they looked *really* happy! Fergal heard Dan say from underneath his long curly hair, "These guys would normally like to kill us, dude!"

"Yeah, like totally!"

"They're just depressed, 'cause Vietnam's all finished-n-fucked."

"Totally, dude! You are *so* right! – If they don't get to kick the shit outa somebody else they might kill us."

"I'm just glad … they're all like … so smashed … like … otherwise they might take that Viet shit out on us for real!"

"Yeah! – Somebody needs to give the order though."

They stopped talking for a while, dragging so hard on their joint, it lit up the darkness. But they didn't see Fergal.

"Let's go get stoned in a German field. That sister o' his said she's goin that way."

"Real chick."

"Yab-yum, dude!"

They disappeared.

Fergal loved the apricot tree triangle. It was tucked away in a quiet corner of the garden surrounded by a wall of bushes. He stepped forward from his hiding place. He wanted to lie down on the ground and look at where the stars were shining through the foliage, when Col. Brechner stepped into this peaceful refuge.

"Need to take a piss wanna join me."

Fergal needed to go, so it wasn't a problem, "What's the bet I can wee much quicker than you, Colonel?"

The Colonel had only ever been the Colonel to Fergal. The whole Colonel and nothing but the Colonel, so help him God! He was Opa's height. – Whilst Opa could be described as a piece of leather with an interesting arrangement of hairs on top, the Colonel was a length of barbed wire with a shining row of loud teeth on top.

"I don't bet on piss boy but I like a man who only bets when he can win unlike our government."

"Yeah."

"On three."

"Yeah cool!"

"You ready?"

"Yupp!"

"One two three go!"

Fergal pressed hard and the first gush squirted out further than the Colonel's. The Colonel's picked up only slowly, but then it *really* got going! He *definitely* had the physical advantage in length, width and depth. He could piss further, faster and harder, which meant he could possibly win this bet.

"Damn there's still so much just keeps comin'."

The Colonel also had the disadvantage of age and alcohol.

Fergal pressed out the last bit, zipped up and shouted, "Finished! I win!" To celebrate his victory he started running a little circle within the perimeter of the apricot trees. The Colonel was by no means finished. He was swaying and still urinating hard, "Stop that running shit Fergal you makin me dizzy."

An order like that had to be obeyed! Fergal stopped just across from the Colonel. Cows and horses sounded and looked just like that! The Colonel was gathering a good puddle at the centre of the trees.

"In '68 I pissed on the bastards had a dead one didn't realise she was dead we had one gook down almost dead put a hole in his heart pissed on it and now they're pissing all over us." He shook his head and looked down at himself, "I had too much too drink it was great feels like I'm gonna keep pissin like this for the rest of the goddam night I knew I'd lose the goddam bet." He kept shaking his head, "This is more than I've fuckin drunk all night my body keeps getting stuff wrong the way you see it in the movies is crap killin ain't easy I mean it is easy but not as easy as in the goddam films you hear me Fergal don't believe 'em if you cut a guys throat like that he's gonna kill you back you have to go deep." The Colonel made a side-to-side movement along his throat with his wet index finger, "What you wanna do is stick it in the side of the sucker's neck turn it push it forward then the throat's out." With his wet hand he stuck an invisible knife right in the side of his neck, "You have to inflict pain to immobilise at the same time but don't do it for the pain or you're a sad fucker like that Marcello pizza guy the Mafia tied to the rear end of his car and drove around till he was just a pile o' meat still keeps comin look at all the piss … ah now that's it!" His mouth went wide showing a shiny row of brilliant teeth in the darkness, "You've definitely won, Fergal!" The Colonel held the root of his penis with his left and started shaking the wobbling rest of it with such ferocity Fergal caught a few drops. He was convinced the Colonel was trying to do himself an injury.

"I wouldn't do that if I were you, Colonel!"

"What's that."

"Shaking your willy that hard. You might rip it off."

"Makes the drops come out when you get older there's more drops have you seen my wife?" He zipped himself up.

Fergal didn't answer. Had the Colonel said Marcello was dead!? "Is Marcello dead?"

"Yupp."

"What d'he do?"

"Insulted the wrong guy Calogero you know him?"

"Yupp, Colonel."

"Guess your father didn't want to tell you bout it."

"Guess not." Beautifully singing Marcello was dead! So the Mafia were serious about killing.

"Gone all quiet."

"Bit sad."

"Happens so have you seen my wife Lydia?"

"No, sir, I haven't."

"OK Fergal come here I want you to have something it's very precious and I once overheard you'd really like one cause your Mickey Mouse one is gone." The Colonel wiped his hands dry in his trousers. He took off his dog tags and wristwatch, "You keep my dog tags and don't givem to anyone and you keep my pop's Hamilton it's an old one from the Second War still working they were real good made for the right cause there take it keep it."

Fergal couldn't believe his luck! – Well, where his mother was concerned he should have said *no thank you* at least three times. It was only polite. But Mutti really didn't understand about this war thing! It was just something between men that girls would never understand, and Mutti was a girl deep down really.

"Thank you so much, Colonel, sir, thank you!"

"Falling right over yourself you're very welcome now I'm gonna check on my wife you can follow me you might learn something for later." With that he did a one-eighty turn. Fergal had to jog to keep up with the Colonel. They went through the noisy crowd neither looking left nor right.

They were on a mission!

They went down the narrow path that connected the garden with the driveway and front of the house. It ran alongside the garage and the Noldes' terrace. Their flat lay in utter darkness. Fergal wondered how his friend Chuck faired in Bavaria. Frau Nolde had written he was going to a Catholic school and apparently he liked the discipline. Frau Nolde was a Catholic, she had confessed in the letter.

The Colonel was now creeping low like an Injun. He and Fergal came to a dead stop by the wide-open garage door and listened. In sign language the Colonel gave Fergal the order to remain absolutely quiet and listen as hard as he could, … or else, … knife through throat, twist, push forward, throat out, Fergal dead. Fergal saluted to show that he would, come what may, obey the order. The Colonel saluted back as a reflex.

Fergal strained his eyes and ears in the dark as hard as he could. There was definitely something going on behind Dad's new BMW in the pitch-black.

The Colonel turned to Fergal, nodded and indicated for him to wait. – Despite the gravel the Colonel hardly made a sound as he disappeared like a frontline soldier under sniper fire in the twilight with only one streetlamp flickering around the side of the house on Georg-Büchner-Straße. There was no moon. This was like an old black and white movie with a hand-turned projector.

Fergal could hear more noises and whispering from behind Dad's BMW. Then suddenly the Colonel was back at his side holding a massive automatic pistol. Fergal could just about see it was a Colt .45 and the hammer was cocked. The Colonel signed to Fergal to tell him where the light switch for the garage was. Fergal understood immediately! The Colonel's sign language was unambiguous from years spent in the line of fire where the sound of a single word could give away your position to the enemy. The switch was just up and around the gate springs.

Everything that happened next happened so quickly Fergal felt he ought to be running around madly, doing something.

He stuck close to the Colonel.

The Colonel jumped up. The light was on. Colt stretched out ahead of him, he was already behind the BMW. A woman's loud but short, startled scream! Lt Hardy got up into view pulling up his trousers. He didn't look afraid. The Colonel gave him an understanding nod, "Fuck off."

Lt Hardy saluted and ran past Fergal into the garden.

"Suck it like you never sucked me before you low-down nympho-whore gonna teach my boy Fergal what traitors get." It was Lydia, the Colonel's wife! He grabbed her by the hair and smashed the barrel of his gun into her mouth, lowering himself on his knees, pushing the pistol deeper and deeper down her throat. Fergal heard something crack. A tooth maybe!? It had to be a tooth! She swallowed without any sign of pain.

"Could never suck me off but everyone else out there no problem do you think I'm blind girl."

Lydia didn't make a move.

As though the Colonel was non-existent.

An invisible force without consequence.

There was no fear in her eyes.

Nothing.

She was waiting patiently for something. Not the back of her head to come off. Fergal knew she was used to this. Everything in the way she behaved betrayed use and even boredom.

She looked at something behind Fergal.

The next thing Fergal saw was Dad rolling off the Colonel who was on the garage floor.

Dad had the gun!

Lydia was covering her bleeding mouth. *Now* she seemed in pain.

Lt Hardy stepped forward, got to his knees, and put his arm round his superior officer. Fergal looked round. The garage was filling with a silent audience. Then, of all unimaginable things, the Colonel started crying, but not as ordinary folk might cry. He got to his feet, hugged Lt Hardy, shut his eyes, and started making these hard *m-m-m* sounds with his cheekbones working hard inside his mouth.

This was just too much for some of the female bystanders! The first shaking heads moved out of the starkly lit garage. The first tears were cried in the dark, little passage that led back to the garden. Fergal heard, "Why can't he shoot that whore", "He's such a good man", "Doesn't deserve this", "He could have come to me any time", "Come *on!* We know what it's like with Lydia", "Damn nympho", "Under a lot of stress".

Lydia just got up and went with the same woman who'd just suggested the Colonel shoot her.

It was only men left in the garage.

Hardy waved with one arm not releasing the quivering Colonel from his hug. There still were no tears. Only *m-m-m* jerks. "Come on guys, give us a minute here!" The men left and made their shuffling way back into the garden.

Suddenly the Colonel stood erect as if to attention. He looked approvingly at Hardy then turned round and gave Dad a nod. Dad handed him back the Colt. The Colonel shook his head, "You keep it Seán you saved me."

" 'K, Pete!"

"Lemme just …" The Colonel stomped off outside. This time Fergal heard the gravel loud and clear. The Colonel's steps. A car door. Then he was back, holding a big box in brown, oily paper and, what looked to Fergal like a pineapple type hand grenade, "Seán here's a keepsake from Nam pried it from the guy who wanted to kill me it's empty and two-hundred rounds of Remingtons for the Colt."

Dad nodded, "That's a great gift, Pete."

The grenade was the fragmentation type. Fergal knew. The short wooden grip attached to it was new to Fergal, who was watching Dad carefully as he heaved the ammo onto the top shelf where the blowtorches were kept. The gun he inserted behind his belt at his back. Fergal didn't know this side to his father.

For a brief moment only did he feel he was standing in the garage with complete strangers. Then the three men went outside. Dad turned off the garage lights and looked over uneasily at the Bruckner's house. They were the closest neighbours. Three Mercs, *and* a swimming pool! No lights had come on. The hunting dogs weren't barking. He nodded and gave Fergal one of his dry, blank looks with eyes half shut. Fergal liked the Bruckners. Fergal knew Dad was trying to smile. But not even in his current state of massive inebriation did he manage it anymore.

The men put themselves in a line facing the house wall. Then they urinated as if there were no tomorrow. Fergal just watched. He couldn't do that again! The last time he had weed was just ten or so minutes ago. He looked at his new Hamilton. The strap was too long but that didn't matter! He'd find a way to tuck it under. Tomorrow!

"I'm taking Lydia I'm too pissed to drive we're goin' home." The Colonel was swaying badly. But so were Lt Hardy and Dad. They disappeared into the garden

Fergal remained at the front of the house and walked to his sandbox. The lights at Joachim's were off. The flickering street light was annoying! When had that started? Fergal sat down on the sandbox's wooden frame, shook his head, and got up again. He walked over to the white, low wall separating their property from the street. The bright white gave it slight Mediterranean look. A lot of walls here in Hessen were painted like that.

All the way up and down Georg-Büchner-Straße the lights in homes were off. Although it was a summery warm Saturday no one else was having a party. All had been invitation-warned that the Bulhof-Murphys were having a party. No one in the street had turned up. The Bulhof-Murphys were just foreigners who had too many American friends.

Fergal went out through the black metal gate in the wall and stood on the wide sandy footpath outside Georg-Büchner-Straße 9. The council were going to lay slabs soon so it was a proper pavement. They wanted Geesterheim to look nice and clean and modern. Old just smacked of backward and might remind people of the war and the Nazis. This was the *Vorsprung* Germans loved above all. Progress! Opa said, why dress up nature if nature dresses rather better by herself.

Out of the blue Fergal saw Big-Eye Nathan flying past on his ten-speed. He found the time to wave. But then Big-Eye was gone again in the direction of Frankfurt.

What was Nathan's thing?

Fergal looked at his new watch. 23:10 h.

Why did Nathan cycle so much?

All Fergal knew was that he liked Dad, and Dad said Nathan never wanted to be inside anywhere again ever and stand still. Apparently, it had something to do with the war and the POW camp he had been to in Bavaria. Dad knew very little of Nathan himself, he had admitted. Apart from that he wasn't talking to Fergal anymore anyway.

The Colonel staggered past with his wife Lydia. She appeared very drunk too. Her mouth was open but no longer smeared with blood. One of her incisors had been knocked out. It was as if nothing had ever happened.

They didn't see Fergal.

Both got in the car.

He was going to drive!

Theirs was the red Mercury Cougar with the blue Maryland plates.

Last time Fergal had seen the Colonel sober he had had one of Dad's Chryslers. The dreadnought Town & Country.

Now, the Colonel switched on the engine and revved the heavy V8 hard. Fergal could see the Colonel's face. It was empty, as if all concentration had gathered in his ears to hear the engine. A wonder that no lights came on in the neighbouring houses! Then he saw the Colonel leaning over to his wife in the passenger seat. There was a flash and a loud bang at the same time. The Colonel was back in the driver window. He looked out briefly and saw Fergal by the black gate. He nodded at the boy before he shot himself through the mouth.

Fergal stood by the gate three meters away from the Cougar. The interior of the car was filled with gently drifting smoke. Slowly Fergal walked over and looked in. On the passenger seat Lydia was reclining as though asleep with a dark wet patch forming around her heart, increasing in size. The flicker of the streetlight made it look as if her body was twitching. Maybe it was. *She's dead,* Fergal thought.

The Colonel had slumped forward to the side of the steering wheel with a black, glistening hole ripped in the back of his neck, blood running out, pulsating hard in the silent movie of the street light. In a movie the horn might be going at full whack. *When did I see a film with someone on the steering wheel and the horn going,* Fergal wondered!? Here, there was just silence. With the memory of shot still ringing in Fergal's ears.

Still, no neighbourly lights!

Fergal walked around the back of the car expecting there to be a hole with lots of blood and brains in the rear window. There wasn't. He went back to the gate to tell his parents, but turned once more. There was an uneven bit on the roof of the car. That's were the bullet had gone! Maybe it was still travelling up to find the moon. The moon was completely gone this evening.

Fergal went into the garden. It was gender clustering again.

Fergal wandered over to Lt Hardy who was standing with Dad and some five others and told them what had happened.

Hadn't they heard!?

What, and *is your kid for real*, and *he's a bit too cool*, and *this ain't funny*.

Fergal felt very calm, "I am not lying! The Colonel's just shot himself and his wife."

Fuck! – All hell broke loose.

Lt Hardy volunteered to drive the Cougar back to camp in Frankfurt. Within ten minutes everyone was gone. The Military Police would take care of this.

As Fergal was watching everyone leave, neighbours still hadn't switched on their lights.

Mutti said, "I know we're being watched from behind curtains, I can assure you! This is Germany! Let's go to bed. We'll clear up tomorrow." – Mutti was very worried that witnessing this horrible spectacle would be bad for Fergal.

"I'm fine! Really!"

Mutti didn't sound drunk one little bit. "I hope so!" she muttered. Almost lovingly did she push Dad ahead of her. "Have you seen Johanna, Ferkel?"

"No."

Post-party Dad stumbled straight up into the living room for another drink. He didn't feel like sleeping yet and wanted a nightcap. Mutti shook her head. She couldn't believe it! "You're going to drink yourself to death, Seán!"

"You don't care."

"It's in you. It's Irish."

"I know how to drink. Stop nagging now!"

J was in her bedroom. These days it was Fergal's bedroom also.

"Are you asleep yet, Fergal?"

"What *now*, J? – Did you hear the shot?"

"No! – What shot?"

"The Colonel killed himself and then his wife, Lydia. I saw it."

"You poor, fucking kid. Anyway, you get over it. – I had sex in the wilds today!"

"I *really* do not want to know. – Good night!"

"I thought, before going sapphist, I want to try out a man or two."

"What's sapphist?"

J knew that if she threw into any conversation with her little brother a new word, he just couldn't resist. Fergal loved learning new words. Joachim was no longer having Granny Hammerich word-parties. In any case, his repertoire had only been limited to granny-abuse.

"A lesbian."

Fergal sighed. She was a frustrating woman, "What's a lesbian?"

"A homosexual woman."

Fergal sat up. *That* word he knew! And that really was one of Joachim's old words as in *Granny Hammerich does it with homosexual rats.* Homosexual meant you only do it with yourself or friends who had a willy. "You can only be homosexual if you are a man. So, that is your *nonsense all Bollerboe nonsense* again, isn't it!?"

"No. – It means same-sex relationship."

"I'll look it up!"

"You do that."

"So what's it like, J? – You want me to ask you that, don't you!?"

"Yes."

"So?"

"It was OK. The two guys were really nice. A bit like two girls though."

"Two?"

"Oh *yes!* And now I'm no longer a virgin."

Fergal knew what a virgin was. "I know what a virgin is. And I know all about the Virgin Mary and *you* are not *it*, 'cause you ain't immaculate!"

"Don't talk in that horrid American accent. It's coarse and base and primitive. – Do you want to be a primi-prolo?"

"What's a primi-prolo?"

"An asocial primitive proletarian!"

"I'll look it up. – Good night, sapphist homo!"

"I'm a woman now!"

With that Fergal drifted off to sleep. J was still whispering on and on, but that didn't matter to him as he had Colonel's dog tags around his neck and his new watch around his wrist.

Fergal dreamt how he took J by the hand and how he actually liked her. Then he drifted out the window with her and they flew all around Geesterheim and over into France and then back to London. – London looked great at night! But what was that down there!? It was an open place with a lot of lights round it. Fergal recognised Trafalgar Square, immediately! There was a man with a pistol down there. He was taking aim. He fired. The shot was deafening!

Fergal woke up. J was sitting upright in her bed shrieking. She was hitting herself around the face like mad. Outside their door Mutti screamed, "Lock your door! He's going to kill us all!"

Another scream, but this time from Dad! Inarticulate and animal-like! Fergal turned the key, pulled it out of the lock and looked through the keyhole. There was Dad underneath Mutti in the hallway. Mutti was resting the Colonel's gun from him, threw it behind her and started hammering her fists down on him. Dad was much too drunk to react. He was in his own painfully slow world of alcohol and sickness.

Mutti kept screaming!

Inside their room J kept hitting herself! Clawing her face with her finger nails intermittently, now and then renewing her screech when she'd run out of breath. Fergal could see gashes beginning to appear on J's face. The world was left without words reflecting only images of flickering madness inside, illuminated by the broken streetlight outside

After a good minute of pounding Dad in the face and chest, Mutti got up and went over to the telephone table. Dad just lay there on his back.

Fergal couldn't see Mutti but he heard her pick up the phone. She was dialling. Then, the wait! Fergal looked at his watch. It was gone three. Mutti was still waiting for an answer. If it was the police they were possibly too drunk themselves to pick up, either of them. Herr Bruckner had recently said Oberwachtmeister Knopf and his underling Kümmerling would have to be transferred. Herr Bruckner was on the council!

Fergal saw Dad get up. But not even his solid stagger could help him stay upright. He fell forward and started dragging himself into the living room like a wounded reptile. He kicked the door shut. Mutti got a line.

"Yes!? – Sorry, Herr Pastor! It's very late. – My husband just tried to shoot us … it's Frau Bulhof … yes, I know … if you wouldn't mind … it's an awful lot to ask … it's worse since last time we spoke … he is not himself … that's very kind of you … thank you!" The telephone conversation finished.

Mutti dashed up the hallway, picked up the gun and disappeared in the bedroom.

Only ten minutes later Pastor Meinheit was standing in the hallway in his tent-like black robe. He looked at Fergal's and J's door. J had stopped screeching by then. Her bloody face was resting on her pillow chewing on one of Fergal's favourite old, crunchy hankies that he had given to her minutes ago for the occasion. She was watching Fergal intently, whimpering.

Pastor Meinheit asked, "Are the children safe in there?"

"Yes, Herr Pastor! Seán's in the living room." Mutti was out of view.

"Let's have a look at the patient then. In God's kingdom all are equal, and all can be helped, Catholic or no!" He strode up to the living room door and knocked on the glass. There was no answer. He looked at Mutti.

"Just go in, Herr Pastor!"

He hesitated, "You said *shoot*. He tried to *shoot* you!? Does he still have the gun on him?"

"No. It's safe."

"Good. Good!" Pastor Meinheit opened the door. No sooner had he disappeared inside than a howl started. Dad was howling like a dog.

The noise level the one-sided conversation proceeded at was enough for Fergal to hear distinctly the foulest language from the deepest pit of hell he had ever heard! Dad was throwing a stream of abusive language so constant and thunderously ear-splitting at Herr Pastor Meinheit the latter did evidently not get a word in edgeways. The pastor did try! Fergal could hear as much through the basic rhetoric curtain Dad was pulling around Herrn Pastor.

He tried, "But Herr Murphy …"

And, "Now, let's talk about this …"

"… like two adults …"

"… no, there was a good reason why that fucking, fat-arsed wanker of a renegade German heretic piss artist reformed the Church …"

"… please forgive me, my Lord, … I am trying …"

"… Lord God of Hosts help me out here …"

"… in the name of God stop this blasphemy …"

" … right, if you won't stop, I'll just go then, shall I?"

Dad howled back in a constant, "… piss off you who have emerged from the deepest chasm of rotting faeces turned uneducated language for corpses not even you in your blithering attempts at pretentious healing can fathom to comprehend de profundis clamavi ad te Domine, Domine exaudi vocem meam, you merit masturbator …"

The howl was muted ever so slightly when Herr Pastor Meinheit shut the living room door behind him with a furiously irritated face turned towards the kitchen where Mutti wasn't. When his face had left all that wasn't sanctimonious by Mutti's oven, he turned in the right direction again so she could see his solemn profundity and eternal compassion.

"My daughter … this … I'm afraid … is a Catholic … problem … I am, although qualified and able to master entirely on my own … entirely … to a degree … goes well beyond … well … the realms of Luther's advice … regarding the … rather esoteric … hermetic nature … of this profound, even very … profound … profoundest problem …"

"Herr Pastor!?" Mutti moved forward and blocked Fergal's view of the Pastor through the keyhole. Shame. The Pastor looked a complete and quivering wreck.

"It *is* a Catholic problem … as I said … call Father Stemmer … call the Vatican … as I said … I …" The Pastor then rushed past Mutti to get out the door. Fergal heard manic footsteps racing down the marble staircase, … but suddenly they stopped, … and Herr Pastor Meinheit screamed, for want of a better way at holding down any specifically compassionate language in its educated cage, … the pastor, normally a great keeper of the gentle word, screamed at top pitch, "I have seen the Devil himself! Your alcoholic husband is possessed by the *Catholic* Devil!" And with that he ran back home. Poor Bernhardt wouldn't hear the end of this! In other words, Pastor Meinheit would beat his son Bernhardt black and blue for being associated with the Devil's son himself, Fergal. But at least not tomorrow! Tomorrow was Sunday. Morning, midday, evening service. Fergal looked at his watch. Tomorrow was today.

Mutti knocked on the door gently, and Fergal let her in. She was holding the Colonel's gun. Behind locked doors, Mutti, J and Fergal slept soundly with the Colt .45 on J's desk.

Dad left at eleven. Mutti's only comment was, "It's *amazing* how much that man can drink! But I gather it's rather a hereditary condition over there in Ireland. Endemic alcoholism. Well, he always used to scold me for my endemically raised German index finger." She looked at Fergal and J, "I ask you, … children, … what's better … alcoholism or index finger? The choice is yours. I am *so* sorry you've had to witness all this. But we *are* a family!"

After Mutti was out of the bathroom Fergal was next. He showered. After the shower he stood on his footstool so he could shave. Without a blade as yet but practising early on in life was important! Hot water on the face, cold water on the blade. Very important! When all the lather had gone, he washed his face in freshly-poured, hot, steaming water yet again to keep it nice and soft.

He was about to take a final look at himself before he got off the footstool when something in the mirror caught his utmost attention. His throat was wide open, blood gushing forth unstoppably. The clean hot water under him had turned to thick blood. Blood was ceaselessly trickling from him into the sink under him. He looked up again touching his throat at the same time. He stared back at a Vietnamese woman. Her face was sunken in as dead, her throat had been ripped out. Fergal couldn't breathe. He looked down at the sink again. The blood was gone. And up in the mirror. The Vietnamese woman was gone, replaced by a young Vietnamese boy with a hole in his forehead and chest.

Fergal fell off the footstool and banged his head.

He wanted to scream but couldn't. His heart was pumping blood out over his white shirt. He had been naked one moment. Now he was wearing a shirt. His feet were in black shiny shoes. His legs chino-covered. His legs stretched. His whole body grew in an instant. The pain was excruciating. Yet, he couldn't scream to let out the pain. He managed to lift himself up. There in the mirror was the Colonel wearing yesterday's Hawaii shirt. Fergal felt tremendous heat at the back of his throat. He touched the back of his head and neck. It was gone. There behind him on the floor lay a good amount of lumps of brain. In shock he looked back at himself. He was Lydia with a hole in her heart.

Fergal fainted.

There was a noise.

Doors were banging.

A large crowd of people was talking around him. He was hot.

The people were laughing.

All of them were opening and shutting doors.

On the other side there were more people wanting to be let in. But no one let them. There was just loud laughter.

Gradually the laughter turned into the sound of breath as though from a million mouths. He couldn't see them. They were knocking on doors.

Millions of them!

"Ferkel! Darling!? Are you alright!? Say something!" It was Mutti.

What had happened?

Fergal realised he had fainted.

"Yes!"

"You don't sound well. Can you open the door, please!? Have you fainted again?"

Had this happened before?

Fergal couldn't remember.

"Yes. I'll open it."

It was hard for him to get back on his feet. Eventually he managed. With trembling legs he got back on the footstool. It was Fergal in the mirror. Only Fergal.

After this little episode Fergal was given the day off. Gummi bears and Asterix and salt sticks and crisps. Heaven!

It took Mutti and J more than half a day to clean up the mess from the party. But in the end everything looked as good as new with the lawn fully mown and clipped. Mutti and J were very happy!

Letter #26 – Fergal To God Via The Pope

Dear Pope,

Dad hasn't been sending my letters to you for some time. But you know that. Mutti did and still does. I just thought I'd tell you that. Mutti is a Lutheran. It would be nice if somehow you could write back at some stage, but I do understand you are the busiest man in the universe.

Three days ago our Herr Pastor confirmed Dad is possessed by the Devil. Mutti and J have been right all along. He said it is a Catholic problem, so I'd like to ask you again to really, really pray for him.

You do know that things happen to me sometimes. Well, now they're worse! Could this be what that doctor predicted? Prof. Dr. Dr. Eichenraub was his name. Am I suffering from SitMut? First I heard some not-so-nice things from the Colonel, but I always get that with grownups. The war and stuff. Opa, Heinrich, the old ones around the old oak, and Dad when he still talked to me. Now, Dad just has this look. Never mind! There are always wars. Opa says it keeps the economy going and beware of those whose economy is all about war because they go to war to make more money just like the Nazis. So, later the Colonel shoots his wife and then himself in the car and they look dead. That's because they are dead. Mutti and J and I locked ourselves in J's (and my) room with the Colonel's Colt, so we were safe from Dad. Mutti will give the Colt to Oma and Opa so it's even safer.

When I get up I shave like a real man. I shaved and there was masses of blood in the sink and I had turned into a Vietnamese woman and then a Vietnamese boy like myself, and then it was dead Colonel Brechner and then his wife. All dead! That wasn't really nice, you see.

I passed out and heard many voices and doors. People were knocking on doors to be let in. Mutti says it's what my subconscious heard. Mutti says I have passed out like this before, as with Heinrich. I kept the Heinrich thing a secret, and I will keep it a secret forever but Mutti knows it, I think. I passed out when the tank accident happened. But I passed out more times than that.

Heinrich is very understanding and says nonsense all Bollerboe nonsense to SitMut. All I have is an overactive imagination and maybe I take on too much of other people's pain. And this is what I want to tell you about. It's that grownup word: compassion (there is also empathy in Greek and at Big School I learn about the Greeks and the Romans more like even their language). One must feel for other people, Mutti says! Not to have compassion is bad and very asocial. Even though, Mutti says she doesn't feel for asocials because they have brought it on themselves, the lazy buggers! She feels for the Negroes in Africa and all the little brown children in India. It's all in the papers and far away, you see. But it's really here! When I see the dead ones like the Colonel and his wife I felt nothing. I was interested how it looked but that was all. But then the next day when I saw myself in the mirror and it hurt I did feel terrible. But more about myself than what I saw in the mirror. I think. Well, it hurt. So, I think if I can learn real compassion and empathy then these things won't happen. And, if everyone learns it, then the Colonel and his wife won't happen, you see!

Yesterday, I thought Superman, Spiderman (Mutti won't really allow me to read those or other stuff like Walt Disney unless it's Bambi, she's happy with Astrid Lindgren though and *Pipi* is very strong but in Selma Lagerlöf's *Nils* little Nils shrinks which is like me I suppose) and Asterix and Obelix all change into something incredibly strong if they see something not right happening, which is injustice. And I change into the injustice. What I mean is I change into the people who have received injustice. Am I a perfect coward then? But I'm not really a coward if I think about it. I didn't go funny when J used to torture me. I'm thinking. I also saw something funny in the glass door after Herr Herbholz reprimanded me. That's a long time ago. I have to think more.

It is a most difficult situation as ever. The question is totally clear. What is the answer though? Oh, and Marcello and his beautiful voice is dead. Do pray for him!

Yours very faithfully with doubt

J. Fergal Bulhof-Murphy

The Black Pond & The Cairn

Tristan In The Trench

On the 8th of May it had been thirty years since the war. Nothing much was happening at school anymore. After the summer holidays it was going to be Big School for all of the fourth-years at primary school! All of Fergal's friends were going to Gymnasium they heard today. Tristan wasn't in to hear the long, boring allocation list being read out with everyone being congratulated.

The Blood & Bone Bread Stabbers were going to Hauptschule to learn a craft or trade to make blood sausage and cut it, to trade blood sausage and knives so they could afford to buy blood sausage and cut it to eat more blood sausage until they died in Germany or Yugoslavia under the influence of slivovitz or schnapps. – When Joachim put it that way in his most laconic and unabusive delivery ever, at least as far as his favourite scumbags were concerned, half the class cracked up, even his super-depressed girlfriend Julia laughed! She *actually* laughed out loud! Vladimir did a thing with his index finger along his throat, which was the wrong way to do it according to the late Colonel. Bernhardt just cast his eyes around Vladimir's vicinity saying "Garlic!" and Vladimir immediately apologised most humbly. His German had improved vastly much to the detriment of his status as the school's number one language defiler and the general entertainment of both staff and pupils.

Most of the girls were going to Realschule because their parents knew it was best for them not to pursue an academic career. The ones actually going to Gymnasium were the *most* boring girls in the world, or suicidal like Julia who wanted to be a lawyer.

Girls were boring come what may, but Joachim *really* wanted to marry Julia! Fergal knew his sister J had been one of those boring girls once. Now, she was just sad. – The scratches she had inflicted on her own face last month had almost healed. There wouldn't be any disfiguring physical scars, a specialist in Frankfurt had said. However she should perhaps see a counsellor and do some transcendental meditation.

Herr Herbholz had taught Fergal's class from year three through to year four. By now most of them were ten year olds. Oh! The arrival of this all-important two-digit number! The harbinger of freedom, wisdom, and a whole lot of other stuff associated with being grownup and getting your own way and driving a car soon … ish. Eighteen was the next hurdle! For some, fifteen, when they'd be allowed to ride their first 25 cc moped, especially to deliver blood sausage. And after that? The three-digit state of age of late Immelmann, and banging on bells with such anger the only way out was by cutting metal to bits all the time, to die with a smile, or being murdered by Steinhöfer, even if Steinhöfer hadn't murdered anyone.

Although the age of ten had, prior to its actual arrival, heralded a coming of age for Fergal, when it actually came the feeling that should have gone with it passed him by completely, as did his birthday and Christmas and the Easter Bunny.

Pastor Meinheit kept stressing very quietly that age ten was really only a mathematical inconsequence. Especially in Fergal's circumstances, considering that his emotionally distant father was in league with the Most Catholic Devil, taking into account also Fergal's penchant for religious disorientation towards Rome and Her Perversions, confirmation in the Lutheran Church, after all, the true Catholic, universal Church, was the only real coming of age and of paramount importance, as communion would get him into corporeal touch with the Blood and Body of Christi, thus he could *truly* be saved! – Fergal had been baptised. But for full protection, Meinheit stressed even more quietly after class, as Fergal was considered a special case, … for *full* protection the Eucharist and constant observance of the catechism was the *only* way! The way to God!

"Fergal! I shall pray for you! Your soul is struggling in most dangerous waters. Promise me, for your own sake, you will not leave our Church!"

"Yes, Herr Pastor! But you became a Pastor in your late twenties."

"That is true, Fergal."

"After you had been trained in the SS and had some fun!?"

"It *wasn't* fun! It was very terrible! I am still atoning for my sins."

"Weren't you a Catholic?"

"That is true also, Fergal."

"So, why not let me try things out a bit? I'm only ten."

"I will pray for you, so you won't get lost." Pastor Meinheit turned away from Fergal shaking his head, looking at the ceiling.

Fergal heard Oma's voice clearly in his head. *Unsinn! Alles Unsinn!* He ignored it. – So, maybe, he was in danger! A lost cause even! But what about his sister? She was in a different world altogether! It was very cold and wet there with a lot of unfriendly faces that only thought the worst of you and judged you all the time. Maybe, she was in hell already!?

Fergal, almost with a surgical sense of interest and detachment, perceived his sister's depression. It had surface and anatomy. It moved in and out of the visible. Above all, Fergal was no longer the target! J had become her own target.

At school there were about two weeks to go to mid-July. Herbholz had promised, this time definitely, to take them to see the Roman Limes at Saalburg *and* the Iron Curtain *if* and only *if* they behaved themselves! He was still putting silly pressure on … as if they were children.

"Look, Herr Herbholz, …"

"Yes, Joachim. You may speak, although you didn't raise your hand!"

"Look! Main thing is, would you like to go to that iron limes thing?"

"Of course, I would!"

"With us?"

"Yes, Joachim!"

"Then why all this silly, silly blackmail?"

Herbholz sighed, "Actually, … everyone … it's a hot day! It's Friday! Let's go home. Go on, off you go!"

All those world-weary, independent ten year olds stormed out of the classroom, out of the school on the wave of one high and happy scream. Home! The lido at Goddelau, Griesheim or even Gernsheim! – Joachim's Mutti would take him to

Gernsheimer Schwimmbad when she wasn't out working. It had slides and the lot, Joachim said. He wouldn't join his friends. War was boring! Chuck was gone! Tristan was mad! Joachim would go to Gernsheim with *Julia* … for a paddle. Fergal couldn't come! Fergal had never been to Gernsheim! And besides, Joachim added, every friendship came to an end, just like everything else.

Although Joachim's mother hadn't kept her promise about not ever going back to work ever again, Joachim was fine now he had *Julia* and she *him*. Both the LeBatards and the Ronsteins had come to some kind of agreement whereby they would alternate not being at home so they could at least work a little to get some more money in, … for diving in the LeBatards' case, … and equestrian pursuits and hunting in the Ronsteins' case.

Fergal ran home like a maniac. There was no time to lose! It was only ten o'clock. Check out Tristan! See why he hadn't come in!? And then, play in the trench!

The door to the flat was open. Mutti was sitting on the chair by the telephone table. She had been crying. Nothing new! She was always crying.

"Come here, Ferkelchen! Let me give you a hug. I have some terrible news!"

Fergal got his hug. But then he really had to go!

"Sorry, Mutti! Is this going to take long? I *have* to see Tristan! We have to stop the Russian invasion!"

Mutti was shaking her head in disbelief. She was always doing that when Fergal talked of playing war. "Tristan is what I want to talk to you about."

"Why?"

She got up and walked into the living room, which nowadays seemed to be reserved for tears and bad news. "Join me, please! Sit down in Oma's armchair!"

Fergal had *never* been allowed to sit in Oma's armchair! This *had* to be a special occasion! Mutti sat across of him. Why was she just staring at his reflection in the glass table? In there she looked like the queen of hearts in Oma's special Mau-Mau deck.

"I would *really* like to go and …"

"Be quiet, Johann! – What I have to tell you, isn't easy! I'm the bearer of the most terrible news you can possibly imagine!

Something so horrific and soul-destroying has happened, it's the nightmare of every mother!"

"What's more horrible than you and Dad?" Fergal was instantly aware that he had just said this a little too nonchalantly. Mutti was going to break out in tears again! Oh, no! But then at the last moment she caught herself and merely let off a sigh, "I know, Ferkelchen. – You and your sister haven't had an easy time of it!"

"No. – It could be worse, as we say in England."

She smiled, "You do know, Oma and Opa and I will always be there to protect you?"

"Thank you very much."

"What I have to tell you now concerns you and your other friends." Mutti shut her eyes and covered her mouth with a clenched fist as if about to cough. No cough came. She kept tapping her mouth with it. There was no specific rhythm. There was no music playing in her head. She wasn't Oma. Then she opened her eyes again, "Tristan died this morning."

"For real?"

Mutti looked stumped, "Of course, for real! Would you think I'd joke about something like this!?"

"No! But … but Tristan dies all the time! When we play, *he* dies *really* well! Grenades, shots in the head or lung, losing a leg."

"Stop it! Stop it, Ferkel! Awful! – Of all the things in the world, I couldn't believe what I heard Frau Dr. Neussler say! It was like something from after the war when all children went round looking for ordnance."

"Was there much good stuff lying about then? I mean, guns, grenades and mines!?"

Mutti did that thing, which meant *I can't believe I'm hearing this!* Her neck went longer, her shoulders went down, she pressed out her chest and inhaled through her nose for a frighteningly long amount of time with a really tight mouth. Then the tirade would start, "Now, listen, young man! I haven't brought you up my little pacifist, away from guns, for you to ask me questions like that! A lot of children your age ended up mutilated or dead with limbs and heads torn off. Don't *ever* touch this stuff! American or German! Do you hear me!? Like your little stunt on the dinner table two years ago. German especially. It's old and rusty, and God knows what might happen!? German weapons aren't for playing with! They were for killing! Killing, you hear!? Promise me … *now* … you will never, *ever* touch any explosive *ever* again!"

"I promise, Mutti. I really promise. Cross my heart and hope to die! I promise!" Fergal made a real, emotional tear-jerker-on-the-floor show of this, crossing his heart five-hundred times as Mutti had asked him the very same question two-million-and-twelve-times infinity to the power of infinity before. If he didn't get the tone right, he'd be grounded possibly over the whole of the weekend. He could not afford to be grounded! There were things to be done now! He had to check out Tristan. Fergal was on the floor wringing his hands.

"Do not pull my leg like some cheap actor, and do not say *hope to die*! We don't say that in Germany!"

"I *really* promise! I won't touch that stuff again, Mutti! Really, really, *really*!"

"OK."

"How did Tristan die this time!?"

Mutti was shaking her head hard to get rid of the terrible images in her mind. Frau Dr. Neussler had evidently told her the whole gory story! – And there they were again. Tears! Mutti couldn't help herself. She had to relate all of it with tears, "He was playing in his brother's trench this morning. I really don't know why the Neussler can't just fill this nonsense in. You know that they've taken Siegfried away again, don't you?"

"Yes. But he went to Bollerboe a long time ago."

Mutti hissed, "Don't you ever, ever say *going to Bollerboe*, you hear! *Going to Bollerboe* is a terrible phrase!"

What was so bad about Bollerboe? He had said it before, and never had Mutti reprimanded him. Ever!

"Sorry!" – In any case, Siegfried really wasn't news! Mutti was so behind, it wasn't true! This had happened last week! Siegfried had been back with two of his helmets from his mental hospital, for a short time only, when yet again he had advanced an American tank in full SS combat gear and a massive machine gun. The machine gun was a deactivated one. So that had been fine. He'd put himself in the middle of Georg-Büchner-Straße with the gun and started making heavy machine gun firing-sounds with his mouth. As ever the Americans had cheered him on.

The problem this time had been that Siegfried had put up four SS standards and eight NSDAP party flags along the road right up to the Neussler residence. – A stray, unmarked police BMW with Frankfurt plates filled with two German Kriminalbeamte and two homicide officers on an exchange program from New York were just travelling through. It had all started with a relatively innocent, "Jesus! Look at that guy!" and then Siegfried had been handled a little roughly by the German CID officers for possession of illegal insignia and their display in a public place. The rest was psychiatric history.

"Little Tristan *always* plays in the trench system! Didn't you hear the police and ambulance sirens this morning!? It must have been eight-thirty?"

"No, sorry!" Fergal hadn't. At eight-thirty the school bell would have rung. Or maybe it had been the defence-situation war siren exercise.

"Strange!? It was very noisy!"

"I didn't hear it. Really, Mutti!" Considering Mutti's emotional state Tristan really had to be dead this time. Fergal had to get to Bernhardt as soon as Mutti would stop this dawdling!

"And do you know what happened to your little friend? – Oh, he was always *so* thin!"

"He died."

"Don't be cocky, Ferkel! He set off a hand grenade in the trench!" Mutti really expected an *oh my God* or similar now. She was wiping away her tears.

"I can't believe it! How? This is terrible." This was fantastic! – If there was one way Tristan would have wanted to die, it was in a real grenade explosion!

"Frau Dr. Neussler said she was drying up the breakfast dishes when she saw this old steel helmet rushing down the trench just outside. It disappeared. Then the helmet came back waving one of those old grenades. It was Tristan of course! She saw his face peaking over the parapet. He was doing something, and then he pulled something, and she said it looked like he wanted to throw the grenade at the kitchen window, but at that stage it exploded right over her son! She managed to duck. She was injured slightly. The glass from the window. She is fine! But *then*, to see her poor little son lying smoking with a big hole in the side of his face and chest down in the trench!? She said she was alright! But she was crying and crying! She wanted to know if any of you know where Tristan got the grenade from?"

"No, Mutti!" Fergal lied and found it hard not to laugh. Mutti had said *grenade!?* More like crates and crates and warehouses filled with grenades! – "His brother?"

"Ach, Ferkelchen! – Just promise me again, don't *ever* touch this stuff!"

"I promise. I *really* have to go now!"

"What? Where?"

"Bernhardt."

"What are you going to do?"

"Play."

"What?"

"Just play."

"War?"

"No, Mutti! I promise! Bye." With that Fergal ran downstairs to the garage, pumped up both flat tyres on his bike, and was off to see Bernhardt.

Of course, the news was terrible! He felt slightly sick and sad and somehow responsible. Whenever they had played with ammo, especially the live stuff, they knew they were doing something very much not allowed and very dangerous. But that was half the fun! The other half was seeing real explosions as in a *real war!* You could experience all for yourself what the old ones talked about. Even though you never experienced the terror, you could imagine it *and* play it. Fergal knew what terror was, and fear. He had felt it with J at times and, above all, when Dad wanted to kill them. But somehow that was in retrospect. Throwing a grenade wasn't terror. It was good fun! Throwing it *at* somebody was different. It was sick!

The Map

Fergal arrived at the Pastor's big house. It was one of the biggest in the village. Fergal leaned his bike against the wall and went through the imposing gate.

No, throwing a grenade wasn't terror. Having somebody throw one at you was. Gradually his friend's death was sinking in. But this too was in retrospect, and he wasn't crying like Mutti. Maybe he couldn't cry!? No, he *had* cried before! He just couldn't remember when. He pulled the door bell. Bernhardt opened the door.

"Tristan's dead, Bernhardt."

"I know. It's horrible. It's the way he would have wanted to die though."

"Yes. I thought so too. I told Mutti. Didn't help. Do you still have the map? I have my bike."

"If Papa doesn't find me at home when he comes back he'll beat me."

"So!? – He beats you all the time anyway."

"True." Bernhardt hesitated. "What you want to do?"

"I want to cycle down to the Rhine and blow it all up in Tristan's memory."

Bernhardt's eyes went wide, "That's such a fantastic idea! Can you read maps?"

"Yes! Dad showed me!"

"Wait across by the graveyard. I'll get my bike!"

Ten minutes later they were on the road to Oppenheim. – Bernhardt had brought supplies. One bottle of tap water, three bars of Milka, one whole cheese, a full kilo, half a salami, thirty centimetres long.

"I eat a lot."

"Figures."

"We could go and stay at Oma's. At her farm. She has a farm outside Oppenheim. She's very nice and old and she likes children. She's a granddaughter of Napoleon's."

"I know."

"How?"

"You told all of us when Tristan was alive and you joined our gang."

"I see. Sorry."

"Don't always apologise. You don't have to with me. Have you noticed … we're the only real gang members left."

"I know."

An hour passed by without much talk. They had left the main roads behind some time ago. It was mostly agricultural dirt paths and narrow tracks.

"Where are we, Fergal?"

"The Kühkopf, and the Oldrhine is over there on our left. That's south. The Rhine is ahead of us down that path."

They stopped and got off their bikes.

"How do you know all this!? And, hang on …" Bernhardt wrinkled his forehead before he continued, "… where's the path?"

"Opa and Dad showed me about maps."

"That's pretty useful. Papa wouldn't show me stuff like that. Have you been down here before?"

"No. Oppenheim and your granny are over there. This map is pretty accurate." Fergal looked at it carefully. With all the swastikas drawn on it, it was a bit hard to read. But not a real problem! Siegfried's *X* marked the spot with skull and crossbones on top of it, "We've got to go that way! The track left goes down to the Kühkopf island."

"Are you sure?"

"Yes, Bernhardt. Don't be such a coward!"

"But there isn't a track there!?"

"Trust me. It is a track. It's just not been used in a long time!"

"Like, never! It's all grass!"

"But look at the trees left and right, OK! They're further apart from each other. It's a track!"

"Really?"

"Yes. Enjoy the beautiful day!" Mutti would have said something like this with a festive mood.

"But Siegfried comes here all the time to pick up guns and bombs."

"So?"

"Well, if he'd been here recently it would show."

"No. Remember! He's in and out of the hospital all the time."

"OK." It wasn't OK for Bernhardt though. That much was obvious.

"What?"

"How does he get the stuff? You can't drive down here!"

"On his bike!?"

"Oh, yes! Sorry!" Siegfried had an old Zündapp motorbike, fully restored to its 1942 German Wehrmacht glory.

"Anyway, the track's wide enough for a lorry even."

"What if there's another lorry. It'll have to reverse."

"Yes, Bernhardt!" Fergal got on his bike and cycled straight into the dense, dark wood, down the completely overgrown track as indicated on the map. "Follow me! The Rhine is down there."

It was intensely humid and clouds of midges were swarming around both cyclists, but neither got bitten. Midges only had it in for J and that hadn't been so bad this year. Nevertheless, she still complained.

After half a kilometre the ground got so soggy it was hard to peddle and keep a good speed. The air was misty and smelt of moss and rotten wood. This was the most magical place on Earth. Why hadn't they come here before? Four, maybe six weeks from now, but certainly when the new year at Big School up in the north of Germany would start, would Fergal have to leave all of this behind. Oma and Opa said the north was cold and wet. Mutti still hadn't told either J or Fergal where exactly they were going.

"No chance you'd get a lorry through this mud, Ferkel!"

"What Bernhardt?"

"You couldn't get a lorry through this mud."

"How would you know!? It's not mud anyway."

"Very wet grass then. And if you have a lorry, it will sink. Trust me, I know. I'm heavy!"

They arrived at an old wooden barrier and dismounted. The red and white paint was hardly visible any longer. But it had been *red and white* once. Military! A round metal sign post, though faded and rusty, still did its best to announce from the middle of the barrier *Halt!* The boom was held in place by a rust-covered lock.

The boys just walked round it.

Fergal's heart was beating with excitement, "That's all old Nazi stuff. Very old! Let's go on foot from here, and be very quiet, just in case!"

"In case of what?"

"The police get us and put us in prison."

"Don't say that! Then you have no life until you die."

"What's that?" Fergal was pointing at something in the grass on the verge.

"What?"

He went over, "It's another old sign. Very faded. But the words left on it are …" he raised his finger triumphantly, "… *rrgeb* … *Wehrma* … " as in army, prohibited area, "and … *engstens* … *boten*" As in *most severely positively prohibited*! "And *ußwaffengeb* … and … *bensgef* …!" As in *Use of firearms* and *Danger of death!*

This was really good news!

It all looked positively promising!

Bernhardt came over to have a look. Bernhardt had a very good look! "I want to go home now, Fergal. There's a skull and crossbones. That *really* means *Lebensgefahr!* Dad knows! He said they didn't have a sense of humour and just shot you back then. What if some of the old ones are still here and they don't know the war's over … like Siegfried, you know? They kill us!"

Fergal couldn't believe his ears! This vast, colossal friend of his, the legend of *Rübezahl,* the turnip-counting giant from the Riesengebirge mountains, come to life! Afraid!?

"No, they won't! – We're here to make sure they *never* kill again. Follow me and be quiet!" This was Fergal's mission. He wasn't going to let a silly old sign, put there by some silly, old Nazis more than thirty years ago, scare him!

He lifted his head. He could see the sun's reflection on the Rhine ahead. In here it was like the light at the end of the tunnel!

"Look, Bernhardt! We're almost there! – I race you! First one there, wins!" Fergal jumped on his bike and rode off as fast as the swampy ground permitted.

The bright light of the sun reflecting the waters of the big river had given Fergal a false sense of distance. It took him another five minutes to get to the Rhine's banks. Steep and stony at this section. And what a mess the river looked here! It wasn't as wide and graceful as in Mainz. It wasn't dark, deep and mysterious! It was just brown and murky, and there was a smell of unhappy, dead fish bathing in fresh poo.

Bernhardt came up behind him panting, "That looks muddy and it … it stinks … it really stinks!"

"I won!"

"So what!?"

"Yes."

The two friends looked upstream and then downstream. The woods behind them had been great. Fairytale monsters in black uniforms. Castles with fluttering swastika flags. Knights with machine guns. GI Injuns. Injured war heroes of the Big-Eye Nathan brotherhood. Lancaster and B17 dragons. Sherman tanks. Rifles. Pistols. Everything!

What was in front of them however was as dull as ditchwater.

And … it stank to high heaven!

The river was slow and narrow at this spot and there was nothing sedate about it. Eddies and nasty currents wherever you looked.

"If you jump in there, you're a goner!"

Bernhardt nodded, "I could probably make it. You wouldn't. But I might save you!"

"Thanks! What makes you so sure?"

"Papa says saving people is the best thing in the world. Papa says *you* need saving."

"Oh, yes!? How come you never talk about your mother then, Bernhardt?"

"I don't want to."

"Your Papa couldn't save her."

"She left us. I don't want to talk about it."

Fergal nodded. He knew the feeling. "We have to walk right a bit. The map says it's all old Wehrmacht property."

"You know, Fergal, … Siegfried must have really gone out of his way to find this!?"

"I guess so."

"No! I'm saying the Wehrmacht as the losers and your lot as the winners really cleaned up after the war. Papa said so! Remember, us Germans are tidy. Of course, there were accidents, but accidents happen. It's God's way."

"I suppose like Tristan."

"Yes. So, to find anything here, Siegfried really had to go out of his way, right!?"

"Yes."

"And he isn't a kid anymore. He's a grownup and that's really sick!"

"True."

"So, Ferkel, … if we find this stuff we'll destroy it!"

"Yes. That's why we're here!"

"Good. – And no taking back any grenades."

"No, of course not!"

"Or pistols."

"Do you think there are pistols!?"

"That's what I mean, see!? You get that mad look! Very Ferkel!" Bernhardt had a very grown-up glare at Fergal but it immediately softened, "Well, … there might be pistols there."

"Promise!?"

"You are such a kid, Ferkel! We'll just destroy *everything*!"

"And if there's too much?"

"We'll camp out … and we'll work!"

"Work how?"

"We'll carry everything down to the river and dump it in. And if you disagree, I'll break your thumb."

"Mmh." Bernhardt hadn't said that one since he had joined the Double Bubble Gang.

They turned right, downriver, pushing their bikes from hereon. North. Fergal would move north soon. But where? Why was it such a secret?

"There should be something … I think … some ponds. Twenty meters from the banks. Seven, eight, nine, ten of them. It's at the back, set in the woods a bit. That's where Siegfried made his mark with the *X*."

It only took them another five minutes and they had arrived by the first pond as indicated on the map. Both dropped their bikes.

These weren't ordinary ponds! When Fergal heard or read the word *pond* he thought of beautiful, secret Frog Pond, dangle your feet in, feel the heat, the soft grass. And never bring your sister! These ponds were square, cut almost straight into the soil and filled with a black substance. The steep sides would make it hard to get out once you fell in.

"What you think that is, Bernhardt?"

"The Devil's holiday camp. – Let's get this over and done with as soon as possible!"

"Yes."

"Can you smell that? It smells like oil!"

Fergal lay down on his front and put his head over the edge of the pool. His reflection was clear and still, as in a mirror. The surface of the liquid was a meter down, but who was to say how deep it went after that!? A boggy swamp that might suck you to the centre of the Earth!

Fergal spat down into the pool. The liquid moved like water.

"Would you mind fetching me a stone, please, Bernhardt?"

"That was very polite! – Of course, I will get you one. Even two!" Bernhardt shook his head and tramped off as though going on a long, boring walk.

"You don't have to!"

"No! – It was too polite! I can't refuse now!"

Within minutes Bernhardt had returned, carrying a cairn of stones, perched precariously on top of each other, supported by the two shovels of his hands, held in place by his chin. Fergal laughed. Not in a million years could he have carried any one of the boulders, let alone two of them together. It reminded him of the Brothers Grimm's *The Town Musicians Of Bremen.* One big donkey-boulder, one small dog-boulder, one big flat cat-stone, one small flat rooster-pebble. With his upper body straight, Bernhardt slowly lowered his heavy load and lay down next to Fergal.

"Always keep your back straight, Papa says. His back is bad!"

Just like his friend, Bernhardt now hung his head over the edge.

"They're like the *Town Musicians Of Bremen.*"

Bernhardt smiled, "Won't make any music though. Do you like my pyramid then?"

"Yes! You are incredibly strong! But it's more like a Scottish cairn, to be brutally honest, Bernhardt."

"What's a Scottish *Kern*?"

"A Scottish pyramid. It remembers people or places, Dad said. It's a pile of stones really."

"How can a *Kern* be a Scottish pyramid if it's inside an apple or pear?"

"No, silly! It's not *Kern.* It's *cairn!*" Fergal spelt the foreign word for Bernhardt.

"Aha! – So, like the *Kern* of the apple remembers the apple, the Scottish cairn remembers the Scottish, like their people or places. That's like a pyramid then. I've got the book. All about pyramids!"

"Suppose so, yes. Cairns are like headstones."

"Pyramids are only for the rich, and only one of them like a king. And they were heathens."

"Can you smell that?"

"Like petrol station. Maybe we found an oil well and that's the end of the Arabs!"

"I like the smell of diesel. This smells better than the river!"

"Go on then, throw in a stone, Ferkel!"

Fergal dropped the pebble in.

"Did you see that!? It's just water! What's underneath is black. And the bottom is close to the surface."

Fergal threw the bigger stone in.

"That didn't do anything."

"I'll get the big one." Bernhardt got up, lifted the boulder, "You'd better get back from the edge," and dropped it into the pool.

Whatever water there was at the surface didn't show. The fountain that shot up in the air was thick black as liquid rubber might be. Fergal thought of Steinhöfer's tyres and their dense, black smoke. He recalled a geography lesson with Herbholz, "That's like bitumen. Herbholz showed us when they put a new road down on Berliner Strasse."

Bernhardt nodded, "Maybe they dumped oil in these or something so the enemy couldn't get it."

"Or they set fire to it for smoke."

"So!? Where's Siegfried's thing?"

"Three pools down."

"Shall I roll the really big one in?"

"No."

The boys moved cautiously, looking over their shoulders a lot. The pools were about twenty meters apart. By the third pool they had reached a set of very sad and brown looking pine trees on a little hillock which set a stark contrast to the other trees they had seen around here so far. They knew from school that elm, ash, poplar, oak and willow could cope with flooding, which was prevalent in the area. Pine trees couldn't. They had been put here! The hillock had to be man-made. And inside was Siegfried's cache with loads and loads of pistols!

Something strange was beginning to happen in Fergal's mind. He had noticed for a while that ever since they had arrived by the pools his neck had been trembling. Then it had gone down his shoulder blades into his arms and fingers, and his knees. His shoulders felt cold. It dawned on him. It was fear! But why? And then it struck him!

This wasn't playing war!

Bernhardt and he weren't playing!

This was serious!

"We're not playing, Bernhardt!"

Bernhardt shook is head, "No."

The two friends went around the hillock, fully expecting a big and obvious entrance. In a game situation a nice big sign would have announced the dangers. Fergal could even see the words underlined on white background with the all-important bits in blood-red.

Extremely Dangerous **Weapons** With
Crates And Ever More Crates **Of**
Grenades Inside, Including
Rifles And **Especially**
Pistols! Lots Of **Fun** To Be Had
For All Children
Who are Extremely **Positively**
Totally Prohibited
From This **Military** Facility Because
They'll Be **Shot Until** quite
Dead! You hear! **Totally**
Dead!!! And If They Find The
Weapons Inside There Will Be A

Great, fantastic, super **Fight** *To The Death!!!*

The sign disappeared as a weak echo.

There was *no* entrance!

They could go home now.

"Shall we watch the Rhine for a bit?"

"Maybe the entrance is …" Bernhardt was on all fours pounding the side of the little hill with his *Rübezahl* fists, "… here! – It's just a bit overgrown."

He pushed grass and earth off to reveal a rusty metal trap door, "There we go, Fergal! Bet Siegfried camouflaged it."

"Doesn't look like he's been here ever. – What now?"

"We open it and see what's inside?" The heavy door caused even Bernhardt to huff and puff and sweat enormously. But after a good minute it opened with a heavy thud. It was more like a hatch opening the view to a dark cellar. Bernhardt turned round, "I'm scared! – You first!"

"You!? Scared!?"

"Just a bit. You're braver, Ferkel!"

"Am I?" But it was a compliment.

Five steps led the way down. It wasn't deep. Fergal could see the floor. Enough daylight reached in here.

"You won't shut the door on me, will you?"

Bernhardt sighed, "I don't do *mean*!"

"Yes, you do! Breaking fingers, headlocks!"

"Yeah! But that's a man-thing. Shutting the door and letting you starve is what a girl would do!"

Fergal plucked up his courage and jumped down on the concrete floor. His eyes had to adjust, but he realised at once that it was very dry down here. The chamber in the hillock was well above ground level so if there had been floods in the past it would have been unlikely the water would have reached here. The pine trees were just unhappy and dead because they had had to serve as a military crown for this pretend-hillock for such a long time. Or maybe Nazi gardeners didn't know how to plant trees.

Nevertheless, with the humidity outside, all considered … maybe they had used a special concrete.

"It's dry down here, Bernhardt. *Really* dry!"

"Can you see anything!?"

"Yes."

"Well, … what!? – Jesus! You can be slow. *Speak if you have a mouth*, as they say in the Bible!"

"Jerry cans, crates, and boxes. Some have the old Nazi eagle on them. But they don't look old! Everything's stacked really neatly to the ceiling. Mutti could have been here, it's so tidy!"

"What's in them?"

"Wait …" Fergal had a closer look at some of the labels, "Numbers. Lots of numbers! Wait! It says *Stiel-Handgranaten 43*. Lots. Wow. And there are long crates with *Panzerfaust 60m* and *Panzerfaust 100m*. Hang on …" He moved carefully forward into the bunker. It wasn't any bigger than their kitchen at home, just the ceiling wasn't as high. "There's boxes here with 88 burnt into the wood …" wasn't that for the famous *Acht-Acht* Flak!? He looked at the label. It said *Patr* followed by more abbreviations and numbers, "… it's not ammo for the 88, … it's cartridges! And there's stuff called *Panzerfaust 30m* at the back. Loads. No pistols or rifles."

Suddenly a strong hand gripped Fergal's shoulder from behind. He stood rigid with fear. A deep German guttural voice shouted at him, "Keine Bewegung oder ich scheiße, Du Ferkelhund[13]!"

Immediately Fergal relaxed and turned round facing Bernhardt, "Phew! You gave me a fright!"

"I know."

"That was a really good voice … like grown-up!"

"I know! – Papa says my voice'll break soon. It's much too early! But I can do this really deep voice."

"Great."

"Did you shit yourself, Ferkel!?"

"No!" He farted. "But I nearly pissed myself, OK!?" Fergal wasn't angry. Just relieved that they hadn't been discovered by an old Nazi, who'd shoot them or string them up as traitors. Mutti

---

[13] *Ger.* Don't move or I'll shit, you piglet-dog

said a lot of that happened in the final days of the war. The real rats had emerged to kill people right to the last second. And then they had just disappeared again. – Mutti and Opa both said the real Nazis had never apologised. Opa was very rude about them. He said they'd just all gone to Bollerboe and that's where they could stay and rot! Only the wrong ones had grovelled, because as good subservient and law-abiding German citizens they had been used to behaving like that anyway.

Slowly, Bernhardt moved to the bottom of the bunker looking left and right as if he were admiring paintings of the Passion in his father's church, "This is totally amazing! It looks like new! Almost. Can you smell the wood!? I bet Papa would know what all this is used for."

"*Was* used for, Bernhardt! Past tense."

"Who cares!? People *still* use this stuff. Just with the names changed. – Do you have a plan, Ferkel?"

"Yes!" Fergal walked back towards the light at the entrance and tried pulling one of the boxes containing hand grenades out of the stack. "They're too heavy! Would you mind pulling one out, please!? You're bigger than me. – The top one is easy."

"You are so very polite today, Ferkel! – Of course I shall!"

Even Bernhardt had to stand on the first step up to reach the box at the top of the stack. He pulled it out with no effort at all and put it on the concrete floor. Fergal tried lifting it. It wasn't as heavy as he'd imagined.

"You open it, Ferkel!" Hastily Bernhardt rushed outside, "I'll just check if someone's watching."

"Yeah, yeah, yeah! – Coward!" – Try as he might, Fergal couldn't pull the heavy clip up to open the crate. "Have you run home or are you still there, fatty!?"

Bernhardt's voice answered from what sounded like twenty metres away, "Yes?"

"I can't open the clip!"

"What clip?" Bernhardt really didn't like this at all. Neither did Fergal.

"The clip of the crate, idiot! What else!?"

"I thought the clip of the grenade?"

"That's the fuse-pull for the detonator, idiot! – Come on! Help me open this thing!"

Bernhardt was back panting heavily. It took *Charles Atlas Rübezahl* only a second to open the clip, "There! Easy! Bye!" and another second to jump out of the bunker again.

"Don't you want to know what's inside!?"

"I know what's inside," the distant voice shouted back, "Grenades!"

Fergal took off a layer of thin paper. Underneath, the grey-green grenades did not look as new as the crates might have promised. The rim of the head tin, which contained the warhead, was rusty. But the wood of the stick still looked polished and like new! – This model was different to Tristan's and Siegfried's. The fuse bit was at the top and already fitted.

Fergal looked at the instructions pasted on the inside of the lid. You had to twist and pull the top bit out. It was much less laborious than the other grenade with the lanyard. The fuse would give you *Vier-Komma-Fünf Sekunden*. Four-point-five seconds.

"Bernhardt!" Fergal called. No answer. And again, "Beeeernhaaaaardt!" No answer!

Fergal climbed up the stairs. His friend wasn't outside the bunker. He walked round the hillock and there he found Bernhardt by the first black pond piling up a cairn on top of the boulder they had left behind for later.

"I need your help, please!"

"Do I have to, Fergal?"

"Yes, please! – That's a good cairn."

"It's for Tristan. When you've blown the ammo up, we kneel and sing a hymn for Tristan."

"OK."

"Let me finish first. Maybe Tristan is watching us now?"

"Maybe."

Bernhardt collected a number of boulders and stones. This time Fergal helped as well as he could. He was responsible for the smaller stones and pebbles at the top. Twenty minutes later they had erected a cairn sizable enough to honour the memory of their dead friend. Unless somebody pushed it over or there was an earthquake, it might remain there forever.

"OK. – I'll help you now Fergal."

"Thank you."

"But you'll sing with me later, agreed!?"

"Sure."

To both Pastor Meinheit and his son singing hymns was most important! It lifted the spirit and delighted God Himself. Bernhardt had a most beautiful voice. He was humming *A Mighty Fortress Is Our God* when they went down the steps into the bunker to finish their work.

"What do you want me to do, Ferkel?"

"Right. Take the ten jerry cans outside and open them. We'll pour all in at the end. If the petrol's still good it should burn nicely like … bamm! When you're finished, take down three more of the grenade crates and open them, but leave them on the floor."

Humming all the time his friend Bernhardt worked like an ox without complaint. Fergal took three grenades and laid them in the grass outside the bunker. When Bernhardt had cautiously opened three of the crates and placed them carefully next to each other both friends started pouring the petrol down into the bunker. After six jerry cans the floor still hadn't filled up, even slightly. The petrol kept disappearing down the bottom end.

"There must be an outflow somewhere, Bernhardt. – Just push the cans down the stairs. It'll all blow anyway."

Finally! Their work was complete! One last jerry can, which hadn't made it all the way down to the floor, was glugging its last contents in a small cascade down the steps.

"You sound like that when you drink, Bernhardt!"

"What now!?"

Fergal picked up one of the hand grenades by his feet, "You twist and pull and throw. Make it land on one of the crates. I've got two. You have one. We have four and a half seconds. Throw and run."

"No!? Ferkel. Nooo! Two seconds is safer! And remember Tristan this morning! He's dead now! One of those things went off immediately. We might die. – Let's do it."

"Two it is." Fergal tossed the third grenade in the bunker and handed his friend the remaining one.

"Twist and pull?"

"Twist and pull, Bernhardt!"

They twisted and pulled at the same time, aware that this might be their end! Together they threw the grenades in. They didn't see where they landed. Bernhardt and Fergal ran like they had never run before, making for the nearest tree by the black pond. And just in time! – No sooner had they thrown themselves on the moist soil than two massive explosions pierced the air around them.

They crawled forward away from the vast noise as they always had when they had still been playing war to get proper cover behind the wide tree. It was a dead oak. More explosions followed. – Small detonations that sounded like harmless firecrackers on New Year's Eve. The bigger ones they knew so well. Hand grenades! And now and then, a deep, hollow thud, that shook the ground they were lying on.

The wind carried grey and black smoke smelling of cordite, sulphur and petrol over to them. From their position they could see that the back of the bunker facing the Rhine was still intact, untouched by the colossal pressure inside it. Explosions were still coming from further inside the woods.

Fergal took a careful peek around the tree trunk. Fingers in ears, Bernhardt had stuck his face into the soft, mossy ground between two roots of the oak. What Fergal saw there wasn't good and didn't look like any Steinhöfer-fun at all!

"Shit! Bernhardt!" He tapped his friend's back. Bernhardt was trembling like aspen leaf. "We've set fire to the woods!!!"

Bernhardt turned his mud-covered face to Fergal, "What?" He took his fingers out of his ears.

"The trees are burning! – We've got to get out of here!"

Another set of explosions followed from inside the bunker. Flames and sparks were shooting out of the entrance as from a blast furnace. Fergal saw something being catapulted into the woods and explode fifty meters away from then. A great hissing noise was now coming from inside the hillock. The hillock itself was steaming.

"Oh, shit! Bernhardt! That's flares! Let's bolt!"

"Yes! Now!!!"

It seemed safe enough, as the bunker's entrance was facing the woods away from them. Ten meters to the black pond, maybe a hundred to their bikes, fifteen or so kilometres back home. Back lanes only.

Bernhardt jumped to his feet and started running as fast as a big gigantic boy with that amount of physical weight can possibly run after he has already made a dash to safety faster than ever before! Fergal was right behind him. He had never been outrun by Bernhardt! Bernhardt was running too close to the edge of the black pond! Fergal saw his friend's feet hitting the ground. Left foot, right foot. Fergal knew what was going to happen! Somehow Bernhardt had lost his balance. Left foot, right foot … his right foot, almost as in a cartoon, seemed to hover in midair for seconds. His intense momentum carried him forward only for another millisecond before the gravity of the black pond pulled him sideways and down into its gaping mouth with all the force this body could offer it. Twice did Bernhardt's right foot kick down searching for ground in the air over this unctuous tar pit before also his left foot as if still clinging to the edge followed inevitably. Bernhardt's right shoulder hit the black mud first, then his head disappeared under the surface to tear down with it his huge frame. A grenade explosion from the back behind the hillock. Then, … silence!

Fergal hadn't heard the water splash where his friend had gone in. Bernhardt hadn't screamed or fought. The water was still describing rings.

Fergal fell to his knees close to the cairn his friend had erected. He felt tears welling up and pressing against the insides of his eyes.

There!

He cried.

He could cry!

He felt awful. Dejected. This had to be similar to J's world.

What could he do?

His last friend in the world was gone! He pounded his knees and screamed.

This wasn't going to happen!

Fergal was not going to let this happen!

He would rather die.

This was injustice!

Anger was rising.

How could this happen to him!?

Furiously, he jumped to his feet and hurled himself into the black pond giving his hatred of the black goo expression by touching the surface, arse first. Had he seen the fountain his *Arschbombe* made, he would have been proud!

Fergal went in close to where he'd seen Bernhardt disappear. – His descent in the oily slime was stopped much sooner than he'd expected. It felt almost comfortable in here! The bottom was also unexpectedly solid. He put his feet down to push himself back to the surface again. This was by no means as easy as in water but it worked.

He had kept his eyes shut.

He was standing upright!

He could feel the water around his bottom.

His upper body was definitely out and safe above the surface! He spat out the mud in his mouth. It tasted and smelt like oil. He sneezed a couple of times before his nose was clear. He was still blind with the sludge. Carefully he rubbed his eyes towards his nose as Mutti had taught him. When there was something in your eye you could only get it out that way. After a while Bernhardt came into view. He was standing right in front of Fergal.

"Mud bath. It's healthy, they say. People go on spa holidays for this!"

Fergal laughed, "Bollerboe! Oil bath isn't. Oil bath is deadly!" – He had his friend back!!!

"I saw you fly right past me, Ferkel, … with eyes shut! What were you doing? You could have killed me!"

"I wanted to save you! You Wetchamoonsi Fatso!"

"Mmh. – Well, … thanks for the thought!"

"You are very welcome!"

"Look, what I found in the mud, Ferkel!" Bernhardt was holding up a skull.

"Wow!"

"Yeah! And this! It's a Hitler Youth knife!"

"Amazing! – Do you think they drowned in here."

"I don't know. Safe to say, he's not alive."

"We still have to get out of here, Bernhardt!"

"And wash. You should *look* at yourself! Like out of hell!"

"And you, Fatso!"

Bit by bit they pushed their hips forward through the black slime. Bernhardt heaved Fergal out first. The other way round would have been impossible.

"Take my hand and just pull, Ferkel!"

"Sure! – What're you going to do with the skull and knife?"

A set of four thudding explosions came from the wood behind the bunker. Both boys ducked. Bernhardt looked down at his hands, black and shiny with mud, holding skull and knife as you would medal and cup after a race won.

"Nothing." He dropped them. "Heave ho!"

An exasperating and slightly scary five minutes later Bernhardt, the interminably heavy, was out of the sludge! The boys cleaned themselves with tufts of grass as well as could be expected and sat down at the edge of the black pond to rest for a little. This had all been quite exciting!

"The fire's out." Fergal got up and weed into the black pond.

Bernhardt looked to the right at the woods past Fergal. They no longer were in a hurry.

"So it is. I wonder why."

"Maybe it's too wet?"

"Could be! You shouldn't piss on a grave like that, you know!"

"That's not a grave, Bernie!?"

"Yes, it is. It's got a skull in it!"

"S'pose it is then."

"Stop it then!"

Fergal zipped up, "I was finished anyway."

"You've got a black dick now."

"So?!"

"Neger!"

"So what? Let's think of Tristan!"

"Yes. And also you shouldn't piss on it because it's a place of memorial for our friend Tristan now. – Do you know what that's called?"

"What?"

"Pissing on a grave with a black dick!"

"No?"

"Desecration! – Papa told me after I dug up the officer's grave."

"Did you keep the femur?"

"Course not! Papa hit me with it."

"He didn't?"

"Did! It didn't break!"

"Wow! – You still look frightening."

"You too! – Papa is going to give me a good thrashing, and then he'll wash me in the bath and apologise. – Don't your parents *ever* beat you?"

"No! – I think they hate each other too much to notice what's going on around them and Mutti is all-protective, since your Papa has told her my Dad is the Devil. J actually thinks he *is* the Devil! As in the *real* thing!"

"I know. – Somehow I'd rather have Papa beat me than have a foreign Dad like yours. – Is it true you saw him do unspeakable things to your Mutti!?"

Fergal was deeply embarrassed, "Who told you?"

"Papa sometimes talks a lot too much when he gets angry with me. It slipped out."

"It's like desecration, I guess."

"I guess so. Just, your Mutti isn't dead."

"No. But she looks dead sometimes."

"Then maybe your Dad has desecrated her."

There was another hollow, thudding explosion from the hillock.

"That was inside the bunker."

"Your sister is really beautiful!"

"I don't know. Well, … I suppose so. She's a bit like something beautiful, but it's cracked, you know, like Oma's and Opa's China. They've had it for two-hundred years. She doesn't ever want to like men because they are pigs."

"Or Ferkels!"

"That was very funny! Ha! Ha! Ha!" Fergal boxed his friend on the arm.

"That didn't even hurt!" Bernhardt raised his fist.

"Please don't! Because …"

"What? Why not?"

"That will really hurt when you do it!"

"OK. – Is it true, you and Johanna and your Mutti and Papa are moving to North Germany?"

"Yes. I don't know where though. It's a surprise."

"Must be a bad surprise then."

"Oma and Opa live up there."

"Will you write to me."

"I might."

"That would be nice. – Let's say an Our Father and sing a hymn for Tristan's cairn."

"Do I have to sing?"

"I'll sing for both of us then, Ferkel."

Without getting up they moved over to Tristan's cairn sliding on their bottoms.

"Let's kneel."

The two friends went through the Our Father, adding a personal prayer of wishes for Tristan, which they took in turns.

Fergal started, "Dear Almighty God in Heaven. This cairn is for Tristan. Please, when he comes to you, don't let him play war ever again. Amen."

Bernhardt was next, "And give him more to eat. Amen!"

"And give him a nice bike!"

"And don't let his brother Siegfried near him when he comes to die!"

"And be really nice to him! Thank you!"

"Amen!"

"Amen."

Bernhardt sang the first stanza of his hymn *A Mighty Fortress* humming the remaining three harder and louder but without words. Fergal threw Siegfried's map in the pond.

After some quiet meditation as ordered by Bernhardt, both friends got up in silent agreement and ambled over to their bikes.

On their way home they encountered neither police nor fire engines.

They never spoke again.

After a good edifying thrashing, when visiting his son at hospital for an unfortunately slipped disc, Pastor Meinheit expressly forbid his offspring ever to communicate with that evil dastard, black and tar-covered son of the Devil himself, Ferkel, ever again, and he told Mutti so too.

Fergal was grounded until end of year four, with the provision that he should be permitted to say goodbye to his friends when the move to the secret surprise place in the north of West Germany should finally occur.

Letter #27 – Fergal To God Via The Pope

My dear Pope, this is going to your employer!

Dear God,

Thinking all the time doesn't really help. I haven't had changes in the mirror again. It was a bit hard to look in the mirror after I wrote to you last. But I look fine now. So, thank you for the prayer.

My friend Tristan Neussler died in a grenade accident. His parents didn't want any of us – his friends!!! – at the funeral. I don't think I would have been allowed anyway because I am grounded until we go to the north of West Germany. And the Pastor beat his son, my friend Bernhardt, so bad he had to go to hospital! I think that's because we said goodbye to Tristan our way. We built a cairn! That's a Scottish memory pyramid for heathens. We prayed the Our Father and Bernhardt sang a humming hymn of Luther's. We prayed for Tristan and then we meditated silently. Bernhardt knows all about meditating! Tristan is with you in heaven now. Look after him! He needs to eat more!

Eva Kromann, the asocial girl with the alcoholic father down Mönchsgasse was accidentally beaten to death, and then her father threw himself out the window with a noose, but he didn't die. Geesterheimers say, normally people like that hang themselves from the door handle or radiator. We all saw Herr Kromann hang there! His face was crimson and they got him down. He's in prison now. I think the Pastor should also go to prison, besides, he might be able to help Herr Kromann there, mightn't he? With things like this, people say, *Oh, how terrible* and then they turn their backs. And I've even seen them smiling! Not about Eva though. But about how her father was hanging there, and they snicker *Oh-how-terrible* laughs about Pastor Meinheit, because after all he's only human like all of them. It is not a sense of humour. It is the opposite.

I am praying for Tristan because he's with you now. Tristan is no longer unhappy about everything and Germany and his brother. Germany is split, and Siegfried is split, and Tristan's blood is spilt. Only you, God, should split and spill things! That I know. Do send a prayer to Bernhardt too! He needs it a lot, because he's not in heaven yet. And Joachim! I think he and Julia look quite happy, but is that happiness not from unhappiness? Can that last? You know best!

You must think I only write to you in times of trouble, as Mutti would say. But this is not so! I think about you a lot and ask myself what you mean by this terrible life? I do look on the bright side a lot though!

Bernhardt and I blew all the arms we found to high heaven. That's the opposite of the arms' race! Not like leg race, but like real weapons!

I have also decided never to become German, come what may, however much I love Oma and Opa. It just sounds wrong for me. I don't really remember people back home that much, but I know they weren't like this! Germans are a little like Americans, but not as fast-talking. They think more. Maybe that makes it worse. I don't really know yet.

With great faith and hope and charity, I hope. – Oh, and what exactly is doubt?

Fergal Bulhof-Murphy

P. S.: Will you ever write back? You could send the letters to my dreams!

P.P.S.: Please, just pray for everybody!

The Blackbird

Saying Goodbye

Being grounded was no fun! Like Hansi the claustrophobic canary in his cage.

Mutti was making absolutely sure Fergal would go to school every morning and return home safely when school was out. She even took Fergal by the hand! Every time. It was so embarrassing!

There really wasn't any need to attend any more!

It was Big School soon!

Please, Mutti! Pretty please! Bitte, bitte, bitte!

But Mutti was adamant!

Herr Herbholz had been true to his word also. Two days before the summer holidays he had taken class up to see the Roman castle at Saalburg north of Bad Homburg, to be followed by a tour of the Iron Curtain near the border crossing at Eussenhausen. The outing had been much too rushed. They had spent most of the time on the bus. – Leaving early at a quarter to eight they had been supposed to get back to Geesterheim at four in the afternoon. They had got back at nine in the evening to a very angry crowd of parents.

The jolly Bavarian bus driver Herr Franz Wurstelhuber, *call me Franzl,* looked like a wet cardboard box with sausages for arms and legs, and a beer barrel painted red for a head with two raisins for eyes. He had apologised profusely to all, blaming it on bad traffic and the Autobahn, and all was fine again. Herr LeBatard had even invited him over for a drink.

As the radio on Franzl's old bus hadn't been working he had sung a lot of Bavarian folk songs. Herbholz had to ask him to stop singing because a lot of the kids were feeling sick. After all, they had been on the bus for five hours already at that stage. The remainder of the tour Franzl had sulked and drunken from a huge hip flask.

Half an hour at the Roman castle. Romans in uniform with swords and spears. Everyone had been allowed to hold a sword. All too rushed. Then back on the bus with the Roman site's tourist booklet. Reading. The Saalburg had been begun at 83 after Christ. The wall the Romans built to keep the north German tribes out was called the Limes. It was 548 kilometres long and started by the Rhine in Rheinbrohl just north of Andernach and continued all the way southeast down to Eining close to Regensburg on the Danube. Facts. Great. Not! Boring. – Holding the sword for two seconds had been fun! And Franzl had been driving like a maniac.

Joachim and Julia had thrown up.

The Iron Curtain had been the saddest sight ever! Everyone had received an A4 copy with more facts to read whilst Herbholz had had a border picnic. The fact sheet said the Great Wall of China was about five times longer than the German-German border. The fence of Russian Germany measured a total of 1,378.3 kilometres with 1,185.7 kilometres of wire fencing. It was four meters or so high and there was a lot of metal in it. Millions of kilos!

Class had sat down for a bit on the crest of a hill overlooking the border fence. A vast forest aisle, extending to the northern and southern horizon, had been cut especially for the purpose. Fifty meters in front and fifty meters behind the Curtain, so they could see you and shoot you!

Close to the fence on the communist side there had been a neatly raked strip of beach sand. That had been the minefield! "Look children! The minefield!" There had also been little boxes that fired shrapnel at you automatically to make sure you would bleed to death in under two minutes if you wanted to climb West. They were called *Selbstschußanlagen*. Self-shooting devices.

From across on the other side they had been watched by two border guards from inside a big white tower. One with binoculars, the other with a camera taking photographs. Everyone had waved, but the border guards hadn't waved back. This had been the least exciting place in the universe!

After fifteen minutes, when Herbholz had finished eating, it had been agreed that everyone was feeling a little sick and wanted to go back home. The Roman wall had been fun though! "No, we won't go back there!" Herbholz had ordered. When they had been about to leave, Fergal thought one of the guards had waved from the communist tower. No one had believed Fergal.

Back on the bus everyone had gone to sleep.

Fergal had thrown up first!

The next day they had received their year-end reports.

Everything had seemed so rushed.

Herbholz had dismissed them with a brief nod and *Good luck to you all!*

It was Big School next.

Fergal knew he was going to Gymnasium, but he didn't know which one. Mutti's secret surprise!

Back home J was packing. She was singing. Her report had been excellent as ever.

"What's happening!?"

"I'm going to stay with Oma and Opa until our house is ready. Pa's up there already preparing his new shop and decorating *my* room. Apparently, I'll be able to see the Baltic from my window."

"Yes. Lovely. Great. – Do I have a room!?"

"Yes, of course you do! And yours looks out over the compost heap and loo drains."

"Where're we going, J!?"

"I really don't know!"

"You do!"

"I don't! I promise, I don't! – All I do know is that Mutti appears altogether quite unhappy about the choice of place. But she wouldn't tell. It's all a *big* secret!"

His sister wasn't lying. Fergal knew because her eyes didn't look left. She would always look left when she lied. "Mutti's always unhappy. – I am also unhappy!"

J sat down on the sofa bed next to her pile of suitcases. She folded her hands in her lap like a grown-up, … like Pastor Meinheit. Yuck! – "Why are you unhappy, Father Martin?"

"Because, Vicomte, … I'm losing all my friends! And I can't smile anymore! That's why!"

She looked down at her hands, "I know, Father. It's that thing in the eyes. I have that too, now."

"Yes. I know. But at least you're singing!"

"We haven't exactly had a brilliant time of it!"

"It's Mutti's and Dad's fault!"

"Look! – We're all just people. We make mistakes. I'm sure things are going to get much better! In two years time, I'll have finished school, and I'll be studying medicine."

"I won't! – I'll still have to live with *them!*"

J sighed, "I know. – Maybe you can come and live with me."

Fergal thought for a moment. All things considered that didn't seem such a bad idea now, but, "Mutti will *never* allow it! I'm just a little kid!"

Half an hour later a taxi collected J to take her to Frankfurt train station. J gave Fergal a kiss and said, "We'll be fine, little soldier!" She had never kissed him before! Fergal waved her goodbye until the taxi had disappeared from view down the far end of Georg-Büchner-Straße where it joined the main road to Frankfurt. Then Fergal cried.

The summer holidays were going by slowly. There was nothing to do, no one to play with, and nothing to smile about. Everyone was on holiday! Fergal read James Fenimore Cooper, Jules Verne and Mark Twain. *Tom Sawyer* was great! At least books could send you on a sort of vacation! But all those books weren't real. His life was!

Just before the end of the most tedious and wasted holidays ever, Dad arrived in the morning in a boring light-blue 5-series BMW, registration BOL. To Fergal that seemed a bit of an unfortunate abbreviation! Then again, Germans didn't know about *bollocks,* and he wasn't allowed to ever say it! Bad J-word!!!

He searched his mind. He had definitely never come across the registration BOL before. Mutti said, Fergal was absolutely *not* allowed to check the county stamp on the number plate. She'd watch his *every* move!

"Let it be a surprise!" Mutti said and looked desperately unhappy.

Behind Dad there was a massive, scrapheap removal truck bearing the same number plate. It came to a grinding halt in the driveway, leaving deep track marks in the gravel. Not even Steinhöfer would have accepted such a pile of junk!

Three fat, unsmiling men with tattoos fell out of the driving cabin like overall-clad dungaree droppings from a constipated sheep's bottom. They clustered for a little, lividly glaring at the driveway, before they dispersed around their unarticulated juggernaut. They were making angry sounds, kicking tyres hatefully. Fergal thought of soldiers under fire in the worst of enemy territories.

Eventually, each one of them gave Fergal a brief, sly look with narrow eyes. This was the only acknowledgement he got! Mutti received a curt nod and "Moin, moin!" from the fattest of the triumvirate.

"That means *hello* up north, Fergal!"

"Sounds a bit like *mine* in Irish."

"Does it now, Fergal?"

"Yes! – Why are they so unfriendly?"

"Just the way they are. They had a long drive through the night."

"Where's BOL, Mutti? – Please!"

"Stop it now! It's a surprise. Don't ask! You'll see when we get there." Mutti really didn't look at all happy about the BOL-surprise.

"Can I go live with J when she's at uni?"

Mutti frowned, "No! – Now, let them get on with it. They have to pack our things."

"Are all people up north like that? People with tattoos are asocial jailbirds, you said."

Mutti huffed, "Now listen, Fergal! – Why don't you go and say goodbye to your friends!"

"*Everyone's* on holiday, Mutti! – Bernhardt's in hospital, and I am *not* saying goodbye to the Stab Gang."

"Go on! Say goodbye! I'm sure you'll find someone or something to say goodbye to."

Fergal stomped off to do his goodbye-tour of Geesterheim.

Martin wasn't in, the fire station shut. – None of the old ones sat around the big oak in the market place. He hadn't seen them for a while anyway. Maybe they had all died!? Old people did that.

Fergal found Pastor Meinheit inside the village church kneeling in front of the altar.

"I wanted to say goodbye, Herr Pastor."

The Pastor didn't get up from his knees, "Oh, good! Make sure you get confirmed."

"Mmh. Will you say goodbye to Bernhardt for me, please!"

Pastor Meinheit shut his eyes, "I shall."

"If I promise to get confirmed, will you promise not to put Bernhardt into hospital again!?"

The Pastor kept his eyes shut, "Go away, and let me pray in peace, Fergal."

"Promise!?"

"I promise. – Go now!"

Heinrich The Vegetable Man wasn't in. The surgery was shut. That was a shame! At least to Heinrich Fergal could have said how much he hated the idea of a place with a number plate reading BOL. He would have loved to stay behind with Heinrich!

Herr and Frau Dr. Neussler came to the main gate but didn't ask Fergal in. They wished him all the best for his future before Frau Neussler turned away in tears. Herr Neussler took her in his arms and slowly they wandered back to the house. – Fergal had been about to ask if they'd filled in Siegfried's trench system, but thought better of it. Siegfried was still alive and might need his trenches.

Fergal walked back up Georg-Büchner-Straße. Home at number 9 the packers were busy, looking actively unfriendly. He could check the county stamp on the number plate, but decided not to. He turned into Mönchsgasse to say goodbye to his old school.

It was Big School next. Fergal felt no joy at the thought.

They said it always rained up north. The Bulhof-Murphys could have stayed on until winter, couldn't they!? Fergal could have started at Heinrich-Heine Gymnasium in Frankfurt like J! – Maybe J already knew what BOL was!?

It was coming up for eleven o'clock. – The glorious sunshine and piercing heat of August passed Fergal by unnoticed.

He had caught his first ever snake here by the swamp! He had eaten sun-dried frogs and slugs. He and his friends had dug trenches all around Geesterheim. They had built shit-dams in the drainage ditch, nearly caught a hare, annoyed the hell out of the stork on the chimney of the empty ghost house, until one of their stones had gone through one of the stained glass windows, and the dead ghosts were going to chase them. Forever! They had raced their pedal cars, go-carts and bicycles down every secret lane Geesterheim had to offer. Forever! – In the past now.

Up north it was cold.

Fergal was standing in the shade of the chestnut by the ancient Schafshütte reserved for religious education. The schoolyard hadn't changed over the past five years. Small grit with fine, yellow sand. All you had to do was to stand around without moving, and you'd get covered in dust by all the children rushing around during break. A five-minute break followed by a fifteen minute break. Always the same. Forty-five minute lessons in-between, always. Monday to Saturday. At Big School lessons would go on until one o'clock, and sometimes well into the afternoon, J had told him.

He took a step back and looked up at the chestnut. It too hadn't changed. It was two-hundred-and-fifty years old, Pastor Meinheit had said. Fergal took another step back, and another. Fifteen more steps.

There!

This was the exact spot where Kellergeister had smacked him so hard for an insufficient photographic smile he had landed face-down in the dust.

It's cold up north!

But maybe it wasn't so bad. Maybe it was good to leave here!?

Fergal left his old school, crossing Mönchsgasse into Berliner Strasse. He was going to take the back route to Herrn Dorfgeist's.

"Hallo, Ferkel! Not up north yet!?"

"Hello, Herr Dorfgeist! – No. The northerners are packing our things."

"Are you looking forward to your new school then!?"

"I don't know where I'm going, Herr Dorfgeist. It says BOL on the number plate."

"Yes, Mutti told me *not* to tell you!" he smiled. "Your Mutti looked a little … unhappy."

"So, … do *you* know where we're going!?"

"Yes, of course!"

"Is it nice?"

"I've never been, Ferkel! Don't like travelling much. Thought the place was made up! I'm sure there are people who like it there. I like it here. I was born here, and I'll die here."

"I've just come to say goodbye, Herr Dorfgeist."

"That's very nice of you, Ferkel! – Would you like a Negerkuß?"

"Oh yes, please!"

Herr Dorfgeist lifted the big glass dome and gave Fergal three Negerküsse, "There you go! One for a good journey! One for the hope that Boll … the place you're going to is full of lovely people like our village! And one … just for good luck throughout your life."

"Thank you very much, Herr Dorfgeist!"

"Don't eat them all in one go!"

"Of course, I will!"

"Of course, you will! – Goodbye! *Lebe wohl, gute Reise und denk an mich zurück*, as it says in the song!" Have a good journey.

Fifty steps up Georg-Büchner-Straße and Fergal had scoffed the lot.

Two hundred and eighty steps to Georg-Büchner-Straße 9.

Home at number 9 everything was much too busy. At least Dad said, "Hi, Fergal!" Dad had almost smiled! He was too busy though to complete the smile. – Still, maybe things were going to be better. A lot better! Fergal knew, this attitude was called hope.

Fergal went into the garden and sat in the blue shade of the apricot tree triangle. It was laden with vibrant, divine, orange fruit, and already there were quite a few windfalls. This year Mutti had not bothered to pick any apricots to make jam and jelly.

Opa's wooden Marble of Wisdom was the same size. Bit bigger maybe. How strange of Opa to carry that heavy thing around with him all the time. He had promised he would bequeath it to Fergal. Why would he want it? Comfort, rest? He had that here!

The quiet amongst the apricot trees was complete, perfect for a siesta. The taste of Negerkuß-sugar in his mouth would take some more time before it would finally go. He was going to enjoy it!

He made himself a bed free from windfalls, away from the spot, where he had had the weeing competition with the Colonel, and lay on his back trying to catch the tiny candyfloss clouds drifting up in the sky through the leaves. Slow puffs of sugar from heaven. Not a breath of wind.

No! Fergal had a craving for apricot! – He jumped to his feet. Before he could rest he needed to savour the fruit's gentle, unobtrusive sweet. Feel its tender, almost dry flesh that somehow managed to contain so much taste. You forgot about the world when you ate it. At this time of year they were perfect! He pulled down a low branch and picked three. One for a good journey, one for the hope that the place they were going to was full of friends, and one just for good luck for his life.

He lay back down and ate the apricots with eyes closed. Heaven! Mutti said *never* to do that! Always open the fruit first to see what's inside, because there could be a wasp or hornet hiding in there. And then your throat would swell up, and you'd stop breathing, and you'd die blue in the face! That was Mutti's hell because inside everything there could be terrible horror awaiting.

Was it better to die like a torch, bright with flames, screaming in the dead of night, burning on under water, or was it better to have a wasp sting you in the back of the throat? Fergal settled for neither. It was altogether better to eat three apricots and fall asleep for a bit!

Fergal heard a swish go past him, then he felt a tiny breath of air. He kept his eyes shut. Seconds later it came back, going the other way, only to return as quickly.

He knew it was the garden's blackbird. The blackbird had been here ever since they moved to number 9. Forever! – Mutti didn't think it was the same one. Birds died quickly, apparently. Brain tumours, heart disease, beak waste, stomach rot, because of all the bad food they didn't cook but ate regardless. And then those poor, little, sick, cancer-infested heralds of the morning migrated down to Italy to be welcomed by hordes of Catholics with nets, who turned them into pie. Mutti wasn't so sure whether there was blackbird pie, but there certainly was sparrow pie and paste and patties and pastries. After pizza, another Italian delicacy she wasn't *ever* going to sample!

Marcello had never offered Fergal any Italian bird pies. Marcello had died, tied to the back of a car, because he had insulted the Mafia, or something.

Chuck had wanted to take one of Tristan's BB-guns to see what blackbird looked like on the inside where all the music was coming from, before you turned it into sparrow liver pâté and ate it. Fergal had promised Chuck they'd never be friends again if he did that! And Chuck let the matter rest. Almost. Only once had Chuck downed the blackbird with a shot from his tennis racket, "I hit it! I hit it! What a shot, man!" – It had fallen to the ground, unconscious. Fergal had run over and stroked it back to life. After that, it had flown around like new, and early every morning it sang for Fergal, perched on the balcony balustrade, whenever he slept in his parents' room, which had been most of the time. Those times were over now.

At least he was going to have his own room up north!

The blackbird made another swishing pass over him. It was twittering all the while. But why did it take the difficult route in through the hedge, through the apricot triangle and out through the hedge again? Great flying, certainly, but going round would have been much quicker!

Fergal was watching the blackbird closely. Every time it returned from their garden to fly past him towards the Bruckner's property, it carried a dry blade of grass in its beak. Fergal counted ten such transports, before he decided to investigate.

The place the blackbird was carrying the grass to was indeed just over on the other side of their fence! Fergal could see the Bruckner's swimming pool from here. The surface shimmered trying to catch as much of the sun as possible. The Bruckners too were on holiday even though they had a pool.

Fergal moved closer to the high fence. Again, he was passed by the great flier. This time he even felt its wing clip his hair gently. Holding the yellowed blade of grass in its beak it stopped on the fence, turned around in a hop, and looked at Fergal. Then it jumped off backwards to turn midair and flutter down to the ground. In an instant it passed Fergal again to return with yet another bit of its worthless cargo. It certainly wasn't building a nest at this time of year! Fergal knew! And in no way down there on the ground! Blackbirds weren't just great singers, they were also very clever.

Fergal carefully traversed Mutti's vegetable patch. He needn't have been tiptoeing, as it was dead and overgrown. Force of habit.

He reached the fence and waited for the blackbird to return to see what it was doing. He didn't have to wait. There, down on the ground, right in front of him, where back wall and fence met, was a little mound of hay under the Bruckner's mulberry tree. At this very moment the blackbird came swooping down, and gently, almost humanlike, dropped another dry blade of grass on top of it. This must have taken the bird the whole morning! And off it was again.

There had to be a reason for this! Blackbirds didn't just make little haystacks for fun. Nothing in nature happened without reason. There had to be a cause!

Fergal tried to reach the bird's dry-grass collection, but his arm wasn't long enough, stopping short only a couple of centimetres. There was something underneath this carefully gathered mound!

Fergal went in search of a stick. It was easier than having to climb over the garage, as he'd done in the past to play with the Bruckner's hunting dog Capo. He ignored his respect for Mutti's vegetable patch and pulled a length of bamboo from her rampant tomato vines.

When he was back by the fence, there was the blackbird already waiting for him. It had stopped its grass-transport frenzy. Perched on the lowest branch of the mulberry tree it was twittering its song. Fergal loved the blackbird's song in the early hours of the morning. It awoke you with joy, whatever the day would bring. You just couldn't go back to sleep after that! The nightingale sang most beautifully too, but only in the middle of the night, and you always had the feeling it was only singing for its own benefit. The blackbird might also throw a midnight performance, but it never forgot the morning!

"What are you doing, my little friend?"

The blackbird interrupted its song and looked at Fergal.

"Do you mind if I have a look?"

The blackbird resumed its song. It wasn't the melody it used for the early hours of the morning.

"I suppose, that means you don't mind!?"

Slowly, as in a game of pick-up-sticks, Fergal pushed his stick under and lifted the little mound as carefully as possible without disturbing it. The mound was constructed well enough not to disintegrate. What he saw underneath staggered and bewildered him so completely, he instantly withdrew his stick. The blackbird continued singing.

"I am sorry!" Fergal said and withdrew. – Underneath the mound had been the blackbird's wife, the brown blackbird, dead.

Fergal went to collect some dry grass himself. When he had gathered a handful he went back to the fence and pushed it through near the blackbird's burial mound. The blackbird never stopped his death-chant from the lowest branch of the mulberry tree.

It was time to go for Fergal.

He stuck the length of bamboo back in the ground where it had come from. The tomatoes looked out of control. Dangerous, diseaselike almost! Someone would move here after the Bulhof-Murphys and tidy up the garden again.

He went out through the narrow path by the garage. With difficulty he opened the huge, wooden gate that led onto the driveway. This gate had never been shut before! At the last moment he turned around remembering that he had forgotten something. He returned to where he had found most of the lawn burnt dry by the sun and carefully picked the longest blade of yellow grass he could find.

Upstairs, Hansi had died. On his back. Claws in the air. Fergal was sure, one of the tattooed removal men must have scared Hansi to death with their northern unfriendliness.

Fergal started his last letter to God via the Pope.

It was a short letter written on the last piece of paper Mutti had been willing to find for him. Torn out from the pages of her small notebook that lived in the universe of her handbag. A light blue bit of paper without any lines on it. Forever used by Mutti for shopping lists and household expenses.

Fergal wrote down only one word. He wrote it as carefully and beautifully as he could.

God

No full stop. No exclamation mark.

Outside he found his golden Mafia Zippo in the crack by the cellar window. No one was watching him. He had refilled the lighter more than two months ago, but on turning the heavy, little wheel a tall flame sprang into happy existence instantly.

Unseen, Fergal burnt the light blue piece of paper together with the blade of grass on the dry ground in the vegetable garden. He scooped up the ashes with some soil in his hands and dropped them over the bird's grave.

The blackbird was nowhere to be seen or heard.

The End Of Damage Fun

The Beginning Of Schadenfreude

Schadenfreude

(*Schadenfreude,* the follow-up to *Damage Fun,* to be published on 1st April 2010. Please watch amazon.com etc. for updates.)

Schadenfreude. 1975. The British Zone.– Oh, God! *Nooooooooo!* Bollerboe! – Bad Bollerboe is for real! It actually *is* a real place in the British military zone in the north of West Germany! – Panic! – Bad Bollerboe is a perfectly square Baltic island that smells of rotten fish. Fish that pretend to be alive still. Locals have lost their sense of smell a long time ago. Bollerboerian locals are stuck in their 1,000-year Third Reich to infinity to the power of infinity, because the Nazis were the greatest guys ever. Of course, Bollerboerians have made modern modifications, so the world views them as Good New Bollerboerians. They just loooooove Indian food … and this permits them to make ample use of the Indian swastika! – Fergal is forced to go to Big School at Bad Bollerboe, where he finds out that he has personally bombed Dresden and invented the concentration camp. Is Fergal going to have fun in Bad Bollerboe?

www.ingramcontent.com/pod-product-compliance
Lightning Source LLC
Chambersburg PA
CBHW030810310726
48980CB00006B/445/J

* 9 7 8 1 9 0 7 2 2 7 0 5 9 *